The Pride . . .

It may have been stubbornness that made John refuse to believe he had lost the only girl he ever loved. Deep in his heart he had hoped that Maddalan would someday be his, and when they met again it was like a dream come true.

and the Passion . . .

It would have been the perfect ending . . . except John was now married and he had no reason to leave his wife—until desire drove him in desperation to choose between a life he could no longer bear and a love that could be but a dream.

Author Ursula Bloom, whose portrait appears on the back cover, is noted in the Guinness Book of World Records *as the most prolific woman writer in the world. She holds the record for the greatest number of books—over 600 to date—ever published by a living woman.*

Other Pinnacle Books by Ursula Bloom:

Prelude to Yesterday
Passion's Pilgrim
Love, Old and New

and

A Lamp in the Darkness:
A Treasury of Inspirational Thought (Corwin Books)

Love Is But a Dream

Ursula Bloom

PINNACLE BOOKS LOS ANGELES

LOVE IS BUT A DREAM

First American edition.
First published in Great Britain by
Hutchinson & Co., Ltd., as *Pack Mule*.

A Pinnacle Books edition, published by special arrangement with Hutchinson & Co., Ltd.
First printing, November 1978

ISBN: 0-523-40414-X

Cover art by Gil Cohen

Printed in the United States of America

PINNACLE BOOKS, INC.
2029 Century Park East
Los Angeles, California 90067

"Hate has come into the House! As long as love was here, we could bear everything; but now, ugh! How cold!"

Eleonora. STRINDBERG: *Easter,* ACT III.

CONTENTS

PART I

Fredal

Chapter One

Out of the mid wood's twilight
Into the meadow's dawn,
Ivory-limbed and brown-eyed
Flashes my faun.
O Hunter, snare me his shadow!
O Nightingale, catch me his strain!
Else moonstruck with music and madness
I track him in vain.

OSCAR WILDE

I

JOHN CARRICK heard the music as he went along the esplanade. It tinkled out in thin arpeggios of sound into the warm June evening. John went slowly. He was twenty-one, but he had none of the elasticity of twenty-one, none of the fluid, irrepressible life flowing in his veins, for he was hyper-sensitive, self-conscious. It was all very well for his mother to tell him to forget himself, but how could you forget when shyness was an ever-present affliction?

He heard the music—Freda's music—and came to a halt.

Dusk was merging into the sea, and the long shadowy outline of the island was blurred and pricked with the first yellowness of lamps being lit, one by one. John loved this time of day, which was in reality no longer day. People were kinder. Lovers were sitting in the shadow-hid seats in the gardens that lay in a wide strip between esplanade and sea. The seats they occupied were half hidden by shrubs. He could smell the warm wine-like essence of privet flowers and of honeysuckle in an up-rushing perfume. The scent was delicious. A few old ladies pottered up and down the front, airing their dogs. They had been tempted out by the pleasant warmth of the June evening. But all these people were kindly and tolerant; they did not slash at his sensibilities by their enquiring stares; he felt happy about life.

The music trickled out upon the still air. It trickled through the open window of the Balmoral boarding-house.

John had met Freda when she came into his mother's shop to buy picture postcards three days before. She had struck him as being different from the other visitors to Portarth. She did not wear a beret and a choker, and she had not the glinting, impertinent eyes of a girl who desired conquest. She was tall and supple, her face was elfishly pointed, with grateful hazel eyes, and a white skin like pear bloom. She had reminded him of white blossom on dark thorn: the darkness was her hair, the whiteness her little triangular face. She had told him that her name was Freda Perkins, and that she was a professional pianist. Later he discovered that she was staying at the Balmoral boarding-house.

During the three days, and in spite of his mother's antagonism, he had met Freda quite often.

"A dressed-up piece," his mother had declared. "You who never look at a girl, then to take up with her!"

"I'm not," he had protested, because his mother would never understand that it was Freda's music which attracted him.

"Go on! You can't kid me!"

To-night he heard her play.

He stood quite still by an ornate Victorian balustrade outside her window. Syringas, heavily budded, over-sweet, clustered together thickly in the tiny garden. There were but two feet between the stone balustrade and the window of the Balmoral boarding-house, flung wide and illuminated by the one electric light. He glimpsed a good black marble clock, an over-mantel cluttered with china ornaments, a thready carpet, and chairs that had become concave with the generous curves of the figures which had rested in them. At the far end Freda sat alone before a time-honoured piano. The music echoed out to him. It was the inviting, questioning music of the *Minuet and Trio*.

As John stood there with the exquisite evening scents eddying about him, he was conscious that he was listening to something which lay entirely outside his usual rut. All his life he had been passionately fond of music, but he had loathed that music with which life had brought him into contact. It had been unreal. He had been forced to listen in torment to his mother's masterpiece "Jennie Jones, with twenty variations", to the "Lily of the Valley Mazurka", and the "Bells of St. Malo". Music was not like that. He longed to tell people, but they would not listen to him. He had longed to explain how Sidney Smith jagged his sensitiveness, but it was useless. Freda's music was not dreadful. The chords rang true. They struck home. He could feel the truth of real harmony in them. He knew now that the ripple was the thing that had evaded him all his twenty-one years of life, the thing that he wanted most. His mother was wrong when she accused the girl of attracting him; it was not the girl, it was her music. Freda finished. Her hands dropped into her lap for a moment, then she raised them again, only to close the piano lid. Disappointedly he called through the window to her.

"I was listening. Freda, it was wonderful. Do play some more?"

She came across the room and leant out over the sill to him. She stooped forward so that her frock fell a little away from her figure, and he caught the suggestion of two young breasts flung forward. Her eyes sought him, questing in the dusk.

"I can't play any more. I'll come out and talk to you, if you like. I'm dull. It's horribly dull in here. What a dreadful boarding-house this is!"

"I loved your music," he confessed.

"I daresay, but I'm tired."

It struck him that she sounded sulky, and not a little cross. He stood there waiting for her, and his heart pounded and assured him that he was glad that she was coming out to him. The music tinkled on still within him in a vibrant echo. It seemed that he had become enmeshed in it. In vivid contrast he thought of her leaning out of the window, her bright dark hair close about her face, her body flung forward, her breasts. . . .

Freda came down the somewhat pretentious steps of the Balmoral, through the wide arch of a doorway, with the brass plate announcing that it was a private hotel and would tradesmen kindly use the back entrance? John greeted her on the bottom step. She was slightly taller than he was, a little older. Freda at twenty-three was his mental senior by many years. He saw the darkness of her hair that reminded him of thorn, and the whiteness of her face, and he knew that the dusk lent her additional beauty. She did not seem to be the same personality as the Freda who had come into his mother's shop to buy postcards—the dusk made her different.

"Let's go and sit in the gardens," said Freda.

John knew that the gardens were dedicated to lovers. He said, "Oh, but . . ." and was surprised when she linked her arm in his and drew him, slightly resisting, across the road with her. His heart beat faster. "Adventure," he thought—"this is going to be adventure, the real thing, worth while."

He felt that he could not explain to her that people would accept them as lovers, and that there in the magic gardens they would be lovers. They passed three seats, all of which were occupied. John went hot and cold with shame that she should see the unabashed embraces, but Freda was composed. She selected a green iron seat under the shelter of syringa and privet, and a single crimson rambler which by daylight was a blaze of wine-coloured blossom. In the darkness the white flowers gleamed. They were smudgy disks, and the scent from them was heady.

"I'm glad you came," she said.

"I'm glad you were playing. It was wonderful."

"Nice that you liked it." She was a little patronizing, but the patronage was lost on him.

"It's rummy, but I could never stand Mother's music. She used to give lessons when I was a kiddy, just after Father was killed. Those lessons made me scream. They thought I hated music, but it was that music, the wrong sort."

"Perhaps it wasn't music?" she suggested.

"But isn't it all. . . ?" he asked gauchely.

"Silly! Why, some music is awful!"

He glanced at her not quite understanding, yet thrilled by the presence of mystery. To him music had always been a sheet of close writing which was entirely undecipherable, the keyboard striped ebony and white, the rickety old piano wheezing and quivering out the notes. "Yours was different," he said, "it just made me feel that I could go on listening to it for ever."

"It's the classical stuff that matters."

She sat there lithely erect. He glanced at her sideways from time to time, for in this soft dusk she was a new personality. Until now she had been just a customer at his mother's shop, a customer who was gratifyingly condescending. Out on the esplanade when he had listened to her music she had been a great master. Now, here, she was merely woman. She was expecting something from him, and he realized it, but was at a loss to understand her. Freda had brought him out of the stuffy atmosphere of the Balmoral boarding-house, with its pampas and plush and its Victorian relics, into the June-sweet night. Freda desired the roses of Hafiz and the wine cup of Omar. She was no longer a person much above him, but an elf with a pointed face whimsical in the dusk. She put out her hand and laid it on his. In some intangible way it reminded him of the coolness of lilies, yet for all its cold it fused him with a new hot emotion.

"Be nice to me," she said.

John had little idea what she meant, for he could not believe that she was suggesting a flirtation. He had never in his life been nice to anybody, not in that way. His mother, widowed young, had been the taskmistress of his life. She had demanded every ounce of strength from him, and, with a faithful sense of his duty to her, he had permitted it. He lacked initiative; it had been trampled under by his training; he knew it, but could not rectify the error. He laid his own hand on hers.

"I'm funny," he said. "I don't know what you want me to do. Am I being an utter fool?"

"Kiss me," she suggested.

He saw her eyes, grown strangely luminous, looking out of the white frailty of her face; they seemed to him like two stars standing from the Milky Way. He thrilled, glanced again at the ripe curve of her full lips, desiring them, yet instantly crushing the desire in his being lest its coarseness should horrify her. He lifted her hand to his mouth, touching it with his lips with infinite care so as not to hurt it. She snatched it from him angrily.

"Fool!" she said, and held her hand against her heart close pressed in its fellow, as though it was wounded.

"You don't understand. It's not all my fault."

"I know," said Freda, hot with defiance, "you're a pack mule. There are pack mules in the world, living ones, human ones. They get all the kicks and curses, and they always do what you tell them. They get nowhere but do all the work."

He should have denied the suggestion, but could not because it was true. She thawed a little from her scorn, and came closer, pushing her warm, soft body against his. Her face, grown nearer, became more distinct, and he felt himself with some unsuspected flame leaping within him. Temptation fired his soul.

"I'm pretty, John?"

"You're not pretty, you're beautiful."

"Then why don't you kiss me?"

"Because I'm afraid. You're too beautiful. You are far above me. We aren't in the same street; just two folks met for a day or two. I daren't."

"Those who don't dare, don't care," she said sullenly.

"I do care," and he felt the tongue of flame licking the soul within him. He was supremely conscious of caring, of loving her enormously, passionately, with the ache for possession.

"You aren't behaving like it."

"But don't you see?"

She pulled herself away with a little indignant effort. "You ought to learn sense," she said.

At that moment he was undecided as to whether he dare suddenly clasp her close to him, draw her to his heart, and kiss her as instinct warned him. Some dreadful convention held him in its clasp. She had felt the swaying flame between them; for a moment she waited, then as suddenly she turned, flouncing her skirts, and moved quickly across the esplanade into the Balmoral. She went so fast that he did not attempt to follow her. He heard the brushing of her frock against the leaves grown dark with night. He heard the clipping of her heels across the asphalt, the slam of the Balmoral door, and then swiftly upon it the crashing down of the window so that he might not hear her playing.

He sat on.

He had wanted her held closely, with the swaying flame a raging and consuming fire. Yet his fool temperament had let her go.

There were times when he did not understand himself, and he sat there looking into himself and seeing little, understanding less.

He was not tall—smally made, with brittle bones, slight of wrist, with long aesthetic hands. His face was long too, and spare and lean, with deep eyes warmed by brown fire, set on either side an aquiline nose. His mouth expressed little, his chin less. It was in his eyes that there lay the something which was his claim to full beauty. Reproachful eyes; the patient dumb eyes of some animal broken to the bit; eyes grown sad, with the fires of enthusiasm damped down by environment. His soul had suffered from rut and routine, from dogmatism and bigotry. He was in very truth broken to the bit.

But as there are some animals who never lose the old instinct, the hot desire for prairie, for sweet wildness, for the wind tossing their manes and rippling along their flanks, so in John Carrick, under it all, a smouldering fire still burnt. The flame of it might one day flicker out into unpitied extinction, or might rise and consume the very soul of him in its burning. You could not tell.

A quiet young man, with a tender mouth full of the whimsical. A long sensitive nose. Perhaps there was a little of the faun about him. There was a hidden attraction, maybe lying in the tiny flame which flickered within, but again you could not tell. Warm June night with the essence of flowers, far away the boom of the sea, and the incoming tide caressing the shingle. But here within himself void that demanded something that he could not give it. He got up, chilled by the dew, and walked home.

II

Mrs. Carrick's shop was in the High Street. It had originally been an ordinary dwelling-house, and in her early years she had displayed her wares from a window that was flush with the street. Then, just before her husband died, she had had proper shop windows set in so that she could attract more custom. Inside was a miscellaneous litter of toys and souvenirs, of fancy goods and Goss china. Behind the shop was the one sitting-room which had been built as a kitchen, but which they had made their sole living-room, using the diminutive scullery beyond as a kitchen.

It seemed to John that the little twelve-foot-square living-room, with its overburdening of furniture, was the arena in which the whole of his life had been fought out. For it had been fought out, a long and sickening fight. It was the battle of an over-sensitive nature against the constant irritation of material and well-meaning—devastatingly well-meaning—people. He knew that it had been a losing battle, too. His mother had a hold over him by the very fact that she was his mother. He owed her something, a debt that he could never repay. His loyalty had been thoughtfully trained in that way, for her maternity had trespassed on his youth, sucked the life from it, and demanded a blood price. All the while when he longed to set her in the Madonna niche within his heart, his second nature had seen her as she really was, a little skinny woman, with eyes sharp like some animal's, and wispy hair tied back from her angular face. Her music, which should have been the most exquisite harmony, was discord to his soul. It was the most terrible music imaginable. This room, which should have been beautiful by the very fact that it was home, was a hideous room. He hated the rosewood piano with the splitting silk in its frontal, and the cheap walnut sideboard laden with E.P.N.S. wedding-presents. He hated himself for realizing the meanness, the shoddiness, in it all.

Perhaps Freda was right, he was a pack mule. He had been born with an artistic soul, crucified by material surroundings. He had suffered in silence, suffocating the sensitive being within him, and had tried to train himself in the way that his mother desired. He had attended an unsatisfactory school; he had allowed himself to be shifted into a berth for which he was wholly unfitted, because his mother thought that it was a gentlemanly career. He had served in the local draper's shop, hating every moment. The smell of it nauseated him. The cheap fustian mats with their galaxy of dust which clogged the air and choked him. The American cloth with its shiny rubbery smell, the sight of ribbons peeling from catherine-wheels of cheap paper, of coarse cotton lace, of boys' corduroy knickers, and women's merino vests, all blended together in one unlovely whole. Mercifully the draper had decided that John had not the proper outlook to make a successful assistant and had dismissed him.

"We want smart young chaps here," said the draper, who sucked in air noisily through a badly decayed front tooth, and wore his hair in a jaunty tuft in front. "Chaps with go. Your manner don't help you much."

"I was never cut out for drapery," John admitted.

"That's right! You never said a truer word. You ain't got the air with you, the polish. I'm sorry to seem hard, but you'll never do for us."

"I know." John hated to admit the exquisite joy the dismissal gave him. Standing talking in the grim little shop, lit by a jaundiced gaslight, he stared at his employer between cord mats stacked in a pyramid and a counter over which dangled a cheap line in 'Gent's braces—reduced'. "I'm not sorry to go," he confessed.

Afterwards the draper told his wife. "Queer chap, that there young Carrick. No go, none of that there veneer, but rum! Mad on music and pictures and all that sort of rubbish; no refinement," and he still sucked noisily through his decayed tooth.

The loss of the drapery job had happened at the very time that Mr. Putman was looking for a young man to help him in his shop. Mrs. Carrick would never have consented to John going to Mr. Putman's save that at that time nothing else seemed to offer itself. Mr. Putman was an antique dealer, old, himself a little antique, with an old-world courtesy and a superb serenity of outlook. John had never regretted casting in his lot with the antique shop down the street. In his six months there he had learnt much about himself, and much about the world in general.

He entered the sitting-room behind his mother's shop and became suddenly sharply aware that she was not alone. A desultory meal was on the table. A cheese much cut about occupied the centre dish. There was a loaf, some butter, and a glass plate piled pinkly with radishes. They caught the light, reminding him of ugly pink fingers, carmined with the cold. Somehow he knew that he did not like the look of them. His mother was sitting at the end of the table, and she was talking to someone. Instantly John felt himself resenting the presence of the third person, and especially such a third person as Mr. Duckett.

Mr. Duckett was the dissenting minister. He was a little man, with a rubicund and annoyingly cheerful face; his pale blue eyes were watery. He was inseparable from his umbrella. Even to-night, a June-hot night, he still held it clasped to him. As John came in he got up.

"Ah, here is the son and heir!" he said in that tryingly pleasant way of his, when all the while you knew that it was put on. "I mustn't intrude any longer. Well, I hope, John, the Lord is helping you along your path?"

"I'm well enough."

"For shame, John!" from his mother. "You ought to be grateful to kind Mr. Duckett for taking such an interest in you."

"I am grateful." Only he wasn't, and he was a poor liar at the best of times.

Mr. Duckett came closer. Being short, he had to raise his head, and he had a trick of peering into a person's face. He came too close. His breath was hot on your cheek; his red face with its little lines, its small blemishes, and its badly shaven jowl, was unpleasant.

"Doing well at Mr. Putman's?" he enquired.

"I'm frightfully fond of the work there."

Mr. Duckett sighed. "Ah, well! I suppose every man to his own taste. But Mr. Putman is not a good man. He is not God-fearing."

"He's a kind man," flared John, "and that's perhaps more."

Mr. Duckett sighed heavily. "No denomination. Never been seen inside a house of prayer. An old man occupied only with his antique shop and his pictures and his furniture. Sad when you see anyone so godless nearing that hour when he must make his peace with his Maker."

"Mr. Putman will live for years," announced John vehemently, as if the very fact of his announcing it meant that Mr. Putman would live for years.

Yet, as Mr. Duckett spoke, John remembered how, only the other day, when they had been discussing some furniture that Mr. Putman had brought home from a sale, suddenly he had clutched at his throat as though he had felt it in a stranglehold. He had reeled back among the Chippendales and the Sheraton table in the corner, murmuring something about 'being better soon'.

"That isn't any way to speak to dear Mr. Duckett," said Mrs. Carrick reprovingly from her place of authority over the speckled cheese and the radishes. "I'm sure he knows what is right and proper. Mr. Putman never does go anywhere like a God-fearing man should."

"He's none the worse for it," said John, and he sat down to his supper littered in all its unloveliness on the table.

There was a silence, an awkward silence, then Mr. Duckett moistened his lips with the blue tip of his tongue, and said, "Well, I must be going," as though it pained him.

"I'll see you out," said Mrs. Carrick.

John heard them grope their way through the shadows of the shuttered shop, and the wheeze of the street door as it was opened. He heard the purr of their voices. He guessed rather grimly that they would be discussing him, his gruffness, his bad manners. He was sorry, because he did not want to displease his mother. He sat there eating bread and cheese, and as he sat there, with his thoughts quietening down, the ugly surroundings seemed to fade. It was no longer the arena of fighting, but the lists of love. The bottle of beer that he drank was aphrodisiac. Into the room there came the delirious essence of syringa and roses. There came also the enquiry of music, Freda's music, in a rapturous harmony. It was odd how she had made the piano sound no longer like a stringed instrument but like a flute. It was bird song. It had carried him along with it.

Now he wished that he had kissed her when they had sat on the seat in the gardens. He wished that he had taken her into his arms and held her close to him, felt the round globes of her young breasts in twin loveliness against his own. Her throat palely lovely, pulsating with a small twitching pulse that enchanted him. Her mouth, a red arrow shot into the white blossom of her face. Fool that he was to have let the moment of enchantment slip by! Opportunity does not come twice. And now she was angry with him; she might refuse to speak to him again. Fool, utter fool, that he was! He felt angry with himself for his squeamishness, his reluctance.

He had got to kiss her some time. Not gently, with the tender lips of son to mother, or of friend to friend, but warmly, with the crushing passion of man to his love. He had got to kiss her like that, he had got to make the opportunity again, he told himself. He would go to her. He would penetrate into the dusty, thready recesses of Balmoral House, and he would demand that she should give her lips to him. But not there. . . . He could not kiss her like that there with the plush hangings and the bulrushes, and the pictures of bloated cupids and fat pug-dogs hung round the room. He would draw her out again into the gardens, into the night, into the hundred drenching sweetnesses and darknesses in vivid contrast to the moon-washed paleness. He would say to her, "Freda, I've got to talk to you. . . . Freda, I've got to thrash this thing out. . . . We belong to each other. We are each other's. I love you."

He trembled a little with the intoxication of anticipation, for love is a trembling emotion. It is the high altar at which youth offers its being, swinging its fate in a censer, aromatic, burning, afire with hope. It is the chrism of our soul.

Mrs. Carrick came back into the room and shut the door to the shop with determination.

"Well, I must say you weren't any too amiable with Mr. Duckett to-night," she announced.

"I'm sorry."

"And where have you been out until nearly ten? You know I like to get your supper over and done with long before this. I'm sure you never think of me. I suppose you've been out with some girl or other."

He admitted it, because it did not occur to him to

lie. He said, "Yes, Mother," and went on with the cheese and the radishes.

She stared at him amazed. "My goodness!" she said, and then sank down into the chair with the broken spring and the spider-web cushion in green and yellow "Sylko". "My stars!" she gasped. "Of all the cheek! And to have the sauce to come and say so to me!"

"But you asked me."

"I won't have you running round with every little fast piece in the place. It isn't right nor decent."

"I've never been out with any girl before," he said truthfully—"you know that. It was the girl from London, Miss Perkins."

"What? Her?" He knew by the way his mother said 'her' that she had no patience with him. "A London piece, too! She don't mean no good. You'll be the death of me, John. First of all you get fired out of the drapery shop, and take up with that horrid, godless Mr. Putman——"

"The salary is better," he reminded her.

"Yes, but look at the work! Old furniture! Dirty rotten old bits and mouldy pictures as half the time you can't see what they are supposed to be of because they're so covered up with dirt and dust. It ain't a gentleman's job and you know it. No decent young fellow would muddle himself up with an old man what doesn't go to church and who messes about with a pack of old rubbish."

John did not reply. He had long ago learnt that it was useless to argue with her. She believed that every black-coated young man who served her with lace and ribbons across the counter was a gentleman. She believed that his black coat and his pimples and his sleek hair were the hall-marks of gentlemanliness. You could not expect her to see that the drapery business had galled John, tormented him, all the time that he had served in it. Here, with time-greyed woods and old mellow loveliness, he was happy. Besides, he and Mr.

Putman had always loved each other. There had been a common bond between them, as there must always be between some people, and the old man had been kind to John. In return John hated to hear him criticized by a woman of so little perception as his mother.

"You're not to go out with that girl again," she went on.

"Why not?"

"Because I forbid it."

He went on eating the radishes, but into the room floated melody again. The *Minuet* quivered into space. It was asking a question, lightly, with a gay abandon of its own. It was answering the same question with a throbbing, thrilling little trill. It was running up in an arpeggio of crescendo. John turned to his mother.

"I shall go out with her again if I choose," he said—"and I do choose."

He could hear his heart disturbed within him, because he had dared to challenge her. It thumped in time with the imperious demand of the *Minuet*. There was scent too, perfume of syringa and rose. There was the deeper wine-like scent of privet. All of it came swinging to him through space, urging him on.

"You shan't talk to me like that! You're a cruel boy and a bad son. I'm sure I don't know what I've done to be cursed with a son like you. First of all your going out with a girl, and then you so wilful!"

He set his teeth. He could feel the blood draining from his lips, running down and out of him, it seemed. He could hear the *Minuet* in its decrescendo. The essence had been of his imagination. It was in reality only of bread and cheese and beer, and the stale frowst of the little room.

"Oh God!" he said wretchedly.

She looked righteously shocked and drew in the corners of her thin mouth in disapproval. "And now you taking the name of the Lord in vain! I spoke to Mr. Duckett about it to-night."

"I wish you wouldn't speak to Mr. Duckett about me," he protested, but his voice sounded weak and far away. He thought of the pack mule that Freda had mentioned so scathingly, and instantly he cursed himself for thinking.

"You're set against Mr. Duckett." It was his mother who was defiant. "You're set against him, kind and good though he is, and what's more you'll be sorry. Mr. Duckett asked me a question to-night. He did me a great honour."

"Oh?"

"I think I'm going to marry him. I would to-morrow if it wasn't for you standing in the way like that. You can't expect him to be happy about it when you're so rude and rough to him and think of him the way you do. I'm sure it's hard on a woman what had done her best and toiled and slaved to bring you up respectable. . . ."

The *Minuet* rose in crescendo again. It was as though furtive fingers plucked at the strings of a gay guitar. It seemed that the music laughed at him. Whimsical music, fantastic music. He got up from the table. He pushed his chair back with a harshly grating noise against the lino. "I won't stand in your way," he said. "I'll go and live with Mr. Putman. Only the other day he asked me, told me that he wanted me."

The door opened. A slot like an arrow into the darkness of the shop beyond. A step out into that darkness. The urge and the thrill suddenly pushed him forward.

"You mean you'd leave me? Your poor old mother what's worked her fingers to the bone?" She stared at him owlishly, her lower lip dropping.

"A moment ago you wanted it."

"Oh, you wicked boy! You wicked, ungrateful, cruel boy!"

It was a moment of decision.

"I've got to think," he said.

"You'd far better stay and eat your supper and not talk such nonsense. I've no patience with you boys always thinking you know best. Leave me, indeed!"

John reached out a thin hand and it closed over his latchkey lying on the walnut sideboard, brightly, brassily yellow against a paler yellow sugar-basin of spurious silver.

"I'm going out to think," he said, "and I don't suppose I'll come back. I'll go to him. We've never really loved one another. You've got Mr. Duckett now, and you won't want me."

He heard her little gasp of anguish as he passed out into the street.

III

His first impulse had been to go to Mr. Putman's, but out in the cool air he came to the conclusion that half an hour's communion with himself would be advisable. It is no good doing anything in a hurry. The fevered impulse is not the one on which to act. Duckett, of all men! His mother married to Duckett, with his rubicund, pocked face, and his fawning, hypocritical manner. Could anything be worse?

He went out on to the sea front, for he knew that he wanted to get away from houses. He went back to the same old seat where earlier in the evening he had felt Freda's arms about his neck, and seen her face raised like a white flower out of the shadows.

He sat down. It was darker now. All the outlines had become blurred, all the trees were smudges of darkness, and the little light wind had caught them and hustled them together. The leaves shook like the light veils that women wear over their faces . . . dust-fine veils. He sat there very still. Opportunity was opening its door to him again. Life was offering itself like some woman who proffers her body. He prayed that life was not a bawd, and that when he took her unto himself he would not find her rotten. He was distrustful.

His mother, who had tyrannized his youth and his adolescence, who had thrust her will upon him, if not forcefully, yet with those mean persuasions upon his sensitiveness that all mothers use, was settling her own future. With Mr. Duckett there would be no need for her son to contribute to the support of the house. That dreadful house! Its ugliness, its smugness, its Madras muslins, its crochet mats. All through the long line of twenty-one gaping years which lay at his heel, that house had galled and irritated him. Its hyper-orderliness, and between its privacy and the outer world the long wooden counter, with its store of brown paper and string in a tangle beneath it.

Only last week Mr. Putman had suggested that John should go to live with him. John thought it would be Valhalla to live in the old timbered house, with its slant eaves so that the upper rooms were shaped like a Noah's ark, with whitewash and smell of old wood, and sun-burnished windows. In Mr. Putman's house were just those few beautiful objects that had passed into his keeping and which he had not had the heart to sell. The half-tester with the vine leaves in carved oak climbing in a wreath up the delicate Parthenon posts. The pictures, particularly that one on the uncovered stairs, the woman's face peeping in alarm back over her shoulder, while she struggled to draw a lace chemise over her nude urnlike body. A Franz Hals that, so Mr. Putman thought—he had never been quite sure. Sometimes he laughed about it, but its attraction was that of a great master. There was something about the whiteness of the linen and lace chemise, and the flesh of her body against the darkness of her room, a Dutch room, with all the warm depth of interior in which the Dutch delight. "One day," John had promised himself,

"I will go to Holland and see them for myself. I think I'd like that."

Mr. Putman had asked him if it would be possible to come to live there in the old house with the antique shop in front. He was a lonely old man, and he seldom found people who appealed to him. John did appeal. John had had to admit the truth, and had had to stay with his mother. After all, his duty had lain with her. She had need of him. But now that was finished and done with. His mother was shaping her own life, and he was shaping his. He sat there drinking in the joy of the night, as a thirsty man gulps in water. It was his first draught from the cup of freedom.

Then he became aware that he was not alone. A girl had come quietly to his side. Freda was sitting there, tall, like some white lily in the darkness. He could see the living ivory of her skin, and the dark circles that were eyes.

"You?" he said.

She put out a hand and laid it on his. A little cold hand, yet it was like fire to his senses. "You've come back? I thought perhaps you'd be sorry."

"I was sorry."

Opportunity had jarred the door open again. He was peering through its chink and seeing the gold dazzle of light, glitter, glamour, all the tinsel that he had supposed to be love. He put out his arms at first in a shamed manner, but when he found how easily she dropped into them he became strong. He caught her to him. He could feel all her softness, and against that tenderness his arms grew taut and infinitely strong, infused with the strength that love gives to a man.

"Oh, you beautiful girl, you beautiful girl! . . ." he whispered passionately.

He kissed her hair. It held a vague intangible scent of its own; he kissed her cheeks, and they were soft; his lips slid to her mouth, which was hot and demanding and moist.

The night drifted about them, a night that was pellucid when the moon came out from behind the cloud banks, dark when she hid her face. He thought that he liked the darkness best, for then perhaps Freda would not see how his own mouth trembled, nor realize how amazed he was with himself that he dared to handle her in this commanding, possessive fashion.

He did not mention his mother to her, for now there seemed to be no need. He did not want to utter anything that would detract from the exquisite joy of the moment. He was a hedonist—beyond that nothing mattered. They clung together.

At last she spoke. "I must go, John; the Balmoral will be locking up and I shall be shut out."

"I'll see you again? Promise me that."

"I'm staying till the day after to-morrow. After that I've got to get back to work. To-morrow night?"

"I can't wait so long. Really I can't."

"Nonsense. To-morrow night. Here?"

He caught her back to him again in another fevered embrace, and he laughed gladly as he held her. "Don't you understand? I've never cared like this for anyone before. I've been shut up in a prison-house, and now at last I've got free. I want you all the time."

"Don't be so silly." She was laughing a little. A woman could laugh at what was life and death to a man! Funny, the queer difference between the sexes! He tried to gulp down his dismay that she should see anything amusing in it.

"You've cast a spell over me," he said hoarsely. "I'm different . . . and it's you!"

A spell, an enchanted cloak. Perhaps the mantle of the Borgia, stained by the blood of Perotti. Somehow he found himself squeamish before the overpowering influence of love. Squeamish that perhaps it was an unclean thing, that there was something deathly about it, that it was not all delight.

"Oh, I'm not so clever as all that!" she laughed. "You mustn't think me clever. I'm quite a little goose!"

"Freda . . . I do want you so."

He was pitifully simple. She felt his simplicity appealing to her, and standing before him she bent over him and touched his hands with hers. "Perhaps I'll come round to the antique shop in the morning. I'll find you anyway . . . if I want to."

She leant forward, stooped so that she bent over his head, and kissed his brow just where the moonlight showed it pale and tranquil against his hair.

He could see her throat—bending as a swan's throat bends—on a level with his eyes, and her small, shapely breasts, but dimly veiled by some filmy white stuff, on a level with his mouth. Before he could stay himself he had leant hurriedly forward and had buried his whole face in her softness. He heard her exclamation as she pulled herself away, felt her shudder, and then as suddenly she had slipped from him, through the darkness of the trees, across the asphalt into the Balmoral.

He wondered if he had been brutal. It had been a beastly thing to do really, and now he was ashamed. Perhaps she would not come to Mr. Putman's to-morrow after all. Perhaps she could not forgive him. He was very much ashamed when he thought of that. He ought to have controlled himself. He ought not to have kissed her like that. Decent men did not kiss women in that way.

It was time that he was getting along to Mr. Putman's. He got up, stretched himself. Now he thought that the evening was chilly, and his limbs stiff; now he knew that he was very much ashamed indeed.

IV

The tide had turned, and the waves were coming in with hump backs. He could see them as he walked along the shore. The moon rising unabashed from behind her veil of clouds cast a dazzling, glittering, golden pathway across all the hump backs, so that it looked as though the pathway crossed Alps and hills and Pyrenees before it reached the shore.

He went along slowly, because he felt that there was no need to hurry, for Mr. Putman was always up late. He would sit for hours into the night in the small back sitting-room, where he worked, studying his pictures with the aid of a magnifying glass, poring over them, examining every detail of them. When you are young and standing on the edge of a new epoch, there is no need to hurry. Hurry is inconsistent with the importance of the occasion.

He entered the little main street with here or there some solitary soul returning home. He went on until he came to the old house which leant forward, hunching towards the pavement like some ancient Atlas bereft of his globe. An old house of quaint points and angles, like a very old man with joints knobbled by rheumatism. It was black and white and vivid in the moonlight, and under its pointed eaves lay deep lines of shadows that seemed violet. Its swinging sign clanked a little, for the wind had got up and drove it to and fro, and its chains were unoiled. The sign had been made by a school of handicrafts, and was in itself a thing of beauty, yet the sound of it was threnody to John. Somehow it struck him as being gruesome, the monotonous creaking of the sign, never a beat too soon, meticulously in time, as it swung this way and that.

It was a dirge, a fugue, in one. The night is eerie. It is too white and too black. Its lines are too hard or too indefinite, it deals never in mediums but always in extremes. He opened the side door and passed up the path between the wall of the kind old house and the cheap tin fencing that the neighbours had put up. He passed round the far end, his cheeks swept by a jasmine bush, its frail leaves like phantom fingers clawing lightly at his hair. They were cold, like weed that has not long left the sea.

Again in his love-swept imagination he heard the pulse of Freda's music throbbing in his heart. He heard it as against the ugly tolling sound of the mournful sign which wheezed above. It was the gay, audacious, plucking music of the *Minuet*, and it put fresh courage into him.

He saw the light of the sitting-room glimmering between the drawn curtains, and he tapped on the door. His tap seemed to him to be tremendously loud in the silence of the night. There came no answer.

It was an eerie homecoming, an eerie arrival on the doorstep of a new destiny. He tapped again, more loudly, and still his tapping was punctuated by the gloomy creaking of the meticulously tolling sign.

He thought, 'The old chap's fallen asleep over his work,' and he set his young hand to the latch and lifted it. It responded easily enough. He passed in at the thin passage with its polished floor, and he caught the gleam of brass from atop an old chest, where a chintz curtain fluttered from the indraught of the wind.

He tapped furtively on the sitting-room door. Again there came no reply. He opened it cautiously. It was as he had supposed. At the table with his back to him old Mr. Putman sat crouched over a picture; he had fallen asleep. The lamp before him was burning low. Beside it on a tray was an untouched decanter of sherry, and a small plate of macaroons. The old man must have fallen asleep early in the evening before he had gone far with his job, and he must be very sound.

John shut the door and went closer. It seemed that Freda's music had stopped, for no longer did it tinkle bravely in his imagination.

"Mr. Putman," he said.

There was no answer.

"Mr. Putman, I've taken you at your word. I've come here to stay."

And still his answer lay only in the stark silence.

He went closer still.

"Mr. Putman . . ."

And then instantly cold horror gripped him by the throat. He could hear his own heart hammering out that horror. He was close to something that was not Mr. Putman at all, that was not man, but cold and clammy, soulless, forsaken. It was the empty cage of a migrated bird, the deserted castle of a tenant who had fled. Mr. Putman had been dead for several hours.

Chapter Two

Cups, let them be dark,
Like globules out of night, about to go plash,
I want to drink out of dark cups that drip down on their feet.

D. H. LAWRENCE

I

JOHN had but a dazed recollection of what happened next. He believed that he summoned the aid of Banks, the policeman from the corner of the street, for he retained a smudged impression of running out into the cool air, brushing past the jasmine, hearing the sign creak. Threnody indeed! He still remembered, though vaguely, clutching at the cloth-covered arm of the policeman.

Amazingly matter-of-fact, Banks came back with John, not flustered, not disturbed. He might have been facing dead bodies every day of the week. It did not surprise him a bit. He brought out a small notebook and took notes, behaving in the way in which one would have expected him to behave if it were mere larceny and never such a shattering matter as death. All the while John stood beside him, unable to stay his quaking. He could feel the blood draining steadily from his face and lips, and the squirming, nauseating horror gripping his vitals. He was ashamed, because the limp body could not hurt him; in life it had attracted him, and now it made him feel like this. The policeman demanded his aid in handling Mr. Putman. And Mr. Putman was cold and clammy, like the weed he had once found on Margate beach and brought home to hang in the yard for a barometer. The weed had dried in the hot sun, and had stiffened—as Mr. Putman would stiffen soon. The policeman told him that with a certain gruesome delight. The weed had rattled and crackled as the wind stirred it against the wall of the backyard, and somehow John expected Mr. Putman to rattle. But he did not rattle. He was still, and the stillness was much more dreadful than any rattling could possibly have been. It seemed to mock at John.

Banks, the policeman, telephoned for the doctor and the village nurse, in a crisp, businesslike manner, as though he rather enjoyed it.

"But it's no good now," protested John, "they can't do anything."

"The doctor'll have to certify death from natural causes, and someone'll have to lay him out, won't they?" demanded Banks.

Sickly, John groped for the decanter.

Death was all the more terrible coming so swiftly on the heels of life, the burning, ardent flame of life that had scorched him in the gardens with Freda. Odd that it did not make him long again for the warmth of her embraces, but it did nothing of the sort. It merely sickened him more.

It was all over. The grim door wheezed to, leaving the nurse to her doleful duties. The policeman went back to his beat, and John was faced with the problem of where to go. Now he remembered that he had not meant to return home. He had meant to take up his abode in one of the queer little rooms under the eaves, which were shaped like Noah's ark, at Mr. Putman's house. The idea was shattered. Also he had lost his employment. He had no idea as to what would become of the antique shop, nor whether the successor to Mr. Putman would be wanting a young assistant. He did not question the future. He accepted it with the docile placidity of one who is accustomed to accepting other people's decisions. He had been divested of his new home before he could take possession of it. At the same time his career had been blasted. Life had been a bawd, and had offered him a rotten body for his investment.

He turned into his own backyard dismally enough. It was late now, and he tried to use caution. The door had been left unlatched for him, for his mother had only supposed him to be in fit of temper, which she believed would quickly pass. He struck a match in the thin alleyway of a passage between the two rooms. The light it gave was quivering. Long angular shadows leapt out at him from the corners. Every shadow was the dead body of Mr. Putman propped against the wall to fall limply across John's path. His own coat, hanging like a man on its peg, frightened him. It looked grotesque in the flickering, jaundiced light of the tormented match. He creaked painfully up the stairs, struggling to be quiet, and horrified how every noise was magnified by the silence and his own horror of it.

On the shallow landing he saw that his mother's door was ajar. She called out to him from her room.

"This is a nice time to come home, I will say. Been along of that girl again, I'll be bound. I should like to know what you've got to say for yourself, I should indeed. It beats me how you can go on like this."

He went inside. The candle by her bed was alight, and she lay in the thin iron bed, a sallow old woman, looking older by reason of her hair in two gaunt braids like plaited string on either side of her cadaverous face. The room had not been aired for many days. It was fetid. The smell of washwater and human body and frowstiness sickened him again. He knew the room by heart, with the crudely painted religious pictures over the mantelshelf, the cheap tin alarm clock, the dressing-table with its prim frill, and the pock-marked cushion stuck with rusting pins and the big cameo brooch which she wore on Sundays. In one corner stood the coffin-shaped wardrobe from which the paint had been chipped long ago, and by it the chest of drawers which was oak but which had lost its polish. It seemed that every article of furniture stood round like sentinels, reprovingly.

"Well, now what is it?" she said.

"Mr. Putman is dead."

Instantly the hostility in her sharp eyes faded to curiosity. She was keenly avid for news. "You don't say so? Murder?"

"I went in there. He was sitting before the table. The policeman said that he had been dead for over two hours."

"Was he stiff? What was he doing? Did he look bad?" She was eager for all the more ghastly details. He had felt the burning need to confide in someone, and now, tonelessly, he gave her the information that she sought. He was distressed by the remembrance of Mr. Putman as he had sat there dead, and yet so dismally lifelike, poor husk that had until lately held such fertile seed. John wanted to tell someone—anyone. He poured out his anguished soul, fluid-wise, as though into the ewer that was her keen interest. He hated the fact that she was not nauseated, but only eager for more, for all, and he gave the facts to her baldly, with no attempt to hide their ugliness. Only when he had told her everything, did she consent to his going to bed. She seemed to have forgotten the affairs of the evening in this, the greater, affair of the night.

"I shouldn't wonder as how it was murder," she said, and he knew that she hoped it had been murder; such a situation would add enormously to her satisfaction.

He went across into his own room, meticulously clean and tidy, simple with the crude simplicity of a beautiless decorum. He could not sleep.

II

Despair engulfed John with the morning. It was a deep river that submerged all the high bravery of his soul, and it drowned him. It drenched his personality and he could not fight it. He must find some new employment. He might even have to go back to the dreadful ordeal of the drapery emporium. Even then he could not earn enough money to escape from living at home, and home with his mother married to Mr. Duckett was unthinkable.

"I shall marry him soon," she said—"no good hanging about at my time of life. No time to lose, and that's all there is to it. I warn you he won't have any of your loose ways about the house. You'll have to mind your p's and q's. He's a stickler for what's what."

"I haven't loose ways," protested John.

"I don't know what you call it, being about with that hussy until past midnight. I don't know where you get such goings-on from. Not from me, I'll be bound. I was always more particular. I wasn't going to have your father reproaching me with nothing after I was tied up, not me! I knew what men was, but I never expected to have a son like it."

"I'm not like it," John protested. "You've got hold of the wrong idea about last night."

But why protest? She would not believe you any more for the fact that you denied your guilt. She might only accept it as evidence. Women were queer. Twenty-one years of life with her had taught him that. Women had strange powers of gauging and analysing humanity. They relied too much on their powers of perception, on what they pleased to call their instinct, but which was in reality their sordid suspicion. He spent a dismal morning in the dark room behind the shop praying that Freda would not come. If she came he knew what his mother would think. She might be rude to the girl. It was not that he was ashamed; it was that the early part of last evening seemed now to be remote and disconnected from the night. The virginal glow of the garden, the warmth of her body pressed against his, and her moist demanding lips, were now as nothing against the vivid and startling contrast of death. The smell of syringa and privet was changed to the death-smell of lilies. The gleam of white blossoms on the dark oak of a coffin lid. The warmth of ardour had chilled within him into the hard bright ice of dismay.

Whilst his mother was busy in the shop, he heard someone coming across the little yard, and the echo of a gruff knock at the scullery door. Going to it, he found Banks the policeman standing there.

"Ah, a word with you, young fellow," said the policeman not unkindly.

John's nerves were tricking him. He was for a moment horrified that they might have made the discovery that Mr. Putman had been murdered, and that they had come to himself, keen with suspicion. "Th-this way," he stammered, and led him into the parlour, taking the precaution of shutting the door between it and the shop.

"It's about this here business of last night," said the policeman, and he set his helmet down on the chenille cloth by the side of the glazed mustard-coloured pot which usually held the aspidistra. It had been raining, and the aspidistra had been put out in the yard, in accordance with wet weather routine.

"Yes?"

Without his helmet Mr. Banks looked much less alarming. He seemed in fact to be almost human. "We've been going over the house," said he, "and we've found a will. You're a very lucky young man, if I may say so. The deceased must have taken a great fancy to you."

John clasped his clammy hands together. He had a vague idea that Mr. Banks was still getting at him. He did not know why, but the hideous idea of murder was rooted fast in his heart and he could not tear it up.

"I don't think you get my meaning," said Mr. Banks blandly: "that there old gentleman has left you everything. The house and the goodwill, and all the rest of it. We've 'phoned through to the solicitor what drew up the will. It seems that the deceased had a tidy bit put by. A nice little fortune, if I may say so, close on ten thousand pound. Very lucky, I call it."

Still John stared, blankly and without comprehension. His mother came in from the shop; she came sharply; and directly she saw Mr. Banks the same idea occurred to her as had occurred to John. She flinched. "Now what's all this?" she demanded hotly.

Mr. Banks repeated his piece of news. He could not understand why neither of them appeared to be overjoyed on the instant. The idea of their suspecting some ulterior motive on his part had not struck him. As he told his wife after, "Never in all me born days did I see two people take a bit of good news so quiet."

It was Mrs. Carrick who understood first. In any emergency the woman's perceptions are usually keener than are the man's.

"You don't mean to say my John's an heir?" she gasped suddenly, and then, as Mr. Banks nodded grimly, "oh, my stars! I always did take to that dear, kind old gentleman. I always did say as how he was one of the best. I hope my boy will spend it wise and proper. Oh, John! Nobody has deserved it more, that I will say. . . . ."

Bewildered, he stood there staring at her. Suddenly in upon the awkward silence the shop bell stuttered. Even at such a time his mother could not entirely disconnect herself from business. She passed out into the shop, and they heard her chattering half incoherently, telling the customer the good news which had suddenly glittered in upon her little day.

Mr. Banks stared at John. "If I were you, my lad," he said kindly, "I'd hang on to my money good and tight. I wouldn't share up with no one nohow. Do you understand?"

"Yes, rather."

"Don't you go parting. I've seen enough of parents what squeeze their kids dry."

"I shan't stay on here," said John, for now the portcullis was up between him and his freedom and he could pass out into liberty.

"That's wise."

"She's marrying Mr. Duckett, and they won't want me. I guess I'll travel a bit, and learn things. I've always wanted to go about. Then perhaps I'll get another antique shop, because I liked that, somewhere else, away. . . ."

Mr. Banks waxed confidential. "I'm all for the young 'uns getting out of the nest," he said; "it don't do them no good stopping at home. The old 'uns only fleece 'em."

"I shan't stop here, whatever happens," said John; then he got up. "This has all been a bit sudden. I want to think about it. You tell her when she comes back that I'm going for a bit of a walk."

"Look sharp! She's coming now."

He went round the table to the outer door. He passed through the yard with its refuse pail in the corner, round which the flies made a metallic humming. It was like the sound of the tops that he had possessed as a child. The smell of the pail was nauseating, warmly sweet, and in some horrible yet intangible manner it reminded him of Mr. Putman. He hated being reminded of the dear old man like that, but he had been brought face to face with all the crudities of death with a jerk. Death was appalling. It left you staring at a mere skeleton; it reeked and stunk, and it was putrid. His own imagination allied it with greening flesh and mouldering bones, and with the rancid, sickly smell that came from the rotting refuse bin.

If he thought about it much more he would be physically sick.

The idea of the money and the freedom had not yet soaked into him. He could only think of death. He opened the tall wooden door with the rusted latch which was hung against a creosoted paling. He passed through the narrow asphalt alleyway, which served as back entrance to the whole row of houses and through which pitiful dandelions and shepherd's purses made a desperate attempt to flower. On either side they protruded, brassy loveliness, and a gay grey lace of blossom. He passed into the street, sweltering in the midday sun.

Waiting there was Freda.

III

Freda wore a jaunty woollen cap pulled down over her dark hair. Her frock was not too long; it gleamed, and under its whiteness he could see the roundness of her arms and the soft inviting curves of her body. Directly she saw John she came closer, and thrust her arms intimately through his.

"I was waiting for you. Somehow I guessed you'd come out here."

He was not surprised to see Freda, and yet he was amazed at the new intimacy which had sprung up between them with the night. He realized that yesterday he had not been himself; he had broken down all the barriers of reserve, though now it seemed to be unbelievable that he had kissed the lovely little face beneath the gay cap.

"Let's go somewhere where we can talk," she said, and directed his steps alongside her own.

They went to the backwater, where a wide arm of the sea flung itself caressingly behind the little town. The tide was out. The pathway lay left between still pools like great pearls, and the same colour. There were long patches of pale sand, and of jade weed, and here or there the up-pricking rosiness of sea pinks, and the faded sea lavenders whose colour had been drained out of their hearts by the too ardent sun. There were no trees, only here or there the highish banks, along which the little path ran fringed by ragged grasses on either side. Freda jumped down to the sand and settled herself beneath the bank in the bright sunshine. John sat beside her. It was peaceful sitting here, with the jade and the pale amber, and the water which was like pearl with never a whisper of the great sea beyond. Far away sailing ships passed. They were so far, or the water was so pale, that it looked as though they sailed on air, part of the horizon itself; they were ships gliding through atmosphere.

Freda still held his hand. She held it between her own, and he could feel her fingers pressing his. She was eager, and he thought that in her eagerness she did not realize her intimacy.

"John, I've heard! Isn't it wonderful?"

"Yes, marvellous, only I can't believe it yet."

"A fortune, John, so your mother says. What are you going to do with it?"

He had not made any plans, although some dreams had already shuttlecocked through his sub-conscious mind. They rose exultingly to the surface of thought now, like corks rising through deep water to the light. They were in no wise mature. About them were bubbles, the light froth of fancy.

"I shan't stay on here," he said. That was definite.

The obnoxious presence of Mr. Duckett had settled that for him.

"That's wise of you."

"I think I'll take another antique shop somewhere else, because I am interested in that. I don't know where yet. I shall have to look round."

She pouted a little. When she pouted, her under lip forced a new line about her mouth. "But why do anything at all?" she asked. "You'll be rich. Ten thousand pounds! My goodness, how much more do you want?"

"I'd hate not to work. I love old things."

Freda scooped a little hole in the sand with her disengaged finger. It was lovely, a thin pencil of a finger, white, pink-tipped at the cusp. "I don't like old things," she said, "I like those nice, new-fashioned things that you get at shops. Lots of shine on them, and plate glass, and ornaments and things. When I furnish . . ." she cast a sudden glance at him from under her soft lashes—"when I furnish, that is the sort of thing that I intend to have."

An idea, which had probably come to him years ago from a picture of Amsterdam which he had once seen, rose out of his mind and clothed itself in words. "I thought of going to Holland for a little while to study art there. They have the most wonderful pictures and pottery."

She said longingly, "Holland must be lovely. Windmills and things. I'd like to honeymoon in Holland," and again she looked at him.

"Perhaps you will one day," said John uncomfortably.

"I wonder."

He caught her hand, imprisoning it. He caught it sharply, almost afraid that he might hurt her, and yet desiring to hurt her, for he felt like that about her. Possessive, demanding, needing her.

"Last night . . ." he said.

"Yes?" she smiled. "Oh, that. I got into an awful row when I went indoors. Somebody saw us."

"I say, I'm frightfully sorry about it all. I don't know what came over me; I felt dreadful afterwards."

"They said that I was throwing myself away," she told him, ignoring the apology. "They can't say that now, can they?"

"I don't see why not, because you're lovely. You're beautiful, far, far above me, and of course you know it. I can't think how you can come and look at a fellow like me."

"You are rich," she said.

"I wasn't rich last night."

He wished that she would not harp on the money, for now he realized how it detracted from her beauty, this grasping for wealth. He hated to connect her with avarice. He hated to believe that she had brought him out here only to talk to him about his money. Last night there had been no question of anything but their two selves.

"Don't let's talk about it," he said, "I'm just the same as I was yesterday. You know that. If you had all the money in the world it would never change you, you would just be Freda."

"Kiss me again," she begged.

He knew that he ought not to kiss her, but he did. He drew her under the shelter of the sandy bank, beaten on its summit into a path. The bleached grasses, long and dishevelled, blew down them both like a woman's hair. Tiny pin-points of sand were blown across their faces. He kissed her, trying to recapture the ardour of last night, but that ardour was elusive. John had not yet learnt that passion is a fickle jade; she is sweet the first time, but she cannot sustain that sweetness. It is the first kiss that intoxicates, the first caress that goes to the head, and after that all caresses sate. Passion is the silver faun flashing through the forest of desire. Once you have caught him, and pressed his bright young body to you, and looked down into his eyes, you find that he has pointed ears, and that his feet are cloven hoofs making ugly prints in the earth. The faun is ugly really. Once you have possessed him you do not covet him again.

John released her. She, too, realized that the kiss was deficient in some quality that she could not actually define.

"You are cold," she whispered.

"I did not mean to be cold. I felt different about it, that was all. I don't know why." Was it that the blossomy face and the warmly moist mouth had lost their charm for him? Was it, in reality, that he did not know himself?

"Money has spoilt you," she suggested.

Money again! He had never wanted to be rich, he had merely desired enough for a small home of his own, a home in which he was master and not pack mule. He felt somehow that Freda was no longer divinely acquiescent in his arms, but that she was groping for the reins and attempting to drive him. She was a master with the whip in her hand, and if she was not careful he would be the pack mule lumbering before her and laden with the burden of her.

"Last night," she said teasingly, "do you know that I thought of marrying you?"

He had never thought of marriage as applying to himself. Until now it had constituted for him a frowsty house in the main street, with an ugly back room occupied by chairs and tables, and cheap bedrooms above. Marriage was something which you associated with the backyard lumbered with old toy crates, and the refuse bin stenching in its corner, pocked cheese for supper, and his mother railing.

"I don't think I shall ever marry," he said, taking her in all seriousness, through in truth she had never thought of him in connection with marriage, not until she had heard about the inheritance.

"Your sort generally don't marry," she said disdainfully; "they come and get round a girl and mean nothing by it. It isn't fair."

She pouted a little. Her body slid away from him. He sensed that he had irritated her, and he did not understand how he could re-establish himself in her good graces.

"It was your music," he whispered—"I loved your music."

"I daresay. You'd never heard any decent music before, that was the only reason. I don't want you to like my music, I want you to like me for myself."

"I do like you, Freda."

"Last night you loved me."

He could not explain what had come over him, but so much had happened since last night. He had found himself faced by the dreadful proximity of death, high words with his mother, the realization of her intended marriage with Mr. Duckett. Since last night life had changed itself as a chameleon suddenly leaping from dead brown leaves to bright vivid grass. Yesterday he had been a boy sitting on the sea front, indulging a boy's fancy in a boy's love; to-day he was a man! It seemed that the outer coating had been stripped from him ruthlessly, suddenly, like old skin peeled from a chestnut, leaving it white and virgin-like beneath. He was not the same being.

He saw that her eyes were hostile. A girl's eyes should never be hard like that, but always lovely, young, and sweet. Their reproachful anger worried him.

"Why are you angry with me?" he asked.

"No girl likes being played with, and you have been playing with me. You never meant anything last night."

"I thought that I loved you," he said truthfully.

"And now you find that you don't?"

He was too immature to lie. The kiss had lost its thrill, the passion had abated. "It isn't the same to-day.

I mean . . . well . . . you know . . ." and he floundered desperately.

"Funny that it should coincide with you coming into all that money," she sniffed.

'Oh, Lord,' he thought, 'now I've said the wrong thing again and she's fed up with me.' He got up swiftly, sweeping down the sand from his suit, and he stood there before her. The light wind shook his hair. It had sprung up since they came to this spot, now it rippled the pearl pools of deserted sea beyond. No longer were the ships sailing on atmosphere, they were riding in on a tide that was already commingling with the little ponds of the backwater.

Freda was sulking. "You're sick of me?" she said.

All the while in his ears there was sounding, like a brittle waterfall of music, the theme of the *Minuet*. And he knew that the music had been the sole attraction which he had found in Freda.

IV

He would not go out into the gardens that night.

Somehow he supposed that Freda would be there waiting, but he knew now, suddenly, with a sharp truth, that he could not hope to recall the ecstasy of that first kiss. It was Dead Sea fruit. Glorious, bloomy, luscious to look upon, and when you put it to your lips mere acrid dust upon those lips. There had been much that had thrust itself between to-day and yesterday. Happenings had rolled like hoops across his path; he was giddy with their bewildering circles. He felt that life was afire with these happenings, their flame as swiftly trodden out by the cold feet of death. The legacy, this strange will of poor Mr. Putman's—why would Mr. Banks keep referring to him as 'the deceased'?—his own resolve, strengthening with the day, to start afresh, to do something away from this place and its drab associations.

No, he would not go out into the gardens to-night.

"As to that girl, that Miss Perkins," said his mother, "she's no good. You should have seen her prick up her ears when she heard about the money. 'Oh, indeed', she said, and she tossed her head. I knew what she was thinking. I know what they means when they looks like that. You'd better be careful."

She nodded wisely through the kitchen door, where she was wiping wet cups with a fetid and clammy cloth over the sink.

"I am going to be jolly careful."

"I've been thinking," said his mother, "if it wouldn't be a good thing for you to build yourself a nice new shop at the corner of the esplanade; a sort of a refreshment shop, with one part for souvenirs and suchlike for me, and the other where you could sell cups of tea and minerals, and so on. It would be a good idea, for there isn't nobody in the place except Gould's, and they're so dear."

"I don't think I'd care about that," said John solemnly, "because I am thinking of getting right away from this place."

"Going away?" She stopped her vigorous wiping and gazed at him blankly.

"I thought of starting an antique business somewhere. This isn't a good place for a young fellow."

"You won't leave me?" She stared at him open-mouthed across the ugly little room. Her eyes were bulging. A pulse twitched in her stringy throat.

"But you will have Mr. Duckett?"

"Oh, I daresay. After I've done so much for you, and all that! Surely, aren't boys the most ungrateful creatures as you could wish to meet? I shan't let you go, so there!"

She was emphatic, vehement. Small gusts of fear

shook him like a wind; he felt the corners of his mouth trembling, the harness of the pack mule slipping into place and the reins being jerked warningly across his thin shoulders. "We'll see," he said evasively.

"We won't see, we'll just do. After I've spent the best years in my life doing things for you, and all that, and then you come along and say you're going away, thank you, with ten thousand pounds in your pocket and never a penny for me. Let you go without a word? Not me! Not much!"

He paled. There was the cheery sound of the milkman in the yard, the ring of his boot on the asphalt, the yodelling call, "Milk-o". It diverted his mother for the moment and she went bustling to the back door. The morning's delivery had gone sour, and she wanted to know why. She wasn't going to be put off with last night's milk, so the milkman had better get that into his head once and for all. John heard her wrangling, and stuffed his fingers into his ears. He would go crazy if he stayed. He slid out through the shop, shrouded in dust-sheets for the night, the revolving post-card stand like a white sarcophagus, and as eerie.

It was raining weakly, as though it had never anticipated such a procedure and could not properly enjoy it. There were thin black lines of rain against the opposite walls, and the soft smell of moist earth, which is so indescribably sweet, rising from the road itself, and from the gardens further down the street. Where could he go? Not to the antique shop, with its close-shuttered windows, and its mournful sign, and upstairs that stark something, husk of Mr. Putman, stretched out on the four-post bed. He wondered morbidly if Mr. Putman were stiff now? He had been dreadfully limp before; he had sagged in their arms, his spineless body broken in the middle.

John went down the street, with the old houses on either side, brooding under their eaves grown shaggy like old men's eyebrows. He went on, thinking of his mother, and of the future, and wondering how he should get away from it all and whither. He went round to the sea front.

Freda was sitting mutely on the iron seat in the fine rain.

He saw her at once, and some new emotion stirred within him. It was pity, a new branch springing from the blasted oak of his dead love. She was wet like some little bird with all its feathers ruffled up, and out of the softness and the ruffling two brightly beady eyes staring at him. He wanted to take her inside his mackintosh, and shelter her. He opened it wide, as a tent is opened, with himself the supporting tent pole; he received her into the voluminous depths of the unfashionable coat which had been his father's before him. She curled close to him; she was small. They occupied the corner of the seat, with the rain increased so that it was no longer fine threads but soft, like feathers falling lightly through the air. The earth smelt delicious, and the syringa and the privet mixed with it. Looking into the depths of his coat he saw her face like a white flower floating on dark water, and he wanted to kiss her, not with the passion of yesterday but with the possessive, more pitying, passion of to-day.

"I thought you wouldn't come," she whimpered.

"You shouldn't have thought that, silly."

"But I did. The money changed you."

"Let's forget the money."

"It's lovely like this."

So they sat, at utter peace with the world. Presently the rain stopped. The moon came out like a white swan riding on a tide of dark clouds. There were no stars, only the one white bird—a passive moon which swam superbly on. They clung together more for warmth than for love. Long, long after, she spoke.

"I'm sorry I'm going home to-morrow."

"So am I."

"If I stayed, do you think . . ."

"Do I think what?" he asked.

She blushed, and her arms clutching him to her drew his body closer still. "Oh, John, I do care for you. Don't send me away from you."

All the while sitting here he had been hearing the whimsical phantom music of the *Minuet*. Now it died down into the boom and slide of distant oceans. It held the discord of Raff in his *Cavatina*, the bigness of Beethoven in his solemn chords of *Pathétique*. He said with scrupulous truth, "If you mean marrying you, Freda, I'm not old enough to marry. I want to think about it first."

"But you love me?"

"I care for you, but not quite in that way. Life has been a bit bewildering since yesterday. I don't think I have actually found myself yet."

She pushed him from her petulantly. "All very well to lead a girl on and then mean nothing by it," she remarked indignantly; "it isn't as though you hadn't the money."

"Oh, damn that money! You've done nothing but harp on it all the time! I believe that is the only thing that attracts you!" Then he stopped dead, ashamed of himself.

They rose and stared at one another. He saw her stripped; she was just the grasping girl-woman, reaching out with tenacious hands for the glitter of his gold. She did not care for him. She had wanted physical passion last night, because she had felt that way and had supposed that he would do as well as anyone else. She wanted him to-day because he had ten thousand pounds to give with himself. He hated the fact that he realized it.

"It's good-bye," he said shakily, and held out his hand.

"Do you think I'd shake hands with a rotten flirt?" she demanded contemptuously.

V

He walked home by the sea. There was a stream of gold across the hills and troughs of the waves, but he knew that it was fool's gold. It mocked him, sang in the eternal salt rage of water tumbling on beach, 'Ten thousand pounds' worth, ten thousand pounds' worth.' The sea was flinging up driftwood. He felt rather helplessly like driftwood himself, something that had been bright and brown, now sodden and soaked and swollen, nothing more than a spongy mass, distorted from all semblance of shape. It was driven on the hard stones, torn back again, flung triumphantly aside, crushed, tossed, mocked, derided by the very waters that had spoilt it. He thought of the water as the world, of the light of the moon as his gold, which had changed everything.

He would have to be very careful; he would have to tread cautiously until he was more certain of his foothold, for there were pitfalls. There was his mother, and Mr. Duckett, and there was Freda.

But if his courage failed him, he could run away. He would have to run away to save his own soul. Boyishly he cloaked the adventure in fascination. Running away should be easy.

VI

Mr. Putman was buried the early part of the following week, and for a little time matters hung fire. Mr. Oglivy, the solicitor, who was a nice old gentleman, came to see John. He was a pleasant person, round and rubicund, with a bland expression and a large stomach. He acquainted John with a simple outline of investments, and advised him to leave the money where it was for the present. He suggested that the debts and expenses should be paid from the proceeds of the sale of the house and the furniture therein.

John did not want to keep any of Mr. Putman's treasures for himself. "A lot of old truck," his mother said: "it is only natural that you wouldn't want it. Why didn't the poor old gentleman buy himself some nice new things instead of all that rubbish?"

"Perhaps he didn't like new things?"

"Oh, nonsense! Everybody likes new things, only it isn't all as can afford them. Now a nice bit of fumed oak, or one of them smart chiffoniers—or suchlike . . ." She eyed her son hopefully.

John went through Mr. Putman's collection methodically. He hesitated before the picture on the stairs of the woman in the lace chemise, for that picture ate down into him. It had a grotesque fascination all its own. The peering face of the woman, with the eyes which held cunning under their rapturous beauty, the gleam of flesh, the darkness of the shadows. There was some cabal attraction, and John knew that it was not entirely a good attraction, for he liked to look at the picture alone, and he did not know why it made him feel like that. Finally he sacrificed it to the auctioneer's hammer. The bed he would have liked, with its Parthenon colonnades, and its vines exquisitely carved and climbing up it. Yet he could not dissociate the bed from the memory of Mr. Putman lying there dead, stiffened, or limp and sagging between John and the policeman; he decided that with the attendant memory he did not want the bed after all.

Just as he was leaving the house, he caught a glimpse of an ornament standing in the corner of a bedroom. He went back into the room and took it down, surveying it critically. He did not know whether he admired it or hated it. It was a bronze. At first he had supposed it to be china, a foreign china, painted in gay colours and highly glazed. It was a Chinese god. The pouched, jaundiced face was lustrous, the slots of eyes indifferent, the pale lips curved in an odiously contemptuous smile. The body was completely covered save for two male breasts, jaundiced and pouched, too, with protruding nipples of titanic size and ludicrous shape. The rest was clothed in a cloak of jade and lapis lazuli. All colours seemed to be blended together in that cloak. Flowers were picked out upon it with microscopic care: there were stars of jasmine, buds of bougainvillea, claret and wine, mulberry-hued roses, paleness of lotus, and the flame of cactus. It was accurate with the meticulous accuracy of most Oriental workmanship. John did not know why he liked it, for the thing was ugly; the god himself, squatting on his haunches, was sinister—he suggested demonology. His hands were strangely distorted, and in the fat fingers he gathered close the cloak, looping it about him. He suggested a portentous suavity, allied with fear. He was gruesome, and yet attractive in his gruesomeness.

"I think I'll keep him," said John, and he did not know why. The god was so small that he slid it into his pocket.

He forgot all about it.

VII

The furniture fetched far more than they had anticipated. Mr. Putman had been a connoisseur, and he had always kept the perfect pieces for himself. They went cheaply in proportion, but the prices that they fetched staggered the little town. The picture on the stairs, of the woman peering over her shoulder, brought a couple of dealers down from London, who bid against each other. They left John with an extra thousand pounds in his pocket, and sheer wonder that such a thing could be.

Mrs. Carrick did not believe it when she heard. She had thought the whole house to be full of rubbish, and she had not considered it possible that it would fetch more than twenty pounds. The house itself went cheaply. Being situated on the main street, and having but little garden, it did not attract the class of purchaser willing to pay a big price for it. John found himself far richer than he had expected, and free to do what he would. But whenever he suggested a move he met with protest from his mother.

Although arrangements were forging ahead for her marriage to Mr. Duckett, which was to take place early in September, she maintained that nothing would induce her to part with her son. His newly acquired income had given her affection for him an added zest. She stipulated that on no account must he take up any form of employment, but must live like a gentleman with her—what better place for a loving son than his home?

She was demanding a weekly payment from him that was far more than would have been expected for the like accommodation elsewhere. He hated himself for realizing that his mother was the shrewish type of woman who exacted a toll from him, and he disliked the fact that she held strongly between her fingers the reins which drove him. He hated it all the more because he knew how he would have appreciated the gentler, Madonna type of mother. She might be a wise mother, but her thin-lipped prudence cut into him like a thong. He did not want a mother who was wise in that way, but one who was sweet, and who drove him by sheer love.

He made the necessary surreptitious preparations in

case he should be driven to run away. He was a little ashamed of the preparations, yet he nourished a certain grotesque joy, as of one who harbours some delightful secret. He made up his mind that when he made the move it would be to Holland. He wanted to learn much, and to lay the knowledge as the foundation for some antique business, to be obtained later. He instructed Mr. Oglivy, the lawyer, to look out for such a place, and he insisted only that his business must be some distance from his old home. Mr. Oglivy believed that in such a stipulation John Carrick was wise.

Whether John would have actually separated himself from his mother when the time came, cannot be said, save that he was suddenly thrust into the vortex of a storm, and from that vortex he could only save himself by flight.

Mr. Duckett was spending the day with the family, as Mr. Duckett had taken to doing of late. He said that it was to make arrangements about his marriage, but in reality it was to save on the food at his own cheap lodgings. Mr. Duckett had very nice ideas as to economy. He hoped that his economy was not obvious to others. He ate at the Carricks', with a vulgar and healthy appetite, smacking his lips noisily, and gulping down his tea and cocoa in desperate chugging gulps like waves at high tide on a loud shore. When he left he always laughed as he pocketed an apple or two from the dish on the sideboard. He protested that he liked to take an apple home for his cat!

Mrs. Carrick had been insisting that John should give her a substantial sum as a wedding present. She was entirely oblivious of the fact that, whilst death duties and debts were in the process of being paid, John had merely a small balance upon which he could draw. She argued that he was mean; after all, he ought to be glad to do something for his dear mother. It was his pig-headedness. Mr. Duckett, who realized the immense advantage of a definite sum of money, took her part. John saw the argument reaching the point where it emerged into the brassy light of a brawl. He saw it as one of the numerous vulgar scenes that were for ever eddying through this ugly little room. He realized that he could stand very little more of it. He lapsed into mulish silence. If they went on much longer something within him would snap, and he would be ended. The innate desire to save himself urged him forward. He could not stand against her tactics. He wanted to get up and scream, "Shut up, shut up, will you? I can't stick another word. Shut up! Shut up, I tell you!" but he kept rein on himself, eyeing her from under lowered lids.

He made some excuse, and slipped up to his room and packed the few things that he could collect with shaky hands into his imitation leather suitcase. He acted on the brave impulse of the moment, otherwise he would not have been able to carry out his plan.

If he stayed, she would suck the life out of him, harness him for ever, flog him before her. Whilst a customer kept her busy in the shop, and Mr. Duckett took forty unlovely winks over the local newspaper on the horsehair sofa, John slipped out into the hot street beyond.

It was now. Opportunity had definitely arrived.

Chapter Three

But I will walk upon the wooded hill
Where stands a grove, O pine of sister pines,
And when the downy twilight droops her wing
And no sea glimmers and no mountains shine
My heart shall listen still. . . .
Half to remember days that have gone by
And dream, and dream that I am home again!

JAMES ELROY FLECKER

I

JOHN came to the conclusion that Thomas Cook and Son was a most excellent organization. They had taken his belated self, and had organized the whole trip for him. They recommended him to a cheap but respectable London hotel, where he slept, and for the first time in his life tasted the glorious taste of freedom. He chose a breakfast which both bewildered and delighted him. He played with the shining taps in his bedroom, ingenious new toys; he studied the hotel rules; he found a dozen amusing and appetizing items of interest, though some of them were more than a little alarming. Then he went to Cook's to collect his tickets, and to Mr. Oglivy's office to collect a sum of money.

On the way he discovered that he had the wrong sort of cap. Full of enthusiasm for the new adventure, he went into a shop in the Strand and chose for himself a more usual outfit. When he emerged he was a new personality. He was at last himself. The mark of his harness no longer rubbed home its imprint on his lithe body. He wore a passably cut dark suit and a plain hat and tie. He had ordered warm luxurious underclothing, and three neatly patterned shirts. He was a young man setting out on an adventure, and it is always an encouraging spectacle to the onlooker.

He spent a day in London seeing sights, which impressed him very much. No one interfered with him, save outside St. Paul's Cathedral, where an old woman wanted to sell him food for the pigeons, and a ragged man urged him to buy an out-of-date Old Moore's almanack. He shook them off with difficulty. He gaped owlishly at Trafalgar Square, and went to Westminster Abbey, revelling in its blue light, but disliking its cluttering of statues and its insistent reminders of death. He rode on the top of a bus as far as the bus went, and back, and saw all manner of places which he could not name, but which enchanted him.

He did not want to stay longer in London. He had got a glimpse of it, a series of snapshots which he could arrange within his mind and take a look at whenever he wished. Besides, the expense of the place shocked him. He did not think that he could afford to stay too long.

He went back to the hotel with its cut steel façades, and its wealth of glitter, and its carpets deep and soft like moss in woods. In the next room a man and his wife were quarrelling. Their strident voices smote in on his silence, and made him hurry in strapping his bag. He did not like quarrels; he wanted to get away from them. He had never supposed people could quarrel in an hotel like this, so rare, so luxurious, dazzle of crystal glass, gleam of steel. Yet as he carried his bag out into the corridor he heard the sounds of their arguing growing louder. A drunken man, dangling noisily a key with its thick iron label attached, was coming jauntily down the passage. He hailed John as a friend.

"Number six hundred and twen'two," he said pleasantly.

"Along there, I should think."

So life went on just the same behind the burnish of a great hotel as behind the little shop at home. Just the same wherever you looked, wherever you went. You could not escape it.

John Carrick left for the Hook that night.

The ship sailed down the long line which is Harwich harbour, with the fog lying wraithlike over Shotley, and all the evenly spaced lamps down Harwich front like so many planets in a new hemisphere which was earth. The ship passed on and out to sea, with the Gunfleet lighthouse swinging its one wide eye round in circles, and little gay groups of lights significant of clustering towns all down the coast. As he stood in the stem of the boat watching this new and dazzling spectacle it seemed that in with the throbbing of the engines there was the faint chiming of Freda's music. For had not all the adventure started with the impertinent enquiry and answer of the *Minuet*? It was in the up-churned spume, irresistible.

He did not for a moment consider what his mother might be feeling, for now she was remote. He knew that she would merely condemn him as being wickedly ungrateful, and in a sense he was sorry, very sorry, to part with her. If only she had been the woman whom he wanted in his life, tender-wise, sweetly loving, mother of his desire! But she was not. Far, far better admit the truth that she was shrewish and sharp than struggle for ever to set the halo of romance about her head.

He had in his pocket an introduction to a Dutch family in Haarlem. They occasionally took in paying guests, and Cook's informed him that they would be more congenial to him than if he took up his abode at an hotel. The hotel in Haarlem was the Funckler, eminently Dutch. It would be easier for him if he were a member of an English-speaking Dutch family. John had agreed. He was prepared to agree with anything.

Just recently the idea of Holland had magnetized him, perhaps because of the picture of his youth, perhaps because it opened out such an excellent foundation for knowledge of art. He would collect pictures from Amsterdam, tiles from Delft, old-world curios from Rotterdam, for his shop.

He did not know when he would return. At the moment he was a leaf eddied by the wind of adventure, and every moment was precious. He was in that enviable position of having no need to return save when he desired.

In that spirit he arrived at Haarlem.

II

The house of the van den Berghs stood on the *gracht* which leads to the prison round and flat, and which can be viewed from between the sails of windmills, and the merchants' establishments and granaries along the cobbled quayside. The van den Berghs' was one of the Renaissance type of houses, tall and gabled, with frequent windows, diamond-paned, and four proud flat steps which led gently to the main door. Between it and the water was a road, bordered by a cobbled path and a fine lacework of trees, which stood as sentinels beside the *gracht* itself. The trees were like green veils, light gauze veils, for between the pattern of leaf and twig you could glean the sparkle of water. Now and then the shadow of a great barge pushing its clumsy way upstream, laden with bags of grain and flour, and hiding the bright water for a while in passing. Beyond, on the left, was the open space with the green glow of gardens, and the redness and goldness of flowers in blossom, and the wide vista of the Hillegom Road. Still beyond, there was more green, significant of the beginning of the Haarlemmer Hout, which is the exquisite forest forming the entrance to Haarlem itself. John came to the house and tapped timidly on the door, which was opened by a large but neat Dutch servant, who understood no language save her own, but who called the *Mevrouw*. The *Mevrouw* spoke the most excellent—perhaps too excellent—English.

Cook's had cabled as to John's arrival, and he had been allotted the big front room on the first floor, which was panelled with dark oak and had a fireplace as big as the average room in a modern English house. There was a little bedroom beyond, which was frowsty with too much steam heat, and heavy with plush furniture and velvet curtains, but John was not concerned with the bedroom. It was the main room that interested him. The *Mevrouw* apologized that it had so little furniture.

"Most always," said the *Mevrouw*, who was large and round and placid, "it is occupied by the artist gentleman, and he likes much to place his easel where he most wish. He do not want too much in here. If you like more, I will fetch him," but her manner did not suggest that the idea would please her.

"I like it as it is," said John.

"Perhaps you too are artist?" said the *Mevrouw* in enquiry, and she folded her ample hands on her enormously high stomach.

"Sort of," said John.

"Ah," said the *Mevrouw*, and she nodded wisely as one who understands much. "You find us simple people," she said. "There is me and the *Mijnheer*. He do not appear too much. I have trained him as is right and proper. It is not the man's place to interfere in the house. I am the master in my own establishment. I have the one *vondeling*, no more."

John had no idea what a *mijnheer* might be, but supposed that it was either her husband or a servant; he rather imagined that it was the former, and he felt a spasm of pity thrust through him. The *Mevrouw* was large and a little terrifying. He had no doubt that she was the master. He could not conceive who the *vondeling* was.

"She brings you up the meals," said the *Mevrouw*; "we call her Maddalan."

Then he guessed that the *vondeling* was their child.

At the moment when John arrived at Haarlem, the *vondeling* had mumps. The *Mevrouw* decreed that Minna should bring him his meals. Minna was slow of movement, she smiled a great deal in a large and bland way, and she wore so many clothes that she gave you the idea of being immensely fat. Minna was large, florid and plain, as were indeed all the Dutch women whom you met. She spoke little English, and therefore could not converse, but during those few strange days John had time to get used to his surroundings.

He was afraid to venture out too far. He sat for hours in the great window of his room, which was different from anything that he had seen before, so that it intrigued him. He rested on the oak seat and stared out between the lacework of green leaves to the gleam of the *gracht* beneath. In places the leaves were already turning gold. The light that filtered through them was dazzling. It was as though the room were flooded with filaments of jade; cascades of green water quivered through those brilliant boughs, tinted with crystal snatched from the reflection of still water. There were prismatic colourings from the diamond panes, new amethysts and carmines, bright inconceivable blues. They pierced into the dark interior of the room; they lighted on Delft plates and bright brass and the spruce table, which always seemed to be set for his meal. The lights enchanted him.

When John ventured out it was into the Stadstraat, which is all commercial confusion and which frightened him by its busyness. He tried twice to find the Groote Markt, because the *Mevrouw* told him it was the place to see, and instructed him to follow the great tower of St. Bavo and find it in that way. The tower of St. Bavo reminded John of some giant chessman against the sky. It was strangely crenellated, and it had eerie shadows about it, but it was almost impossible to find the base from which it rose. Twice attempting to get to it, he found himself in the yards of indignant Dutch merchants, who did not appreciate trespassers. Knowing no Dutch, he was alarmed.

He retreated back to his one room and wondered why he had ever set out on this expedition at all. He had had an idea that there would be beauty here, and so far he had found no real beauty outside the loveliness of his own room. Holland was a dull country, flat, and the people in it were dull and flat too. There were no antique shops at all, only eating-houses and sweet shops and banks. It was singularly disappointing to him.

He wrote to Mr. Oglivy that he thought he should return early the following week—he named Wednesday as a probable day—and then he would get to work to find some antique shop suitable for him to make a start in, in England.

But before Wednesday John met Maddalan.

III

Maddalan brought in the dinner one midday. She came into the room shyly, for she was very young. She was just eighteen. John saw her first as she stood in the doorway, with the wide shelf above it ornamented with blue Delft dishes—Maddalan wearing a grey stuff frock cut away at the throat and finishing in a crisp white collar. Maddalan was small; she reminded him strangely of a Christmas rose by reason of her deadly white skin and her palely yellow hair. She was intensely proud of that hair, cut in a short fringe as she believed was fashionable in more flighty European quarters, and ending in a couple of great plaits which trailed far below her waist. They swung as she walked, those plaits, like ropes in the summer wind.

Maddalan was not ordinarily pretty, she held the promise of something that was far from ordinary, of a fuller, riper loveliness, of a vivid beauty when she had matured. In the whiteness of her face, and in vivid contrast to the pale honey-yellow of her hair, were her eyes. They were the colour of the irises lifting their purple lips from the flower border. John thought when he saw her standing there, "If she wore a green frock, flat and straight like their leaves, she would be all iris. Yellow like the flags that one sees in country streams, white like some of the more cultivated varieties, purple like her eyes."

But Maddalan did not wear green. It was unfashionable for a woman to wear too bright colours in Holland. The *Mevrouw* had instructed her that only the wicked women in the houses of ill fame wore bright colours; those same wicked women who are to be found round the Onderkerksplein in Amsterdam, and who beckon through the windows there and call men with their lustful eyes.

Maddalan was greatly shocked.

She saw John, and she brought him the rough pottery dish full of soup and set it on the table before him.

"I have been ill," she said, "or I should have come before"—and she spoke perfect English.

It had been raining outside. Suddenly, as she stood there beside him, the sun broke through and pierced the rain-sodden boughs with a spear of gold. In that light she was unbelievably lovely. He remembered Freda, how he had thought of her as a spray of blossom on thorn, and he saw Maddalan and thought of her as irises and found her vastly different. Freda had been nothing to this. What he had felt for Freda had been merely physical desire, what he felt for Maddalan he knew was something approaching love.

"Perhaps," said Maddalan, when he told her haltingly how he had journeyed alone into the little town, and of his reception by indignant merchants—"perhaps you have not understood. You have been homesick?"

"I have been very homesick," he said.

"I once went to England. I went with my aunt who married an Englishman, and who lives in an aristocratic part of your London. He has a cheese and butter shop in Tooting. I was homesick. Tooting is not like Haarlem."

John had never been to Tooting, and he did not know. "I don't like Haarlem," he said, "not awfully, you know. I feel out of it, lost, and it is not a very comfortable feeling."

She leant forward, balancing herself on the flats of her hands pressed firmly on the table. The plaits of hair slid on either side of her face, framing it in pure amber. "You must not say that. Come, I will show you Haarlem as it is, as foreigners never see it. Shall we?"

"Let's start right away," he exclaimed, "only . . . only what will your mother say?"

"The *Mevrouw* will not mind. She bade me entertain you."

It was quite true. The *Mevrouw* spoilt Maddalan as much as such a grimly determined woman could ever spoil anybody. She liked to brag about the girl. "In all Holland," the *Mevrouw* would assert, "there is not one like our Maddalan. No, not even in the *Huis den Bosche* itself." (The *Huis den Bosche*, as John learnt, was the summer palace of Queen Wilhelmina.) The *Mevrouw* was proud of Maddalan, proud but strict, as she believed right and proper.

"We will start this afternoon," said the girl.

Between dinner and the starting, John wrote to Mr. Oglivy, and he said that after all he thought that he would stay a little longer. It seemed that there was more to see than he had supposed. He wielded his pen tactfully and hoped the solicitor would not read between the lines. When the old man got the letter, he chuckled to himself, read it again, and yet chuckled again. "And I wonder who the lady is?" he commented, still laughing.

So much for John's tact.

IV

Maddalan, dressed for the street, wore a long grey coat and a small grey hat which came down like a bonnet around her face and covered her ears. The two amber plaits swung down behind her. She came to John's room when she was ready, and tapped softly on the door.

"I have some shopping to do for the *Mevrouw*," she said; "perhaps you will accompany me?"

They went out together.

She was far more at ease than he was. She seemed to hold no hint of embarrassment as she tripped along, her feet clinking against the rounded cobbles with the great iron rings set in them for the barges to tie up. She carried a large basket which she refused to hand over to him.

They went along, turning into the narrow busy street. It twisted, never staying long in one direction. It jostled with people, and on the left, looming over it, rose the great tower of St. Bavo. Maddalan did not give way for the people passing, for it seemed that no Dutch person ever did. She pushed along before her, and all the while she clutched the basket as though it were the most treasured possession in all the world.

"I am going to the Groote Markt," she said. "This

day they have the market there, and it is good. There is useful shopping to be done; it may interest you."

So little, and so slight, it seemed strange that she could push her way through the crowd. She did not allow them to disturb her. She passed up the winding, straggling street, with its inordinate stream of cyclists for ever passing to and fro, and the first gold flurry of autumn leaves blowing here or there about them. She passed round by the Stadhuisen, imposing and grand, and under the shadow of the great church with its innumerable little inconspicuous and bolted doors. There was the statue of Koster, upright and rigid, there was the jangle of the meat market and the stalls at the far end where Maddalan bought. She bought, with tremendous solemnity, gleaming fish from the Zuyder Zee, butter and vegetables. She and the stallkeepers exchanged conversation in a sing-song monotonous manner. They did not become excited, for there was nothing excitable about it all. At last the basket was filled.

"I will carry it," said John.

She resigned it to him without a protest. "And now," said she, "I will show you something; it might interest you much, and you could not find it for yourself."

They passed out of the confusion of the Groote Markt and, crossing the narrow streets in full spate of people, turned aside. Maddalan steered her way down a side street, stopping before one of the smaller and more insignificant houses there. The house had all the frequent windows and the small doorways, yet was of no set period whatsoever. It was dull in the extreme.

Old Jan opened the door to them.

Maddalan introduced John in English, and it seemed that Jan spoke a little. He ushered them into his sitting-room with its heavily sealed windows and its frowst of steam heat like a damp blanket on everything. The sitting-room was small, and meticulously clean. In the corner there burnt a small light, which

Maddalan told John was to keep water hot for the "*thee*" of which Jan, in common with all the true Dutch, was inordinately fond.

"This gentleman," said Maddalan, referring to John with a wave of her hand, "is anxious to see some old things. He intends starting a shop in England. He has come here to study our china and pictures. You will help him? So?"

"Delft is for the china," said old Jan solemnly. He had grown big with his age; his red-rimmed eyes were rheumy; his silvered head was snugly covered by a round black cap. In his ears, the lobes of which seemed to be grotesquely elongated, were small tin earrings. He fascinated John.

"Yes, yes," said Maddalan impatiently, "but you have china too?"

The old man pottered across the room and, stooping wheezily over his cupboard, brought out his treasures into the light. He held each as though it were brittle, as though a breath might blow it away. He laid them on the table. There were tiles—tiles of such blues that John had merely dreamt. Tiles that had all the rich, pale colours of the sky, and of delphiniums in a garden. Some of them were baroque, but pleasantly baroque. Their grotesqueness was their charm.

"They are all my—my *vondelings*," he said rather pathetically.

"You see, he has no wife, no children," said Maddalan in simple explanation.

"But I have a sister-in-law in Cologne," he said. "One day I go for to see her. Perhaps next week. One not know." Then he tapped John on the shoulder. "I have more. I show you. . . ."

He led them across the room into some inner, holier place. He pottered, his white hands like late skeleton leaves, silvered with frost. He waved them towards the wall. Then it was that John gasped. For on the wall was hung the collection of years. Some were small in wormy frames, others were in heavy tarnished old gold, but one and all they were beautiful. They were dark and exquisite, and full of deep rivers of colour. Two old women sewing in a quiet room, a room whose home atmosphere you could smell, whose kettle chuffing on the hearth you could hear. A nude girl on a dark window-seat, wakened late, and looking out upon the day. A Madonna and Child, with none of the Romish fripperies and trimmings, but simply Mother and Child, the more divine for Their simplicity.

"Wonderful," said John.

The old man peered up into his face, hopping first on one foot, then on the other. "You will come again?" he demanded. "*Ja*, you come again. I haf more to show."

He indicated the picture in the corner, the picture of a girl, with her flesh pearl-tinted, all round curves, all softness, standing and staring down at an oak cradle. She was naked. Her head was bent; you could see her eyes. Suddenly John realized, with an acute and heady fear, that she had honey-gold hair too, in thick plaits on either shoulder.

Then he knew that he would come again.

Chapter Four

It was so old a ship, who knows, who knows?
  And yet so beautiful, I watched in vain
To see the mast burst open with a rose,
  And the whole deck put on her leaves again.

JAMES ELROY FLECKER

I

JOHN received an agitated and reproachful letter from his mother, who demanded that he should return and all would be forgiven. He had behaved horribly, and she and dear Mr. Duckett hardly knew what to think, but, being good people, they would overlook his offence and behave charitably. There was also a letter from Mr. Oglivy, urging that he should not waste his time but should learn as much about art as possible before settling down. With this end in view John made a definite tour of the picture galleries and museums. He made special expeditions as suggested by the *Mevrouw* and Maddalan.

He went to the Hague with the intention of seeing the Mauritshuis and the Rembrandts. The Mauritshuis was disappointing by reason of its smallness and the few pictures. But those few were exquisite. For a long while he studied the Negroes, and felt wake within himself the dawning of a new intelligence. He studied the surgeon operating on the greenish-white body of a prone man, and it filled him with sickness. Mr. Putman had been greenish-white like that and had lain as limply. He passed through the galleries, with their long windows looking down upon the Vyver, flashing crystal with its central island gold and bronze with autumn. He thought that the Buitenhof must be one of the most beautiful squares in Europe, with its avenues of trees and its straight tall houses, and its graceful swans swimming on the old moat in the middle.

He stood drinking in colour, for there is no picture in the Mauritshuis that is not a masterpiece. He thought with an effort that if he could dissociate himself from up-bringing, from the pack mule, and from the hundred and one little reins and harnessings that bind us so closely to our fate, he might even yet be great. There was a being within him, a keen appreciation of beauty, that waxed strong in the presence of so much loveliness; but caged, it wilted. It had been suffocated by his home, his mother, by the drapery emporium, and by life in the drab seaside town. The being demanded to be fed, and its food was colour and music. Here was the food set before him in rich profusion, yet he was so weak that he could not feed himself with it. It evaded his clasp. He could feel himself reaching out, striving to understand, and the understanding being near but not near enough. He was appalled at his lack of education. He thought desperately, "If I try to soak myself in beautiful things, one day I may learn to understand them. . . ."

He went to see the van Goghs at Amsterdam, and somehow they did not impress him so favourably. Yet all the while he realized that the lack lay in himself, not in the pictures; perhaps he was not educated up to them. Amsterdam was noisy, the *grachten* did not run so smoothly nor so quietly as in Haarlem; there was not the air of sleepiness, but rather of confusion and of trade. Even the bells of the old Mint House had become infected with it.

"You were homesick?" Maddalan suggested when

she brought his supper to him that night on his return and heard all about it.

"I did not like it."

"But Amsterdam is a fine city."

"I daresay. But oh, Maddalan, all these things make me miserable. When I don't like a thing I realize I am at fault. I'm stupid. Ill-bred. Lots of people born like I was born never realize it, but I am not quite stupid enough. If only I had been born a little sillier, or a bit wiser!"

She came round the table close to him, and stood there, a pale flower against the shadowy darkness of the room. "Another time I will come too. Perhaps I can show you. You do not see things properly. Once an artist stay here and I show him. . . ."

An insane jealousy sprang like a swaying flame within him. "He made love to you?" he challenged.

"He did not," said Maddalan, and there was coldness in her tone, and a treacherous chilliness about her eyes, like blue Northern seas that become frozen.

After that she did not speak so often to him, nor so gladly, and she did not offer her companionship. Even the *Mevrouw* noticed it.

"Come," said the *Mevrouw*, "have you two quarrelled? It is a pity, for days should be of peace. It is not meant so much for the upset. Make friends, my little ones—better so, *ja*."

John, looking across his closely packed table with its weight of good butter and eggs and its newly baked rolls, crisp-smelling and hot, looked into the eyes of Maddalan.

"I'm sorry I said that the other day," he told her.

"So?"

Even then he did not know if he were forgiven.

II

He had brought the god with him. He did not know why, save that perhaps deep down within him there burned some superstitious demand for the god to accompany him, as a mascot; it had somehow associated itself with his good fortune. At first he did not bring it out, because in his heart he was ashamed of the two naked male breasts pouching over the jade and lapis lazuli cloak. The first day that he produced it, he set it on the window-ledge. The sun glinting in through the thinning trees lit up the pallid jaundiced face, which smiled inscrutably, as it would smile through all the ages.

"A cynic," thought John, "a satanic thing, and yet perhaps it knows the secret of the world, which is quite a poor little secret, and that is why it smiles."

Maddalan noticed it. "What is that?" she asked. "It is queer."

"It is my luck-bringer," he told her, "and here I particularly want it to bring me luck."

"So? It is not very beautiful."

She took it up between her light, slim fingers, and somehow he hated to see the contemptuous god in those hands. He felt that she would be contaminated by it.

"Put it down," he ordered her. "It is a beastly thing really, and you shall not touch it. Put it down."

She laughed. When Maddalan laughed, twinkles came to her eyes. It was as though the irises stirred and between their purple lips you saw the sparkle of water. "I, to be ordered by you!" she said. "Oh, that is very good!"

"I will make you." He went across the room and

gripped her wrists; they were so slight that it seemed that they would snap like twigs in his clasp. A little afraid, she winced, and let the god drop. It fell with a dull clatter to the floor. For one tense moment they stood looking at one another. John did not hear the door open, and only when the *Mevrouw* spoke did he know that she had come in.

"The noise," said the *Mevrouw* ponderously. "I think the earth shake. What for you two stand like that? Have you nothing better for to do than to look so foolish at each other?"

He pulled himself together with a jerk. "It was this which fell," he said.

Maddalan had recoiled from him; she clutched at the dark wall for support; she was like a white petal flung against the brown trunk of a tree. The *Mevrouw* picked up the god.

"It is not pewtiful," she said solemnly, and she screwed up her eyes in disdain; "it is not for the picture of a chentleman. I do not think it even to be nice."

"It is not nice," John assured her.

The *Mevrouw* breathed heavily with disapproval. She was perplexed, and she always breathed like that then. She had come into the room and had seen the look on their faces, and the *Mevrouw* knew that look. Awakening on John's face, the dawn of a new entity within him; fear like a startled animal, the frail fear of the faun, on Maddalan's cheeks. The *Mevrouw* was not at all sure about it. She did not mean to have any fallings in love in her house. Maddalan was far too useful and baked the bread too well for that. No fallings in love, predicted the *Mevrouw*.

"Come, my little one," she said, and she put an affectionate arm about the girl. She drew her away with her.

Alone, John stood with the god in his hands, and a nasty sensation of dislike of the *Mevrouw*. Horrid, fat old woman, in voluminous skirts, ponderous, arranging, interfering old woman! He had no idea how much she had seen.

III

During the next few weeks John managed to learn a great deal from old Jan. They spent long hours in the stuffy house in the inconspicuous street. They drank "*thee*", and they discussed pictures and china glaze and Delft tiles much as magicians discuss magic. A great world of knowledge was opening up before John; he was amazed at its bigness. All the while the picture of the nude girl and the empty cradle remained in the background. The girl with amber hair in plaits, and the virginal pearl skin gleaming against dark oak. From Jan, John learnt to discern the different glazes, to gauge colours, to select true from spurious, to standardize his mediums. It was slow work, but well worth the trouble. Jan had spent his life among beauty, and he loved it faithfully. He did not grudge imparting his knowledge to John; his only grudge was against the new generation which grew up inappreciative of true beauty. Soon he would be going to stay with his sister-in-law in Cologne. Cologne was a lovely city.

"But he will never go," said Maddalan; "he has been saying that for years."

Once, discussing a picture of a young girl making her first communion, John, struggling to find words to describe it to Jan, said, "Yes, iris, white-gold, like Maddalan. A beauty like hers."

Jan peered at him curiously. "Ah," he said, and then slowly, "it is not well, the painted beauty likened to the living. Beauty of woman hurts too much. Love hurts too much."

"But surely," enquired John, "love is the greatest beauty of all?"

Old Jan's rheumy eyes flickered together; he wavered a little, like wind-blown grass grown sere with autumn. "The greatest beauty, *ja*, but the most exquisite pain. Death is sweetness to it," he said.

John longed to ask him what he meant, but Jan did not invite confidence. Silence came; the silence only riven by passing bicycle bells, stuttering into atmosphere. When old Jan spoke again it was as though nothing had disturbed him.

John bought tiles as specimens, and Minna surveyed these with approval. In broken English she attempted to explain her ideas on the subject. She had an aunt in Edam who had most lovely ornaments, she said. Taking a holiday one day and bicycling to Edam, she promised to bring John back "the souvenir".

"Poof," said Maddalan, "she knows nothing. Jan knows. Don't pay any attention to Minna and her souvenirs."

Late that night Minna returned, having had trouble with the ferries, which had delayed her considerably, and also having come back by the Amsterdamsche Porte, which had been thronged with people. She had brought with her a small *stoofje*, which she had kept buttoned inside her jacket. At any time Minna was an extraordinary figure, but the bearing of the little *stoofje* inside her jacket had added to her extraordinariness. She held it out to John, a small, perplexingly perforated box.

"*Stoofje*," said Minna, "for sell. Pewtiful."

John had no idea what a *stoofje* might be. He handled it with extreme caution. "But what is it?" he asked at last.

"*Stoofje*," said Minna, and held it in her hands. She poised it coyly, as a concertina.

"It goes like this?" he suggested, and whistled.

At that Minna laughed immensely. Oh, but it was

most amusing! "No," she persisted, "no," and she went across to the steam heating and puffed at it, blowing out her cheeks so that they became round and red and shiny. "So," said Minna, "what for."

John did not see what for. The *Mevrouw*, coming in, stopped and stared at them.

"What is this?" asked John. "She is trying to explain what this is. She calls it *stoofje*. What is it in English?"

"Ah, *stoofje*," the *Mevrouw* took it into her hand and nodded wisely—"you call him the muff."

John surveyed the little box curiously, and enquired: "But where do you put your hands in?"

"Ah, not the hands," smiled the *Mevrouw*, amused at the joke, "not so! For the feet."

"*Ja, ja,*" said Minna, joining in with enthusiasm, "*in den kerk.*"

"Of course," said John, not wishing to appear stupid, but after they had gone he said to himself, "Damn it all, what is the thing for?" He had to wait until Maddalan brought up his supper. Maddalan took the small perforated box in her hand and, opening it, showed him the little tray arranged for peat which lay inside.

"It is a very nice one," she said, "and it was good of Minna to bring it for you. The *stoofje* is a little stove. In the winter it is very cold here, and these *stoofjes* are lit and, in church especially, the women sit with them under their skirts and keep warm that way."

"Lord, I should never be able to face real cold," he said apprehensively; "you won't catch me staying a winter here."

"So?" She glanced at him in quick alarm. Instantly he knew that she would be sorry if he left. He felt the trickle of warm interest poured through him, the thrill, the ebb and flow of a tide beating upon his heart's shore. He interested Maddalan, as Maddalan interested him. That was good. "One day," he said tenderly, "perhaps you will come to England?"

"Perhaps." Then she spoke slowly, "I come perhaps to Tooting, to the cheese and butter shop."

"You will come and see me in my little antique shop? I shall want you, Maddalan—say that you will come and see me there."

"I don't know."

Then he saw that her eyes were wet.

IV

He met Maddalan by accident in the Haarlemmer Hout. He had gone out alone to look upon the bulb fields with their deep even stretches of earth, and their low nestling barns alongside, where the bulbs were stored in summer. Coming back he had stepped from the road into the woods, bright with gay leaves. It was more like some lovely part of Kent than Holland. It had not even the typical flatness of the country, but rose and fell in undulations. John sat down on a seat there, and, looking up, was surprised to see Maddalan coming towards him.

Maddalan looked paler than ever, with a coat tightly buttoned about her, and her eyes suggesting the redness of tears. "Something is worrying her," he told himself, "something is disturbing her. Now what in the world can it be? I expect it is that old cat of a *Mevrouw*."

It could not be lack of money, for that never seemed to disturb the Dutch too much. Maddalan did not spend excessively, for clothes did not interest her. She did not desire great riches, nor even to be richer than she now was. The Dutch are not competitive. They live a life unto themselves, shut up behind their tall houses, with their little nightlights keeping the kettle hot for "*thee*", and the good wife doing the work of the house.

Beyond that nothing disturbs them. But it was quite obvious that something was disturbing Maddalan. He plucked at her coat, or she would have passed him, and he drew her down to the seat beside him.

"Here we can talk," he said, "here I can ask you what is the matter; for something is worrying you, Maddalan, something has changed you since I came. What is it?"

She would not say. She averted her eyes so that he could not look into them and read her thoughts swimming in their depths. "Nothing," she said, "nothing," but it was the usual woman's futile denial.

"That is not true." And then softly, "It is not that I am worrying you, Maddalan? It is not that?"

"How could it be that?" she asked dully.

The leaves swept round them in little gusts. The wind severed them gently from the branches, and they danced to earth in a gipsy pattern. "I have heard from Mr. Oglivy again," said John, "and he is negotiating for a house and shop at Condering. It is a big, old city, not far from the east coast, near Harwich, you know."

"You mean that you are leaving us?" she asked, and then she lifted her eyes, and in them he read the truth that she had tried to keep from him.

"Oh, Maddalan," he said, "my dear, my very dear!"

He drew her to him and she did not resist. She was little and light, most delicately soft. Her face was velvety, like the tender petals of white roses, or the thick plushy buds of lilies. Against his own her cheeks seemed to be indescribably soft, and her mouth when he found it was warm and delicious. "Why didn't we find each other before?" he demanded hotly.

"Why not?" She was weeping now, but in ecstasy. There was no hint of despair about her tears, it was a supremely joyous weeping. The autumn blowing about them had taken on all the virginal gladness of spring. No longer were the bulb fields behind them long lines of darkness, here or there lightly dusted with white ash, and padded with straw from which the sun had drenched all colour; they were flowering. To these two, so joyously in love, there was the scent of hyacinths, the deep blue rivers of scillas, tulips in lines of rose and blood-red, the amber trumpets of daffodils blowing bright music for them.

The world was glorious. They did not speak, for there was no need for words. They sat there side by side, with the ferns like small green crosiers springing at their feet, and the world a temple of sweet-smelling incenses. Words are ugly things; they are immaterial, they are but the poor expressions of beautiful idealistic thoughts, and somehow John felt that now they did not matter. They had gone further than that; they did not need speech any more.

He had found Maddalan and she had found him!

Two or three people passing by did not give them so much as a second glance. A lover is too usual.

"I have always loved you," he said.

"And I you."

"Darling, Maddalan, little sweet Maddalan. You reminded me of irises, you have always reminded me of them, and I'll never make you understand how much I have wanted you."

"And I thought that you would go away and forget me."

"Never. How could such a thing be?"

He thought of Freda as vagary, passing fantasy, white blossom on dark thorn. Freda sitting out on the sea front, with the essence of privet and syringa; yet, in vivid contrast, Maddalan sitting here in the Haarlemmer Hout, with the smell of honey warmly sweet from an adjacent linden, and the crumbling scent of earth under moss-greened trees, with the first drab huddles of drifting leaves lying beneath them. The wood surrounded the two of them. It was like a great cathedral; one almost expected to hear the deep sound of its organ booming through it. Yet this cathedral knew only earth's greatest music; it did not sway to the magnificence of Beethoven and Wagner, it had never heard the impertinent trickle of the *Minuet*. Its chords were the great winds tearing at the branches arching across its cloisters, its *crescendo* was the thunder in June, its *cavatina* the thin arpeggios of rain and sleet, its *piano* the soft, almost dumb sound of snow on light twigs.

They walked home together.

"We have found each other," said Maddalan simply, as they came out of the *hout* into the road, with the *gracht* pearl-white in the soft dusk, almost as though it were a canal of milk. They saw the great round base of the prison lying beyond. It was almost completely round like the cheeses that they made in Edam. "Those poor prisoners," said the girl—"nothing like this ever happens to them."

"Nothing like this ever happens to anyone else," he told her, and they kissed again, in a humble fashion, humble by reason of the greatness of their love. They stood on a low bridge, with the water beneath them, and the thinning golden veil of the trees on the *gracht* side hiding them from curious eyes.

"Now whatever happens we have each other," she said.

"Whatever happens. I must talk to the *Mevrouw*."

Not a pleasant prospect, that!

She set her little hand across his mouth, and he was surprised at the coldness of it. Somehow he sensed that she was afraid. "Not to-night, John, not to-night. The *Mevrouw* might not understand: she is old, and it is difficult for the old to understand. They are so far away from love. She might spurn it. Not to-night."

"Oh, all right . . . only there is no time like the present." He had no wish to approach the old woman, Maddalan need not run away with that idea. In fact if he could have postponed it for ever he would have done so.

"Let it be our secret," she nodded.

"Our secret," he promised.

And when they got indoors, the *Mevrouw* was having a violent altercation with Minna. The chicken had been burnt. What waste! What carelessness! Such a beautiful bird too, and now blackened and ruined. She had a good mind to pack Minna about her business, the hussy! A very good mind. But, being the most amiable of women—dear God, how amiable!—she would pardon her. All the same, it was disgraceful, such an exquisite bird!

That night, sitting in his room and looking down into the street through the uncurtained window, John thought of life as being all the more delicious for their secret. Little Maddalan, she was his! One day they would be married. They would step out of the *kerk*, and come back to surprise the *Mevrouw* and the *Mijnheer*. Yes, that would undoubtedly be the best plan. Minna would throw her apron over her foolish face and laugh with her wide mouth and its even set of teeth grinning out at you. One day . . . the little shuttle of imagination darted in and out of the grey fabric of his thoughts, and where it darted it left a gleaming silver thread. The dreams came and went. Dear delicious dreams! They were like the beautiful golden leaves falling in curls silently from the trees to the cobbles below, like the shorn tresses of some lovely Lorelei. Leaves, on the Rijwielpad beyond. Autumn combing the gold hair of the trees.

Sie kamt mit ein goldenem kame.

The leaves lost their lustre when they reached the earth and became contaminated by its dullness and its dust, and its tiredness. But the dreams went on. . . .

Chapter Five

It is something to have smelt the mystic rose,
   Although it break and leave the thorny rods;
It is something to have hungered once as those
   Must hunger who have ate the bread of gods.
G. K. CHESTERTON

I

MR. OGLIVY was urging John's return. In a panic over his insistence, John tried to put off the moment of departure. Living in Holland was expensive, but the antiques which he bought under the careful and judicious tutorage of Jan and Maddalan were cheap. He imagined that in England he would be able to sell them for three times the price. Maddalan was a queer combination of businesslike instincts and a frail, flowerlike personality. The two were amazingly commingled in her.

Together they made several expeditions.

Afterwards, when he looked back on life, he remembered those expeditions with Maddalan as being dreams. They were, it seemed, long peaceful hours, lying serenely like broad flowing rivers between the troubled shores of his life. He knew afterwards that he ought to have appreciated those dreams more.

They went to Rotterdam, slowly travelling in the queer little train which puffed along at such an absurdly slow rate. Maddalan sat opposite to him, her eyes bright with pent-up excitement, her whole body poised, strangely still, yet full of suppressed enthusiasm. They walked about Rotterdam, which is so Venetian, with the tall bluely dark tower of St. Laurentskerk reigning over it all. It was a tower which held deep Delft blues in its peculiar squareness, and green gloom as of old stagnant waters, merged together.

"But the shops," said Maddalan, who had grown impatient of the tower, "it is the shops that are so splendid."

John thought the shops to be hideous. They were like the cheaper emporiums which lumber up small towns. He wanted to linger with the old bridges and watch the barges, for here was a beauty which urged him on, a tranquil beauty in a commercially confused city. They walked about all the afternoon, which was hot with the muggy warmth of October. They wandered through the maze of cobbled streets and of *grachten*, in the avenues of trees with here or there the red glow of dahlias, and the gold of chrysanthemums in rich profusion. With the early evening they came to the flower market grouped round an old broken windmill, in warm banks of colour. The windmill was sailless. It towered there, in a trumpery but rather pitiable majesty, over the baskets of flowers all tied in stiff bunches and presided over by matrons of irrefutable respectability.

"Such lovely dahlias," said Maddalan.

"I will buy them for you." He bought them, a great armful of them, mulberry, wine-coloured rosettes, held closely against Maddalan's grey coat.

"That was most extravagant of you," she said, but not disapprovingly.

"One cannot be extravagant when one is in love. It is the one experience worth while, worth anything."

Above the red and purple flowers her eyes danced. "John, it is so hot. It is such a day. One of the days we shall never forget."

"Never," he promised. "We have each other. We are

alone. There is no chance of the *Mevrouw* nosing in. Could anything be nicer?"

Yet he was not passionate with Maddalan; with Freda, yes! But Freda had been different. Her music had attracted him in one way, her body in another. Maddalan's body did not enthral him. It held none of the significance that he had associated with the woman in Mr. Putman's picture, the woman with the lace chemise, who peered cunningly at him with lustful eyes through the gloom. Maddalan was the nude girl who looked into the empty cradle. She held him by her sheer loveliness, as a little springtime pool may attract you, as flowers on a wind-breathed common, as all the beauties of a natural world attract but never tempt.

"Let us go into the market," said Maddalan.

He would have stayed with the flowers, and the sail-less tower of the windmill above them, but she wanted to push her way forward. They passed down the narrow alleyways, between two lines of stalls, strewn with every conceivable article for sale. There were fish, with the white-capped girls bending over them, their arms silvery with scales. There were men and women jostling together. He was glad when at the far end he extricated himself.

"There is yet another row of stalls," said Maddalan, and then he saw that they had to retrace their steps through a second alleyway.

"Oh no, not there, for heaven's sake! . . ."

"The train is not for over an hour," she said composedly.

The idea struck him, and, like a dart with a barb to it, poised itself quivering on the disk of his brain. "We will hire a car."

"A car? Oh, but that would be most expensive."

"I don't care." There had been a cheque in only that morning accompanied by the urgent request from Mr. Oglivy that he would return. He did not care about money. He was thinking of the hours with her in the darkness, speeding up through the flat canal-riven country to Haarlem. He felt the agreeable weight of gulden in his pocket.

"Oho!" said Maddalan, and the idea of the car appealed to her. "You're wonderful. But I don't think we ought. What will the *Mevrouw* say?"

"Damn the *Mevrouw*!" said John.

II

They were riding through the dimness and the dusk which was fast bearing down upon Holland. The flatness of the country was rolled in it; they passed through little villages comfortably lighting up for the night; little houses tucked away, with their *klompfen* faithfully remaining outside, and their little light for *thee* growing dim against the greater lights which blazed in their windows. The trees became unreal. They were no longer gold and green and bronze, but smudged into nothingness. The stunted, chopped trees beside the road took on the appearance of old, gnarled witches hobbling out to menace them. Their twisted arms were easily discernible against the sky. But inside the car it was dusk; he could only see her pale face, and trace the darkness which signified eyes and brows, and the shadow that was her mouth. It was indescribably lovely.

"You do love me, Maddalan?" he asked.

"Yes, yes, of course."

"Why should we not tell the *Mevrouw*? Why should we not demand that we want to be married right away?"

"The *Mevrouw* wouldn't. It would be different if I were her own child, but I am a *vondeling*."

He said, suddenly stirred out of his apathy, "But you are her own child?"

Maddalan shook her head in denial. "Oh no. She likes to believe that I am her own child, but I am not. She got me from the *Weeshuis*: it is what you call in England an orphanage. Nobody knows, not even the *Mijnheer*. She pretends that I am her own. It was one day that she told me, 'Not mine, Maddalan,' she said—she had a malady at the time and thought that she would die—'not all mine.' "

"Then, if you are a *vondeling*, she has no hold over you?" he urged.

"Oh, but she has. I am not of age. I have no right to marry without her consent, and she knows that. She is very hard, and she would return me to the *Weeshuis* rather than let me marry, because I am useful to her. She told me that once. No, she would not part with me that way."

"We could elope?"

The idea had never entered Maddalan's head. She turned her face to him slowly in the darkness, as the suggestion soaked into the recesses of her mind. "But that would be wicked," she suggested.

"Now how on earth do you make that out?"

"It would be altogether wrong."

Dutch scruples! He found them rather difficult. They had stupid principles against which they could not go. The idiotic belief that gay colours were wicked save in their national dress; that elopement was wrong; that to go against one's parents was sin in the extreme.

"Lots of people elope in England," he told her.

"But the English are loose."

"Lord, no, it isn't looseness! You've got a pretty rotten idea of my countrymen."

She shrugged her shoulders indifferently, and he knew by the action that he had not convinced her. He put his arms round her and tried persuasion; it was the only way to deal with Maddalan. "The *Mevrouw* would not send you back to the *Weeshuis*, because I would not let her. Understand that, once and for all. I love you, and I would not let you be unhappy."

She said, "I know, but you are not tremendously courageous. It would require a Bismarck to face the *Mevrouw*. You are not a Bismarck." For a moment she quavered, then she went on, "They would take me back into the *Weeshuis* willingly enough and find me a situation. I should have to work very hard."

"But the *Mevrouw* is too fond of you to send you back again. She would much rather that you married me."

"She would rather lose me to the *Weeshuis* than to you. With you she would know that I should never return. From the *Weeshuis* she could always get me back."

They were crossing one of the great *grachten* in a ferry. The ferry went slowly, pushed in elemental fashion by a clumsy man. John kissed her, and as he kissed her the moon lifted a pale white lamp above the horizon and turned the *gracht* into pellucid whiteness. It flooded the car. It was one of those magic moments, in the wash of the moon, with the soft chugging sound of water, and the feel of her lips parted beneath his. It was so lovely that he almost wished that he might drown now, and that there might never be a future to mar the beauty of this moment.

"Something will shape itself," he said.

The bright hope of youth illuminated the flameless lamp that was his soul. It burnt bravely.

III

They went to Leyden, to the borders of the old Rhine, and saw the mill where it is rumoured that

Rembrandt was born. A long, low old mill, that had long since ceased working but stood there shouldered by the trees. Maddalan told him that the story of its being Rembrandt's birthplace was not true.

"It is just legend," she said.

"Then why do they say so?"

"Legend," persisted Maddalan with a shrug of her shoulders.

The mill was pretty. It stood artistically with the old Rhine flowing before its doors, calm and unperturbed. About it the trees ambered. Its sails went round at times merrily enough, when the wind provided a good enough joke for it to laugh at. At other times they were just four brave arms pointing to the sky.

Maddalan wanted him to see the Hooglandsche Kerk, and he went unwillingly, for he loved the mill and its associations, and the old Rhine droning along. He did not want more. They walked along discussing the ever present problem of the *Mevrouw*.

He knew now that Maddalan was terrified of the *Weeshuis* which the old woman had used as a threat. The girl had been born there, or brought there when she was very young, with no knowledge of who her parents might be. Probably her mother had been some poor servant maid who had got into trouble with the master of the house; perhaps a gentler born girl, whose scandal had been hushed, and whose baby, evidence of her lapse, had been hastily hustled into the orphanage. It was a cold, hard place. Children who had once been in the *Weeshuis* could always be sent back to the place, for it had some sort of skeleton grasp on their luckless shoulders.

The *Mevrouw* had no intention of allowing Maddalan to marry yet awhile. She was devoted to the girl, but marriage, oh no! The Dutch believed in a long youth, in a bridal later in life, some rich merchant perhaps, or a trader from Amsterdam. She would not look with favour on an English bridegroom.

"You see," said Maddalan, "it cannot be. There will only be the most terrible quarrel, and I shall be left to bear the brunt of it, while you will be turned out and sent back to England whilst I face all the anger, and it will be unfair."

"But we must do something, make some plan. We love each other; we can't allow people to part us like this," he protested—"we must run away."

"But we can't."

"If you really loved me we could."

"I do love you," she said wretchedly.

"You do not, because you are not prepared to make this sacrifice for me; you are not prepared to leave everything and come with me. If you loved me——"

"I do love you," she persisted, and she clasped and unclasped her hands in alarm, for in her own strange way she did love him, yet she was frightened. He could only see her affection with his own perspective. He knew that he shrank from the formidable *Mevrouw*. Mercifully the *Mijnheer* had long since ceased to be of any importance in the house, but had taken to the chimney corner, realizing that there was room for only one master. Running away was the simplest method, and John would have urged it strongly save that he had some hazy idea that the passport might prove to be difficult. He wished that he could decide how to act. He thought of consulting old Jan, but the moment the conversation veered round to love, Jan always flung up his old silvery hands. "Love! Ah, but it is so difficult. Never mention it. It is too hurtful."

That night, in his own room, John went to the window-seat and stood there looking down gloomily on the trees, now almost naked, and the coldness of the water in the *gracht*. It was a cold country.

"You do not love me," he told her when she brought in his supper. "I might have known. You have given your life to the *Mevrouw*, and what does she do with it? Tears it to ribbons."

"You will not believe me?"

He turned and caught her hands in his, pressing her body back, breathing on her cheeks. "Can't you see that this isn't enough? I can't go on like this. I want you. I want you for my own. Not just to kiss and play with like a doll. If you really loved me you would want me too, you would be willing to run away with me—but you don't love me."

"I do."

He kissed her; he kissed the throat curved back as her head fell, kissed the white lids above her eyes and felt the strangely soft fringe of lashes against his lips. He kissed her shoulder, with its thinly brittle bones, and down to where the bone became covered by warm rounded flesh. "That's how I love you," he said, and let her go.

He heard her gasp. It was a gasp of outraged virginity. He heard the door shut behind her. "Oh Lord," he told himself, "now I've been a beast to her, and nothing I can do will change it. . . . I thought I cared for her differently, and it wasn't differently really. . . . The woman peering over her shoulder, and the woman with her empty cradle, it's both the same at heart. . . ."

He turned again to the window looking on to the *gracht* grown naked and cold with the on-coming winter, and he knew that he was ashamed of himself.

IV

He wondered if the joss were evil.

Sitting there on the window-seat staring out at the day dying, at the water gleaming so palely, at the cobbles becoming blurred, and the faint outline of the

Rijwielpad becoming mere mist, he wondered about this ornament in connection with himself.

There is a certain superstition about gods and josses. It looked evil; he felt that in some sinister manner it urged him on to behave like that—because the John who had pressed his lips to Maddalan's shoulder had been a new being. Someone whom he did not know. Someone who acted without premeditation, led rather than was led, drove rather than was driven. Later Minna brought in his pudding on a tray. He ignored the white island of a letter from Mr. Oglivy propped against the cream jug, slipping it unread into his pocket. He resented Minna's presence.

"But why?" he asked bewildered.

"Not well," said Minna in explanation, and she put her hand to her head, and the other to her round fat stomach in ludicrous gesture.

The dumb show tormented him. He could not eat. He pushed away the pudding hardly touched, so that Minna, when she came to remove the soiled china, demanded the reason, and, finding her English failing her completely, pointed a deprecating finger at the dish. She fetched the *Mevrouw*. It seemed to John that the *Mevrouw* was suspicious, tight-lipped, with a searching gaze, and that she came as an avenging matron.

"Minna tells me," said the *Mevrouw*, "that you not eat the good supper. You also ill?"

"I'm tired," he said.

The *Mevrouw* raised her eyebrows a little, and surveyed him with hawkish eyes. She folded her large ample hands on her ample stomach. "Young people do not tire so much easily," she remarked acidly—"maybe you are in love?"

He wanted to shriek out; to proclaim to her that he was in love; to let the quiet room echo with it, and the *gracht* beyond, and even to set the bell of the Groote Kerk ringing with it. But when the *Mevrouw* looked at him like that, through and through, he was afraid. He understood now why the *Mijnheer* crept out by the back door and skulked furtively into a corner. He had had a lifetime with the *Mevrouw*, and he knew the futility of argument and opposition.

"No, I am not in love," he said dully.

But it was not true. He was in love with her, and in a physical way which gnawed at him and would not let him be. The restlessness of the emotion possessed him and commingled with himself, so that he stuttered and reddened before the *Mevrouw*, and the life in him grew soggy with his surging desire. The vibrant demand kept thrusting itself in upon him. He was glad when she had gone and he could sit there alone and think about Maddalan and his love, dwelling upon it, torturing himself with it. He was glad when the dusk blotted out all the crudities of day, and he sat alone with only the street lamp lighting his room, and the lace of the branch and twig flung like a mantilla about the high heads of the trees without. He sat on and on, thinking, and all the while his thoughts were circles that eddied on the surface of the pool that was his soul. The thoughts that he flung into its stillness were the pebbles of lust. "Do I want her?" they demanded. "Can I marry her now? Why not face the *Mevrouw* and be done with it? Why not?" And everytime the out-stretching circles expanded and widened so that he was afraid of their circumference. They were bigger than he was. They were far greater than his own soul.

Presently his head went down on his arms.

"I shall have to face the *Mevrouw* whatever she says," he told himself. "I thought it was not like that affair with Freda, but it is the same physical need, just the same."

He sat there, exhausted by his desire, tensely still.

V

She came into the room quietly, like some little ghost. She opened the door in a soundless rush, slipping through the narrow slot of space, stepping across the threshold, and closing it behind her just as quietly. Outside the great bell of St. Bavo struck eleven.

She could just make out the hump that was John sitting crouched on the window-sill, and seeing him like that she guessed the thoughts that had been tormenting him. She flittered silently across the intervening space to him. She was in white. The long gown, fastened demurely about her throat, fell to the very ground itself; across it was tossed the unbraided yellow of her hair. It reminded him of primroses on snow. She walked as a somnambulist walks, stiffly, with little jerks, and then, stopping before him, knelt there raising her small hands, primly buttoned into their cuffs, and laid them lightly upon his arm.

"John?"

"Maddalan."

"I know how you feel. I've been thinking, and I understand."

He leant forward, laying his hands on either side of her hair, which was soft as the wings of some tender bird. "Maddalan, you don't understand. You don't love me in the same way."

"I do love you. Because I love you so much I am here."

"You run a great risk, you little silly."

"I want to give myself to you, John."

Her upraised face reminded him of an angel. Not one of the loutish angels that he had seen in the Hooglandsche Kerk that day when they had stood beside the old Rhine and watched its lethargic progress, as one who will not be hurried, towards the sea. Not one of the solemn Dutch angels that he had seen in every church, but one of those whom Rembrandt might have visualized; one of the angels looking down in spiritual beauty from the walls of the Mauritshuis, with the crystal gleam of the Vyver in the Buitenhof beyond. Maddalan's face was pellucidly white. Her hair was untarnishably gold. He saw her as youth, and could not believe that such exquisite youth could fade. It was inconceivable that one day she would be a *Mevrouw*, old and fat and run to seed; to-day she was his.

Opportunity does not rap twice upon the door of men's futures. Chance is the caprice of youth. His hands, growing hot, held her head closely.

"My sweet!"

"I shall not regret."

Coldly pure, *jung frau* Maddalan. He knew that she was not giving him passion, but she was offering herself in the spirit of sacrifice. He ought not to accept it . . . not that way . . . but the new demanding man in him fought his sanity. Her fingers pressed close in his hot hands were thin and cold like icicles. Outside from the night-filled roads came the insistence of a sharp bicycle bell.

He lifted her in his arms, and through the thick white material of her nightdress he could sense her body, thin as a scimitar, and adorably curved. The feel of her was rapture. Now, even if he had wanted to stay himself, he could not have done so.

He carried her to the big couch at the far end beside the great fireplace. They were close to the steam heat there, and she would not be cold. He laid her down, kneeling beside her, clasping and re-clasping her, and all the while in some intangible manner remembering the face of the woman in the Franz Hals picture at Mr. Putman's; the woman with the lace chemise.

"Maddalan, aren't we wise to snatch at happiness?

When the *Mevrouw* knows how much we mean to each other, she will allow our marriage."

"Perhaps," she whispered, "but don't let's talk of the *Mevrouw*."

"We have been married all the time. We were married in the great cathedral of the Haarlemmer Hout. God has married us. We do not need man to marry us as well."

All logic seemed to be swept away in this spate bearing them ruthlessly forward. They did not remember the sober teaching of their youth. Nothing mattered save their two selves, and the world was mere prelude to the divine mystery of their bodies.

He held her closely; he kissed her until she was no longer separate entity, but part of himself. They slept, with only the soft night wind crooning in the trees without, and the crushing sound of water pressed forward before some insistent barge passing up the *gracht*. They woke again, to cling, to kiss, to love. So, at dawn, the *Mevrouw* found them.

VI

The *Mevrouw* had had a bad night. She had lain in her prim befrilled bed disturbed and restless, for, in her own words, she did "much suspect". She did not know why, but for some time she had been aware of a latent current flowing through the tall Renaissance house behind the trees. She had suspected John of an intrigue with Minna. Invariably the *Mevrouw* suspected Minna, because in her opinion all servants were bad at heart and not to be trusted, and all her lodgers were morally lax. Later, to her own horror, she suspected Maddalan.

The *Mevrouw* had for many years tried to make herself believe that Maddalan was her own child. She had cheated herself into such a complete belief that now this sudden realization of the existing circumstances was a greater shock to her. She was obliged to dig down into that garden which was her memory and recall incidents therein. She had been married many childless years, over fifteen, to the *Mijnheer*. She had been unfavourably aware during the latter part of the time that he was cooling in his affections; when she reproached him—and the *Mevrouw* was much too tactless to do anything but reproach him—he had accused her of barrenness. The *Mijnheer*, it seemed, had wanted children. He could not accuse the *Mevrouw* of bad housewifery. She worked conscientiously, early and late, in her housekeeping with the one servant, which was as her code demanded. She washed and baked and cleaned at all times herself; she was diligent—if anything, too much so; no task was beneath her. She had an enormous store of linen, of which she was inordinately proud. Her whole house was amply stocked, over stocked, but she would not have thrown away a single utensil useless though it might be to her. To discard was not in accordance with her code of honour: it would have typified bad economy.

All her larders and closets were packed close, wrapped in innumerable wrappings, and she had but little idea of the extent of her possessions, but she clung to the savage love of actually possessing.

The *Mijnheer* had told her brutally of his desire for children, and she had been appalled at the realization that she was unable to conform to his demands. The *Mevrouw* was a highly respectable woman, and the very fact that he had a single complaint to make was humiliating. It was all the more humiliating because she realized that his grievance was a genuine one. She had prayed to her prim and highly worthy God that He would send the stork to visit her. But still the stork could not be persuaded. It was all the more maddening when her sister Wilma had four fine children whom she was never tired of displaying. It was at the birth of the fifth, a lusty son, that the *Mevrouw* conceived the idea of the *Westhuis*. Nothing could be simpler than to adopt a child.

Surreptitiously she made her way to such an establishment, and enquired therein. There were legal documents to be drawn up. It could not be done on the instant, and at the moment they had no children for adoption. The *Mevrouw* had in her own scheming mind planned to procure a young baby, and at the end of a reasonable time to display it entirely as her own. Even the *Mijnheer* was to be bamboozled by it. She was not easily deterred. She became sickly and peevish, and visited a doctor in The Hague, coming back with the news that she was pregnant. The *Mijnheer* could hardly believe it, and kept mumbling to himself, "After fifteen years," as he sat by his hearthside. The relations expressed surprise. Wilma said, "Fancy old Elna, at her time of life, too," but after the first incredulity had passed they said no more. They were all too much occupied with their own concerns to care about old Elna. Elna protested that she desired to be confined in Rotterdam. She produced a fictitious aunt, and thither she proceeded. She protested that the *Mijnheer* worried her, with his eternal "After fifteen years, after fifteen years". When the family learnt that old Elna had given birth to a daughter, but that the child was weakly, they shook their heads and laughed. "What would one expect?" asked Wilma, and smiled triumphantly at her five fat children. "It is a miracle that the child survived the birth."

In Rotterdam the *Mevrouw* contracted milk fever and stayed an unpardonable time. The *Mijnheer* did not visit her. The joy of paternity was ousted by his sudden taste of liberty. For fifteen years the *Mevrouw* had bullied and tormented him, and now he enjoyed a great and glorious peace. He pleaded much business in Amsterdam, but his business quite often took him round the Onderkerksplein, where there were such women! (Ah, what eyes! What hips!) No, he did not go to Rotterdam. Later Elna returned with her baby. Everybody was deceived. Whereas the Englishman's home is very much his castle, the Dutchman's home is definitely his fortress. Few cross its threshold. None peered in upon old Elna's secret, and she kept it entirely to herself.

Maddalan would never have known had not the *Mevrouw*, in the throes of a dangerous illness, felt the necessity to confide the truth in her, in a misguided moment. She imagined that she was about to die, and wished to propitiate the Deity. And, having confided the truth to the child, she wielded it as a two-edged sword of Damocles above Maddalan's head. One word, one scene, and back she would go to the *Weeshuis*. The *Mevrouw* never forgot to threaten.

VII

The *Mevrouw* found them together. She found Maddalan lying on the sofa, clad only in her thick white nightdress. Instantly the *Mevrouw* was smitten with the awful presentiment that had for a long time lain on her heart, that the *Weeshuis* had shelved one of the light daughters of a harlot upon her. There was no mistaking the fact that the couch had been the altar of love, that the room had been the shrine of a sweet passion, and that the *Mevrouw* had entered far too late. For a moment she agitated within herself as to what she could do. The idea of marriage flashed across her brain, then she decided against it. The *Mijnheer* was no companion to her, and she would not part with the girl and receive nothing in her place. She attacked John vigorously.

John was dazed. He was exhausted. Passion had left him cold and depressed, and suddenly he was thrust into the vortex of a hideous tornado of words in which the *Mevrouw* was wholly unrestrained. He pressed his hands to his ears to try to avoid hearing the ugly words which she was using. He saw Maddalan, her face grown white, her lips greenish like water of the mirage, and he heard her whisper:

"Go, for my sake, go. Later . . . but not now . . ."

He made a desperate endeavour at explanation, but explanation was impossible; it was mown down like grass under a sickle—the sharp vituperative sickle of the *Mevrouw*'s tongue. Before her she swept everything. The room echoed with her words, the air was volcanic. Nothing else mattered, nothing at all. Far away, a ghost in the corner, Maddalan was beseeching him to do as the *Mevrouw* said. "Go, go now . . . Later . . ." Neither of them would listen to him, and his head ached. Oh, how it ached!

Afterwards, when he found himself in the cheerless street, he went round to old Jan's house. If only the old man would take him in for a few hours, until his head had cooled, until he could think coherently, and nerve himself to face the *Mevrouw* again. In the bitter light of the remorseless dawn, old Jan's house looked gaunt and still, with the queer stillness of death. He rapped on the door, shivering as he trounced the thick oak.

He rapped again and again, until a young girl, half dressed, a coat covering ill-matched underclothing, came out of the next-door house and informed him in halting English that old Jan had gone to Cologne for the night—to see his sister-in-law.

At last! Old Jan had been predicting this for years, but to have happened now . . .

Tiredly John moved towards the station. Passing the Funckler, he enquired for a room. The young waiter did not know. The *Mijnheer* was asleep—later, perhaps the chentleman would be so good? The chentleman would not be so good. Action seemed to be vital, but what action? He felt in his pocket, and there lay the unopened letter from Mr. Oglivy. He twitched it tiredly. Mr. Oglivy had found a business, would John come at once? It was really very urgent that matters should be clinched immediately.

Later, hours later, still unwashed and unshaven, he found himself standing on the desolate station of the Hook, watching disinterestedly the customs officers making pretence to examine his luggage.

John was returning to England.

END OF PART ONE

PART II
Belle

Chapter One

The fruit of my tree of knowledge is plucked; it is this, adventures are to the adventurous.

DISRAELI

I

UPON his return to England John was faced with difficulties and with doubts, and with the necessity for quick decision. He had to forget his wounds in the new present; he had to forget Maddalan, who had stepped through the darkness of the room like some white-clad angel. He had to forget the hot and angry face of the *Mevrouw* as she burst in upon his ardour, with the chill and the sate of the haggard morning pulling with cold fingers at the grey mist above the *gracht.*

Mr. Oglivy met him in London.

"Now we must really get down to work," said he. "There is much to be settled. I have found an ideal business for sale, and I fancy that there you might be thoroughly content. Also it is—er—far away from family connections."

"You are very kind, sir."

"Not at all. I am interested."

They lunched together at a restaurant of Mr. Oglivy's choosing. It was a mature restaurant with a certain solemn dignity of its own. It had little of the pretentious glitter of modern restaurants, but was staid and primly superior. There were no curved façades of glass, no gleaming steel fittings, but it was more middle-class in its reserve. With the war new scintillating restaurants sprang up, with a strong feverish element in them. They ousted the soberer eating-house, with its "dining-roomish" atmosphere. But Mr. Oglivy clung to sobriety, to joints wheeled by white-capped chefs, and smelling pleasantly of hot gravy and roast potatoes.

Over a glass of sherry Mr. Oglivy glowed warmly. He was obviously one of those men who delight in good food and well-matured wine. John was all impatience to get down into the country, to view the new project, clinch matters, and then arrange about Maddalan. He chafed against the restraining hand, and on him good food and wine were wasted, because they were immaterial to his happiness.

But Mr. Oglivy was not to be hurried, and the ritual of the meal dragged on. Fried sole, roast beef, sweet omelette, with Beaune. Coffee afterwards, and a liqueur brandy gold as the leaves in the Haarlemmer Hout. It seemed that they would never get away. It was not that John disliked Mr. Oglivy, he liked him as a man very much indeed, and he had great respect for his discernment as a lawyer, but all the same he was eager to be off. Then, at the last moment, with Mr. Oglivy bland and pleasant, not hurrying over a Corona and his liqueur, a telegram was brought to him, an orange island drifting on a silver sea of salver. Mr. Oglivy opened it, and his bland brows knit perplexedly.

"Very trying indeed," he said, "most trying; I don't know if I shall be able to come down with you after all."

"I could go alone, sir."

Opportunity again. A chink in the door that life opened every now and then, a long golden chink through which chance glimmered, bright with caprice.

"But that wouldn't be the same," said Mr. Oglivy disappointedly—"not at all the same."

Oh no, not a bit the same! Much, much better! "I ought to see the place at once, sir."

"Yes," agreed Mr. Oglivy, and he fingered the telegram irresolutely. "Well, if you really think that . . ."

John did think it. He went alone.

II

The train carried him across that misnamed "Flat Essex" to within a handful of miles from its sea. The city was old; it straggled out a long way in every direction. At one end its houses reached the sandy waste that was St. Barnabas, mud flats, long and drab, stretching on like thin colourless fingers for ever grasping out in desperate endeavour to reach the sea. On the north there were rose nurseries, ambient with essence in June and August, dead gardens in winter, with ghosts of roses flittering about their stark bushes. On the west there was the suburb which was considered smart, and which once had been the village of Leyton, but which had now become involved and part of the town itself. There were good old houses standing close to the streets, bending caressingly over, with fronts flat to the pavement, and oak doors studded and gnarled with time. Also there were new houses, pretentious new houses, built in the years when England was so prosperous but so inartistic, the happy years lying between the two wars, South Africa and the Great War. These homes were be-towered and battlemented, ornate with French windows and ugly stucco porches.

John was only interested in the house on the North Hill. It stood flush with the road, just far enough away from the main thoroughfare to be merely pleasantly stirred by the faint hum of traffic. It was half-timbered, as Mr. Putman's home had been, but this did not suggest the eerie or fantastic. Its small windows were latticed, and there curled greenly about it a vine, thick with deep velvety leaves and tiny pliant tendrils. The vine was the frame from which he could look out upon the world. The previous owner of the house had been an artist, and she had converted the long front room into an antique shop. Alongside it ran the little garden, in summer fragrant with stocks and sweet williams and old-fashioned flowers; this she had converted into a sale yard for stone garden ornaments, sundials, and things of that kind. Standing in the shop itself, with its sloping wooden floors and its old plaster walls and ingle-nook, you could see the garden, now stripped of verdure by the ruthless hand of winter, and standing about the few unsold pillars and posts, the Eros in stone, the Mercury in bronze. It was a garden of the gods.

A middle-aged woman came in answer to John's knock and showed him round. She took him over the shop and the garden and the living-room which lay behind the shop, and the four quaint bedrooms above.

"Miss Fergusson had a bathroom put in," she explained—"that was the mistake. Ho yes! She spent too much on the old place. You can't make it pay when you are always putting your hand in your pocket like that, can you?"

"But she made it charming."

"Ho yes, sir, charming enough, but you can't make a place pay like that. Ho no! Now, as I says, the next person as takes it gains by all that. The next person had ought to make money here. Ho yes!"

She had a thin face, triangular, and a halting voice with its strange Essex accent which he had difficulty in following. He asked if she lived near by. Instantly she glanced at him doubtfully, and he realized that she had over-estimated her personal charm. He said hurriedly, "I mean, if I take this place—and I think I shall take it—I shall need someone to work for me. It will have to be kept clean, won't it?"

Immediately the triangular face became more triangular than ever and wreathed in smiles. She told him that her name was Muriel Barnes, and that her husband was a policeman. "It's lonely," she explained. "I gets long patches of time to meself, and I gets all fed up like. It isn't that I works because I has to, ho no, but because I likes it, see?"

John explained in turn that he did see.

He stood there surveying the empty house, furnishing it in his own mind, wheatsheaf chairs clustering together in a corner, the Delft tiles in their blueness, Minna's *stoofje*, and, propped against the plaster walls, the old pictures in mellow loveliness.

He visualized it as it would be. He saw it with almost a womanish joy of possession, and the room beyond which would be his own holy of holies, with gay chintz curtains on which sprawled delicious flowers, larkspurs and peonies, candytuft and thrift in little round cushions of blossom. A refectory table long and thin with mountainous legs supporting it, looking queerly like a hipless woman with fat calves. And flitting in and out of the house, in and out of the room, and up the narrow old stairs with their rickety balustrade, across the humpy landing, in and out of the rooms above, and more especially their room . . . Maddalan.

"Yes, I shall take it," he told her.

"And I hopes as how you'll be very happy, I do, ho yes!" said Mrs. Barnes.

He went upstairs for the last time, and stood in the low doorway of the room that would be theirs. Long slender room, with the eaves sloping at one side, and a window reaching to the floor, almost like a door of crystal, at the other end. He saw it as it would be, with a Persian rug stretched across its uneven little hills, with the gleam of red-gold oak, and a bed in the centre like an island, small and low, delicately moulded . . . their bed.

He wrote to Maddalan that night.

III

Maddalan did not reply. The *Mevrouw* saw to that. The *Mevrouw* had anticipated letters from England and had lain wait for them, determined to deal with them according to her own discrimination. Her method was crude, but effective, as are most crudities. She consigned them to the fire, having read as much of them as she could, her argument being that a letter in ashes was far better than a letter in little pieces in the waste-paper basket. The steady flame of his passion suffered a bewildering drenching, and he began to believe that the girl he once had loved had forgotten him. A new perspective shaped the affair. It had not been love which had forced her to surrender herself to him. She was quite passionless. If she had really cared for him, would she not have fled with him? Have not countless women sold their souls for love? The plea that it was sin was insufficient, and it was that she had not cared for him.

He spent some time in furnishing and arranging his home, and in writing to his mother—now Mrs. Duckett—and keeping her ignorant of his address, as advised by the discreet Mr. Oglivy. He moved in, and he made new friends, in particular Roy Graham.

Roy was a young estate agent who lived in Condering. He made friends with John from the first day when he had been employed to superintend some alterations in the old house and to test the drains.

"Queer," he said, "but they're good. Generally in these old places they are damned rotten. You're in luck."

To John, who had never known a man's friendship before, there was something akin to hero-worship in his comradeship. Roy was the antithesis of John. He was light-hearted, debonair, and he did not care much what happened. He was young and attractive, with none of the bruised mentality of John, who had suffered defeat from the birth which had brought him into the world handicapped by his environment. Roy, with bright yellowish hair, and a fine aesthetic face, was a type. He would always be young, and his very youth set John, grown sere in his own springtime, worshipping.

"Women," said Roy, with the bitter bright cynicism of youth, "are not worth loving."

"They forget," John nodded across the little room that he had furnished with such care. He nodded in patriarchal wisdom. He knew.

"They forget. They make use of us. They don't love as men love. They have no depth, no roots . . . yes, that's it." Roy laughed at the simile. The idea appealed to him; women without roots, like elms, all gay leaves and twitching branches and allurement, but unsafe and treacherous because they are not deeply rooted.

"I loved her tremendously," said John, for he had told Roy all about it—that late autumn evening with the wind whining at the window crevices and jiggering the door latches. The pain of the confessional had been a little exquisite.

"Let her go. You were just an episode in her life. We often are just episodic, and it doesn't pay." Roy lit another cigarette from the old pewter box and lolled back in the comfortable chair. "When I love, I'm going to be everything to her, or nothing. I don't intend to be *pour passer le temps.*"

In one sense these two cynical young men were right, for although Maddalan had not forgotten the night, and the day at Leyden, and the hour in the Haarlemmer Hout, she had forgotten how much she had cared. The river of her affection had been engulfed in the sea of her indignation at finding that he did not attempt to make further overtures to her. She had forgotten that she had herself bade him be gone. Now he represented to her a passing phase standing between her approaching womanhood and her departing girlhood; with him she had crossed the Rubicon of her desire, and now suddenly the passion of the emotion gushed away from her as blood from a mortal wound. She wanted no more.

If he had married her it might have been different. If he had persuaded her, taken her into his arms, then she might have reshaped her theories, and kept him on that plinth within the shrine of her memory. He might have remained as the ikon in her heart's temple. But the *Mevrouw* assured her that men were like that. What they had had they did not want again. She had been a fool, and now who would want to marry her ever? Had she not surrendered to this man her precious virginity? And would not the whole world know of it? In the *Mevrouw*'s eyes the only way in which to blot out this sin was to cover it, to bury it deeply with the earth of silence. To hustle it away, unshriven and unshrouded, to pretend that it had never been, and to forget the man. That was most essential to the *Mevrouw*: they must forget the man.

The *Mijnheer* had no idea what had occurred, and when he made any tentative enquiries his head was immediately snapped off, and he was told "not to be a fool". So he lapsed into silence. Silence was far more strategic with the *Mevrouw*; she insisted upon it.

Once, when just at first the wound was sharp and hurt, Maddalan lay awake at night, her eyes red with weeping, and Minna, hearing her, came to see her. Minna crept in, tall and angular, with her great woollen nightdress in fat folds about her spare body, and protruding above it her round benign face. Minna carried a candle set in a deep socket, and held it high so that it lit a halo round her head, through which hung her two long plaits. They were thick ropes of hair securely tied with an old bootlace at the bottom. Minna put the candle down and knelt beside the bed, drawing Maddalan's shuddering body to her own. Minna knew that there was a man who had caused the weeping; she knew because (in spite of her unromantic appearance) she herself was a victim of love and passion, and felt all the deep flurryings of desire and anguish in her own poor heart.

"There, there," said Minna. "Tell me—it will help."

Torn between the stern instructions of the *Mevrouw* and her own feminine craving for the confessional, Maddalan did not know what to do. Then, because her need was great, and because youth clings to youth whether it be mistress and maid or two friends, she admitted the truth. Gradually, word by word, Maddalan unearthed her skeleton, dug it up, displayed it to Minna's view, and was strangely comforted by the fact that the intervening weeks had decomposed it. Now it was not so lovely, and she could see as she had not been able to see it when she was close up against it.

"I was a fool," she wept.

"Many of us are fools with men," Minna consoled her, and she clasped the young soft body close to her harsh nightdress. Then she whispered to Maddalan of her own foolishness. He was a cheese-maker at Edam, but oh, such a cheese-maker! The way he looked! And he had dark eyes . . . dark eyes that pierced you through and through, that possessed you. How could one refuse him? Just outside Edam there are dykes, and banks with soft seeding grasses, offering shelter. She had met him there, though all the while her better self had advised against it. She had meant to come away at once, but somehow she had delayed. She did not know why or how. She had delayed too long. It had been quite dark when tiredly they had got up again, and the barges riding down the canals had looked like unshaped hulks in the twilight. Next time they had met he had been cold, though she had been more ardent. Tearfully she explained the cruel law that persists in making the woman desire more when the man is, alas, satiated.

Now she was afraid, she was tremulously afraid. There were signs about herself, and she believed that she might be going to have a baby. Maddalan sprang up in bed and caught Minna to her.

"No, no, not that!" she besought. Because perhaps the same thing might be happening to herself. Perhaps she might already be unable to prevent the workings of Nature within her. Something that she could not pluck out from under her heart; something that, desire as she might, she could not tear from within her. She felt her eyes glazing with fright; the anguish of the moment sent her lips dry. She wanted to sympathize with Minna, she wanted to help her, but what could she do about it? Had not Minna opened this new and fearful field of suggestion to her?

For weeks Maddalan suffered torture, deceiving herself about every sigh that she drew. Then suddenly the spate of fear left her, and with the silk-soft air of spring she knew that she was safe.

"Ah, but that Minna," said the *Mevrouw*, knitting solemnly some capacious garment for the *Mijnheer*, "she was bad girl. She was very bad girl. A cheese-maker at Edam! As if one believed such nonsense! Much more likely that it was that *Mijnheer* Carrick. Get one bad man into the house and all the woman are with child. But thank the Providence we have weathered that storm."

The *Mijnheer* sucked at his foul old pipe and said nothing. Bit by bit, chance word by chance word, the truth unfolded itself. To him it was merely transitory. He was a calm old man; things did not ruffle him. He sucked at his pipe in the chimney corner and thought of the lovely lustful women in the Onderkerksplein, under the bells of the old Mint House.

Maddalan thought of John. She thought of him dispassionately, having no idea that he had ever written. If he had married her it might have been so different. Then she would have dared to love him in her full flood-tide of emotion.

John believed in marriage; he believed in it with all the indomitable faith of respectable people who have been brought up to think of it as of outstanding importance. Since his romance he had set it as his goal in life, and he believed that it would render everything to him. Although he had written to Maddalan and offered her marriage, desired marriage, she had spurned his letter. There had been no reply.

And, from Maddalan's viewpoint, he had not offered to marry her. Between them both, like an impassable mountain, stood the *Mevrouw* with the handy incinerator and a blind faith that she was doing her best and putting right a very grievous wrong. One day Maddalan would marry some splendid gentleman from Amsterdam or The Hague, which would be most wise, oh yes, most wise indeed! She would follow the routine of all respectable Dutch housewives, living in one of the hyper-cleanly Dutch houses beside a sparkling *gracht*, and she would have children. The *Mevrouw* would attend all the confinements and order her son-in-law about. In the end Maddalan, having reached a ripe old age, would be buried in a simple graveyard and the town would mourn her for her respectability above all things. They would never know—which was the essence of the whole affair to the *Mevrouw*—they would never know that she was a *vondeling*; they would never know that she had made the one bitter mistake in her girlhood.

IV

John Carrick did not look at women. He felt cynicism squirming in his heart, the adder in his Eden, for Condering proved itself to be a little Eden. He fitted up the house for himself and delighted in its gay furnishings. He equipped the shop, and already it was showing a profitable return. Roy sent him customers. Roy was engaged in building houses for young couples, and it was easy enough for him to put a deal in John's way. Young couples knew little of furniture, but brides seemed to develop a craze for old things, and bridegrooms are notoriously desirous to please their new wives. Then Roy got the order for a mansion some miles in the country, and, as money was no object, the client bought all John's Delft tiles for his old-fashioned fireplaces. The price was amazing.

"That was rather good," said Roy.

"Excellent."

"Now you'll have to go across to Holland and get some more."

"And see Maddalan again? I wonder."

"You're bitter about her."

John sighed as he sat at the refectory table with its great fat legs and slender top. "You'd be fed up, too. I'm through with women. There aren't going to be any more women in my life. First there was Freda: she wanted all she could get, and nothing else. There was my mother. It is a rotten thing to say, I suppose, but she just ordered me about. Freda was right. I've been a pack mule, and I'm through with it."

"That's wise," said Roy approvingly; "and don't you elope with Barney."

"What? Mrs. Barnes?" Mrs. Barnes was for ever a

thorn in their flesh. She did John's housework. She came in early and late, taking a too proprietary interest in the house and shop, and also in John himself. Secretly down in his heart he was not sure that she was not the woman with a whip and himself the pack mule jogging along before her. Mrs. Barnes was the new type of charwoman. She was the product of that class bred of war, which, stepping out of its yeoman rut, mounted into a smug and dreadful respectability, aped the defunct middle class, and was, in fact, the new middle class. Like most new classes, it was deadly. Mrs. Barnes and her policeman husband were very much lady and gentleman. They lived in a most excellent cottage close by, and had bought a piano second-hand, on which the policeman could play certain hymns, but was inclined to repeat himself badly. Mrs. Barnes read books from the library, and magazines, and did not only ape her betters but in her own opinion became her better. John could never understand how it was that she consented to work for him at all. He knew that in her heart she despised him, she considered his whims and fancies to be vulgar and his love of art ungentlemanly.

For Mrs. Barnes had a passion for knick-knacks and veneer. She had a Goss china complex, and worked atrocious sofa cushions for an atrocious front room. Here, between Madras curtains looped on either side the window, much as the centre parting of a woman's brow, Mrs. Barnes' oval face would look out.

Yet she amused both him and Roy with her mispronunciations and her misinterpretations of words, though her conversation disturbed them. Mrs. Barnes *would* talk. She could not be persuaded to leave off.

"Talk?" said Roy—"she is a positive Niagara of conversation."

"She means well," explained John, who liked to believe the best of people.

"Epitaph to all the old cats in the world, who drove their fellow beings mad."

"Well, I can't tell her of it."

"I could. I should say, 'Barney, my lamb, do let me beg of you to serve me faithfully and well, but *be mute*!' I should have one good row."

John shook his head. He was no lover of the one good row. Quarrels still frightened him, and he had the natural shrinking from scenes habitual to a sensitive nature. He believed that anything was liable to become a brawl. He had too often been appalled at his mother's hankering after the good row. He had, lurking like grim fantastic shadows in the back of his memory, recollections of gruesome arguments over the backyard wall. Shrill arguments, screamed in wrath over a slack clothes-line on every day save Monday, when it was tautened, and flew flapping flags in the wind. Flags of white linen, bellying shirts, flaunting petticoats grotesquely imitative of pregnancy. They had formed the drumming, the muffled, muted, derisive drumming to the shrieking arguments. He had always shrank from conspicuousness ever since those times, and he would go on shrinking, because vehemence had no part in his nature.

If he had not been terrified of a quarrel, he would never have run away from home to where angry words could not reach him. He would never have crept forth into the unfriendly world without good-bye or God-speed. He would never have left Maddalan in that hour when the dark pool of night was disturbed by the first opal iridescence of dawn. He would have faced it out, demanded her of the *Mevrouw*, and would no longer have been pack mule, obeying the commands of the woman with the reins. Maddalan would have been his to-day. But pack mules do not turn like that. Public opinion is too often the scourge which, plied, frightens men into obedience. John was not alone in his dislike of comment.

"Only it's queer about you, a sort of complex," said Roy. "It hinders you—must do. I don't care a couple of hoots what people say. Let them say! It won't hurt me."

"But it reacts on you," John complained, covering his shrinking, for he was a little ashamed of it. "I am all for peace."

"Yes, but not at any price."

"No, of course not at any price."

"Yet it is at any price with you. Anything to avoid a shindy. In the end you land yourself in a worse one. Tell Barney what you think of her."

John was silent.

V

"I've got two tickets for the theatre," said Roy one early spring evening. "What about it?"

"What's on?"

John had to admit that he had but little intimacy with the theatre. He had never gone in his youth, save to the pierrots who nightly sang on the pier; he had only a small conception of dramatic attraction. His mother did not approve of theatre-going, nor did Mr. Duckett; they believed it to be ungodly. Lately John had had qualms about his people. Up till now he had kept them in ignorance of his address, in strict accordance with Mr. Oglivy's instructions. Recently he had remembered that after all she was his mother. His sentiments had been played upon, and in answer to a pathetic letter from her he had in a weak moment written giving the name of the house where he was living. Now he regretted his action, but it was too late to undo it. The remembrance of their strictness with regard to the theatre, suddenly drifting in across his mind, recalled the foolish sentimental moment when he had posted that misguided letter.

"A play. I shall enjoy it," said Roy. He was sophisticated. Son of an old couple, and, as is so often the case with sons born late in life, to people who had hitherto supposed that they were to be childless, he had run more than a little wild.

The bright veneer of a post-war decade had polished him. A good fellow at heart, yet he suffered from the too gaudy gloss of modernity.

"Wine, woman and song," he told John, "that's what a fellow wants. I've got two tickets. We might have dinner at the Chantry first. That would be a change."

Chapter Two

There lies the port; the vessel puffs her sails;
There gloom the dark, broad seas. . . .

Ulysses

I

THEY dined at the Chantry, which was an old-fashioned hotel situated in the main street of Condering. It stood back, with its wide cobbled posting-yard at one side, and oak beams stretching with a bulge across the arch. Its knobbled doors were propped wide. In the dining-room there was a certain bareness, accentuated by the loftiness, for there was too great a space between floor and ceiling. There were long windows, reminding John vaguely of the Renaissance houses with their too prevalent eyes. There was a wide hearth at the far end which sent no warmth down to them.

They dined in an atmosphere that was gloomy rather than gay, with the gloominess which staid old England considers to be the hall-mark of respectability. Roy had had a hankering for something different, for cocktails with golden bubbles in crystal glasses, for orchids in silver bowls, for mellow-shaded lights and obsequious attendance. The small old-fashioned country hotel could provide nothing of that sort for him. A slow and abashed maid handed them the two vegetables a little clumsily, with the boiled fowl. Her cap was awry and her hands reminded John of frozen meat on butchers' marble slabs. The table was badly laid, with a green stone jar of daffodils in the centre; the light hung from the roof and was inadequately shaded, but permitted a somewhat liverish glow upon it all. John chose beer, despite Roy's intention of having a bottle of wine between them. Afterwards he insisted on ordering liqueurs with their coffee.

"Such a damned dull meal," said Roy; "so typically English, isn't it? Soup, fried fillets, boiled fowl, prunes and custard. Those blasted prunes always put the lid on it."

"I thought it was nice."

"A damned sight too nice. It was worse than nice. It was respectable!"

Roy sipped chartreuse, brightly green against the gleam of glass. John remembered a day lying under the path by the backwater. He recalled the vivid greenness of weed against the sparkling froth of a shimmering sea. It is odd how memories come and go. One cannot account for the demands which bring them forth out of their retirement; they are forgotten, lying away in the dusty recesses of a tangled mind, and it is amazing when they leap forward into prominence.

He said, "I hope we are going to enjoy ourselves."

"I hope so, too. If I enjoy the show as much as this rotten dinner, I'm going to be sorry for myself."

"Things that begin badly often end well."

"Oh, do they? I have found things that begin badly go on worse." Roy flicked cigarette ash into the saucer of his coffee-cup stamped with the name of the hotel. "So honest themselves," he explained bitterly, "that they anticipate that you will run off with their mouldy china."

"Do you think so?"

"I know it."

He called for the bill from the dingy maid, who had been lingering near the Victorian sideboard, obviously discarded from some great mansion which had succumbed to the demands of death duties and infamous taxation. She brought it readily enough.

A moment later and they were ready, gathering up coats and hats to pass round the screen which made a pitiful attempt to keep out the draught from the door.

"Hardly cold enough to put them on," said John. "The evenings are drawing out. Spring is almost here again."

"Yes, Spring. Suppose you've got that Spring feeling? Queer how it goes to a young head." Roy blundered out into the ill-lit corridor beyond, and as he did so he fell over a middle-aged man who had been in the act of entering. "I say, I'm sorry," said Roy. "Did I hurt you? They keep this place so infernally dark, you never know where you are going, and it's a foul old place, all steps and unexpectednesses. A rotten old house."

The middle-aged man came in. He was cadaverous, with a long, lantern jaw, and a grim mouth set across it, to break the almost equal distance between upper lip and chin, and mouth and throat. His eyes, deep sunken into pits, were languorous and full of an almost pathetic appeal. He had a hungry look about him, which John instantly attributed to either an artist or an actor. He bore the same hall-mark in the very way that his thin clawlike hands quavered forward and his furtively questioning eyes sought those of the two men.

"That's all right, sir," he said; "my fault. I was coming in for a drink. Couldn't make anybody hear, and came too fast."

"Well, have a drink at my expense," said Roy, and from behind the older man he winked at John. They were shuffling back to their old seats again round the bare table, now messy with soiled coffee-cups, and grey trails of cigarette ash, and gleaming glasses in which still quivered the faint essence of green chartreuse. The dingy maid appeared once more, agape with surprise, and they ordered. John hardly noticed what it was that they ordered.

He thought that their companion was a quiet fellow, a reticent being who did not tell too much about himself, but when the drink flamed down his throat it seemed that his lips were opened. Sparkles came to the old eyes, old not so much in years as with knowledge, the grim, acute knowledge of this world's hells. He was willing to tell them about himself; he unleashed his history swiftly and joyously as a dog who is released after being a long time on the lead. He was an actor. He was travelling with the repertory company, and did not appear until the third act in to-night's drama, therefore he had had time to pop in for a drink. One presumed that he often popped in. He had played Hamlet once. He had made a hit, he might tell them. He had known all the great people: Tree, Waller, Forbes-Robertson. He had played the Dauphin to Waller's Henry V. Some people had preferred his treatment of the Dauphin to Waller's treatment of the King. "But"—he waved his thin fingers with meaning, and somehow John thought of bird claws scraping against rock, the grimly rocky substance of that wall between hardship and success—"it is all a matter of fortune."

He eyed them craftily. "I could have been a Waller if I had stooped to the gallery. I could have been a Tree if I had done this and that. Anyone . . . if I had had the fortune. As it is, well, here I am."

"I expect you are damned good, sir," said Roy appreciatively.

"Most people seem to think so. Your wretched little county rag of a newspaper was absurd about me. Yes, sir, as you are so pressing, I think I will have another. I went round to the office and saw the editor, a well-meaning country bumpkin with no idea of true art, of course. He was amazed. He said to me, 'Mr. Jefferson, I apologize.' I accepted the apology. I shall be anxious to see what he says this week. I shall be most interested."

"We are going to see the play to-night," said John.

"That is good news. You will enjoy it, you will enjoy it immensely. It is, of course, melodrama, and some people hold melodrama cheaply. So easy to be cheap. So simple to sneer. They ought to have our jobs, that would make them change their opinions."

"I expect it would," said Roy.

The actor, thumbing his glass until it seemed that the stem must snap, said thoughtfully, "What seats have you two gentlemen got?"

"Stalls," said Roy.

"Stalls? Umph. I daresay I could get them changed for a box if I said that you were my friends. Friends of the great Leslie Jefferson, hey? Would you like a box? Of course you would like a box."

"Rather," said Roy, "but there is only one box in our rotten little theater—supposing it is booked?"

"It shall not be booked," said Mr. Jefferson in a lordly manner, and he tossed off another glass with a cavalier-like flourish.

"Certainly," agreed Roy, "it shall not be booked."

Once more he called up the slatternly maid and asked for his bill.

"And after the show," suggested Mr. Jefferson, "you might like to meet some of the girls, eh? You might like to come behind for a bit, and we could manage a little supper together?"

The idea went to Roy's head. It was champagne to his youthful anticipation. "Ra-ther," he glowed."

They took down their hats from the Victorian hatstand, which stood like some slender giant by the screen at the door, proffering large mahogany hooks to right and left of it. They passed out into the street, a vista of blue dusk beyond.

III

The theatre was close. It had but a poor façade, for it had been built many years since, and primarily with the idea of affording a corn market to the town. It struggled to put up a prosperous appearance, with its long tail of bills fluttering in the wind, and its one-eyed commissionaire standing in an ill-fitting uniform on the single step.

Mr. Jefferson swept past the commissionaire with the air of a duke about to enter his own castle under a raised portcullis. He went within, through dusty plush curtains which smelt of time and disuse, into an ill-lit passage where two over-coiffured programme-girls were giggling together. He pushed on, down the stairs at the side, and paused before a small door, optimistically labelled "Box A", regardless of the fact that there was not, nor was there ever likely to be, a Box B.

"Here we are," he said.

The small door yielded. They went within into a small square, plush-hung and threadily carpeted. Three wooden chairs, of the style that is to be seen in the cheaper drapers' shops, were sitting in mock interest before the house. On the right the curtain quivered and trembled, blown by the wholesome draught from behind. In the long rows of stalls and the round rows of circle and gallery, humanity was flooded, and sat obviously agog with interest or stoically indifferent to the affairs of the moment.

It had become plain to John that Roy was excited. John did not know whether the wine had gone to his head or whether he was thrilled by the prospect of the evening's entertainment seen from the greater vantage-point of a box. They hung their hats on the pegs provided for the purpose, and then took their seats against the plush-covered rail. In doing this, John discovered both painfully and ignominously that the chair which he had selected had only three legs. As he picked himself up from a humiliating position on the floor, he heard the outraged murmurs of the scandalized matron alongside in the circle. "Disgusting!" said the scandalized matron. "Too drunk to stand up! Ought to be ashamed of hisself!"

"I may as well see the curtain up," said Mr. Jefferson, with the air of one whose time is definitely his own. "There is no need for me to hurry."

The band was collecting in its narrow pit. A melancholy-looking violinist, with conspicuously thin hair and peering glasses, was resining his bow and sucking his tongue absorbedly while he did it. The music-stands stood like so many skeletons, a pitiful array, and lying on the floor in pathetic groups the bulging hulk of double bass and 'cello, and in one corner the tired piano, with its yellowed keys like so many ancient teeth stuck in some wizened old head. John did not listen to the bantering conversation of Roy and Mr. Jefferson; he was thinking of the music. It would be execrable. He had a feeling that it might be *Poet and Peasant* taken *presto*, with much drumming and very little harmony. He was prepared for the worst.

But the conductor was not a bad young man; he had a finely drawn face, the profile of which John could see chiselled against the darkness. He rapped the orchestra to attention. The brass skeletons filled with white flesh. Papers flittered like ghosts among the gloominess of the narrow pit. John, leaning forward, sensed the orchestra as a churchyard with ghouls and rotting bodies and yellowed teeth, and the squares of music as tombstones standing etched against the blackness of the earth.

The music started. Instantly he was galvanized to attention. For it was not *Poet and Peasant* at all. It was the *Minuet and Trio*. It perked out its little pertinent enquiries, and answered with its abrupt crescendoes. The 'cello wept for it; the violin gavotted; brittle, laughing, mocking music cascaded on his ears. It pirouetted with itself, chuckled and swung, now high, now low, now passionately crescendo, now tremulously *piano*.

John sat back in his chair. After all he was going to enjoy the show, for the *Minuet* had humoured him. It had sent the full spate of delicious memories into his mind.

The curtain rose, somewhat wheezily, but John did not hear it ratcheting like some asthmatical old woman climbing a hill. He was there to be entertained; he was staring down on a stage, gaudily lit. He was in the mood to be pleased.

People came and went. The story was hackneyed, familiar to the entire world. It provided all the accustomed rôles, hero and villain, the young *ingénue* and the mature bride, the harmless, senile old man. They passed before his eyes, threaded in and out of the melodrama, all part of the established theme. The programme told him that Mimi Adair was the ingénue, that Belle Stevens was the bride.

"Wonderful girl, that Mimi," said Roy as he leant across Mr. Jefferson to impart this news to John, "marvelous girl. What eyes! What limbs!"

"I'll introduce you later," said Mr. Jefferson, "both of you. She is quick, that kid; she will go far. Belle too. I think your friend would like Belle"—and he smiled benignly on John.

"I—I'm not a woman-lover," apologized John.

"Oh no," jeered Roy, "you're a nice one to talk! Not content with only Englishwomen! Why, when you crossed the ocean——"

"Ah, Paris?" said Mr. Jefferson, and he wagged a roguish finger. "Paris! I, too, have tasted the sweetness of the demi-monde. No one to beat her."

John felt himself turning hot. He hated the treachery born of liqueur which had made Roy voice what should have been inviolably secret. "My friend was not demi-monde," he said, "neither was she Parisienne."

"Dutch," explained Roy in a voice which he thought was a whisper.

Mr. Jefferson seemed amused. "Oh, droll," he said. "So stodgy. All petticoats and clogs."

"Neither," interrupted John harshly.

This tickled the other two enormously. "He knows, you may be sure," said Mr. Jefferson, digging Roy playfully in the ribs as he chuckled grimly. He reminded John of a gargoyle grinning over some church roof; a satanic, goggling head, with sinister eyes and gaping mouth, in queer contrast to the sanctity of the building it was supposed to adorn. These people discussing Maddalan. Maddalan, pure as ice, cold as water, his Maddalan.

He lapsed into morose silence again.

III

John wanted to be excused from going behind the scenes, but Roy was determined to make an evening of it. The cocktails and liqueurs had gone to his head; although he was in no sense drunk, he was far from being absolutely sober. He was ready for anything that offered itself. Mr. Jefferson, noticing this, urged him on in a knowing fashion. Mr. Jefferson, who, incidentally, had not partaken of a good square meal for some time, was keen for the supper at the Chantry, and knew that by gently and judiciously pressing Roy onward he would in all probability obtain his end. In a way, John suspected Mr. Jefferson. He was ill at ease about him, more particularly so when, after the second act, Mr. Jefferson suggested the *détour* behind the scenes.

"Oh yes," said Roy jokingly—his cheeriness was becoming more than a little tiresome—"I am all for making the lovely Mimi's acquaintance."

Mimi, bright, brassy hair, too large blue eyes, a shade too innocent, too everything. Mimi, with eyelashes like stiff horsehair, blackened until they stuck out at you. Saucy, impertinent, common little Mimi! Even John could see how common she was.

"We're all right here," he suggested.

"All right? All rot! Let's make a party of it. You're a regular wet blanket to bring out. Do or dare, says I. This place is stuffy enough at ordinary times; opportunity doesn't come twice. I'm for a beano while I can have one."

And there was Mr. Jefferson standing in the wheezy door of the shabby little box, beckoning them with long shrivelled fingers, ogling them, leering. His cadaverous face smiled. It grinned out of the gloom at them as skeletons grin. They followed.

They cranked down rickety stairs, opening out suddenly and unexpectedly into the full, gusty space which was stage. The dusty plush separated them from their audience, and here were men in shirt-sleeves setting a new scene. Props were stacked about; wicker baskets marked, with an effort at distinction, "The Reubens Repertory Company", in huge letters, as though to impress readers. Members of the company sat on these baskets, or lounged against the wall, or tried to get out of the scene-shifters' way, with small success. Mr. Jefferson winked at Roy, and curled his finger authoritatively in a beckoning movement. Roy tripped after him, John sloped in his wake.

They went behind the stage, to a passage diversified with little doors. On each little door there was a name hurriedly scrawled in chalk, and on others, the more superior kind, visiting cards, neatly printed and slipped into small slots arranged for their reception. Everything struck John as being singularly dusty and untidy. There was so much dust that it seemed to choke you. Mr. Jefferson stopped before a door, and tapped tenderly. An irritable woman's voice from within called out sharply: "Whatcherwant?" in a strident manner. Mr. Jefferson, who had assumed a playful attitude before tapping, and had murmured something about being "Cupid's messenger", now changed his tone.

"It's me, Mimi. Two gentlemen want to see you. May I bring them in?"

"Half a mo'!"

There were sounds, whisperings, hurried movements, things being swished away into obscurity, rustlings, and then a cooing, "Come in."

It was quite obvious to John that Mimi had two voices; he had been prepared for it, because his mother was gifted in that manner. She had her "company" voice and her usual voice, and they were as remote as China from England. Mimi's "Whatcherwant" had been familiar; it had all been in keeping with the common little girl who had danced. Mimi's tender and sighing command to enter was obviously "company voice".

They went inside.

The dressing-room was ridiculously small. On one side before an untidy dressing-table, over-mirrored, bedecked with mascots, and liberally dusted with powder, sat Mimi. She was wearing white muslin and blue ribbons and a great many curls. Her manner was white muslin too! She had reached for a great teddy bear and sat there shyly expectant, obviously posed to greet them. Roy saw her, noted the rouged cheeks, the superfluity of Number One grease paint, the eyes with their coarse wires of lashes heavy with *cosmétique*, and approved. He did not notice Belle standing close to the door, drawn up against the wall, in an attitude of sullen disregard.

At that moment her more matronly deportment contrasted favourably in John's eyes with Mimi's overdone *ingénue*. She was dressed in dove-grey against which her hair flamed. It was red hair, coiled loosely round a largish head, and framing a face that, having left thirty behind it, had "settled". Mimi's eyes were frank hazel, the brows and lashes artificially darkened; her mouth was a dart of crimson in a face that was coldly white. Belle's jaw was too heavy, her chin had begun to think of a shadow chin, and her bust was masterful, with two thick shoulders behind it.

But John, peering into this ill-lit cavern and seeing Mimi as harlot and only harlot, saw Belle standing aloof in her sullen disapproval as something altogether different.

He liked her hair shining at him in the shadow without yellow artificiality. Roy went forward. He leant upon Mimi's chair, perhaps not too steadily (it was becoming more and more apparent that he had had enough to drink); he entered into a bantering conversation, with Mr. Jefferson satanically approving and leering gargoyle-wise at him. They had forgotten John standing awkwardly on the threshold, unused to such company or to such places, and entirely at a loss as to what to do next.

He looked from one to the other of them. He was, unfortunately, stone sober. In upon this incongruous scene little light arpeggios of sound seemed to him to ripple . . . the sound of the *Minuet*; the sound of the great cathedral of the Haarlemmer Hout; the face of Freda passing briefly before his eyes, dusky, soft, tender; the face of Maddalan, white like ice, with eyes of irises; and, somehow allied to these two, the face of Belle as she stood against the wall flashing her sullen contempt upon them.

"Well, that's that," said Roy with some swagger: "a little supper after, all of us. All jolly good fellows. . . ."

"Oh, I say, I don't know that I ought," Mimi simpered. "You know how people talk."

"Let them talk! We'll give them something to talk about."

"That's the spirit!" said Mr. Jefferson, yellowly cadaverous. It was all working out just as he had wished. A good supper—he'd see that it was a good supper, too. Wages these days didn't run to much; shows were lighting on hard times.

A call-boy banged on the door.

"Nah then," said the call-boy, "toime, young lidies, toime."

"Of all the cheek!" said Mimi, then she caught Roy's eye and simpered again.

They were edging to the door. John saw Belle glance at him; she had apparently noticed his face for the first time, and she turned away disdainfully. He took an impression of her back into the theatre with him. Red gold gleaming against the dirtily smudged whiteness of the wall; her face and figure all heavy, sagging a little, thickly coated with some chalky substance, her lips too brilliantly reddened.

Roy was nudging him. "What I call a bit of life," he said gaily.

"You would!" commented John.

IV

They were in the Chantry again in urgent conversation with the manageress. Mrs. Darsy was a middle-aged woman, and she was unused to suppers. In her mind suppers had cold beef and pickles as component parts, beer too, perhaps a cold fruit tart, cheese. Roy had formed an over-bright opinion of the Reubens Repertory Company, and was burning to treat them to something brilliant. Caviare sandwiches, *pâté de foie gras*, cold grouse, tipsy cake. He had no idea how welcome the sustaining cold beef would have been to Mr. Jefferson, nor that their usual supper after the show was fetched from the fried-fish shop and conveyed home in newspapers to be eaten over the fire in the bed-sitter.

Mrs. Darsy was determined to be difficult. It was not that she was unreasonable, but that she did not like the class of people connected with the Reubens Repertory Company. She held a very high regard for John, whom she knew slightly, but she considered Roy to be fast and flighty, and she thought his friends might be even faster and flightier. She put all manner of obstacles in the way, but finally consented very grudgingly to serve them with cold fowl, some of the inevitable prunes and custard, and some cheese straws.

It was not at all in accordance with Roy's original idea, but he had to put up with it. They went up to the dining-room, where the others were waiting. Half the electric lights had been extinguished from motives of economy, and the place now looked dingy enough to Roy and John, though to the famished members of the Reubens Repertory Company it was as a shining star. They were grouped about a corner table, Mimi in a day frock, an imitation silk affair overtrimmed with cheap lace, and her coat creased and shoddy, with a bunch of cotton flowers pinned to the lapel. Her hat was of the tam-o'-shanter class, in too bright wools. John noticed it with scant approval, but to Roy it was dashing. It was an impertinent little cap, jaunty with its bold oranges and blues; it invited him, and he eagerly accepted its invitation. So do objects appear different to different eyes.

A little aloof, still looking resentful, Belle was standing. Her clothes were also of the flashily cheap type, but they looked more sober beside Mimi's. She was background to Mimi; she was a gentle and sombre background, John thought. She wore clothes that had been originally intended to be sporting; a tweed coat and skirt, and with it a silk blouse much decorated with lace and hemstitching, and marred by a large emerald brooch pinning it together across her massive bust, and pulling it in a way in which it did not mean to be pulled. Her hat was a small felt, set well down over her red hair, darkish, becoming, but again spoilt by the heart of glittering diamonds securely fastened across its frontal. Belle had a passion for jewellery, lots of it. Stones intrigued her; she loved the sharp whiteness of diamonds, and spent far too much on shoddy imitations of them.

John found himself sitting beside her. He was somewhat ashamed of Roy talking over-excitedly, urged on by Mr. Jefferson. He was more than ashamed of Mimi with her paper-white face-powder, so that she looked as though she had been dipped in bismuth, and her too defiant scarlet mouth, her little squeals of girlish laughter, and her continual, "Reely now! Oh, I say! Did you ever! Reely now!"

"I'm sorry about this," said John humbly. "I know this isn't the sort of thing you are used to. The truth of it is that Roy has fallen for your friend—"

"She's no friend of mine," interrupted Belle savagely.

"I'm glad."

"You don't like her, then?" Belle darted a quick glance at him as though anxious to hear his vehement dissent.

"Well, she isn't . . ." he ended lamely, aware that it was disloyal, and tailed off before he could explain himself.

"You're right, she isn't. I've been sharing a dressing-room with her all this tour, and I've had about enough of her. Always doing the 'little innocent' and all that, and she forty if she is a day."

John cast a quick look at Mimi convulsed in merriment. ("Oh, come now! My word, if you aren't orful!

Reely now! Oh, *reely* you shouldn't!") He decided that Belle had overstretched the date by ten years, but he did not contradict her.

"She's flashy and cheap and common, and she isn't no better than she ought to be either. If it wasn't for that she'd have been out of the show weeks ago. She's got our manager on a string. He's one of those feeble fellows, can't say boo to a goose—you know the sort. He's infatuated with Mimi. She puts the baby stuff across him. That always gets a man every time. She's putting it across your friend too."

She came to a standstill. From the table there sounded a little cooing laugh from Mimi, and instantly, "Oh, but reely now, you mustn't say things like that; Mimi doesn't like them," and all the while her big eyes telling Roy lustfully that she did like them, and that she wanted more of them.

"There," said Belle, "you see?"

"I'm afraid some of it is Roy's fault; he is encouraging her," commented John. "He is like that, easily whirled off his feet, and he has had quite enough to drink, too."

The slatternly maid came up, obviously annoyed at having been brought back on duty. With her she bore a large tin tray covered with cold fowl, and wizened prunes in their black juice, and a prominent loaf of bread.

She banged the whole tray down noisily on the table as though to impress them with the fact that she did all this against her will. She banged it down, made no attempt to remove the plates from the tray and arrange them, but stood there, pulling together her apron strings behind her back, with a pin held firmly between her teeth. Through the pin and her clenched teeth she whistled enquiringly, "And-what-are-you-having-to-drink?"

"Ah!" Instantly Roy was all ears and alertness. "That is the important question. A bottle of wine? Yes, we must have a bottle of wine. The thing is, what is it to be?"

It seemed that Mr. Jefferson had very definite ideas of what he wanted. He liked a white wine, nothing like a good white wine, and some rich ruby port. He had a passion for rich ruby port, it appeared. It dawned on John rather distressfully that Mr. Jefferson intended to take the host's position upon himself; that not only did he intend to order the meal, but to superintend the drink himself, and that probably the only time when he would draw back would be when the slatternly maid presented the bill.

"Well, I don't know as 'ow you'll get yer bottle," said the maid, still hissing through the pin (she was evidently having great difficulty with the apron strings); "it's just on closing time."

"Oh, reely now, that is too bad! What will little Mimi do?"—from Mimi.

"That can be settled," said Mr. Jefferson with a lordly air, and he winked at Roy and John as much as to say, "You leave this to me, I'll see you through this." He really was a most unpleasant man. He leant across to Roy. "A little tip," he said ingratiatingly, "a small matter of a coin changing hands . . . *comprenez*? Ah, you didn't know that I was French. On my mother's side. I had a French grandparent—better than a Dutch uncle, what?"

Then, remembering that there had been something said about John's relationship with Holland, earlier in the evening, he turned and said with an exaggerated bow, "Oh, pardon, I forgot that the shoe pinched," thereby making matters very much worse.

Roy thrust his hands down into his pockets and was surprised to find how slender his store had become. He came into contact with two half-crowns, brought them into the light of day and handed them across to Mr. Jefferson. Mr. Jefferson seized them with much alacrity and, winking solemnly, passed one into the hand of the maid. He murmured something about keeping the other for later on, but as far as the maid was concerned the "later on" never arrived.

"Well, I'll see what I can do," said the girl, having at last settled the matter of the apron. "I suppose you ain't *bona fide* travellers?"

That pleased Mr. Jefferson, for he screamed with a fiercely hearty laughter. "*Bona fide!*" he said. "Ah, that's good! I'm *bona fide* all right. You see to it, my girl. *Bona fide*, and so are these two gentlemen here."

"That they ain't. They live 'ere. I knows 'em," she said grudgingly, as though to know them was to dislike them intensely. She began to shovel out the cold fowl, setting a plate before each of them, and the bread in the middle, and the prunes arranged in two glass jam-dishes on either side. Then off she went again.

The whole thing struck John as being dreadful. It dragged one down. It was like the suppers in the room behind the shop with his mother. Yet he did not know that he had not preferred those suppers, for there had been about them a certain smug air of sanctimoniousness and respectability. Here there was ogling and leering, a false sensual atmosphere, allied with vulgar promiscuousness, and wine. He refused the white wine offered him, but he noticed that Belle drank it languidly. Mimi sipped hers with vigour, as also did Roy and Mr. Jefferson. He wished Roy would realize that he had had enough; he went on apologizing to Belle for him.

"I am sure this isn't what you are used to. I am so ashamed of it. Roy's party, not mine. I'm sorry."

She snapped at him a little savagely: "Don't keep on about it. Our two friends have let us in for this, and a rotten show it is. It isn't our fault. Tell me about yourself, so that we don't have to listen to them. She makes me sick with her baby talk and her artfulness. Tell me what you do."

He told her about the antique shop. This she treated with some contempt, which she did not try to conceal. She did not like old things, she told him; her ideal was a villa in some smart suburb, with a real maid of her own, and a walnut suite. She could not understand how anyone who had a walnut suite could not be happy in life.

Then he told her about his early years, about the shop at home, and old Mr. Putman and the legacy. At the legacy she turned to him with shining eyes.

"My, but you were lucky!"

"Yes."

"What did you do with it?"

He told her that he had gone to Holland and had studied art and china for a time. She did not understand the fascination of art, and it was impossible for a girl who looked upon a walnut suite as the Mecca of her worship to understand. Somehow he did not mention Maddalan. How could he? When he thought about her, it seemed to fill the room—the smoky, heavy, ugly room—with a trembling, ice-cold dew. It seemed as though a blue berg had sailed into it, something purely cold, yet magically fascinating. He shut his memory to its allurement.

"Then I bought this business. It was good fun altering the house round. That was how I met Roy. He has helped me enormously, and we have got to know each other and care for each other."

"He's not the right sort of friend for you," she said sharply.

Woman's intuition. That instinct which stirs so swiftly in the breasts of all daughters of Eve. He honoured her for it, though he tried to cover his friend's lapse. "He isn't always like to-night," he hastened to assure her.

"I should hope not." She fingered a glass of ruby red port meditatively. "Why don't you marry?" she asked presently.

Her eyes met his. Hazel eyes; a queer colour hazel, lightish brown, with stabs of green in it, and yet with quick little living darts of red through it. It was gold, too, honey colour. Her eyes reminded him of river water, running swiftly down some reeded causeway, snatching some of the brown clay of its banks into its reflections, some of the thin upstarting reeds, and some of the savage brassy gold of St. John's wort growing lavishly by its side. Fool's gold, confusing glitter of it! His glance fell before hers.

"Oh, I don't know. Perhaps I have never yet met the girl."

"What's that?" Mr. Jefferson happened to have heard the last sentence and leant forward craningly across glasses and soiled meat plates, and pudding plates smeared claret by prunes. He had a curved look that reminded John of snakes, and his face was snakish too. "What's that about the girl? Why, the girl is the one of the moment. Of course she is. This is the only girl that matters. Isn't that so, Mimi? Of course it is."

Mimi giggled, and said of course it was, it was reely! Roy, very bright-eyed with the white wine and the ruby red port, giggled and said of course it was too. Mr. Jefferson sagged back into his chair, as though he had made a very clever remark and was well satisfied with himself. He tried to remember that most successful joke of his that he had brought out at the last party which he had attended, but somehow his memory was confused. Heady stuff port! Perhaps a hair of the dog that bit you. He poured out yet another glass.

"I suppose we have got to stay and see this thing through," said Belle. "I'm afraid it is going to get worse. Les Jefferson is an awful man, a regular sponger. Can't we get away?"

"Say your head aches," suggested John.

"Shall I?" She rose. "Well, good night, all. See you later, Mimi, I've got a rotten head."

"Oh, you can't go yet," urged Roy brightly, "you

can't go yet. Coffee and liqueurs. Mush-have-coffee-andsh-liqueurs. . . ."

"Don't be a spoil-sport," gurgled Mr. Jefferson, wagging his finger at her roguishly; "v'y naughty little gel. Don't be a spoil-sport."

"I shan't spoil your party. Mr.—what's-his-name will see me home." She turned, and in an undertone said, "That gets you out of it too. Anyway, I couldn't bear this any longer. I must have air. You don't want me to faint, do you? I weigh eleven stone, and none of you look to be capable of dealing with me as a dead weight."

She moved away from the table. John saw Roy beckoning to him through the viny twists of smoke which curled between them. Mr. Jefferson had ordered a cigar and was puffing away at it foully. The room reeked of smoke, and the perfume of wine and stale food. In the background he could discern the slatternly maid yawning, as she propped up the huge mahogany sideboard.

"Well, what is it?" He went to Roy's side. Roy whispered to him in a stage whisper:

"Lend me a fiver. The——have darned well—hic—cleared me out."

Hurriedly John thrust his note-case crinklingly into Roy's hand.

V

Outside it was freshly cold. The moon swung in the sky with not a single cloud in sight, and the little city was hushed with the peace of night. Quite naturally Belle took his arm, putting her own hand lightly in his. The cold air was invigorating, and she had drunk just enough of the ruby red port to feel pleasantly anticipant of some adventure. It had trickled warmly down her throat, not burning her, yet infusing thrill into her. They walked along, contentedly aware of the stillness of the muffled city, and turned down the North Hill, for she had told him that she lodged in a street lower down.

"I live there," he told her, as they passed the house definitely black and white in the silver-footed shadows.

"My, but it's a big house." She drank in its proportions greedily. "I didn't know that you meant a place like that. I was muddling it with a sort of old clo' place. One side old clo', and one side Uncle."

"Oh"—he laughed a little—"Lord, no! Mine is a definite antique business."

"Does it pay?"

"Yes," he admitted frankly, "it docs. I think anything does if you put your soul into it, don't you?"

She didn't, but she had the discretion not to say so. As they walked down the hill she became silent, and he noticed that she clung more heavily to his arm. Passing a garden there came the deep scent of daffodils, and they could be seen gleaming honey-sweet and honey-coloured among the darkness of grass and leaves. Soon there would be pink-flowering thorn and all the ecstasy of lilac and laburnum. It seemed to John that spring was breaking differently, made different by the fact that he had attended an absurd party which had been in itself horrible. Different, because he had met Belle, and he had, he found, been homesick all these months for a woman's company. He liked women. He did not accept them in the sexual acceptance of Roy, who liked them only because of the rampant instinct within him. John liked women to talk with; he preferred their viewpoints.

He saw her to the door. It was a small, cheerless residence in one of the cheaper streets, and stood flush with the pavement, as did all its fellows. Each window was liberally becurtained with much of Nottingham's worst, and displayed bravely an aspidistra. It was a typical house of a typical community, and it struck him that no wonder she was morose and hated life when it had dealt her into such beautiless surroundings. He had escaped from similar conditions, and he could sympathize keenly with her dislike of them. For, after all, she was artist too, although she thought in walnut suites and bamboo complexities; all actresses were in some sense artist.

They stood on the doorstep. He thought that her eyes were a little wistful. "I suppose this is good-bye?" she said.

"I don't see why. The company is here for another month, isn't it?"

"Yes, but you'll have seen enough of me. I'm not a Mimi, you know. I don't hold men that way." She sniffed a little indignantly, and added, "Thank God."

"Supposing you came to tea with me, and saw my place?" he suggested eagerly.

"Yes, I'd like that."

"Is it a bargain?"

"When?" she asked, and then added scornfully, "you'll forget."

"I won't. Let's make it to-morrow, then I can't forget."

"All right," she said, and after a moment's hesitation, "to-morrow then," and she let herself in with her latchkey. He stayed in the street to see the light flare up at the top window, which denoted that she had climbed the cheap box staircase and was now in the very act of undressing. Slowly he went back home. He stayed for a while outside the house with the garden gay with daffodils. He did not know why, but it was music to his mood. A soft wind soughed through the leaves, quitted them again, and once more left the world soundless. He thought of Maddalan as something definitely confiscated into the cold abyss of his past.

Life is not lavish with its opportunities; he would never go back to that episode, for episode it had been.

What a hateful evening! What a fetid, stained, tarnished evening! As he stopped outside his own door, he thought of it, weighed down with dusty plush, filled with a smoky atmosphere, a beastly evening. Yet for all that he had been happy.

He went within and to bed.

Chapter Three

Desire may be dead,
And still a man can be
A meeting-place for sun and rain,
Wonder outwaiting pain
As in a wintry tree.

D. H. LAWRENCE

I

NEXT morning John found that for some reason he was restless. He was well pleased with himself, and yet when he came to think of the night before he thought of it with disfavour.

After breakfast he went into the little square of garden and gathered a heavy sponge of moss and some of the small clustering primroses and grape hyacinths that grew there. The hyacinths were like blue bubbles clung to a thick sticky stem. He brought them indoors and arranged them in a dark pottery vase. He was conscious that Mrs. Barnes was watching him with suspicion. She did not care for pottery bowls, and her idea of a pretty flower was a nice petunia.

"There'll be a lady to tea," said John as though in explanation.

"I thought as how something was up," announced Mrs. Barnes, and she grumbled as she hurried with the tray, flouncing into the inner recesses of the kitchen.

"Now that's got her goat," thought John. "Oh Lord, aren't women the most difficult creatures in a difficult world! It's my own house, and after all I can have a friend to tea without it interfering with Mrs. Barnes, yet she looks at me as though I had suggested something positively indecent."

He went on arranging the primroses, with the moss stretching out tentacles like starfish, jadely green, amberly brown, and the blue bubbles of hyacinths poised between. He clamped the bowl round with stones, so that it looked like a little valley set in between cavernous mountains. It delighted his artistic senses.

A young couple came into the shop and bought the Queen Anne tallboy which had been his despair. It was an exquisite piece of furniture, shining like satin, with ripples of the wood lying like waves in it. It had round rings of handles the tender shade of very old brass, with no gleam of Birmingham newness in it. John had had to give a good price for it himself, and had afterwards accused himself of idiocy. In a provincial town it was a hundred to one against selling any single piece of furniture at such a cost. Yet to-day, his lucky day, the young couple came in, did not quibble at the price, but bought the piece and were joyously exultant in the possession of it.

An hour later, when he was examining some old prints under a magnifying glass, Roy came in. Roy with rings under his eyes, and his cheeks with two pits on either side. Roy in the throes of a vicious headache, penitent, misused, utterly dejected. He sank into a chair, and his head lolled back against the peonies and delphiniums, and the old heavy-headed roses, of its cretonne. "Oh, Lord," said Roy weakly, "oh Lord!"

Behind him the joss crouched on his haunches, bending forward curved like a fat snake gorged with food. Roy saw it with its blatantly nude breast, noticed the gleam of the sunshine on its jade and lapis lazuli cloak that disclosed rather than hid.

"That's a beastly thing," said Roy. "If you ask me, the brute is haunted. Horrible affair. Why don't you sell it?"

"Because I choose to keep it," said John indifferently. "What happened to you last night?"

"Last night? Oh hell, what a night! That beast Jefferson, what a swine! We sat on there drinking and drinking—awful muck they give you at these pubs—and he wouldn't go. I thought when he saw you'd gone he would have taken the hint and gone himself, but not a hope; not while there was a spot left, or half a bit of bread on the table. If you ask me, I don't believe the beast had had a square meal for weeks."

"I daresay not," agreed John, who had rather thought that all along.

"At last he went. I had to fairly shove him, and by then my head was going round and round with what I'd drunk myself. The girl sat there all the time, and when we had popped him off I asked her what about going home with her. . . ."

"Oh Lord!"

"Well, why shouldn't I? I had taken a fancy to the kid, and I didn't see why I shouldn't. She turned uppish then, said she wasn't that sort of girl, and she had thought I was a gentleman. Handed me out a great deal of that sort of stuff. Then I paid the bill . . . and Jove, what a bill it was! They put it on in these places, don't they? And the whole feed absolute muck. But I paid it and we got outside. I saw her back to her digs, and then we started arguing. Lord, how we argued!"

"What happened in the end?" asked John, rather sickly interested.

"Oh, she got her own way. Said something about tonight, if I was nice to her. All that sort of truck. I don't believe she is much really."

"I never thought she was. That was sticking out a mile."

"Oh, that's it! You be wise after the event! Anyway, you popped off with the other in double quick time."

"There was nothing of that sort about it."

"No? Then it looked jolly odd, that's all I can say.

It's what we all thought. Mimi told me a thing or two about old Belle. It seems she is nearly forty, and she looks it. And she is always getting off with people half her age; they call her the 'kid-napper'. Jefferson said——"

"I don't want to hear what that sponger said. If you want the truth, Belle told me a thing or two about Mimi. All these actresses are like this, damn each other behind their backs, in spite of all their dear-ing and darling-ing them to their faces. I think they are a filthy lot."

Roy sat drumming with his fingers on the refectory table. Beyond him in the garden spattered with bright spring sunshine a stone Mercury posed on one toe, radiant in virgin youth against the gay greenery. John thought of the coming afternoon, thought of it in a passionless way, spring-drenched and radiant. He dreamt that a silver faun flashed through the little garden beyond, leaving behind him a ghostly shadow; a glittering shadow for all that, half boy, half beast, yet in no way too boy or too beast. He had thought that he was a misogynist, but he was nothing of the kind. He was glad that a woman's presence was coming to the house and garden, his house and garden, glad that her shadow would fall with the shadow of the silver faun in the garden that lay beyond the window.

"Yes, it's all very well for you," said Roy, who was self-aggrieved; "you can sit there grinning, but I can see nothing to grin at. All the same I shall go and see Mimi again to-night."

"Why? She is a common little thing; she isn't worth it, frankly she isn't," advised John. "I'd leave the young woman well alone."

Yet he knew that it was foolish to advise, for Roy had dressed her in all the gay garments of love. He was seeing her through the eyes of passion, which still aches to possess that which has refused its first overtures. "Damn it," he said irritably, "cold fish like you don't understand."

They sat staring at each other across the table, with the pottery bowl containing its bright valley clamped round with stones. Neither quite understood the other.

II

The midday post brought a letter. John recognized his mother's writing, opened it, and read with a puzzled frown. It was seldom that Mrs. Duckett wrote to him. She had, as she had told her friends, been bitterly disappointed in her boy. His wealth had spoiled him. What had he done to return all her loving upbringing and tender care? Nothing at all. He had run away, skulking out of the house like a thief in the night. He had gone to some outlandish country to which the very letters cost twopence-halfpenny. And he had resented her re-marriage to good, kind Mr. Duckett, whom everybody respected and admired.

Yet time and time again she had turned the matter over in her mind, and had decided that it was a sin and a shame that she should go on slaving away in her small business, and with her music lessons, and still remain poor. Mr. Duckett earned little. Piety is poorly paid. No matter how much people admired and respected him, they were not prepared to put their hands in their pockets to pay for that admiration and respect. The first glitter of romance had worn thready. Mrs. Duckett alias Carrick had begun to realize that money was advantageous. It was an exceedingly comfortable attribute to life.

Mr. Duckett was not so clever as she had at first supposed him to be. He could not do this, and he would not do that. He said a very nice grace over the supper-table, but he could not be left to wash a radish for that supper, or fry a sprat, without his bungling it somehow.

She began to turn again to John. She had been done very badly, sold a pup, and she resented it. She had sent John a very expensive and beautiful card at Christmas, with two waxen hands clasped above an arbour of forget-me-nots, and surrounded by a regular halo of incongruous glittering frost. She had been obliged to send it to Mr. Oglivy's address. This had not met with the response for which she had hoped. John had sent her a cheque, but she felt that it might have been more. One point was certain, and that was that Mrs. Duckett would have considered that it might have been more whatever the figure written in its corner. Just recently she had got that Spring restlessness, and she had become absorbed with the idea of visiting John. She had turned the matter over and over in her mind, but had always been pulled up short by having no address. But now she felt that she had got it at last, and she decided that there was nothing for it but to take the matter into her own hands and go down to Condering and invade his premises.

"I'm his mother, and I ought to see what he's doing and how he is living," she announced in self-vindication.

The letter conveyed the fact that she and Mr. Duckett were coming down that very afternoon!

That very afternoon! John sat there with the letter fallen to the table-top, like a flag of truce hauled down. What worse afternoon could she have chosen? And he did not want to see her. There was nothing here of which she could approve. Why had he been such a fool—such an ill-advised fool—as to have written to her? He must put Belle off, and yet if he attempted that he knew that she would be both suspicious and resentful. Belle, who seemed to have been born with a grudge against life, with a certain complex writhing at her heart and making matters difficult for her. Belle whom he had to admit he did not quite understand.

Last night she had said, "You will forget." To have forgotten might have been permissible, but to shelve, to excuse, and so to appear as a cad, was unforgivable. No, he dared not send her a note, for if he did so he knew that he would never see her again.

In some mysteriously thrilling manner he was afraid of Belle. He was afraid of her reserve, of her disapproval. He looked upon her as a being amazingly strong; and perhaps because he himself was pack mule and a little weak, he was intrigued by her strength.

No, this thing had got to work out its own course, prove its own making or undoing. He called to Mrs. Barnes, who was washing-up in the small kitchen, and singing a well-known hymn tune in that melancholy fashion which very righteous people adopt.

"My mother and stepfather are coming down this afternoon," he said, he hoped without tremor.

Mrs. Barnes stopped suddenly, a cup in one hand, a limp cloth in the other. "My, that's a go!" she remarked.

He went on coldly. "We shall have to get something extra. Some more cakes and jam and cream. . . ."

Mrs. Barnes was evidently turning it over in her own mind. "I'll go out in a minute and get some things. A chocolate cake, perhaps, and some little drop cakes; I can get some cream in one of them little cartoons."

He smiled in spite of his vexation. Mrs. Barnes with her invariable mispronunciations. She went on. Once she started, you could not stop her.

"What'll the other lady say? Her as you was so pleased about. It will spoil your party, won't it? Ho yes! Not a bit what you meant, and this coming down as a surprise, too, like a bolt from the brew, as you might say. Dear, dear, what a fair mess-up!"

Yes, that was it. She was right, it was a fair mess-up. He only prayed that Belle might arrive first so that he could explain to her. He wondered if he dared run down to her diggings, tell her what had happened, and apologize. But to apologize for your mother seemed to be wrong; it was the sort of thing that an honest son did not do. He did not know what was the best plan of action. The result was that he helplessly let things drift.

III

The Ducketts arrived first. He had guessed that they might. He saw them from his window when he was looking out between urn-shaped blue vases and the joss, set along the broad window-sill with long lines of cretonne curtain between them. There was his mother in her best toque, hassock-shaped, frilled tulle, a red rose, and some jet, a fearsome affair which she had bought when King George the Fifth first came to the throne. She was standing on the other side of the road gripping tightly Mr. Duckett's arm and staring blankly across at the shop. Mr. Duckett wore a black hat like a pancake, and as shapeless; his seedy black suit was spotted with grease and shabby with dust. He grasped hold of a badly furled umbrella and a small imitation leather suit-case, and he also was gaping at the shop as if for the moment it occupied the centre point of his universe.

John had seen neither of them for nearly a year. During that year he had tried to think kindly of them, and unknown to him his memory had undergone changes. He had re-dressed them, softened their harsher lines, tenderized them with compassion, and had set them back within his soul caparisoned in fairer clothing.

He had not remembered how dreadful they were, and he saw them, so it seemed, for the first time, illusion torn from them, leaving them thready. She, a hard-faced lower middle-class woman, intensely material, obsessed only by the driving of worldly things, with avaricious peering eyes, and a hard-set mouth; Duckett himself, mealy-mouthed, indecisive creature, putty in her masterful hands.

They looked cautiously to right and left, and then, though there was no vehicle within fifty yards, broke into a ridiculous little run and scampered across the road to safety. The run was ludicrous.

There they were standing on the shop step, and even there he could sense their disapproval. He went forward to let them in.

"Hello!" he said, with a desperate attempt at ease. He kissed her, reaching down to her face, parchment skin drawn taut across the thin bones, the chin a little bristly, with fine grey hairs pricking out. Nothing beautiful here, and yet how sick he was for beauty, tired for love! He remembered suddenly, like a film flashed across the screen of his receptive brain, old Jan pottering among his treasures, touching them reverently, startled at the idea of love.

"The greatest beauty," he had said, "but the most agonizing pain. Death is sweet to it." And yet here was John aching for some of that beauty which seemed for ever to be slipping through his fingers and evading him, yet standing near enough to mock him. Pure, chilling beauty of Maddalan; exquisite *andante* of the *gracht,* white glass between the tall trees; the smell of lindens, of privet flowers like essence of wine, of daffodils in damp grass. And not one atom of beauty here on which he could feast, while down within his heart yearned the most tragic void of all, the desperate desire for his mother to be the most perfect beauty.

He ushered them into the room beyond, so strangely dissimilar to the one in which his drab childhood had been spent. The floor was darkness; there was the gleam of oak, yellowish in places, red in others, and upon its water-like surface rugs, queer islands of mature colours. The table was set with its little pottery bowl of flowers and around it cakes of the sort that his mother never bought; slips of sandwiches; an oyster shell of jam.

There were chairs glowing warmly against the wall, here and there an odd picture, and an old sampler at which some tired infant hand had plucked tediously. Brass glinted from dark corners; a well-proportioned vase raised its urn, like some young girl's body, wide of hip, slender of breast. The joss, blatantly nude, smiled ironically from his position on the broad sill.

Mrs. Duckett sank down on the sofa. "Well, I must say as how you've done yourself well," she admitted grudgingly.

She was annoyed that he should have done well, peevish that she was not participant in this comfort, and she accepted every little luxury as a personal insult.

"You like it?" What else could he say? Words stuck in his throat, and he felt helpless, rather lost.

"I can't say as how I like it. It looks to me fast, not the sort of place as Mr. Duckett would approve of. That awful thing over there"—she jerked her head contemptuously in the direction of the joss.

"It's disgusting," said Mr. Duckett, and took a second lingering look at it, to satisfy his curiosity as to its vice.

John stared irritably at his stepfather. It was a hot Spring day, and Mr. Duckett was feeling the heat. Beads of sweat were starring his brow and standing out in an unlovely glistening effect on his pink skin. He laid his pancake of a hat and his umbrella and accompanying attaché-case of peeling imitation leather on a chair alongside him. Mr. Duckett felt that it was quite time that he and his wife benefited a little by this money which had come into the family. John had been atrociously mean about it. Five pounds here and there were nothing, a mere flash in the pan; what he and his wife wanted most of all was a good allowance, a set sum quarterly on which they could rely, and no nonsense about it. That was what they had come to arrange.

But the months had made a difference in John. He was not so tractable. Stubborn, Mr. Duckett thought, uppish, self-occupied, conceited. Just like all the worthless modern young men, none of them worth their salt, but living so selfishly for themselves.

"I am afraid," said John from the head of the table, "that you gave me very short notice, and the result of it is I have someone else coming to tea as well."

"I am sure," said his mother stiffly, and in her "company" voice, "we shall be only too pleased to meet any gentleman friend of yours."

John cleared his throat. "This happens to be a lady," he said; he felt nervous and clammy about it. Something had told him that Belle was not a lady, she was an attempt at one, but his mother would quickly see through that attempt with the uncanny intuition of all women. He saw her sharp glance at Mr. Duckett. She thought hurriedly that it was much worse than they had anticipated. John was undoubtedly contemplating matrimony. Young men—nice young men—did not entertain ladies to tea with any other object. A wife meant that, far from obtaining the fixed allowance and so participating in the legacy, the occasional gifts of five pounds would probably cease altogether. His mother took in a deep breath, moistened her thin lips with the tip of her sharp and anaemic tongue, which had always reminded John of an asp, and began.

"I am sure," she said, "we do hope as how you are not up to any nonsense. There's been trouble enough with you already."

"Trouble?" he repeated vaguely—"what trouble?"

"Why, with that girl Miss Perkins. A nasty, fast little piece she was; and you will never convince me as how there wasn't trouble with you and some girl in Holland. And now just when we did think as how you'd turned over a new leaf, and was behaving proper, here you are running after yet another girl."

"She isn't a girl, Mother," he said quietly, though inwardly he felt far from tranquil; "she happens to be a new friend of mine. We only met last night."

"Then you've done very well in the time," sniffed his mother, "that's all I can say. I am sure, John, I don't know where you get your habits from, unless it was your poor father. He was a dreamer. I thought I'd married a gentleman when I married him, but I couldn't do nothing with him. No gentlemanly habits; just like you."

Mr. Duckett, who had been sitting there patting his knees with podgy hands, and mouthing occasionally, now cleared his throat and made an enquiry. "Who . . . who is this young lady?" he asked.

Desperately John glanced at him. A lie never suggested itself to him, for all his upbringing had veered towards unassailable truth. He said helplessly, "She is on the stage," well aware of the bomb-like effect that it would produce."

There was a tense moment, when his mother glanced meaningly at Mr. Duckett, and John glanced imploringly to heaven. "Patience, oh God," said John to himself, "let's get this over. Why do they come here to torment me? Patience." Then the storm broke. His mother was a voluble woman. When she started she had no notion when or how to stop. She realized that this was a predicament, that an actress was probably after John for his money, and that at any cost such an event must be prevented. She railed on loudly, with John sitting there in an agony, for at any moment Belle might walk in. His misery was intensified by the knowledge that Mrs. Barnes had arrived, and was busily boiling a kettle in the kitchen, through whose ill-fitting door she could hear every word. She would enjoy it. She would serve up the whole story to her policeman husband, garnished with the parsley of her brave imagination. She would revel in it.

He rose suddenly. "Mother, you really must control yourself. You can't come here and behave like this."

"Control myself? When I find my boy making a fool of himself? Wouldn't any proper-thinking mother be indignant? Wouldn't any mother say her say, wouldn't——"

"Hush," said John imperatively. The reins were slipping from him. In fancy he could feel them sliding down his neck, slackly down his spine, looping loosely round his haunches. "Belle may be here at any moment, and this has got to stop. If you cannot control yourself, you must go."

"Go?" she repeated, her eyes glazed with hostility. She had no intention of going.

"You cannot dismiss your mother like that," explained Mr. Duckett, patting his knees in a positive tattoo. "She is your mother, and you owe her a certain duty. You are an ungrateful and abominable son. I am ashamed of you."

"I am ashamed of you both," glared John.

His mother sat there staring fixedly at him. Suddenly she flung up her hands like spray, churning the air with them. She twitched, she was convulsed. Her shrill, sharp screams died down into jerky, hysterical sobbing. That was how Belle found them.

IV

Mrs. Barnes had burst in, now thoroughly enjoying the whole affair. They laid Mrs. Duckett on the sofa; her hassock hat fell off and disclosed her string-like hair. Her hands, in their ugly white cotton gloves, groped aimlessly for support, her mouth gibbered, her wild eyes were fixed on nothingness.

"You've killed your poor mother," said Mr. Duckett, being careful to do nothing to help, "killed your poor mother with your badness; may God forgive you. You've killed your poor mother."

No one saw Belle enter. She stood at the head of the sofa watching them, her big bosom swelling contemptuously. The scene was a familiar one to her, for she herself had indulged in many such attacks, and fully realized how disarming they were to their audience. She realized the helplessness of John, moving from side to side in frantic attempt to do something, and finding nothing to do, and of Mrs. Barnes, who patted the clawing hands, and said, "There, there," soothingly. Then Belle said inflexibly, "Get me a bucket of cold water."

Mrs. Barnes brought it, a white enamel bowl filled from the tap, and she handed it, without a word, to Belle. Belle took it, and splashed a liberal quantity in Mrs. Duckett's purple face. Mrs. Duckett gulped, temporarily blinded, and let out a startled and dismayed shriek. She sat up waving the basin away. Belle stood her ground, her face set in a scowl. John admired her presence of mind; he admired her indifference to the twitchings and convulsions, to the gulps and gurgles. It was the tremendous difference between girl and woman. Maturity which knows when to act and does so without demur. Belle stood there; to Mrs. Duckett she represented some sinister figure about to take possession of John's money. She had got to admit it, she was afraid of Belle.

"You're better now?" John enquired tenderly, stooping over her, and he wiped the water from her face with his handkerchief. It was an old tired face which had never held the beauty that he had coveted for it. "Oh Lord," he thought, "now perhaps she'll go. Surely she'll never stay here for another ducking!" His mother looked beyond him to Belle, for she knew that in Belle she had met her match.

"I feel awful," she said.

John became conscious of the masterful presence of Belle, and that he was host at this strange party. He held out his hand. "I'm sorry. My mother and stepfather were paying me a surprise visit, and I wasn't prepared. I'm sorry." He went towards her and stood there holding her hand, looking into those eyes that were impertinently hazel, flashing scorn. He was asking her dumbly if she could understand.

"You ought to have put my visit off," she said.

"I didn't want to do that."

"I'd have liked it better."

"I'm sorry," he added in a half whisper; "bear with it a little longer; they'll have to go home soon. Put up with them for a little while."

His mother had sat up again, stiffly erect on the sofa. "We didn't expect as how John would have young ladies to tea with him," she complained, interrupting the whispered conversation. "It gave me quite a bad turn."

John shot her a glance across the tea-table. "Let's have tea," he suggested.

They gathered closer. Mr. Duckett took the opposite end of the table and abased himself over a plum cake in the attitude of an extremely pious man saying grace. Then he mopped his liberally pearled forehead. His wife sat rigid, staring before her with a thin-lipped prudism, as though in extreme distaste. On John's right sat Belle. Through it all she had magnetized him with a keen admiration for her methods of dealing with a difficult situation. He could feel the quintessence of her being flowing through him. Her powerful lines, her heaviness, the restraint of her gestures, the brooding scowl upon her brows, just beneath the flame of her hair. He was conscious that his mother was eyeing Belle, that she was trying to "size her up", as she would have expressed it, and that she was utterly defeated. Mrs. Duckett did not forgive defeat easily.

"Which train are you returning by?" asked John, by way of a pleasant conversation, and thought afterwards to himself, "Lord, that's a bad brick!"

"It's a nice thing when that is one of the first questions you ask me! We could have stayed the night."

"I'm afraid you gave me short notice for that," he said; "the spare room isn't ready."

"You mean we shouldn't be welcome?" He remembered her grim habit of twisting phrases round until they revealed a different meaning. It was her old dismal search for insult. Her intuition smirked out at him defiantly from behind her antagonism.

"No, not that," he said; "if you send a letter and swoop down on me the moment afterwards, it does make it difficult. I haven't a regular maid. Mrs. Barnes comes in and does for me. . . ."

"She does for you very well, far better than I've ever been done for," sniffed his mother ungraciously. "I have had to put up with discomfort, and as far as I can see I shall have to go on putting up with it, and nobody to care what happens to me either."

"Sons are so unfeeling, so ungrateful," whined Mr. Duckett, who was busily fortifying himself with plum cake.

"Oh Lord," thought John, "this is frightful. In a moment we shall all blow up or something. It can't go on." He saw Belle heavy with scorn, and he turned to her in a desperate attempt to ignore their insinuations. "I want to show you my house and garden afterwards. I hope you will have plenty of time."

She answered coldly enough. "The show doesn't start until eight."

Mr. Duckett left off eating to survey her with chilly blue eyes from over his glasses. "I understand that you are on the stage?" he demanded.

"I am," said Belle, and, with blunt directness: "do you object?"

"I think it is a dreadful thing. Play acting is a device of the devil." He again launched himself upon the plum cake.

"I have never," protested Mrs. Duckett from her side of the table, "sat down to a meal with an actress before. A mother's feelings——"

"Mother!" he said.

But Belle had risen. She was gripping the back of her chair, curved Chippendale in pear wood, shining with a sleek darkness like heavy laurel leaves after rain. "If that is how you feel about it," she said thickly, "I'll go. I didn't come here to be insulted by a woman of your class."

"Belle!" The word was torn from him like blood is torn from a half-healed cicatrix. He hardly realized that he had used her Christian name. "Belle, please . . . Mother, it was your fault. You might at least behave yourself."

"A woman of MY class!" repeated Mrs. Duckett, and she ignored her son—"a woman of my class! And she dares say that to me. A woman of her age, dressed up and aping a girl. Obviously out for what she can get! If this isn't the last straw!"

He felt himself going cold with anger. "Mother, you had better go."

But he had not reckoned on Belle. She strode round the table. She shot out capable hands and gripped his mother by her thin shoulders. Horror gulped up within him. He had a momentary picture of Mr. Duckett putting more plum cake than was advisable into his mouth, and all at once. Then another picture, of his mother shaken to and fro. Her hat fell to one side of her head; her bag and her handkerchief, and all those little stupidities which she insisted on carrying about with her, tumbled clatteringly to the floor. Too startled to scream, she went on shaking owlishly. Her grey face had become nothing more than the face of an expressionless, worn out, stuffed doll, with roundly gaping eyes and grinning teeth. This way and that, then as suddenly released, to fall back in a huddle on to the armchair.

"I'll go now," said Belle.

"No"—John's hand held hers—"they'll go. You must stay." He could feel his brow moist and was conscious of a trickle of wetness down his chest and back, under his clothes. Crisis faced him. He was standing on the edge of a precipice, the precipice of indecision. He had to act, to choose one or the other. Which? He was quite firm, his firmness surprised him. "You must stay here, Belle."

"How can I after that?"

"Please." He wiped the sweat away in an anguish, but it recurred again, as moisture wiped from a weeping stone returns within the minute.

She stood half undecided. In that moment, the moment of definite action, he turned to his people. "Please go," he said, and was ashamed of the conspicuousness of the position. "You must go at once."

Mr. Duckett crammed the rest of the plum cake into his mouth, and began to speak through it, thickly. "You would turn us out?" he demanded. "What do you suppose your loving Father would think of such an unfilial act? What do you suppose?"

"You came here at your own invitation."

"Parents should be welcome in the houses of their sons," said Mr. Duckett sententiously. "It is written, 'Honour thy father and thy mother, that thy days may be long in the land' . . ."

"But you aren't my father," said John, and, stung to wrath, added piously, "thank God." He thought to himself, "This is becoming nothing more nor less than a vulgar brawl. Fighting and scenes and screamings. It is horrible."

His mother, recovering herself, rose unsteadily, collected her belongings with a jerk, and stood there swaying. "This is the last time, John, the last time."

"I only hope that it is the last time," he replied.

"Your goings-on have brought sad disgrace on us. I guessed there was something like this afoot, but an actress . . . !"

"Mother!"

"An actress! Old, too; can't get a good-looking man, so comes after you. Can't you see through it, John?"

He put out a hand, groping for aid, and, finding Belle's, held it fast. He repeated miserably, "Please go," and heard them as they went across to the door leading into the old furniture shop. Looking after them, he saw them like two ugly ghosts, the ghosts of two people soured by age, sloping past furniture that in its senility only becomes more beautiful. At the doorway Mr. Duckett, having at last swallowed the enormous helping of plum cake, turned to mutter something and to shake his fist. Then they trod out into the sunlit street beyond. In the tiny kitchen Mrs. Barnes, who had managed to edge the door ajar and to squint through it, watched them go too. "My stars," she said, and she chuckled to herself, "if this don't beat the band!" That was when John came across the room and closed the door firmly upon her.

V

"I'm sorry," he said to Belle.

She was leaning against the window-sill, but she was not looking out across the garden where the winged Mercury flew and where Eros hid his shamed face. She was looking down at her hand where it played indefinitely and aimlessly with the ornaments.

"Oh, Belle, I am so sorry. Thank God they've gone. What could I do?"

"Nothing."

"Sit down. Let me tell you about them, about myself, please, Belle."

She sat down with the indifference of a puppet acting according to its master's whims and fancies. She was entirely selfless, quite automatic. There seemed to be a certain mild sadness about her that was rather charming. He told her of his life, of his mother, of Mr. Duckett, and how he had broken away from them.

"What was your father?" she asked at last.

"He was—well, really I don't know. Mother said he was a gentleman. I remember nothing of him. I was a kid when he was killed in a bathing accident."

"He was a gentleman," said Belle quietly—"it is quite obvious that you are a gentleman's son."

"Perhaps he was lucky in that accident. Accidents are over in a moment, or a handful of moments, but lives seem to drag out for an eternity. I sound bitter, I suppose, but I feel bitter. An affair like to-day is bound to make me feel like that."

She sat very still, and he watched her hands locked together in her lap. He watched her breast rising and falling. At last, conscious of his eyes, she turned.

"After to-day we mustn't see each other any more," she said.

"Why not? It wasn't my fault that she behaved like that. You mustn't blame me, because I couldn't help it."

"It isn't that. It is that what she said was true. I am old. I am a failure. Can't you see that little cat Mimi is acting younger parts and I have to do the old ones? I don't look a girl."

"I liked you because you were older," he confessed.

She turned her face to him, and at the moment there was no mark of girlishness on it. He saw it with the set seal of the thirties laid irrevocably upon it. "Yes, but you don't realize that in my profession age is a tragedy. Until four years ago I didn't look my age. I hadn't started to grow fat. I could still make myself look pretty decent on the boards, and I hung on to the girl parts, grimly, like you'd hang on to life. But it wasn't any good; they slipped past me. I grew fat, and, my goodness, how careful I was! It didn't make any difference. I don't believe it does. I found myself shelved into other parts, what the manager thought seemed more suitable, and however much I kicked and cursed at him, in my heart I'd got to admit that they were more suitable. I'm in this show now on tour. It's a rotten show, and you know it's rotten. When it comes to an end what will happen to me? It will be difficult for me to get another job. Next time it will be still more difficult. In ten years' time, don't I know that it will be impossible? Of course I do."

"I don't see why," he said; "you are a fine actress."

"Don't be a fool. I am not a fine actress. I never was. What I ought to have done was to have married while I had the chance, because, although you may not believe it, I did have the chance once. Only I was not so keen on settling down—conceited; believed in my own power. I thought to myself: 'Marriage will do when I am sick of the stage.' Your mother was right."

"My mother was a beast," he said hotly.

She sat queerly still, etched against the dark sheen of leaves outside the window, and beside her, on a level with her full throat, sat the joss, smiling imperturbably over his nude, womanish breasts. John was conscious that Belle was crying. He could feel her tears rather than see them, and he went closer. "Belle, you're upset, and I don't wonder. Can't we try and forget this?"

She asked him wretchedly, "Does life ever let us forget anything? You know it doesn't. We may be willing to try to lose a memory, but life itself is a damned sight too strong for us. I'm so lonely, so wretchedly, achingly lonely. I can't chum with Mimi, and the others loathe me. I think I loathe myself."

"You mustn't." She sat down opposite him, so that the pale evening light, falling pellucid through the window, caught her face and painted it with the coolness of lilies. He could see the tears traced down either cheek. "Don't you see," he explained in a sudden passion of emotion, "don't you understand that I couldn't part with you again? Do let's be friends. I'm lonely, too. Isn't everybody lonely at heart?"

"No, the other girls aren't. They are pleased with anything, being taken out and about, being fussed over. They don't realize that it doesn't last. They are making the same mistake that I made, and they'll find it out too late. Sometimes I sit and wonder what life holds ahead for me, and the thought drives me nearly mad. I haven't got a farthing outside what I earn, and the earning will come to an end soon."

"Couldn't you teach elocution?"

"Far more likely that I should turn harlot," she said bluntly. "It's easier, and there is always the demand."

The suggestion jarred in on his susceptibilities; he could feel himself recoiling from it. It was stark, naked; its very unashamed nudity appalled him. "You couldn't do that," he said.

"It may be the only way."

Outside the breeze whispered tremblingly to the daffodils. John heard it and was aware that there was a certain exquisite attraction in the moment. The moment died.

"We must always be friends," he said tenderly; "please, Belle, please."

She laid her hand on his arm. "Friendship? Is there such a thing?"

"There is going to be," he promised her.

VI

Mrs. Darsy was standing in John's shop. Evening had fallen. Belle had gone home through a magic dusk that held in it all the sober colours of a hushed pool by the roadside. A dusk sweet with the scent of swaying jonquils and budding narcissi, of hyacinths with their regal tight-curled plumes of flowers, red and blue, and marble-white. "They will be all ablaze in Holland now," thought John, and tried to dismiss the memory, but it came back insistently; "they will be like a sea of colour round Hillegom. You will see them between the tree trunks in the Haarlemmer Hout, like the splashings of some futurist artist on a canvas framed by rough wood, the rounded wood of bark and trunk, framing the lovely mystery of flooded colour."

He returned to the moment, to find Mrs. Darsy standing there. He did not know her very well. She had been at the Chantry some years, he believed, and, as he had become known in Condering, they had exchanged greetings, though how the actual acquaintanceship had started neither of them knew. A respectable woman of uncertain years, she was possessed of a largish frame over-fleshed. Her face powdered lightly, her hair arranged fashionably under a smart hat, she was undoubtedly in the middle years, yet managed to maintain a very pleasing appearance. She had a certain fascination entirely her own.

"Good evening," she said. "I came all in a hurry to buy a chair for my private sitting-room. I had a fancy for an antique."

"Certainly," said John, immediately all attention. "What period?"

Mrs. Darsy had no idea. She thought that she would

like one of those curly chairs. It ought to have lots of carving on it, because that made it appear to be more expensive. What wood? She didn't mind about that. She was not educated up to antiques and admitted bravely that she knew nothing about them. John smiled a little as he produced a perfect William and Mary armchair, sedately prim, exquisitely balanced, a chair that was reserved in appearance, dignified, not a little forbidding. But Mrs. Darsy had a burning desire for a Charles II chair, a beauty standing at twenty pounds, with its throne-like base, and its tall slender back embossed and carved with curling leaf and twisting vine. When John told her the price, she was horrified.

"Good heavens!" she said. "Isn't it awfully dear? I never expected it to be so much. I thought about five pounds." Her dismay was more than a little amusing.

"I am afraid you would not get an original for that."

"Does it matter about it being original?" she asked naïvely.

"Well, I don't sell fakes."

She demurred a little, eyeing the chair, seeing it only as chair, and not as the object of beauty that it was to him. Then she said, "I don't know what you will think of an old woman interfering, Mr. Carrick, but I wanted to speak to you about last night."

Oh horror! He could feel his heart hammering within him. He said "Yes?" and hoped that it did not sound too guilty.

"You and Mr. Graham brought in a rather disreputable party to the Chantry. They stayed late and there were scenes. I don't want to be nasty, but you know what I mean."

"I left as soon as ever I could," said John hurriedly, "and nothing went on while I was there. I didn't care about it myself, and I do hope that you won't think I was responsible."

"I don't know whose idea it was, but it can't happen again."

"It shan't happen again," he said, and then he remembered that he had thought of taking Belle into the Chantry to dine one evening. There was nowhere else in the city. The Red Eagle was a poor place, more of a public house than a hotel. The Fountain, true to its name, was a teetotal house, and the White Swan purely commercial. It would be a terrible blow to his pride if his respectability was hit in this way and he was refused admittance to the only possible hotel. He tried weakly to explain.

"Roy Graham brought those theatrical people in to supper, and I am afraid that they got more to drink than was really wise. I thought it was probably going to be a bit rowdy, so I and one of the ladies left as soon as we possibly could."

Mrs. Darsy, who was a woman with a far-seeing mind, looked what she was thinking. Instantly he was aware of how grossly she had misinterpreted his reason for leaving early, and felt himself flush. "How awful!" he thought. "That's a nice thing for her to be thinking!"

"Theatrical people are like that," she agreed. "I never have them in if I can help it, because there is always trouble with them. Last night is not going to happen again. Not in the Chantry."

"It shan't," he persisted, "but you must not blame me, really you musn't. I had thought of coming there to dine myself, and I am sure that you would find no cause for complaint in my behaviour."

"None at all," she agreed; she was really being very nice about it. "It was that Mr. Graham and the theatricals. I am quite willing to have a quiet gentleman like yourself, but not noisy, stagy people."

That was awkward, for John had been imagining himself and Belle comfortably ensconced in the Chantry. Still, it was, of course, gratifying that Mrs. Darsy thought of John as a "quite gentleman", which was exactly how he would have chosen for her to think of him.

"However did you come to get yourself muddled up in such a party?" said Mrs. Darsy, and she laughed.

"I'm sure I don't know." An idea darted quickly through his brain, like a shuttle with a live gold thread through a loom. "One of the ladies happened to be an old friend of mine," he said. "she isn't young and flighty as you suppose. We had thought of coming to dine one evening. I do hope you are not going to stop all that?"

He let out the tentative suggestion, and was horrified to find that it was not well received. Mrs. Darsy looked dubious. She was dubious. In her forty-seven years of life (she usually called it thirty-eight, but to be accurate it was forty-seven) she had discovered that theatrical people led to trouble of two kinds. They were either inebriated or immoral, and both were disastrous to the reputation of an hotel like the Chantry. "You do make it difficult. Come now, don't you?" she said.

"I don't mean to."

"Well, shall we make it a bargain that, as long as there are no more scenes like there were last night, no suppers with song, it can go on? The first time there is another disturbance I shall have to put my foot down and be firm about it. You must not take it as being my nastiness, for it will be my discretion. You understand that?"

He smiled at her, and she smiled back, her eyes twinkling. She was being charming about it, and after all, he had to admit that it was too bad of Roy to have worried her.

"I'll be a good boy," he promised.

Then they both laughed.

"Be a careful boy!" she suggested warningly.

Chapter Four

What mighty ills have not been done by woman?
Who was't betrayed the Capitol? A woman.
Who lost Mark Antony the world? A woman.
Who was the cause of a long ten years' war
And laid at last old Troy in ashes? Woman;
Destructive, damnable, deceitful woman.

THOS. OTWAY

I

HE and Belle dined at the Chantry once a week, and there was no demur about it, nor was there any fuss.

He had never seen Belle again in that confidential mood, when, stung by his mother, she had turned to him, her face stained by tears, confessing that she was old, and that life was receding with its opportunities, as a summer sea recedes, leaving hope stranded on the hard, chafing shingle, helpless as a fish gasping for breath. For youth was breath to Belle. Understanding her better as time progressed and she disclosed herself mood by mood to him, he found that she was the lover of glitter, the devotee of brilliance. She was enchained for ever to the altar of youth, and youth only could cede to her all the joy for which she was so hungry. And the lilies on that altar were withering. The altar cloth, once whitely pure with virgin glory, had grown stained. Its golden fringe was tarnishing. Never before had John realized the insidious, clawing terror which age has for some women. Age, a wolf leaping on the threshold of their years, bound to destroy them in the end. Age, with hackles up, and red slobbering mouth disclosing teeth like so many sharp, white javelins spearing up from the mottled fangs. This was what Belle saw, which held her frightened for the future, rather frightened for the present, disguising that ever ready fear with her grim resentment against her surroundings, and with her heavy frown.

"Since I met you I have felt different," she told him across the table in the gaunt dining-room of the Chantry.

"And since I met you I have felt different," he confessed.

Different! In an amazing manner. Belle was not clever, she could not draw you upwards into her own sphere of light, talk to you, and make you dimly aware of your soul swimming out as into a great sea which drenched you in her personality. Her beliefs did not clothe you in a new guise, and make you immanently conscious of the being within yourself. She was no sponsor of genius. When with her, you were not for ever aware of her mental bigness, but rather of her smallness. So big in body, she was insignificantly small in mind. With Maddalan there had been the different nationality, and she had made you vaguely conscious of that up-swimming into something beyond yourself, as though some tremulous cloud hung low in the sky, and, reaching up, your hands could strike its splendour. With Belle, you were conscious of reaching down, lifting her out of a sea into your own safe harbourage.

Being male, he was aware of a pleasant conceit that he could lift her to his level, and that afforded him satisfaction. Her grudging gratitude tickled his vanity; for the first time in his life, to be driver rather than the driven.

The evenings at the Chantry were charming. It might not supply the same kind of dinner as the Savoy or the Ritz, but it was clean, and in a way comfortable; it was far above any standard of his youth, or hers either, if it came to that. After a while Belle lowered her hostilities; she called an armistice. She took back her first story of an upbringing in a country rectory, ever the Mecca of women of her type; she recanted the biography of lighting on hard times with her father's death, and her subsequent necessity for earning. Across the Chantry table, with its fried fillets, its roast joint with two vegetables, and its inevitable fruit salad abundant in prunes, she confessed the truth.

"I was just a poor little girl," she admitted. "I never knew my father. Goodness knows what he was."

"Rather like my history. Funny we have that in common."

"My mother did odd work when and as she could. She was a dresser at a theatre, and that was what gave me my chance. It was panto. I was ten years old, and the girl who had done the part of Whittington's cat couldn't get into the rig-out. They put me in because it fitted me. It wouldn't fit me now!" She laughed gaily, and then her lips curled as she remembered that the outgrowing had marked the passage of the years; it was all significant of age, that deadly factor which, as she expressed it, she was always up against.

"We both had rotten childhoods."

"You've come into luck," she said, "dropped on your feet. I haven't."

They sat there knee to knee, under the swelling white tablecloth starched stiffly. Mrs. Darsy always put on a clean cloth for John, because she liked him. She believed that he had been led astray by Roy, and only hoped that he wasn't going to make a fool of himself with the actress whom he was always taking out. You never could tell with young men, and he so quiet and pleasant, and so much that was really admirable in him, it seemed to be such a pity.

"I wish," he said, "that I could do something about you, Belle. I feel awful about your future."

"Well, if I starve, then I shall have had my fun

now," she answered quickly, and she sipped from the wine-glass.

"Dinner with a quiet stick like myself in a poor country hotel. Beaune, fillets, joint, prunes . . ." He indicated them with a wave of his hand.

"You've been decent to me." Her eyes, for once not fiercely hostile, but rather complacent and approving, rested on his. "When you've lived my life, and had only two types of men in your life, the ones that wanted the most for their money, that sort, and the ones who treated you like dirt, filth . . . well, you'd appreciate being decently treated."

"I've only been ordinary to you," he said.

She drew a small cup of coffee closer, circling it with her hands, so that it reminded him of the *stoofje* that Minna had brought from Edam. She glanced down into it, as a witch would glance into a crystal, seeing mirage in its depths, curiously fanciful pictures drowned in its darkness. She said, half to herself, "I wonder, if we had met earlier—if we had met when I was in my prime, not like this—I wonder then if you might have thought of my having something that you wanted?"

He followed the trend of her thought, sipped at his own coffee and discovered that it was aphrodisiac. Outside the windows, fast darkening with night, a little plum tree lifted its branches, white with five-pointed stars of blossom. In some strange manner he associated the plum tree with her, its brightness, and its meaning. She was at least frank in her sentiments, and dimly he began to realize that she cared for him.

Love begets love. He saw it shining in her heart like candle-flame, pure against the darkness of everyday affairs. For the first time since he had come to know her, he experienced the desire to take her in his arms and feel her softness pillowing against him. He became tensely still.

"For me," she said tenderly, "we met too late. Men love the outside husk, they don't look at hearts.

Haven't you seen it happen time after time? Women love more deeply, they love the self. They will marry a cripple or someone who is deformed. You never see a man doing that."

"I wouldn't mind marrying a hunchback," he said.

He watched her smoking—the cigarette and the smoke from between her lips, like blue curls about her; the fingers replacing and removing the cigarette, a crude white stick, stained carmine where its tube had come into contact with her lip-salve.

"You would when it came to it. Men want prettiness and youth; I don't blame them."

"I'd demand a companion," he said, "because I am sure real companionship is the basis of successful love."

"Yes, but youth doesn't think that."

Companionship! He had thought that was all that he wanted from Maddalan, and had found that he was wrong. He had wanted more, much more. Exquisite commingling, body to body, delicious essence of life, glorious partnership which had merged into the oneness of love. The stars outside the window were gleaming whitely against the heliotropes and heaven-blues of the night.

"It's time I was at the theatre," said Belle suddenly.

II

Roy interposed. The affair with Mimi had been brutally swift; the second day he had overcome her prim scruples, and had been obliged to pay the price in frocks and cheap brooches, and a shoe bill which had been worrying her. Mimi had hunted Roy down, and, having laid claim to him, refused to let him go so easily.

"Can't think what I saw in her," he admitted to John. "Why, she's a common little thing, and I am quite sure that her hair is dyed. It's patchy in parts, anyway. I can't get rid of her, not without being damned rude; she glues herself on to me. It's pretty frightful, isn't it?"

He reproached John about Belle. Frankly he disapproved. Mrs. Barnes had cast out hints which she had believed to be subtle, but which were in reality outrageously crude. Her disapproval had been cut short by John supplying her with the wherewithal to go out for a day trip. Mrs. Barnes went to Southend by charabanc, and did the whole journey in a ridiculously short time, including, as she told John, travelling over a "suspender" bridge, which had interested her enormously. After that she had not hinted so broadly. John had felt that his affair was progressing without comment.

"Belle is old," Roy said. "She is obviously the mother of the company. I don't suppose she has told you how old she is, or anybody else, for the matter of that. Probably she is even older than her face, and that is no chicken."

"She's all right," said John, who was studying prints at the table. "I don't care for her in the way that you care for women, just because they are women. This is a sort of companionship care, if you follow my meaning."

It was the sort of care that, frankly, Roy could not understand, and he said so. "And it is very much the same thing as the other when it comes to it, I'll be bound," he said. "After all, all cats look black at night."

"It isn't that sort of thing."

Roy was irrepressible. "Well, it might just as well be, for everybody thinks that it is. That awful swine Jefferson thinks so.

"I don't care what Jefferson thinks. As you say, he is an awful swine."

"There was the crashing row that you had with your people over Belle. That has gone round the town. Mrs. Darsy mentioned it to me. I expect your precious Barney talked. That woman could never keep her tongue still. Clack, clack, clack. . . ."

"That wasn't over Belle. It was over them being just my people. . . ." He looked up irritably from his prints. Roy could irritate him. He did not care for criticism. He wanted the delicious liberty of youth, freedom of thought, freedom of soul. He wanted to cast aside his shackles and carve out his own career.

And what they did not understand was that he did not intend to marry Belle. He did not intend that their friendship should be anything more than friendship. He looked into his own heart introspectively. Can one ever be sure of the heart? It is the indwelling sanctum of emotions, it hides its inhabitants very closely, so closely that too often the bearer of them does not realize the characters of those inmost dwellers. Belle gave him companionship; it might not be an uplifting companionship, it might not reach down with tender arms to drag him up into a greater understanding, a keener appreciation, or a sharpened intellect, but for all that it was companionship.

This covetousness for companionship which sapped his life-blood was not love. Maddalan had been love; Freda had been passion. They were both dead to him, white handfuls of ashes garnered on his hearth. He did not believe that love counted really, because it was too heady, it lived too short a time. It was like drunkenness, exquisite and wine-sweet while it lasted, but entirely of the moment; it did not linger.

III

He discovered that on the Easter Monday there was to be a concert at the Corn Exchange; a concert above the average, with London artistes, and he promised himself a treat.

Belle did not care for that kind of music. She liked jazz. She believed that it expressed a certain youthful liveliness, a clash and clatter which was invigorating. She believed that from its syncopation she could snatch some of the lost glitter of her twenties. But, as she explained, she did not care for music that had no tune in it. All the same, she went to the concert, because, she said, she could see that John was set upon it, and it played her cards properly, there was just a chance that this time she might be able to work them to a successful climax. Nothing was to be won by hastening matters, nothing was to be gathered from scenes or threats, but everything from this passive intimacy. Belle, her wits sharpened by years and hardships, knew quite well that companionship was her ace of trumps.

Unfortunately for her, the sands of time were ebbing against her. The Repertory Company was giving its final performance on the Saturday night, and after that was journeying into Suffolk. That would be the end. She had six days in which to clinch matters. Six days! She began to be worried, especially as Mimi sneered, and Mr. Jefferson made audible and lively allusions to the fact that she must run her game fast to catch him.

"We shall have to get our wits to work, shall we not? We shall," he commented pleasantly. "A little more lipstick; a little more rouge. Oh yes, indeed."

She invested in a new frock, buying a blue one, because she had read in some woman's magazine that blue attracted men, and she was rewarded by the gleam of appreciation in John's eyes.

She reminded him of bluebells, he told her as they walked to the Corn Exchange.

The streets were thronged with merry-makers, for there were some big sports being held in the park at the further end of the town. The shops, all shut, stared out upon the world stupidly, like so many sightless eyes. Everyone was abroad. There was bright sunshine, gaily yellow, and yet, as if to cry the lie to it, a knife-sharp wind swirled round the corners, nipping up side streets, a wind clad in the "armour of ice" which Kristina wore in *Easter*.

The Corn Exchange had only managed to gather together an indifferent audience. Condering did not care for classical music. Frankly, it was more interested in sports. In the park there would be litter of paper bags, and desultory chocolate packets, and people standing frozen by the wind in its "armour of ice", while the sun spattered their faces sparingly and laughed at all their foolishness. They were more interested in the tug-of-war between the city police force and the fire brigade. They fancied the sack race for veterans, and the three-legged race for little boys under ten. The brass band would play there, too. It would blow out its inside trombone and French horn. That was music if you liked it! Condering could appreciate music like that, a good stirring tune, lots of noise and a drum that banged irrespective of harmony. It was far finer than Schumann's *Widmung* with its silly soft slurs of sound; it was more stirring than *Auf meinen Thranen Spriesson* with its throbbing of nightingales, and all the rest of the harmonies in the Corn Exchange. Something grand, with a tune to it, that was what Condering wanted.

John and Belle settled themselves side by side before the platform sparingly decorated with pot ferns, and one highly veneered grand piano gleaming glassily at its corner.

"Always looks so bare to me," said Belle; "it seems that you want a curtain to go up. I hate seeing the stage first go off. It sort of spoils a show—starts it badly."

But John was studying the programme.

Piano Solo. *Valse Brillante*. Chopin. Miss Freda Perkins.
Song. *Pagliacci*. Mr. Hugh Dorset.
Song. *Beloved, it is Morn*. Madame Elna Vaughan.
Piano Solo. *Sonata in C Sharp Minor*. Miss Freda Perkins

The printing ran into little even spurts, as a single pistol-shot disguises itself in puffs of smoke. For one indescribable instant he was back in the gardens outside the Balmoral boarding-house; he was smelling the smell of privet, and holding her in his arms; he was kissing her. Not only her warm, moist mouth, sweet with anticipation, not even her throat, but lower still, where the bones drew back into mere curved softness. He felt his colour rising.

"Good heavens! I know her," he exclaimed.

"Who? The pianist?" Across the programme Belle's eyes challenged his. He saw bright lights dart into them. He tried to laugh, but she was jealous, burnt with the quick consuming fire of that insane jealousy which ravages some women's hearts.

"She isn't much to look at," he promised her, hoping to pour water on the leaping furnace.

Yet all the while he was remembering Freda, and adorning her with the little trimmings of memory, which is always so eager to excuse, so willing to paint in softer colours, so anxious to appease. Blossom on thorn—soft red heart of a mouth flung into the centre of that white face. Her hair dusky, very soft—blossom on thorn!

Belle beat impatiently on the programme with her fingers. Competition! Life was always bitter in its test, and in the test you were lost. She had supposed that she had got John fast, but here was another woman coming between them, another woman gifted with that strangely elusive gift of good music, which Belle could not hope to understand. She floundered, chafed chokily at the idea, and her mouth became set.

A man came on to the stage and moved the piano forward with an effort, arranging it wih elaborate care, only to retire again. A moment later Freda was there. Not the old Freda; a new Freda, the girl whom he had forgotten. She wore a perfect dark lace frock, with her arms and hands gleaming like white flowers from under the black net. Freda, with a thinner face, in which the softness of girlhood had gone, and the harshness of maturity had crept in. She had worked early and late at her piano, and had accomplished much, but the accomplishment had been hard. It had demanded a toll from her. He was disappointed, because he had imagined her differently, and now, seeing her again, he knew that all the while she had been a little ghost lurking in the innermost recesses of his heart, haunting him at intervals when the hour was propitious. And in this hour, the little ghost was laid with bell, book and candle. It was her passing hour. The little ghost would never more trip out upon the fields of his imagination and laugh at him. Blossom on thorn would no longer dance deliciously in the wind of sentimentality; it was dead.

Freda began to play. No, her music had not been intensified by time; his dreams had minimized its beauty. Chopin pirouetting up and down. Chopin, with long laughing arpeggios of sound trickling out of the piano. The melody, a wailing waltz, not too determined; as you snatched at its phrasing it eluded you again. It murmured into triplets. Then it became reproachful; it mourned its very trickery, it asked questions of itself, answered them with runs to the very piano top, with lark-like sublimity, and from its highest note crashed back to the lowest again. Then suddenly, out of all the questioning and the arpeggio enquiry, it gave its answer in ringing, insistent chords. All the while the rhythm ran through it, the rhythm of a reed swayed by a stream, of a jonquil bending in the wind, to and fro. It was jubilant and triumphant, laughing yet coaxing. There were waterfalls of music dripping down into his heart, music which faded into nothingness again. That was the end.

He turned to Belle as he clapped vigorously. "That was fine, wasn't it?"

"Oh, I don't know. It sounds funny to me, nothing like a pianola. Now that is music if you like. I expect, because you know her, you think it is grander than it really is."

He was hurt at the reply, hurt that she was resentful, and he did not answer. Freda did not take an encore; Hugh Dorset sang *Pagliacci,* Madame Elna Vaughan sang *Beloved, it is Morn,* and as an encore, *Hark, hark, the Lark,* the gay, glad morning song of Schubert. It was after the *Sonata in C Sharp Minor* that Freda gave her encore: *Humoreske,* dainty, twitching notes, lilt and fall of it, impertinent demand and provocative enquiry. It was then that John scribbled across his card and asked the programme girl to take it round to the green room.

"What did you say to her?" asked Belle, sick with jealousy.

"I asked her if she remembered me, and whether she would spare me a moment."

"That's a nice thing to do when you take me out, I must say." She choked down her rising passion, the hurt, hot tears of resentment filled her eyes.

"I don't mean it like that, Belle. We know each other well enough."

"Well, we seem to know each other enough to be rude and indifferent. That's about it." She tore frantically at an over-perfumed handkerchief.

Mr. Hugh Dorset was back on the stage, clearing his throat, striking attitudes preparatory to *The Blind Ploughman.* The people in the rows ahead glanced round at them irritably, and said, "Ssh" to Belle. John said:

"Hush, he is going to sing."

"Well, I don't care if he is going to sing," announced Belle. "It was a nasty mean trick."

The people ahead said "Ssh" more emphatically. John could feel himself blushing. "After he's finished," he begged, "not now. . . ."

"Very well, if you don't want me and won't listen to me, I'll go."

She got up, taking no care to be quiet about it. She pushed herself past him, flounced down the gangway to the dismay of the programme girls and the audience, who were now thoroughly antagonistic to her. She banged out at the far door. It took a few seconds in reality, but to John it was an eternity. He was indignant that she should spoil his joy over the delicious music. She had no business to have come with him if she had been going to feel like that about it; he was resentful of her conspicuous attitude. The girl brought him back a note. Yes, of course Freda remembered him, and she would love to see him. What about tea afterwards? And as there was now no Belle to be considered, John thought tea afterwards was an excellent idea, and scribbled "Rather" across her letter.

Then he settled himself down to rhapsody.

VI

He did not know where he could take her. Mrs. Barnes was out for the afternoon, and therefore he could not take her home. All the tea shops were closed; he would have to take her back to the Chantry, where he was always going with Belle, and he wondered what the maid and Mrs. Darsy would think.

They would imagine him to be a flirt, but that could not be helped.

Widmung died down. The people stood for the King. In a thrill of expectancy he followed the programme girl round to the green room. It was in reality the packing room of the Corn Exchange and could not disguise itself easily from its original use. There was a tray made of tin, and advertising a well-known brand of beer, standing on the table, and it bore proudly a cheap glass and a carafe of water. That was the sole ornament of a wholly unlovely apartment.

Madame Elna Vaughan was drawing a very ample black satin coat about her large body. She still wore her stiff kid gloves, which gave her the appearance of a badly stuffed doll. She was a Jewess, big and bosomy, for ever restlessly wandering about the room. She was instructing the accompanist about packing her music for her, talking volubly. Still humming, Hugh Dorset was pushing his own music (of which there seemed to be a ridiculous amount considering the few songs that he had sung) into a leather case. Freda had no music at all.

She stood before the table, thrumming it with her fingers. She was wearing a hat now, some small felt shape, pulled low over her hair arching across her brow and away from the slender, shell-shaped ears, ending in a point on the nape. A coat was drawn loosely about her, as though the actual act of fastening it was a matter of indifference to her. John knew little of the price of women's things, but somehow he realized that the coat was expensive. Its material was soft and crushable; it clung with deep seductive shadows about her even breasts, curving inward for her waist, and out again over the long lines of hips. She reminded him of a vase; she was urn-shaped. Once more she quivered into life within him as the being that he had remembered.

"Oh, John," she said, and then with a little sophisticated laugh, "this is amusing! Fancy meeting you!"

"It's good, isn't it? I thought you would have forgotten me."

"Silly! As if I should forget anyone ever!" All the same, she had forgotten him! When she received his card she had knit her brows and wondered, and remembered him dimly as some loutish fellow, more boy than man, who had mauled her with his unpolished caresses; someone who, as far as she could recall, had had money. The money had been her incentive to remember him vigorously. "Did you like my music?" she asked. "The *Moonlight*? I don't think any of the big masters have ever handled it that way before. I heard Mark Hambourg, and he put quite a different meaning into it. Quite different. I did not care for his rendering half so much."

"I thought you were wonderful," he said.

"And the valse? Chopin? You liked that too?" He could see her eyes staring out at him, avid for praise. He knew instinctively that if he were to drop one little word of dissent, if for one moment he were to disagree with her, she would despise him. He had no wish to disagree. He had considered her playing to be exquisite, and her execution perfect.

"Let's go and get some tea," he said.

"Where shall we go? I have to catch the six-ten for London, for I am playing at a big concert to-night."

John saw Madame Elna Vaughan surveying him calmly. Her great lustrous eyes reminded him of dark laurels in the rain. Her beauty was bold, too flaunting. It stared out at him maturely from above her big breasts upholstered in tightly gleaming satin. That was the strange thing about these women, they were different from Belle. Their clothes were different. He knew nothing about frocks, but suddenly he learnt by instinct that Belle's blue dress had been cheap and inferior, and that the clothes which Madame Elna Vaughan and

Freda were wearing were luxurious and expensive. They were cut, too; they were not reach-me-downs, suitable for the average but never for the individual. They were clothes that were part of the women, not women made to be part of the clothes.

"We could go to the Chantry," he suggested. "It is the local hotel, and the most suitable."

"You live here?" said Freda, and she pulled her coat closer and moved to the door. "Married perhaps?"

"No," he said, and he was sorry that he could not say yes. He was seeing Freda as two individuals; one who had music with all the rapture of true beauty poured into her, making her perfect, and the other who was Freda herself, merely mercenary, aggressively egotistical, obviously self-centred.

They went out of the green room of the Corn Exchange, and all the while those black lustrous eyes of the Jewess followed John. They expressed all manner of blatancies which made him feel most uncomfortable. "Damn the woman!" he thought. "Why the devil does she look like that at me? Roy might like it, but I'm not her sort."

Freda chatted as they crossed the street. She chattered unconcernedly about the concert, and most of all about her music. What a success she was, what so-and-so had said about her. She might be going to America this fall. Already in anticipation she was posing as half American, adopting their expressions. She entered the dining-room of the Chantry, and glanced round her with disapproval. Maud, the dilatory maid who spent a dreary life propping up the enormous mahogany sideboard, advanced, openly staring at Freda.

"Oh, what a place!" said Freda. "It's got a funny smell about it, hasn't it? Is this the best you could do?"

"It's the only place. Everywhere else is closed because of being Bank Holiday, and these confounded sports."

"Bank Holiday ought to bring them more custom."

"I daresay, but in provincial towns at such times they don't bother about custom, only about going out and enjoying themselves. That's what has happened now."

"Then I suppose we shall have to make the best of a bad job," she said, and sat there pouting. She drew off her gloves, very soft skins, pale almond in shade. They reminded him of the old skin peeled off the horse chestnuts that he had collected as a child. Underneath was the white ivory sheen, the live loveliness, that was her hand.

"What are you going to have?" he asked.

"I like Russian tea. Russian tea and *petits fours*."

Maud had never heard of either, nor for the matter of that had John, and he explained apologetically that there were tea-cakes or buttered toast, bread and butter, seed cake, and tea. It was the ordinary reasonable tea which you received out of a brown teapot, and which smelt of stewed leather and tannin and sponge-bags left too long in the sun and withering. Disdainfully and grudgingly Freda accepted the offer. Belle was not like that. She took his hospitality frankly, confessing that it was far better than anything she would have got at home in her dingy lodgings. He felt that perhaps it was the difference between the actress and concert artiste; one could be honest, the other could not.

Freda was obsessed with herself, and all the while he hated the cheating memory which recalled her as a lovely Circe who had cast illusion over him. But even as he sat there facing her, the music of Freda still encompassed him. It quivered through the air, engulfing him in cascades; it was like shaken petals, showering. The music of Freda was not Freda herself; she was an entity separate from her harmony, and now he knew, with a certain gasping surprise at the discovery, that he had never cared for the girl herself at all. He had never wanted to possess her. Even at home it had been the music of Freda which had held him spellbound. When he had taken her body into his arms, roughly caressing, loutishly demanding, kissing voluptuously, distressed with the sudden ardour of his passion, that passion had been for the music of Freda, and not for the woman. She had never been the woman to him at all. Her soul was little, petty, and obscure; he had no tamperings with it. Her body was not even attractive; it was prettily clad, the face powdered, but it was an ordinary face for the very reason that a quite ordinary soul looked out of the eyes, and rendered them plain by the lack of inner loveliness. He was sitting here talking to Freda, watching Freda, and was acutely aware that he did not care for her, and never had cared for her. He was made aware of the fact by the madrigal of her which floated about him. It attracted him even here in this frowsty room, and it took enchanting form, the delicious form of tones and semitones, of clashing chords, and symphonic harmonies. Out of its enchantment there peered the face of a woman, the eyes of a muse!

This was what he had loved, and it had neither flesh nor blood, it was his for ever to woo, seeing that it did not need a physical presence to bring it close to him, but was merely that airy fairy nothing of imagination.

Meanwhile he had to face Freda, the living Freda, who was disappointed in him, wondering what he was mooning about and piqued that he did not attempt to renew his efforts at making love to her.

"This isn't much of a place," she said at last, pouting.

"I'm sorry. I'm afraid I don't bother too much about places. I wanted to talk to you again, and I didn't think the place mattered too much."

"Well, now that you have the opportunity to talk, you don't seem to make the most of it. I'm sure you haven't said two words. Is it that I have grown hideous?"

"No. You are as pretty as ever. I should have known you anywhere."

He ought to have said, "You are beautiful, just as I had remembered you. I love you, Freda; I have never looked at another woman," but somehow he could not. He felt that she wanted it, for she had a greedy little nature, and she wanted everything for herself. But he could not do it.

"Is your mother here?" she asked.

"No. She married again. I went abroad for a time, and then started an antique shop here. I was always keen on antiques, if you remember."

She hadn't remembered, and she did not trouble to lie about it, because now she was bored with the whole proceedings. "I suppose your money did not last long?" she said.

"It has settled me in a home I love, and I have a good income," he told her.

"You're lucky. I've got to work for my money, and it's hard work too. Still I've improved—you noticed the difference in my playing?"

"I thought your playing was wonderful."

"You'd never heard me before, not properly."

"No," he said, and then in a sudden burst of confidence, "but I heard you play the *Minuet and Trio*, and it has been with me all my life. It may seem silly to you, but it has been my inspiration."

She said, "Pooh, that thing!" disdainfully, but she was at heart gratified, and rather pleased about it. He heard it faintly again, perhaps as the lovely threnody, for it was significant of his divorce from the Freda whom, unknown to himself, he had kept sentimentally in the garden of his imagination. Disillusion was painting out the picture of the girl in the garden, but illusion, a strengthened, dignified illusion, was painting in with a restrained hand the lovely inspiration of that girl's music.

"I'm glad you thought about it so much," she said;

"still, it wasn't anything really. If I go to America you'll hear a lot about me. I'm one of the girls that mean to get on. No hanging about in back alleys for me. I want to get to the front. I've got the talent, the brains and the appearance, though perhaps I shouldn't say so. . . ." She giggled a little, paused ready for him to agree with her, and, as he kept silent, added resentfully, "Well, other people have told me so."

"I'm sure they have," he said.

Now deep down in his heart was cavity, aching for Belle. He was acutely conscious that he had behaved badly this afternoon. After all, music was not in her line, and he had forced her to come. It was quite natural that she should be jealous of Freda, because she was that type of woman. She had fiercely resented Freda's claim to youth, and had she known that they were having tea together here, probably she would never have spoken to him again. Had she known how bored he was, how aggressively Freda jarred on him, with her complex of self, and her little nothingness that she called soul, then Belle might have forgiven him. But she did not know.

"What about my train?" asked Freda at last. She pushed aside her half-finished cup of tea. There was a dragging brown stain about the white arc of the cup; the saucer was smeared and ashy with her cigarettes, for she had smoked a quantity.

"Is it time?"

"It must be," she said. "To-night's concert is important. I was lucky to get the engagement. It isn't often that girls of my age go as far as I've done." She drew out of her bag a slim gold lip-pencil and lined her mouth brilliantly in vermilion. She nodded at her reflection in a small enamel mirror. He thought of Melisande, not knowing why, and somehow he felt an odd choking feeling at his throat. Red heart of a mouth on a pale face!

"You've done splendidly," he muttered.

"I should think I have!" She still nodded at the reflection in the tiny mirror. It was so small that it had no room for any face save her own—rather like her mind, no room for anything but herself. "Is there never a face but your own?" he thought, and again he did not know why. "Oh Lord, oh Lord," he told himself, "I'm being a fool. Why can't I be like other fellows and admire her?"

"I suppose I can get a taxi in this one-eyed place?" she drawled with an affected grace.

"I'll come with you."

He asked for the bill. The girl was so long in bringing it that he had to go down to Mrs. Darsy's office, where Mrs. Darsy was busily knitting herself a silk jumper. She gave him the account, and looked at him piercingly. "You seem to be getting very fond of the ladies," she said—"another of them this time?"

"She was playing at the Corn Exchange."

"Oh, a piano player!" Put that way, Freda lost half of her attractiveness. "You do go in for theatricals, don't you?" She unlocked a small tin cash-box and counted out the change. "You're too nice a fellow for that sort of thing, really. I wish you'd put on the brakes a bit."

Although he did not care about Mrs. Darsy's interference, he knew that she was right. Freda had not been worth it. Cheap, self-centred, common little Freda! Why, she was far commoner than Belle really, in a different way.

He got the taxi and they went down the North Hill to the station. She chattered about herself gaily as they went, and he listened. The early spring evening lay like a lovely cloak upon the world. Trees thickening with buds, a sky palely green, like water, with two white clouds like moths fluttering across its tranquillity. All the while, mockingly, the music throbbed around him. Freda's music. The decoy that had drawn him to her, threnody, madrigal. He had conceived her as blossom on thorn, and now the petals were shaken and were showering about him. There was only the thorn left.

She leant out of the carriage window. "It was nice of you seeing me again, and I liked hearing all about yourself. . . ."

"All about myself, ye gods!" he thought, and made a grimace.

"Ta for the tea. It got me out of that stuffy green room with old Elna and Hugh Dorset. I'm afraid of him. He is the passionate type, and I attract that sort of man."

Would the train never go? Standing there, he had a homesick craving for Belle. Belle, who would be crying her eyes out in the dingy lodgings, he supposed.

"The scenes I've had," said Freda, "you'd never believe it. Once I had a Marquess in tow. But my art is everything to me. I've got on so well, and gone so far, I wouldn't like to chuck it all up for some cheap little coronet."

He thought, "I can see you missing the chance, my lady," but he said mechanically, "Of course not."

The guard waved his flag, there was the shrill of a stuttering whistle. "Well, that means so long. See you again some day." Freda waved her hand nonchalantly.

Slowly the train puffed away. He knew that he would never see her again, and he was rather sorry that they had met now, for until to-day he had held a lovely recollection of her. Now the heart was eaten out of the memory and he was left with only the husk. Freda leaning out of the carriage window, greying with distance, a spot merging into nothingness. The train curving like a great python round the shining steel bend, curving along, gaining speed; long forked spurt of steam from the engine. A python writhing out of his life. . . . Freda. . . .

V

He walked back from the station slowly. In the west the day was dying. It lay yellow topaz flung into the pool of delicate turquoise which is neither blue nor green but a mixture of both. Against its brilliance there were etched the thickening boughs of trees. The hedges with their first pale splashings of green along the darkness; the gardens with their flowers nodding in the wind. The traffic had died down, most of the world was busy in the park with the last of the sports, but here or there children played in little groups and women stood at their doorways looking out upon the new loveliness of the twilight.

He could hear their voices thin as a *pizzicato* string, yet striking in upon his communing with himself. They were the everyday voices grown rarefied by night.

He went to Belle's lodgings first. She was not at home. He did not know if the landlady lied to him—she was quite capable of it—or if the message were true. He did not care much. "Oh hell!" he thought. "Now she's offended and done with me. I've made a proper mess of it all."

As he went up the hill to his own house, he thought of the afternoon, and it dawned on him that he had flung aside the blessed companionship of the woman who really cared, for the elusive emptiness of the woman who cared for no one but herself. He had done it before. He had done it with Maddalan. He had meant to return to the house on the *gracht* side, and to go to the *Mevrouw* and demand his love. He had meant to put things right, only they had not been put right, and there had followed the long desultory period of settling down, of achieving a home, and of this, that and the rest of it. On Saturday the Repertory Company would pack its traps, its wicker baskets so boldly displaying its name in the best advertisory manner to the world, its scenery, its poor withered frocks, and its little mildewed romances. It would journey on to Bury St. Edmunds, to Saxmundham, he did not care whither.

It would journey out of his life, and leave him here additionally dull, additionally derelict by the very reason that it had given him a fleeting glance of something better. Romance is a bitter-sharp knife plunged into the heart. There is sweetness in its exquisite pain. But oh, the wound that it leaves, the emptiness, the bleeding scar! It cannot heal. He knew that now. He ought to have known it before. Nothing that you can do will heal it, nothing at all.

He had not looked upon Belle as a romance until this moment when he approached his own shop door; he approached it with the topaz and turquoise day dying about him, sky green as water, clouds like moths fluttering with white wings across that water. And all the while the bitter-sharp knife plunged into his heart.

VI

His shop door was open. He knew that he had left it closed, and he suddenly felt the quick throb of expectancy. Burglars? Someone must have guessed that he would be out. A fight! That would be good. His fingers itched for it. He went across the shop itself and into the sitting-room behind. Everything was in order. The distempered walls shone palely, like precious stones in the twilight. On the wood over the fireplace there was the greenish gloom of shadows on a still pool. The joss smiled at him, imperturbable. Was the joss friend or foe? He had never discovered that. Inscrutable face, womanish breasts drooping with sagging muscles over the protruding paunch. The thing was more hideous than ever.

The room was quite still. He would have crept cautiously upstairs to surprise some thief in the very act of robbery save that he heard a sound in the garden. It was a little sound, much like a young bird cheeping feebly in its nest, like a river that has come upon shallows and chitters against the stones. He could not tell.

Belle was sitting on the low stone seat. The shadows fell moodily about her, Eros turned his bandaged eyes to heaven, and Mercury leant forward beside her, as one stayed in the act of running, who stands surprised. Her head was bent forward on her hands, and he knew that she was crying. A revulsion of feelings flooded him. He stood there suddenly aware of a hundred warm emotions, and in their full spate he was uncertain of action. Something sent his heart pounding. In the sky he saw Sirius, the largest and most beautiful of the stars, and all the music of Freda seemed to flow about him.

"Belle!" he called.

He was sitting on the stone seat beside her. At first he did not know whether it was his own little garden at Condering, or whether it was the Haarlemmer Hout, the forest like a green cathedral, grown passionate with the slurring whispers of its trees.

"I've been a beast!" he said savagely. He tore her hands from her face. Belle's face with its shining lines of tears on the cheeks, with the eyes that had lost their resentment, and her hair flaming about her. "I don't know what to say to excuse myself. There is no excuse."

"I'm old," wept Belle—"I'm a failure, such a dismal failure. I expect the homage that girls get, and I am not a girl. It is dreadful having to give up all the attentions and the love. It hurts so much."

She hid her face again.

"Listen, Belle," he said quietly. "Listen. I saw Freda. I took her out to tea and she was awful. She was quite the most dreadful girl I have met for some time. I was bored stiff. I've been down to the station with her, and when the train carried her away I said, 'Thank God.' I did, honestly I did. I've been punished, Belle, I've been properly punished for behaving like that, and it serves me right."

"You see, I thought I meant more to you. . . ."

"You did mean more. I have found that out. You mean everything. I've been lonelier with Freda than I've ever been before. And now you are going away on Saturday."

She leant closer. He could feel the pleasant warmth of her through her blue frock; his arm slid round her and drew her nearer still. "You shan't go away Saturday. I won't let you go."

"Oh, John," she sobbed.

"I can't let you go. I've found that out."

"But I am so much older than you are."

"As if age mattered! We have each other, we want each other. I thought I wasn't in love with you, but I am. I have been all the time. It's just that, Belle, and it is the most wonderful thing in the world."

"I'm too old," she protested, but her sobs had stayed. Sirius waxed high, red, yellow, five-pointed. John thought of it as the star of their happiness.

"That is for me to judge," he said, "isn't it, my dear?"

From far away in the park there came the last faint blaring of the band, beating out its brave tune. It was so far away that it was almost attractive. They both listened, not acutely conscious that they were listening, only dimly aware of it. The first dew of night brought from the daffodils and hyacinths deep rivers of essence. It flowed about them.

"I oughtn't to let you sacrifice your life like this," said Belle slowly; "that other girl would be so much more suitable. Besides, you don't know me as I really am." A sudden urge towards the confessional overcame her. "I'm not nice at all. I have a vile temper. You remember how your mother behaved that day? I can behave just like that when I choose."

He laughed. "Water is cheap. I shall know how to deal with you."

"You've seen me always in my best light. In a sense I have been acting up to you, but I couldn't go on acting all my life. I don't want you to do anything that you will regret."

"I daresay we both have our faults," he said gently—"I know I have."

They kissed, with the first frail light of the stars gleaming about them, lighting up the garden with a new and lovely glitter. The world took on new shapes, etched in ebon, chiselled in crystal.

Enchantment, that was it!

This time there must be no slipping. They would be married at once, before there was time for interference. John made up his mind that this time he would clinch matters.

END OF PART TWO

PART III

Maddalan

Chapter One

From out of the deep, dark pits, men see the stars more gloriously, and *de profundis amavi.*

ROBERT BROWNING

I

ANOTHER spring.

Another sweet spring of the year with the blue bubbles of grape hyacinths in the garden border. Later the flowering thorn lying like snow along the branches of the trees; the laburnum chains, loops of yellow fire, and the lilac nodding her assenting plumes, snowy-white or pinkly mauve. Winter-gaunt rockeries becoming masses of heliotropes and arabis, shrubs flamed with flowers, trees half strangled in their bright new green in which the birds mated and nested.

Another spring! Another futile, endless spring. Only a year since they had sat out in the little garden on Easter Monday and had plighted their troth. Only a year! Interminable year!

Some years are over long, whereas others rush by, speeding through with their rotating hours of happiness, their joyous self-satisfaction, and leaving us with but a scrambled yet satisfactory memory. But this year had been long, too long. It seemed to John to lie behind him long as hell, and as despairing.

He stood in the shop, staring out at the North Hill,

threaded with rain, the tarry surface of the road sparkling with the wet gleam, and the houses opposite bending forward like old men grown bowed with the years. Standing there he thought about it.

The year, the hideous year come round again. Why must we suffer so for one mistake? Why must our folly cling, barnacle-like, to the rotting hulk of our discrimination? One folly. One little hour.

He stared mulishly out at the rain, his thoughts racing back. . . .

II

They were married almost at once. In the few days that lapsed between that romantic hour in the garden and the subsequent contract entered into in the registrar's grim office in the High Street, people saw fit to warn John of the risk that he might be taking. He told himself that these were people who did not understand the circumstances.

First of all Roy, who, urged forward by the best intentions, set about the work in just the wrong manner. He burst in upon John's solitude.

"I say, old chap, this is a pretty big brick you've dropped, isn't it? Get out of it, old boy, chuck it! She's nothing but an impostor trading on your good nature, and she's old enough to be your ma. Don't be a fool, John; you're on a dud. Live with her, old boy, live with her, but for God's sake don't marry her."

And John, with flaming cheeks and smouldering eyes, replied through his teeth, "Get out, Roy! I mean it. Get OUT."

Roy got out then, but he came back again. He was a loyal friend, and he honestly believed in the enormity of the mistake and tried hard to influence John. Finally, having utterly failed in his well-intentioned efforts, he accompanied John to the registry office. "You'll need someone at your funeral," he said grimly—"anyway, I'm coming." After all, John was grateful for such staunch friendship.

Mrs. Darsy herself called round to see John. She had heard the news through her waitress, but she did not believe it. Mr. Carrick was such a nice young man, and she knew Belle only as a large and vulgar woman. In the course of a tactful conversation Mrs. Darsy alluded to the matter.

Why did they all bring up the same old points? Old enough to be his mother. That was the weighted barb, the dum-dum bullet that they spurted at you. He knew that Belle was older than he was, but in love did age matter? They were not physically in love, though this he could not explain to the people who were so solicitous for his future bliss. He had no thought of passionate longing for Belle, and he believed her emotion to be in the same category. He did not feel that this was any but the higher sort of love. This love needed no long-drawn sweetness of body to body, with which to cement it and hold it together. But of course people did not understand. They only thought of marriage in one way, the usual and predominant way. They could not conceive it as a coldly pure emotion swimming like a tranquil swan through the still waters of his life.

Mrs. Darsy was so nice about it that she made it more difficult. He could not think of her as nastily interfering, but all the same he wished that she had not come. It is far easier to be annoyed with a person who is nasty, a blustering fool like Roy, who blunders into it in the wrong way—they are an easy proposition to handle. You are entirely justified if you kick them. But a nice woman like Mrs. Darsy! "Oh Lord," he told himself, "I do wish she hadn't. Why do people make it more difficult?"

It did not end there. Three evenings later he ran up

against Mr. Jefferson after the show was over, and he was returning from seeing Belle home. He had a suspicion that Mr. Jefferson was drunk. He was wandering aimlessly down the North Hill, he said in search of a certain fish shop, which was at the other end of the town.

Also at half-past eleven the fish shop would be closed. The two of them ran into each other.

"Oh—you . . ." said Les Jefferson in a friendly manner. "Ah, you're the very man I wanted to see."

Being unable to say the same thing, John held his peace. He chafed irritably against the fate that had brought them into contact.

"Mind if I walk home with you?" asked Les Jefferson amiably. "No, of course you don't." He had the habit of answering his own questions for his friends, which was, to say the least of it, disconcerting. On John's doorstep he enquired, "Mind if I come in with you?" And again replied to it with alacrity, "Just for a minute? No, of course you don't," and in he went.

And having once got Les Jefferson inside, it was extremely problematical when he would be got out again. He sat himself down at the end of the table, smiling benignly round the room, not unlike the joss itself, save that he was jaundiced and thin, whereas the joss was jaundiced and fat. Mr. Jefferson was macabre. John thought of him as a satyr, whereas the man himself believed that he was puckish. Mr. Jefferson demanded something to take as a matter of course. He seized upon a whisky decanter with all the thirst of a man who had deliberately kept his throat dry until he could drink at the expense of a friend. Then he enquired if there were such a thing as a sandwich about.

Desperately John produced what the larder could offer, and watched Mr. Jefferson making his first round meal of the day.

"I wanted to see you, dear boy," said Mr. Jefferson

when he had appeased the first pangs, not without some noise.

John was becoming suspicious of people who wanted to see him. He doubted them. Everyone who had wanted to see him lately had wanted to warn him against Belle. He was getting more than a trifle tired of it. He would have loved to have replied tersely, "Well, I don't want to see you," but civility held his tongue for him. He said, "Oh," in a not too encouraging manner, but he might have known that Les Jefferson did not wait for encouragement. Nothing short of the most severe discouragement daunted that man.

"About this intended marriage of yours," said the actor, his mouth full of cheese and his eyes bright with whisky.

"I'd rather not discuss it."

"I expect not, dear boy, and there I agree with you, but the fact remains that I ought to discuss it with you. It's my duty, my dear boy, and who has ever seen Les Jefferson shirk his plain duty?" Again he answered for himself, "No one has seen it; and why not? Because Les Jefferson has never shirked his duty; he never will." He tapped his breast significantly. He took another gulp of the whisky, while John was racking his brain to think of some good excuse by which he could rid himself of the man. Then he went on: "Belle is not all that she seems to be."

"I don't believe it," announced John.

"Mark my words"—Mr. Jefferson wagged a finger at him roguishly—"mark my words, she has determined to get you into her clutches. I've seen Belle. I know her."

John thought of the Belle whom he knew. Belle, haunted by her age, haunted by the approaching wolf with its slavering jowl, its shrewd eyes. The Belle who had confessed her failure to him, and for her he was so sickly, so hopelessly, sorry. "You don't understand her," he announced.

Les Jefferson rolled his eyes to heaven. A bulge of cheese which had stuck out, round and shiny like some grotesque apple, from one cheek, swung to the other side. "Understand her? That's rich. I not to understand her! Les Jefferson who has worked with her in London and on tour, in all the best theatres, and now in this town where people don't know what acting is. Not our sort of acting, my sort of acting, the cream of dramatic art. I, not to know her!" He swallowed the lump of cheese with a tremendous effort. Horridly fascinated, John watched, thinking to see it swell his Adam's apple (peculiarly emphasized in Jefferson's hen-neck), waiting to see it roll like a giant marble until it was respectably concealed behind his collar-bone. Nothing happened. The cheese disappeared; the Adam's apple remained its normal shape and size. "I tell you I know Belle." He emphasized the gesture with a thump on the table which set the knife chattering to the bread platter. "Who should know her better? Not the King of England himself," and he stared round as though for contradiction. It seemed to be improbable that the King had ever heard of Belle, but John did not want to contradict Les Jefferson. He wanted to be rid of him, and that quickly. It could not be quickly enough.

"Don't let's discuss it," he said doggedly.

Jefferson refreshed himself copiously from the decanter, and when he set the glass down upon the table it struck John that the action was not so decided, that the thin fingers reminded him of queer yellow teeth from which the gums had long since receded; they were shaky. The spirit was flying to Les Jefferson's head.

"You'll be shorry," said the actor, more kindly. "Be advished. It is for your good, m'lad, unpleashant, but for . . . own good. . . ." His words slurred one into another in a good-natured, friendly way. Out of the general blur he headed for intelligibility.

"Lord, now he's going to get sozzled," thought John

helplessly. "As if his rotten advice were worth two hoots! Miserable sot!"

Les Jefferson took more cheese in an absent-minded fashion, set it jauntily on a three-cornered piece of bread; he was amused that it fell off again, and, laughing immoderately, replaced it with a rather cumbersome jocularity. He seemed now to have forgotten his mission. He was indifferent to the reason for his presence in John's house. He became conversational with himself, convulsed with laughter at his own jokes, surprised at his perspicacity, rather annoyed at John's efforts to get rid of him. It went on for what seemed to be an eternity. Finally on the doorstep, lurching, and intensely amused at the absurdity of the door-knocker (an old brass figure of Napoleon which was far from humorous), Les Jefferson recalled vaguely the purpose of his visit.

"Ah yes—Belle," he said, and the words raced one into the other and enjoyed it. "Belle, something about Belle. Fine girl, Belle. All beau'ful girls. But Belle most beau'ful of all. That's why she's called Belle. . . ."

And again he caught sight of the ridiculous door-knocker and became shaken with hysteria at it.

John heard him laughing all the way up the street, and somehow he could not help laughing too. Life was damned funny when you came to think about it.

III

He married Belle at the registrar's with a special licence hurried through from the Primate's. He was not going to delay this time. They were to honeymoon in the Isle of Wight. Belle had chosen Ventnor, which she considered to be both classy and dashing.

At this time Belle was obsessed with what was the

right thing to do. She could not believe that she was really going to be married until the moment when they were all standing in the registrar's dusty room. Mimi was there, holding a bunch of daffodils and white ara-
the Isle of Wight. Belle had chosen Ventnor, which she
bis, the best that the local florist could produce. It was a feeble attempt at a bridesmaid's bouquet. Roy, with an orchid in his buttonhole which had cost him half-a-crown and of which he was inordinately proud, stood in military manner, bravely erect. John was white, more than a little shaky; suddenly afraid that perhaps there might be some mistake. He was not sure of himself. He had been sure until now, but all the good resolutions had been scattered; they were difficult and elusive. The ceremony was awesome, setting as it did its seal upon his life.

Les Jefferson was there, and Mr. Oglivy, breathing heavy displeasure and eyeing Belle in her white serge coat and skirt with disapproval. Belle had made a wholly foolish attempt to appear bridal. The local dressmaker had suggested white serge arranged as a costume, regardless of the fact that white serge was old-fashioned, and that the days were cold with a nip of frost in the bitter east wind. Belle's hat too, a white felt, was pulled down over her hair and spiked through with a brooch of large diamonds. It made her look old. Even John saw that she looked old, but he did not care, for in this marriage he felt that age did not matter. The old are often more companionable than the young, and was this not a marriage of companionship rather than of passion?

By Belle's side was Mimi, enacting the rôle of the juvenile bridesmaid. She was in pale blue, pertly trimmed with little bunches of cotton forget-me-nots. Mimi disported a chiffon hat, with a scarf that not only draped itself round the crown but served a double purpose as sash as well. Even then it trailed off, weighted at the two ends by two more coquettish bunches of the eternal forget-me-nots. Somehow John felt that he would never forget Mimi as she looked in that solemn hour. Mimi, with her face pinched by the east wind and too liberally powdered. Mimi ogling Mr. Oglivy without much success; looking coyly at Roy, who now frowned on her charms. Such a little while ago Roy would have thought her lovely. That was life for you! Life, which is a cup of chance, of whim and fancy, blent together into a wild sort of wine that goes to the head and inflames the senses.

John had no definite memory of anything in that stuffy room. It was blur, a picture hurriedly passed by, picture of a ceremony, reigned over by a mothy registrar. The registrar had an alpaca coat, liberally scattered with ash (he was an inveterate smoker), and his hands were none too clean, for he was also an inveterant gardener. He was promising himself that when he got rid of this party he could go back into the garden and bed out the salvias—he pronounced it salivas—so he hurried things up. Just a handful of people gathered round a glum table, and the smell of mildew, of cracking leather binding together an old cumbersome book. That was all.

Afterwards in his own house there was some sort of lunch. Mrs. Barnes had insisted on the local caterer taking it in hand, and all the morning baskets had been arriving, and strange men bustling about.

"Cold lunch," said Mr. Oglivy, in the tone of a man who would have preferred a hot meal.

"Champagne," said Mr. Jefferson with the grinning joy of a man who is well pleased with anything. "Could anything be more appropriate?" And then, without waiting for anyone to answer him, "Nothing at all, of course, nothing at all."

Again blur seemed to crowd in on John. It appeared to him that in the tense moments of life, fog, a kind of thick vapour, descended on you, and cut short your acuter vision.

The noisy chatter hurt. The room became heavy with the fumes of smoke and of wine, so that it was no longer his own home room but some strange place of entertainment, which was a little terrifying in its very jocularity.

He realized his own urgent need for air, and turning aside, unmissed by the others, who were already full of their own wit and his wine, he strode out through the long door into the garden. There came the sudden smiting of the clean, sweet spring air, striking at him like cool steel, the sickle to his harvest of desire. He pulled himself up with a jerk, clammily sweaty, and heard their laughter and their talk growing confused, by reason of the door blowing to upon them. He saw before him Mercury poised for flight, eyes turned to the clear blue of the sky. Mercury with his pert little wings, messenger.

John remembered, as he stood there, something which was almost terrible in its poignancy. It was the sound of wheels trundling round on cobbles, the music of the *gracht* as it chugged, splashed close against the stone sides by the pressing forward of the great black hulk of a barge....

IV

They went by the train which left at three o'clock. Mercifully by that time the other guests were not so desirous of accompanying them to the station. Mr. Oglivy had left early. It was Roy, and Roy alone, who drove down in the taxi with them

"I know that three is a crowd," he said, "but I had to come. You'll get her alone for the rest of your life, you know, old boy. Good luck to you!"

He was a little drunk, but not unpleasantly so. He

was merry with it. They drove into the station yard, up a hill, curled round like a half hoop, and standing in the half hoop a miscellaneous assortment of taxis and horse cabs. They went into the booking office, John feeling strangely conspicuous. The porters knew who they were. They stared at Belle's white serge costume and her hat. They stared at John and made jokes with one another. He could feel himself reddening, painfully conscious of their fusillade of fun. Odd that people could make so merry over this marrying business, really. What was there funny about it? Nothing at all when you came to think about it, two people fulfilling their destiny, nothing more! He paid for the tickets, thought them expensive, and pocketed the change. All the while Belle stood aside glowering at Roy, Roy who had two pockets bulging with fat bags of confetti.

The train came in. The silent platform suddenly filled with people who surged forward; porters appearing from nowhere pushed barrows along; boys with tea-baskets shrilled their goods. There was jostle, importance, urgency, flowing up and down it like a noisy river chattering over stones.

Then there was a hubbub in the gangway. A red-headed ticket-collector was taking tickets from the out-flowing crowd, all cramming together in the little exit where there was screaming, fluttering! . . . John, leaning out of the open carriage window beside Belle, and trying to talk naturally to Roy, saw the scrimmage. He saw something blue pushing and fighting forward, and the crowd falling back before it. Mimi, her chiffon hat on one side, dragging someone by the hand, and that someone Les Jefferson wearing property topper and sponge-bag trousers, his ill-fitting morning coat, made for a very stout man, almost torn from him. But the two of them did not care if they made a shambles of the emerging crowd. They were far too full of wine to care. They rushed forward, a grotesque couple. Mimi, red and blowzy, her face patched mauvely with cheap powder and inferior rouge; Les Jefferson, sheet-pale, but his eyes like two blazing lamps burning with ravaging fires deep down in some inner chapel of his skull.

"In time," panted Mimi, "in time . . ." and she screamed with hard laughter, and bursting open an enormous bag of confietti, shot the contents into John's face.

That was the signal. Showers of confetti! Spots of red and blue and green shivering through the air at them. Rainbow snow of it! The carriage floor spattered and himself snowy, Belle snowy. All the while the three of them (his friends) hysterical, dancing up and down, clapping their hands at the enormous humour of such a delicious joke. And John was a quiet soul; he loved respectability. He felt as though these three had held a torch to his breast and bared the flesh, scorching and naked, to the world. He felt that somehow they had seared into him with their laughter, their gurgles, their hand-clapping.

Confetti! Round disks of it hurtling through the air, rather like flower petals showering from some May tree, white turning rosy with age. You could not escape it. He felt that if only he could bury himself in it. . . . Wet and clammy he looked round helplessly, hating the moment. "Would the damned train never start?" he thought.

The guard's flag. The train gave a warning rasp, jerked itself together, connecting links rattling, pulling taut, a giant hiccough, and then there came the steady 'chug chug'. He saw Roy and Mimi break into a run, and heard her screaming still. Her ridiculous hat flapped as she ran, confetti dribbled from a burst bag which she held in her hand. Les Jefferson, starting to run, had lost his balance and had sat down with more violence than he had anticipated. He was sprawled drunkenly in the middle of the platform, two long gaunt legs straddled out on either side of him. He reminded John of some fantastic clothes-peg, the long legs and the small body, and the head bent over it, helpless with laughter.

The train, gaining speed, left it all behind. It curved round the steel rails, as Freda's train had curved. And now, as it went along, he saw with sudden horror that where before he had watched Freda and had thought of her in her train as a python writhing along a gleaming track, he now was part of that python! Eden, and a serpent! Extraordinary how your brain squirmed and turned round.

He drew his head inside the window. "Oh Lord, look at all this mess!" he said.

Belle was shovelling it away with her feet. She was picking spots of confetti off her costume and trying to throw them out the window, but the wind blew them back. "Anyhow, I don't see that it matters," she said.

"We can't possibly get out of a carriage messed up like this. Everybody would know." He felt self-conscious about it, guilty. People would laugh, and it would be agony to his sensitive soul.

"And why shouldn't they know?" she asked. "It isn't that you are ashamed of me?"

He was thinking, "Supposing that someone got in at the next station?" He began with fingers that shook to gather the rainbow spots from his coat. They were such tiny pieces. They were difficult to manage. When you thought that you had got yourself tolerably clear, new dots appeared from nowhere. All the while he was conscious of Belle watching him, coldly disapproving.

"You think more of that beastly confetti than you do of me," she said at last. "After all, it was only a bit of fun! I'm sure I can't see what there is to make such a fuss about."

He sat down beside her. He put an arm round her. Perhaps he had been wrong, and had ruined a very exquisite hour, probably the most exquisite hour of his entire life. Spoilt it for multi-coloured spots of confetti. . . . .

He drew her lips up to his own.

V

They got out of the train in London, and made a rapid crossing in a taxicab, catching another train only by luck. London was dull; it had been raining all day, and a blanket of vapour wrapped its huddled buildings close. It was entirely unattractive. The second train proved to be more cheerful, and they had tea in it.

By now they had forgotten the interlude of the confetti and John was his natural self. He was trying to remember that this was the end of his long loneliness. It is the wise man who mates. Life is so tragically isolated. Even with a bosom friend our thoughts are locked in a grim castle which is soul. We can never let another cross the threshold of that castle. Its portcullis cannot rise. Peeps through that portcullis. No more! We can never let another into the hidden intimacies and mysteries, for life is like that. It is always dreadfully alone.

Over the tea they grew friendly again.

"I'm awfully fond of you," she admitted.

She looked fond too. He believed in her own intangible, mysterious way she was fond, and he promised himself that this marriage of sheer affection was going to hold them fast. It was going to be a success.

They crossed to the Isle of Wright with the pale twilight drifting about Spithead. It was a gay sea, spattered with forts. Grey warships flowing homewards in a line. A sunset flaming behind Haslar, with its one turret and its long, wavy lines of trees and roofs, blue and amethyst with distance. A little quiet sea, tranquil with eventide, lilac and jacinth, a tender sea!

They arrived at Ventnor later, and as he got out of the train he drew a swift intake of breath. He had not supposed that it would be like this. It was as some foreign town, built in cascades. A town of crumbling walls, red and gold with wallflowers; little impertinent streets twining in and out, almost vine-like in their tendrils. As you stood on the doorstep of one house, it seemed that you were poised on the roof of another. The Undercliff flowed away to the right with humpy hills rising behind. There was the warm smell of grass, of sun-scoured earth, dry and crumbling.

"It's rather wonderful," he said chokily.

It stood for beauty!

They were standing on the doorstep of a house. The rooms had been recommended to them by theatrical friends of Belle's. John, glancing from the view before him back to the rooms, was disappointed. The house was one of many, built in a pretentious age, dripping plaster, standing back from the thin road and bordered from it by a shallow strip of untidy garden. He surveyed the lank grass, and in its centre a broken urn displaying a promising crop of groundsel. The windows of the front room were fast sealed, and draped with dust-stiffened curtains. They displayed a single card, fly-blown and grimy, "Apartments". The fanlight over the door had once been of stained glass, but it had been broken often, and when they had troubled to have it mended it had been done with plain glass. As he and Belle stood there, and he, annoyed at waiting for a reply, banged the rusty knocker, a triangular wedge of glass, loosened by the jar, fell chattering from above him.

"My, that's dangerous," said Belle. "Ma ought to have that seen to."

John felt as though a cold wind had caught him and pressed him to its icy breast. He clutched at her arm.

"Belle, don't let's stay here. It's awful, it reminds me of what my home was like. Let's go somewhere else?"

"As if we could! Probably the place is full."

They heard heavy footsteps coming down the passage; a warning voice shrilling to someone to "shut that there door", then the rattle of a bolt being drawn. The door opened. They saw a large face pondersouly hung about with flesh peering through the aperture at them.

"We've come for our rooms," said Belle.

The door wheezed open. Belle crossed the threshold into a hall, thin, small as a closet, papered with a large-patterned, varnished paper, dismally peeling. There was a frowsty smell about the place, a sickly smell, frying fish, washing-up water, unaired rooms and unwashed human bodies, all in one.

"Not here," he said shuddering, for the beautiless atmosphere clutched at his throat.

But Belle did not hear him, and she went on. The landlady flung open the door of the sitting-room. She went forward and, striking a match, set it to the brass loop of gas. "This is the front room," she said.

A bare, unfriendly room. He could sense the hostility in it. A chenille-draped table set smugly in its middle, horsehair chairs and couch, bilious-hued cushions. There was a sideboard like the one at the Chantry, only this was chipped and scratched, and on its surface sprawled ugly ornaments and jaundiced silver. It was a mausoleum of a room, full of the decomposing bodies of inanimate objects which had never been conceived in beauty.

"Heavens!" he gasped.

It seemed that the landlady—her name was Mrs. Crumpet—had her eye on him already. "The gentleman don't seem happy," she said; and then, her angry eye fixed on his face in hypnotic stare, "All my lodgers is happy. Home from home, that's what it is." She drew in a long breath. "The bedroom's over this. I'll show you. . . ."

They climbed the stairs, wheezing, rickety stairs, with a thready carpet showing white wood between where the varnish had chipped. They climbed round a queer angle of a landing, where a Japanese vase disported last year's pampas and bulrushes. The three of them—Mrs. Crumpet, fat, perspiring, a Cubist figure of eternal circles; Belle next; last of all John, his face sweaty, his soul panicky. They were going to see the bedroom. Somehow he had always thought of this room as the temple of his love, lit by the candle-flame of rapturous delight.

Mrs. Crumpet charged open the door, which had stuck a little. She went forward and lit the gas, a triangular glare from an abutting bracket. "It's got a sea view," she said.

"It's nice," Belle announced.

But John could hardly creep round the door. He could feel his eyes glazing as he stared into the apartment, which would perhaps be the shrine of their consummation. Oh no, not that! The stiff white bed, with the not too clean honey-comb quilt. The iron posts, the brass knobs. The washstand, with its ill-matched toilet utensils all resting on ugly mats of Turkish towelling and yellowing crochet. The indifferent mantelshelf, Goss china, a picture of Derby Day, the dressing-table side by side with a coffin-shaped wardrobe. And the smell, the horrible frowst of it all . . . a mortuary in which the windows had not been opened since the last body had lain rigid and inflexible here.

A room of death, not of love. How could it be of love, such an ugly, stenching room as it was!

He saw the two women merging together. Mrs. Crumpet, moon-faced with her fringe of other faces, and Belle, the luggage, and the room with its great engulfing bed, and its coffin-shaped wardrobe. He felt sickish, heady. He thought rather amusedly that perhaps he was drunk. He slid forward in a faint.

VI

When he came to he was lying on the bed with his coat undone. He lay there staring up at the ceiling, fly-marked, and cracked into lines like some ancient map. The sounds reminded him of a fish he had once caught and that had lain gulping out its life on the wooden bottom of the boat. Semi-conscious, he did not associate the panting with himself, but lay there, and gradually the room came back into his perspective, or he crept back into the perspective of the grim room; he did not know which it was. Belle was holding water to his lips in a thick tooth-glass. Mrs. Crumpet had gone.

"You poor dear. It's been too much for you."

He drank thirstily. The water tasted strong, as though the glass had not been thoroughly rinsed, but it steadied his vision. He saw more clearly the coffin-shaped wardrobe, the picture of Derby Day over the mantelpiece, the crochet cornucopia with its yellow and green pom-poms arranged as a hair tidy and hanging from the dressing-table mirror. "I'm still here," he said.

"Of course you're still here. A nice welcome for a bride, I must say! You falling down and fainting like that! I expect you're hungry, or you've eaten something to upset yourself. I told her to get us a meal straight away. She's got some fish to fry for us. You could fancy a piece of fish?"

"No," he said urgently, "not here. Isn't there a restaurant or somewhere where we could go? Somewhere handy?"

"I don't think you ought."

"I'd rather. If I rest a little first."

"If you're sure you feel all right, I'll go down and

ask Mrs. Crumpet," said Belle, but she was still dubious.

When she had gone, he struggled into a sitting posture and tried to tidy his collar and tie torn apart by hurrying fingers. He found that his head was whirling. No, he was not drunk. It was not that at all. He was, in fact, nauseatingly sober.

When Belle came back he felt better. She explained that there was a restaurant at the corner of the street, and Mrs. Crumpet had given her a key so that they could get in and be no trouble to her afterwards. They went out into the cold evening together.

It was a small restaurant, lit by a great golden lantern suspended from a central beam. It glowed warmly. It was the sort of restaurant about which John had dreamed, and he took it as a happy omen to have found it on their wedding night. They sat before a small square table fitted into the corner of the room; there was a pottery bowl set on a check tablecloth, and in the bowl anemones, prune, claret and mulberry, with thick stems and strangely furred leaves. John ordered gladly enough: tomato soup, fish, cutlets in their fussy little frills, a fruit salad. He ordered a bottle of wine. Now there was no sign of faintness, for it seemed that he had put it behind him, with the grim house smelling of disuse, of death and decay, of heat and languor. While they were here he could forget the house; he could forget the sinister meaning of that house. Ghost meaning. Phantom ghoul plucking at his flesh.

Across the pleasant table Belle looked attractive. Her face was not so heavy, her eyes were bright. It might be the warm fire of the wine that they were drinking; it certainly was the prune of that wine which had stained her lips so brilliantly. It might be that this was the apex of her heart's desire.

"I can't believe that this is true—you and me," she said.

"Well, it's true anyway." There was nothing more to

be said for or against it. She was his wife. She leant forward, and her hand closed over his.

"John, you do love me a little? It wasn't pity that made you marry me, was it?"

"Pity? Heavens, no! I care for you in a different way from most lovers, I suppose. It is love though, perhaps a higher, better sore of love."

"There's never been anyone else in your life?" she challenged, and although her eyes were sympathetic he recognized in them a dart of quick, accusing fire. A little flame, yet one that could leap up house-high if fanned. The memory of the chugging water of the *gracht* subsided. The memory of that night with Maddalan white like some statue, of the virgin Maddalan, ice maiden, *jung frau*, delectable in his arms, dispersed. Faded.

"No one else," he said.

He sipped again from the glass, and across its arc of mulberry, its one pool too blue for blood yet red enough to suggest blood, he saw her face. It was working in a spasm. Her mouth was dry; he could sense it. Her eyes spoke words, flooded with passionate caressing.

"You will love me very much?" she said, and then suddenly, urged on by the hot tide of her emotion, she added swiftly, "Somehow I have wondered about you; you seemed so cold. I'm not like that, you know. What I want from a man I usually get. What I've wanted from you I'm going to get. . . ."

He felt a faint, muffled drumming at his heart. He saw the memory of Maddalan rise white and triumphant, a Jairus' daughter in the sepulchre that was his soul. The memory urged, "I was the woman you wanted physically. I still am that woman. I am always going to be." He set his glass down, tracing its stem with his fingers.

"I'm not quite that type of man," he said huskily. "I don't know . . . something queer about me . . . I've never thought of you in that way, never wanted you in that way. . . ."

"That's a nice thing to tell a bride!" She stared at him fixedly for a moment. He had the impression that her lips were drawn taut over her teeth. "You are not going to tell me that you are so pure that . . ." She floundered helplessly for words in which to express the state of her emotion.

"It isn't a case of purity . . ." He also was struggling in a sea of phrases that left him only more helpless. "It's not what you think of me. It is the you mean something more to me, Belle, something greater. After all, I married you because I was fond of you in a very sincere sort of way. . . ."

He saw her debating the point in her own mind. She evidently weighed it up to a successful conclusion within her. "Supposing we don't talk about it?" he said.

"And let it all shape itself! A very good idea!" She help up her glass for more.

The waitress brought the cutlets, and Belle ate heartily, but John had no appetite left. Thoughts were crowding in upon him, like stars into a heaven already over full. Snatches of memory pictures, elusive scents, essence of privet and the faint mildewy smell of rotting leaves round the old mill by the Rhine.

Belle chattered with a gaiety not only born of burgundy and good food. She did not notice that he had left his cutlet untouched. He had remembered that soon they must return to that sepulchre of a room. Soon there would be no gainsaying her. It was wrong, all this tremendous river of emotion winding through him. His was the womanish, passive emotion. Hers was the active male delight in mastery, in conquering, in possessing. But perhaps he could account for it in his pack-mule complex.

They ate their fruit salad and drank their coffee. Belle drank a crème-de-menthe and set the glass down, shaped like a crystal chalice, crocus-cupped.

"Well, it's no good staying here," she said, "you've paid the bill."

She was restless and impatient to return. He noticed how the big bosom rose and fell, how she continually moistened her dry lips with the point of her tongue. She was eager, whereas he was reluctant.

"I'm just finishing my cigarette," he explained hoarsely. As if to give him the lie, the cigarette had gone out.

"You've got no excuse left now."

"No, I suppose I haven't."

He got up slowly, sheepishly. He reached for his hat and stick, and walked towards the door.

"You're not in a hurry," she teased him, and she took his arm, drawing it close against her body. He could feel the warmth penetrating from the flesh under the clothes. They went along the street, not quite certain of the way, but finally distinguishing the garden with the urn that in this light might have held orchids in its bowl for all that you could tell to the contrary.

Belle had the key, and she set it into the latch. The gas was turned down, and they blundered into the hall. He stopped awkwardly. "Shall we go in here?"

"I'm going to bed." Her eyes challenged him.

Uncomfortably he said, "I'll stop here and read the paper for a bit, shall I?"

She laughed as though she were uncertain of herself, and drew him towards the stairs.

"I'm not shy, duckie," she said, and she laughed again, queerly, jerkily. On the bottom stair she turned and, catching his head between her two hands, drew it roughly to her breast, kissing him with a passion that surprised him. "And," she said huskily, "you know I love you, don't you?"

VII

It was all part of a dream, a hideous dream, nightmare pressing hard at his heels, following him. Flurry of foam as though a sea embraced him. Small gusts of fear blowing through him. Then suddenly recovering to find that it had been merely a day or so. No more.

They were still at Ventnor.

He was lying on the close grass of the Undercliff. Lying there with his body pressed to the ground, hot with sun. He could see the sea like a blue jewel below, glittering where the sunrays darted among the waters. The pier stuck out like a low white wall. The cliff rose behind him, spattered with gorse and furze and blue-dark shrubs. Lying here he could smell the soft tangled earth smells, see the butterflies skimming the grasses, hear the bees on the gorse. They zoomed as they passed through the air, glorious, splendid zooming of a bee. . . . He had come here to think. Sometimes in life there is the urgent need for loneliness, the urgent demand for self-communion. Until now he had always looked upon himself as a very passionate man; he had been half afraid of the memory of kissing Freda that night on the seat by the sea, and again of that sweet darkness with Maddalan. But now he knew that youth is pitifully helpless; it cannot even gauge its own fancies and whims. He had known nothing of himself really.

His marriage! Sitting on either side the bed that struck him now only as bier . . . sitting there talking. Her arms drawing him down to her, baring of her round ample breasts, her lips inviting. It occurred to him that he was no longer gladiator for her charms, but that she was demanding him, she was insisting and accepting, she was the eternally male.

He did not appreciate the masculine demand of her passions. He had been shocked by it. He had felt as though all his finer senses were seared, flayed, laid open hot and red, and burning to the licking flames of her voluptuousness. Three nights of it. Belle whom in daytime he tried to dissociate from that demanding, protesting woman of the night. Yet he could not dissociate the two, for they were one and the same being.

Then on the third night she had accused him of not loving her. She had declared that he never had cared, not in her way, that he never would care. She was savage in her fury. She had unleashed all the hounds of her hatred and set them snarling at his throat.

What did you do next?

He knew now that they were unsuited. Until passion had entered in upon their scheme of things they had got on so satisfactorily together. Passion corrupted them; it was fungus eating away the fortress of their affection. He cursed the ridiculous laws that make marriage so difficult, tie it up, fetter it with shackles unfitted for its slender wrists and ankles. You could not tell what a woman was like until you had married her; you could not tell her viewpoints; and when you had married her it was too late to retrieve the false step.

He ground his toes, as he lay face down, into the powdery earth. It flew up in a light shower of dust. A man sitting near by watched him amusedly.

"Something wrong, son?" An old man this; old and seedy-looking, a dribbled beard falling from under his lips; bright, vivacious eyes over the grey-downed cheek. Not unlike old Jan.

"Everything wrong," said John.

"Made a mistake?"

"Perhaps."

The old man lifted a shaking finger. "If you've made a mistake, run away from it. If I'd my time over again,

I'd always do that. Run away. Cut the responsibilities and go. If you don't you only let yourself in for greater responsibilities. . . ."

Greater ones! Oh, hell!

But the pack mule has no idea of dissociating itself from its burden. It believes the burden to be part of it.

"I can't run away," said John.

The old man sat there, his arms round his knees, staring out to sea. "You can always run away," he said, "unless you are in the garden of Eden. The garden of Eden is walled in."

"Yes, isn't it?" said John wretchedly. Queer old man! A cynic, but he knew something of life. You can always run away unless you are in the garden of Eden. Love fetters, palisades itself. Horribly true, that!

"Well, I must be getting along," said the old man, and he rose, stiffly scrambling to his feet."

"I'm grateful for your advice," said John.

"Most people aren't. Advice costs nothing to give, and therefore people underprice its value. It is more valuable to receive than to bestow. Think it over."

"I would take your advice . . . if I could," said John.

The old man shook his head sadly as he began shuffling along the dusty path towards the little town. "They never can take advice," he said.

Chapter Two

> They seem to take away the sun from the world who withdraw friendship from life; for we have received nothing better from the immortal gods—nothing more delightful.
>
> CICERO

I

THEN the honeymoon took on a new turn. Belle realized that she was treating him wrongly, and she came to him in her old humility. She excused herself. She was like that, she said—over sexed; they must not let it come between them. If he would be gentle with her for a while, things would shape themselves.

There were some rather pleasant evenings listening to the concert party on the pier. It was not real music, of course, but Belle liked it. She had no appetite for the classics, but could appreciate this type of entertainment. He found that she liked to sit there and pull the actors and actresses to pieces. She was withering in her scorn of them, but she enjoyed it, and probably did not mean to be unkind.

He found himself face to face with an attitude which until now he had never suspected, something that had never suggested its existence to him: the feminine outlook. He had supposed women to have male viewpoints with a gentler reasoning, rough surfaces smoothed, coarseness glossed over. Suddenly with dismay he found that he and Belle saw life from entirely different angles, that it was as impossible for her to bridge the chasm that separated her from him as it was for him to cross those white alps barefoot which divided his masculine personality from her feminine one. She was petty. Her mind rotated in small circles. A tiny pebble of thought flung into the pool of her mind threw out its ever widening ripples and embraced suspicion, jealousy, fear. She could never adopt an impersonal interest in any happening, but must inevitably bring in atmosphere and conditions and drape them round herself. She was the central pivot in every situation that presented itself to her fevered brain. She must always lever herself into every occurrence. She was innately feminine.

Thankfully he remembered that he had never told her of Maddalan. Once he had been tempted, believing with all the innocent man's faith that it were better to make a clean breast before marriage and advance into the new life with everything revealed. Now he knew that secrets disclosed and laid bare to the naked light of cold day would shatter his happiness. Belle would pounce upon them, twist them from things of beauty into distorted monstrosities. She had the feminine conception of truth, decking it out to suit herself.

"I love you," Belle told him, lying on the white bed in the airless room one afternoon. "I love you so much that if there had been any other woman in your life I think I would have killed her."

"There is only you," he told her.

He lay beside her. Both their shoes were kicked off. He would have preferred to be out on the Undercliff, or on the hills, or close to the sea with its whisperings and its little tinkling laughter and its quick crescendoes, but Belle would lie down here afternoon after afternoon. She believed in breakfast in bed, in lying down, in resting, and it chafed against his active habits. He hated the fetid air, the frowst and the day as seen through the dirt-stained windows. But these were the eyes with which she forced him to look upon the world. He lay beside her. Sometimes she slept, breathing heavily, but at other times she lay there talking.

"I suppose," she said, "I seem old to you. I must do. You always seem to me just a brother. I never expected you to love me, not really. But I thought you'd care for me more than this."

"I do care for you," he persisted doggedly.

"You aren't passionate, are you?"

"I don't know what it is about me. I'm different from other people, I suppose, different in a funny, queer way. . . ."

"Yes," she said; then she put out a hand: "anyway I am glad to have done with the theatre and touring about and all that sort of thing. I got sick to death of it."

"I hope," he said, "that we shall never see Mimi, or Les Jefferson, or any of them again."

"So do I." Then she fell to kissing him. She smoothed his head on the parting, and kissed the little white lane of skin lying between the dark heaths of hair. She was in one of her most pleasant moods. He liked her like that. There was so much that was good in Belle, so much that stirred him into a deep pity for her. In her passionate moments she might be terrible, but ordinarily, as he knew her in their quiet communings, she was attractive.

She sat on the bed brushing his hair back with her hands; it was an odd fluttering movement, reminding him of moth wings. "John, we are going to be happy?"

"Awfully happy," he said.

"You won't let people set you against me?"

"Against you? Goodness, no!" He laughed a little. "If I were the sort of man to be upset by outside opinions, I should have been upset before this. Everybody in Condering took the opportunity to warn me against marriage. Roy——"

"Like his cheek!"

"Jefferson."

Startled, she said, "Surely not Les?"

"Rather. He was drunk, if that offers any excuse. It was really humorous, for he came to the house to tell me how awful you were, and got so squiffed that he ended up by saying that you were the most lovely girl he knew."

She was a little mollified. "Oh, well," she admitted.

"Mrs. Darsy."

"Not that——" She used an expression that he had never heard on a woman's lips before, and it struck cold to him. He turned sick. "The stuck-up piece! I'll never let her come into the place again, I'll show her! Her, indeed, nothing more nor less than a public-house keeper, a barmaid once, I'll be bound!" Her breasts heaved up and down, her face was mottled with her swelling indignation.

"She meant well; you see, she did not know you, not the real you," he said uneasily, disturbed at the anger he had roused in her.

"Umph!" Belle was not pacified. "She probably wanted you for herself. I know these women."

"It wasn't anything like that."

"Of course you'd say so. If I see her I'll tell her what I think of her."

"Belle, you mustn't do anything like that."

"Why not, indeed? Unless you really do care for her. I suppose that is what it is. You and a woman old enough to be your mother!" Her eyes flashed scorn at him.

These memories stabbed up out of his honeymoon. Queer memories, like seeding grasses in the arable land of his heart. Belle passionately defiant, and he conscious of a fear deep down within him, a deep-rooted fear of something. . . . He did not know what. A room, airless, with its coffin-shaped wardrobe and its cheap pictures. Mrs. Crumpet in the background of the house, a presiding and ominous presence. Mrs. Crumpet with her hawk-like eye and her round face with its other roundnesses drooping from beneath it; her unpunctual, dilatory meals, smelt long before they were tasted, and her quick resentment of any extra work. Then the Undercliff, earth-sweet, smelling of grasses, budding clovers, and of moss.

Yet, under all the sweetness and the darkness, under all the hills and valleys which go to make up the little everyday occurrences of life, he was aware of the jangling of harness; he recognized that a burden was settling itself definitely down on his shoulders.

II

Returning to Condering they took up the normal routine. Mrs. Barnes stayed with them. She did not like Belle, and John had a premonition that they might quarrel violently, but Mrs. Barnes was well paid and she intended to stay. She undertook all her work as a favour, believing that life could not continue without her assistance. She largely magnified her true worth, and there were moments when John longed to tell her so, but he realized that tact was necessary, and that silence made for a peaceful life, whereas home truths would have brought chaos into the house.

People called on them, and Belle basked in the new glory of being at home. Now she was desirous of making a social success of her life, and she wove herself all manner of pleasant little dreams in regard to the future. She thought that later she might start an "at home" day. She read women's magazines of the more indifferent kind, and pored over the very etiquette columns that had once left her cold. She had visiting cards printed for herself, and considered seriously as to whether she should have a certain Wednesday in the month inscribed in the bottom left-hand corner. No, she thought she would wait. She had fifty printed, which would do excellently for a start. They gave her much pleasure, and she would take them out of their corner in the writing-bureau at times, and look at them. John was glad that she should adopt this attitude, because it was one that he had not anticipated from her.

"You're different," he said, "changed. I believe you are going to like life better."

"My greatest grudge against it has gone," she said.

In those first weeks she was enchanting. He sensed the warm fragrance of her Indian summer about his romance; it was like a garden lit brightly, with the light falling on ambering leaves and reddy berries. Life held a new significance. He decided that marriage was a glorious institution, because they could share their feelings, and even if Belle did not understand some of his emotions there were others which she understood quite well.

The Repertory Company had passed on into the wilds of Suffolk. Condering was peaceful. A sweet June flooded it. The market days were thronged and busy; trade flourished. The streets were full, and people perambulated up and down, calling in at Jackson's the caterer for ices at mid-morning. All the tide of pleasant society ebbed and flowed up and down the warm inviting streets.

Then the vicar called on them. John guessed that there was something wrong when, coming into the sitting-room, he saw Belle's face glowering from the armchair, and the bland baby face of Mr. Atkins like some palely enquiring pumpkin from the opposite side of the room.

"Ah, Mr. Atkins," said John.

"Very charming, seeing you both," said Mr. Atkins, "very charming indeed. I was telling your wife that I had only just heard of the marriage. Not being at my church, you see . . ." and his light blue eyes twinkled merrily. He liked giving people sly digs. Hints about the pews growing cold, keeping a place warm for you in church, the lack of Sunday school teachers, all manner of little suggestions.

"Well, it is nice seeing you," said John, painfully aware of Belle's ominous silence. "How is Mrs. Atkins?"

"Very well, indeed." The vicar immediately switched off the subject on to the new lectern. It was really a very beautiful lectern; an eagle, you know, in brass. A nice shade of brass, nothing too yellow. Mr. Atkins felt sure that John, being a connoisseur, would admire it. He and his wife must come and see it; they must come one Sunday. There was always a nice cheerful morning service, everybody welcome, and lots of bright singing, and not too long a sermon. Mr. Atkins felt convinced that John would be favourably impressed with both the morning service and the lectern. John agreed. All the while he was thinking of Belle glowering at them, eyes gloomy beneath heavy lids, smouldering with dull fire. She would not be able to rein in her anger much longer. He knew her these days, and the fear, deep-rooted like a weed in his heart, tugged at him. He hoped that Mr. Atkins would go soon. As if in response to the inner prayer of John, Mr. Atkins rose.

"Next Sunday," he said, and wagged a roguish finger—"next Sunday we shall be keeping your seat warm for you. You really must see the lectern. You really must." He passed out through the shop, burbling.

John saw him out and came back rather pleased over the visit. It signified that better people were wanting to know them. It meant that they were being accepted, noticed, and his old urge for respectability welled up within him.

"Well, that was all right," he said to Belle.

She was sitting there, her fingers plucking at her

handkerchief as though to tear it into shreds. "Hateful old man," she said at last.

"Hateful old man? Why?"

"It wasn't a social visit at all. It was just a parochial call—you see he never brought his wife; he took good care to leave her at home! Too stuck up, I suppose. He and his rotten old lectern, touting for us to go to church. That's what it was."

"But it may mean that later she will come."

"She won't come. Of course she won't come." Belle beat an impatient tattoo with her foot against the fender. He did not know why, but the tattoo reminded him of drumming, native drumming in the jungle; beating up the chiefs to war, beating up the men to do battle. Drumming all the time. Tattoo of tom-toms, insistent, dreary, rather terrifying, tom-toms drumming. Belle's feet!

"Well, don't let's talk about it," he said after a moment, and turned away to the window-sill where the joss sat implacable, still smiling at the world in that sardonic way of his.

She turned broody eyes to him. "You would stand by and see me insulted—because that is what it is. You would stand there and never put out a hand to help me. I suppose I can't expect more from a man who married me out of pity, and it serves me right. Still——"

"Belle, you mustn't say that, you shan't say that."

"I'll say what I like. I'll do what I like. What's more that nasty mealy-mouthed old man shan't come in here again, touting for his beastly church while his wife looks down her nose at us. I'll tell him so, too. If he does come here again, I'll give him the length of my tongue."

"Belle!" he implored. His throat dried, his eyes receded into his head, dim lamps grown a little blurred with the thick driving mist of the coming storm.

"I mean that. If you want there to be peace, keep that old fool out of my way."

Then she swept past him, up the stairs creaking and bending under her, into the room above it with the four-post bed and the Jacobean chintz sweeping on either side of the long windows to the ground. He knew that, left to herself, she would cry. Somehow he believed that it might ease the pressure, she might find comfort in herself. She made him feel so helpless. . . .

How difficult were women! You could not understand them. Changeable as the surface of a pool. Chameleon-like. What was it Roy had said? Women had no roots. Perhaps that accounted for it.

III

Whenever John met Mrs. Darsy she was always pleased to see him. She was particularly nice to him, but for all that she did not come round to call on Belle. He knew that his wife expected it. He knew that secretly she fumed over it, and that unless something was done about it Belle might allude to it in one of her tactless, rather brutal moments. So one morning, when he had nothing better to do, he crossed the street to speak to Mrs. Darsy, who was just returning from her shopping. It was a day of bright sunshine, streaking the hot streets in gold ribbons of light; a pleasant day, when print frocks looked delightfully cool, and shady hats had a charm all their own. Mrs. Darsy wore a navy blue frock with a white pattern wriggling all over it, and John liked it.

"When are you coming to see my little place?" he asked her jokingly. "Belle wants to see you."

"I'm rather busy at the moment. The hotel is full. It

usually is at this time of year. Later . . ." John recognized it for a shallow excuse.

"Mrs. Darsy," he said, and pressed his point home, "I haven't offended you, have I?"

She shook her head. "Of course not." Then, because she saw that he was serious, "Perhaps, John, I am a little narrow. I am middle-aged, and we old fogies don't see eye to eye with you young people. I don't think your wife would like me, you know."

"She would."

"Then let me put it another way. We should not have much in common, from my side anyhow. Oh, John, it is difficult not to offend you, isn't it? I don't want to hurt, but that is how I feel. You understand, don't you?"

It made it all the harder that he did understand. The matters which we do not fully grasp are easier to ignore. "I'm sorry that you feel like that," he said, "because Belle is a good sort, she isn't a bit what you think she is. Won't you try?"

"I'm sure we should not get on."

"And supposing that I was sure that you would?" He had followed her into her little room in the Chantry. She set her shopping basket down on the side table and stood there looking across at him.

"You make it difficult, don't you?"

"It isn't quite fair if you don't give the thing a trial," he persisted.

She patted his shoulder and he flushed. He felt somehow that between them lay a tie, a mother-and-son tie, because her hand was gentle, her affection beautiful. He thought suddenly, with a passionate distaste of life, "Why wasn't she my mother? I should have been so proud, so fond . . ." and instantly there swept across his memory a picture of Mrs. Duckett with her hassock hat and her thin blue lips, and withered, nobbly hands like claws.

"You're right," said Mrs. Darsy, "and it was horrid of me. Somehow I felt . . ."

"But you don't feel like that now?"

"Perhaps I do, perhaps I don't, but for your sake I am ready to make the effort. You understand, don't you? For your sake I am ready to try and like her. Forgive me for having stood out against it for so long." She went to the side of the empty fireplace and pressed a bell. He watched her as she stood there, her finger on the round button. He appraised the generous lines of her figure, the ample curves, the roundness which veiled what once had been a supple grace. "You'll have something to take?" she said. "Sherry?"

He nodded.

When he left the Chantry he knew that he had made a wise move. He had taken a step forward in the right direction. Mrs. Darsy would call, and he believed that the visit would be the beginning of a new friendship. Should he tell Belle what he had done, or not? Then he remembered her resentment, her quick offence, and he decided not; better leave her to herself, then she would be all the more natural when Mrs. Darsy arrived.

He went out into the street whistling.

IV

Lapse of time. . . .

He had to admit that he was happy with Belle in his own home. They were together, and they held long intimate conversations from the very soul of each. He could not conceive how he had lived as a bachelor. There seemed to be an enormous epoch of time stretching between him as he was now and what he had been then. As to Maddalan, his love for her was quite cold. She was, it seemed, a statue standing in a niche, bathed in blue-white light. No more.

Belle trimmed up the house. Occasionally their tastes clashed, for she had to admit that she had no patience with old-fashioned truck and wanted gayer chintzes. He had a sneaking idea that she could not see the damnation in plush and pampas. He was quite convinced that bamboo held a certain charm for her, though she did not admit it. Her eyes had never been opened to real beauty. Poor Belle! Her life had been walled in with small cheapnesses, with rigorous economies, makeshift rooms, supervised by some old ma. She had been surrounded by fetid air, springless chairs, and the kind of ornaments that make you shudder.

He would never open her eyes to beauty as he had known it in the Mauritshuis, or listening to Freda playing the *Moonlight Sonata.* He knew now that Belle was a solid wall between himself and that greater soul of his which he had glimpsed at some moments in his life. Genius gazing through the veil of clouds at him. Eddying circles reaching out to touch the fringe of the golden garment, and failing. . . . But now he was standardizing himself, and he believed that the greatness of which, at times, he had been conscious had been only youth over-estimating its power. Belle might be the wall between him and that elusive greatness. He did not care.

Mrs. Darsy called. Mercifully John was out at the time and he did not come back until afterwards. Belle met him on the step in an attitude of defiance. Her face was chalk-white; her eyes were flashing. He knew instantly that she was furious about something. Limply he followed her into the inner sanctity of the room behind the shop.

"I'd just been waiting for that Darsy woman," said Belle, "after her advising you not to marry me. I got her number right enough. When I heard she was here you could have knocked me down with a feather. Then

I said to myself, 'Now for it. I'll give her something to be going on with,' and I did."

He felt himself going cold, and yet trickling with sweat. "But, Belle, I asked her to call," he implored.

"I don't care. I asked her in, and then I started. I told her that I knew she didn't approve of me. She seemed surprised at that. She did not attempt to deny it. If it had been me I'd have put a good face on it. I'd have got out of it, and not sat down under it like that. I told her exactly what I thought of her, and I'm glad of it too. I suppose she thought that she'd marry you herself. Jealous cat!"

"You didn't tell her that?"

"I don't know what I told her. A joke is all very well, but this was more than a joke." She paused and then, taking fresh breath, went on again. "She went white and got up, but I made her stay. I made her stay and hear every word of it. *Every word!*"

To Belle it was a triumph. He could hear the clashing chord of victory in her voice; there was something Wagnerish about it. He felt himself faintly sick, weak-kneed. What did you do next? What next? "It was horrible of you," he said at last.

"Horrible, was it? Oh, then there was something in it. You were keen on her yourself?"

"Heavens, no!"

He felt weary, sagging, just as though some support had broken in the middle of him, a spine that wavered.

"There was something in it," she shrilled.

She came nearer. It seemed that her face had become puffed, the colour of tapioca pudding, yellowish white, with streaks of red where she had over-rouged the cheek bones. He made a little deprecating movement. "I can't fight this thing out; there is no truth in it. If you said things, you said them; there's the end of it. Do let's have peace."

"Peace?" she echoed, and the echo was jarring. She drew back from him and looked at him. It seemed that the whole of her body was distorted by the consuming fire of jealousy which burnt within her. "It looks like peace, doesn't it? I thought you were faithful. I thought you were too much of a fool to be anything else."

"Heavens! You can't accuse me of that!" he gasped, stung out of the first stupor of the thing.

"Accuse you?" As she turned from him she swept her arm wide and brushed along the sill. It caught the joss. It dashed the god to the ground. There was the hollow, metallic tang of bronze, then the dull thunder of it rolling along the uncarpeted floor. She turned and looked down at it.

"That thing!" She picked it up, a grim god who still smiled at them both. "I hate it! It is beastly! Why don't you throw it away? One of these days I'll chuck it out myself!"

Then she rushed away. He heard her as she went up the stairs, crying loudly, as children cry before they have been taught control. He heard her slam and lock the bedroom door, her agitated footsteps tottering across the room, her body cast down, lumpily, despairing, to the bed.

He picked up the joss and set it in its place. It smiled blatantly. Until now he had doubted it, he had half meant to get rid of it some time, but now her vehemence had awakened some obstinacy in his heart. He would keep it.

V

Despairingly he clung to respectability. He clung to it though dimly aware that it was the crucifix to which Belle would nail his sensitiveness. By his respectability she hurt him more. Scenes—intermittent, frantic scenes. When there were not scenes there were the long dour hours when she was rebellious about life, when she would hardly speak; then the Belle who had once attracted him seemed to be submerged in a Belle whom he could not hope to understand. Gradually it seemed that her enchantments dispersed, flooded in this spate of her intense dislike of life and the resentment she bore it. Her first attempt at social life died down, flamed out like a candle in a high wind. The vicar's call, and then Mrs. Darsy's, had finally settled her.

John realized that she was lonely. You cannot take the life of a woman of Belle's age and reshape it. Housekeeping did not occupy her. She had been used to dilatory meals on trays, a chop, porter, some cold meat. Housework was outside her scheme of things, and anyway Mrs. Barnes did it all for her. She found her new friends a strain, for she had adopted the pose which she considered to be ladylike, and could not cling to it without an effort. Life was changed. She had lived on the cliff edge of excitement, production, and thrill. The footlights might have been cheap, but they had been glamorous. She was bereft of their glitter. She could not market as did the other housewives, nor chatter scandal, nor could she even be herself. She had never been good at playing a waiting game, and the fruits of her victory ripened far too tardily for her. Belle was becoming sick of the whole adventure.

Mrs. Darsy never mentioned the scene that she had endured with Belle, and John had not the heart left to apologize for it. Besides, how could you apologize for your own wife?

"You made a mistake in marrying her," said Roy one day, when they met in the Chantry bar, "and you won't admit it. That's your fault."

"Poor Belle. She finds it odd always having been on tour. You can imagine that."

"Well, why didn't she go on with the stage? Why didn't you let her have her fling? Or did the stage give her up?"

"Please," said John, and there was something so earnest about his tone, some deep 'cello-like note that made Roy drop his tinkling banter.

"Sorry, old chap! We are going to ask her to join our dramatic society. She might do us some good there, drop us a few hints. We want to do 'When Knights were Bold', in November."

A warm thrill tingled through John. That would please Belle, as also it gratified him. It was in a sense a compliment. "I'm glad about it," he said; "and she will be bucked, too. She gets a bit down at times."

"Glad you're pleased." Roy came closer, leant up against John, glass touching glass in neighbourly fashion on the counter before them. "I can't think why you don't find some little pet," he said. "I know a lovely little bit. Name of Letty——"

"You've got me all wrong. I'm not that sort. Women don't appeal to me in that way."

"They appeal to you, apparently, in the most senseless way of all." Then Roy pulled himself together again. "Sorry," he said, and pushed their glasses across to the barmaid, jauntily wiping tumblers with a cloth marked in red squares. "Same again, miss," he said.

John clung to Roy. He did not want to lose more of his friends than he could help through his marriage, and, opposites as they might be, Roy attracted him.

The theatricals would be a step in the right direction. When Belle received the invitation to join their ranks, she was pleased. It tickled her vanity. She was determined to teach these loutish amateurs a thing or two about the stage. She went to the preliminary meeting and came away indignant but triumphant. The producer had allotted her to the part of the aunt, and she had told him definitely that the only part she would consider undertaking would be that of the Lady Rowena. Belle was not going to be put off with any second-place rôles. She would have the lead or nothing at all. If she had made a scene the details were mercifully spared from John. Every Monday and Thursday the Corn Exchange delivered itself into their hands. Here, apparently, they launched themselves wholeheartedly into the mysteries of rehearsals and all the attendant bickerings.

"They think that they can do what they like with me at those rotten old rehearsals of theirs," announced Belle over breakfast one day, "but I won't have it. I've told them so, too. Old Atkins is a bloody fool. They came to me and asked me if I knew of anybody who could take it over from him. I told them."

"What did you tell them?"

"I told them of Les Jefferson."

"What? That awful man?"

Her eyes narrowed a little and surveyed him across a cup of coffee. "He wasn't awful. He knew what was what, and if he got on to their rotten old 'Knights were Bold' he'd have it shipshape in no time. It needs order, it needs work. I told them so."

"They aren't getting him down, are they?" asked John in some alarm. He did not want to have Jefferson hanging round the place again.

"I don't know. They are writing to him. I expect they will have to do something about it. Mr. Atkins is a fool. Fancy ever asking a vicar to produce a thing like that! It's their own fault. Such tosh!"

"Mr. Atkins is at least a gentleman," commented John, glumly thinking of Jefferson.

She sneered a little as she helped herself to marmalade. "Yes, that *is* what you would think of! Never having been a gentleman yourself, you're damned keen on it in other people. Gentlemanliness in this doesn't matter; what we want is a good producer."

There was a silence. It was one of those moments when Belle was undecided whether to let the matter drop or to launch herself wholeheartedly into a temper. Mercifully there came the sound of Mrs. Barnes, who had just arrived, bustling about in the kitchen. Gas popped. Saucepans scraped against drawing-boards. China clinked together.

"That must be Mrs. Barnes," said Belle, and she called sharply, "Mrs. Barnes!"

A tousled head peered round the kitchen door.

"You're late," said Belle. They stared at each other, these two women. Obviously they hated each other. Belle's eyes were hard and hazel, Mrs. Barnes' were indignantly blue. There is something harsh about blue eyes, something steel-cold, sharp, and you cannot escape from it.

"Yes, and I've had me troubles this morning, ho yes," said Mrs. Barnes—"what with the pig and one thing and another."

"The pig?"

"Yes. The pig what me husband bought at the sale to fatten up for Christmas. That there tinker of a kid from next door hit it no end of a wallop with the besom—it's got a whale on its back that big. . . ." She held up her hands to indicate the size.

"A whale?" echoed John.

"I should say so. All red and the skin broke at the corner. Pigs won't stand that sort of treatment . . . an awful whale. . . ."

"Oh, a weal, that's what you mean," said Belle. "Well, why should we be put to discomfort for your pig? Mr. Carrick had to come down and boil the kettle and cook the eggs."

Mrs. Barnes made no audible answer, but lapsed into muttering. She withdrew her tousled head and slammed the door noisily.

"What a sauce!" said Belle. "The pig indeed! Why should we be bothered about her pig and its whales?"

"But a whale!" Their eyes met and they laughed.

"The other day," said Belle, sipping her tea, "she and I got talking, and she was saying that she would never have any children. She has had one apparently, and was frightfully ill afterwards, and she told me that they took her 'wound' out, so she will never have any more!"

John began to laugh helplessly. Belle caught the infection and she laughed too. The critical moment had passed. They laughed together, and there was something joyous about the echo tinkling through the room. The joss laughed grimly too.

"After this," said John, "I shall call her 'the wounded one'."

VI

Mr. Atkins had long ago decided that producing was not in his line. He had had no idea that the rehearsals of "When Knights were Bold" were to entail so much quarrelling. Being heartily sick of the whole proceedings, he had accepted with alacrity Belle's suggestion of Les Jefferson's services. He wrote off to Hoxton, where it seemed that Mr. Jefferson was temporarily 'resting', and he prayed that the answer would come soon. He could not understand why it was that he had ever been prevailed upon to offer his services at all. Once, long ago, when he was a curate up North, he had arranged a children's party, a very pretty little operetta called "Puss in Boots", which had been no trouble. He had written the play, too. Somewhere in the library he had the libretto still lying about. I had been a very creditable bit of work. He had been especially proud of the opening chorus, which had started:

> There was an old miller who lived till he died,
> Who between his three sons did his fortune divide.
> To Thomas the eldest he left the old mill,
> His horses and carts to his second son Will,
> And then to the youngest one called "Little Matt"

He left nothing more than a fine pussy-cat.
Doo da dilly dee dido.

There had been a lot of the "doo da dilly dee dido" about the vicar's operetta, but the fact remained that it had been a huge success, and that the parish had been so pleased that they had been asked to take it on New Year's Eve to the workhouse and enact it there for the benefit of the inmates. And the workhouse had hailed it with such vigour that they had gone on to the county asylum, where one of the patients had gone most dangerously mad in the transformation scene. It had been at the moment when little Liza Newton, dressed as Puss, had advanced upon the giant and had sung:

That you can take the form of a lion,
I'll own is very clever,
But that you can take the form of a mouse,
I'll not believe, no, never!

A triumph of metre that, and of rhyme too. The vicar had been extremely proud of the "no, never", which had been the result of much thought.

In spite of this past success, and his renowned ability in organizing charades at different house-parties that he visited, he had to admit that so far as "When Knights were Bold" was concerned he had failed most dismally. It was a fiasco. Mrs. Carrick was a trial as the Lady Rowena; she wanted to manage everything. She was a dreadful woman, and she would be far better with a producer who pandered to her. It would mean that Mr. Atkins would save himself any amount of unpleasantness and rows.

Roy did not shine as Whittles. He over-acted, and he would flirt behind the scenes. He was never ready for his cues, and it was most embarrassing. The vicar had an idea that the theatricals were a glorious excuse for flirtations, and he was sick of it. He did not know whether he would have to sacrifice his own part as the dean. But, alas, the rôle of the dean tickled his vanity. It was the nearest approach to gaiters to which he could ever hope to aspire. No, he thought that he would retain the part at any cost.

Les Jefferson received the letter from the vicar asking for assistance at one of those lean moments in his life when things were looking glum. His landlady was a skinflint, and she was pressing hard for the rent. He had been out of a "shop" ever since the Repertory Company had broken up, rather more precipitately than anticipated, owing to the manager clearing off with the proceeds one Saturday night and leaving no address to which to apply for their salaries.

Since then Jefferson had been round to agents' offices without success. He was a poor, pathetic figure, very angular, very cadaverous, with that pitiful courtliness to which he still clung. He wore his ridiculously high collar and the heavy black silk stock; he still stuck to the quaintly cut long morning coat, which gave him the appearance of being a wooden man out of the Ark. Mercifully he had escaped with the pair of property trousers of sponge-bag pattern. His spats covered boots worn into open sores; his socks had long since been reduced to anklets. Yet, crowned with his absurd sombrero of a hat, bound with a corded ribbon that had left it in parts, and that waved dismal strings in other parts, he still bravely assailed the agents.

He would pass up dusty stairs flanked by other hungry, cadaverous men and women, and would press himself in through the thin door at the top. He would wave aside the little boy who in round and comfortable cockney demanded his business; he would stride haughtily across the floor into the great presence, necessity driving him onwards.

"Anything to-day?" The old imperious enquiry, and in his heart the terribly urgent need gnawing in hunger and thirst. Always the same old answer, "Not to-day, I'm afraid, Mr. Jefferson, not to-day." Sometimes nothing so polite, sometimes surliness, rudeness, a bidding never to return, but always the descent into the street again, brushing his hat with the sleeve of his thready coat, with that dreadful mask of a smile glued to his inscrutable face.

Then this morning, this lean and stark morning, with the suggestion of fog hanging in jaundiced webs above the plane trees, with Hoxton dour and gloomy, sweaty in the autumn mist, a dead place smelling of disease, of refuse, of decay, there came this letter. The sum that it offered was a fortune, and down at Condering there was Belle.

Les Jefferson felt that he ought to make something out of Belle's marriage; old Belle, who had been afraid of being left by the tide, who had been afraid of life and age bearing down on her; old Belle whom he had left too well alone.

He answered the letter in person.

VII

The fact that Les Jefferson, past master in the art of subterfuge, travelled the whole route in a truck, and yet managed to extract his first-class fare from the unwilling vicar, accounted for his being in funds.

He went round to see Belle. John happened to be out. He had gone on a visit to a sale in the country; taken by Roy in the tourer that he had just bought and was anxious to try out. Les Jefferson found the land clear. After six months' smug marriage, and a desperate endeavour to live in the rut of respectable conventionality, Belle was only too thankful to hail him as a friend. She forgot everything that she had ever held against him. She welcomed him warmly.

"But where am I to stay?" asked Les Jefferson, when he had fed well. "I have no rooms, no rooms at all, don't you see?"

"You shall stay here," announced Belle in a fit of generosity.

"But what will John say?"

"John daren't say anything. Why should he? I have trained him well."

A smile that was sardonic spread itself pall-wise over Les Jefferson's face. "Excellent! Belle, you were clever when you landed this fish. I gave you a leg-up with him, you know."

"You warned him against me," she said sharply, suddenly recalling the incident.

"I? Is that what he told you? I . . . oh, that's good! Did you hear that? Yes, of course I heard that. What a one! I warn him against you? Belle, my angel, he said that to turn you against me. Why, I advised him. I pushed him into it. If it hadn't been for me, Belle, you'd never have been where you are to-day, not on your life you wouldn't. No, of course you wouldn't."

He stretched out a lean hand, through which the fine bones were showing dark lines in macabre transparency. She took the hand and held it. "You're a pal," she said huskily.

"Shall we kiss on it?"

"Rather!"

He reached across the table, drew her full and bosomy to his own corpse-like body. The warmth of her went through him, fired him; the full-bloodedness, the glow of her being fused his senses. "Do you remember, once . . .?" he whispered, and his eyes were burning in the condensed glimmer of street lamps luminous and yet distorted through the fog. "That night when we were doing 'Under Two Flags' at Wolverhampton . . . that night . . ."

Her body stiffened, drew itself together, and then

suddenly went limp; she was sobbing. "Oh, Jeff," she protested, "he's not good to me, he's cold . . . oh, Jeff!"

VIII

When John returned late that evening he was pleased with life. He had bought several rather good specimens at extremely reasonable prices, and he was discussing them animatedly with Roy.

"Come in for a drink," he suggested as the new car slid to a skidding standstill on the wet road outside the house.

"You don't think the old bus will skid away down the hill?"

"Lord, no!"

Roy got out lumberingly. It was not raining now. There was a hint of soft-smelling loveliness about the air, a hint of sharpness, whisper of frost. Later the moon would rise like a great gold ship out of the darkness, and instantly there would be the faint crystal glimmer upon the hedges. The hand of winter was already laid tenderly on the shuddering shoulder of autumn.

"Come in," said John.

They blundered in through the shop entrance, stumbling over furniture stacked on either side, china in groups, old Jersey brass-bound jugs standing knee high. They went on to where the glimmer of light showed warm and friendly from the sitting-room; as they approached they heard the sound of voices.

"Oh Lord, you've got somebody in there," said Roy, stopping short. "If it's Atkins——"

"It won't be, on your life. More likely Mrs. Barnes.

Belle must get lonely, and they talk scandal. You know what women are."

Johh pushed open the door, and saw Les Jefferson, gaunt like a skeleton, his face sunk in deep pockets on either side the grinning mouth, his eyes in pits. "Oh, my God!" he said.

Roy saved the situation. He staggered forward into the warm flowing river of light. "If it isn't old Jeff!" he exclaimed. "Well, this *is* luck. How's Mimi?"

John felt his mouth dry; it tasted as though it had been crammed full of dead leaves, beech leaves, from their drifting among the sere grasses. He felt his body stiffen, his hands shake a little. He knew that Belle was watching him. Her morose eyes sought his defiantly, flung down the challenge to him, and he knew that against his better self he was accepting that challenge. He went across to the sideboard and picked up the decanter, noting dryly that its high-water mark was left far behind. The beast! The drunken, fawning beast!

"Have some?" he said to Roy, and added with sarcasm: "there's just a little left."

Jefferson turned his glittering eyes to John. "Will I have some? Of course I'll have some. A long journey down here in not too comfortable surroundings. I'm producing the play, you know. It's going to be some play. Belle is Rowena, I hear. Good for her. I'm producing it."

John poured out the whisky and pushed a syphon across the refectory table in the direction of Roy and Jefferson. He noted that the table top seemed to be glazed, just as the roads had been glazed with rain. It must be that he was seeing things in the wrong perspective.

"Where are you staying?" asked Roy, endeavouring to make polite conversation. That was a bad start.

"The good lady has asked me to stay here," said Jefferson, and he lifted his glass in Belle's direction.

"Blessings on her bonny brown eyes. My luggage"—and he winked outrageously—"will follow after."

John gripped the table closer, as though his thin fingers would have pulped the solid oak. "You are staying here?" he asked, and his dry throat rattled.

It was Belle who thrust herself between them. "Yes, he is staying here. Have you any objection?"

None at all when she looked like that. It was like looking into the significant eyes of some giant cat, a tender, furry cat looking softly as though she could gambol softly, but with the acute and desperate knowledge that under the curling lips was speckled fawn of fang, and teeth sword-sharp. He wanted to say, "To hell with Jefferson! Get him out! . . . He has got to go . . . and quickly!" But instead he found himself saying reluctantly, "No, no, of course not . . . none at all . . ." and he thought that the world had suddenly grown grotesque like the world you see at a shadow show. They were all here, all of them, puppets for his play. Roy, the sharp, rather silly young man, Jefferson the sponger, Belle—and what was she?

He did not know. He recoiled a little, and took a long pull at his whisky. It flashed down his throat like a flame searing its blistering way. It burnt into his lungs, leaving behind it a hot fire. It was a knife, bitter-sharp, yet sweet with it all. It struck some latent chord within him, it satisfied some want.

He said; "Oh yes," and nodded sagely to himself as though he needed the comfort of that assurance. Roy was staring at him owlishly. He saw Belle's face recede again. He saw Jefferson, his hollow eyes gleaming in inebriety over the crystal rim of his glass. Life was a stage, and the play was farce, grim farce. Ghastly, stark farce, and never a single joke in its rotten lines.

John gulped down the whisky and poured out a second glass of it. The second was horribly sobering. Something would have to be done about this. The whisky reminded him of it all the time; something would have to be done, and at once. Later he would talk to Belle.

He poured out a third glass.

IX

Roy had gone. The new car had purred its way down the hill to its garage, and Roy himself had gone to his lodgings. Jefferson, very drunk, very bland, in love with life and all that it offered, had taken his gaunt body up to the spare room, and without troubling to undress had sprawled himself out on the clean bed. John was sitting on the cretonne-covered chair in his bedroom unlacing his shoes. The affairs of the evening were confused in his mind, a jumble, but now he was sober. It was a very grim reaction. The gas fire, burning low, made little plops, as though that, too, had drunk and become hiccoughy. Long curtains of cretonne hid the night—curtains on which sprawled tulips and yellow tassels of laburnums on parchment-hued backgrounds. The bed was occupied by Belle. Her hair was knotted back under a tired lace boudoir cap, which irritated John beyond measure. Somehow he associated that kind of cap with tawdry actresses, with harlots, with the flotsam and jetsam of life, and not with his wife. Her nightdress, too, peach-coloured, was cut low. It was a voluptuous nightdress, which repulsed rather than enamoured him. He had hated his mother's nightdresses, severe linen with good calico buttons at throat and wrists, but Belle's nightdresses were detestable. In them she appeared blowzy. Belle knew that there was a storm impending, and she lay there with an amused smile twitching her lip-corners, pretending to read the papers. She was quite ready for it when the first words rapped out like a machine-gun attacking.

"Why did you ask that man to stay here? You know how I hate and despise him."

She glanced up indifferently, folded the paper, and laid it aside with an affected yawn. Her eyes sought his in amused boredom. "I happen to like him and I wished him to stay here. You have your friends, I have mine."

"But to stay in the house! Hang it all, Belle, you seem to forget that it is my house."

"And mine," she nodded.

He felt argument choking within him; then glancing at her from under lowered brows, he realized that he was impotent against her. He began more calmly: "You will oblige me by asking him to go as soon as he can. He can't sponge on us all the time, and he shall jolly well find his own lodgings. Hang it all, the man will be paid for his work."

"If you feel like that, tell him yourself," she replied, and knew that he would do nothing of the sort.

"It was you who asked him, and you can damned well get rid of him," he challenged.

"Well, I shall do nothing of the sort."

Still the gas fire plopped away in its miserable little hiccoughy protestations. He wished that he had been born a strong man, capable of taking her into his hands and giving her the shaking that she so richly deserved. But he could not. He was weak. In his desperate attempt at self-assertion he could not even gain possession of his own house.

"It isn't playing the game," he argued. "I don't want to upset you, Belle, but I can't have that man here."

He went over to the bedside and stood there staring down at her.

"You never think how dull it is for me," she complained.

"You married me. You were frightfully keen on it. If we had not married you would have been miserable—you know that. Then, you wanted to marry me."

"Or you thought that I did."

"You did. You know you did. You seemed to be a different person then, now I don't know what has happened to you."

"I haven't changed," she said sulkily. She glowered at him. She had sat up, her large arms embracing her bent knees. Her hair fell in a wispy screen across her flesh, her lace cap set coquettishly atop it. "Unless you've frozen me out. You've done that, you know, not caring for me. Why did you marry me if you couldn't care in that way? Why?"

She was getting excited, and her voice rose and fell. He said pleadingly, "Hush! Don't you realize that Jeff may hear you?"

"Hear?" she sneered. "Don't be damned silly. He never hears anything at this time of night—much too pulpy. Besides, he knows me. He's known me years. He is going on knowing me. . . ." She became a little hysterical, clawing at the bedclothes with her hands. "I've been had!" she protested. "I've been cheated! Thought I'd married flesh and blood, and found you—a corpse dressed up! That's what you are, a corpse dressed up!"

"Hush!" he begged.

"Why the devil should I hush? I've got nothing to be ashamed about. I think it is abominable the way you have married and neglected me. Now when I want one of my own friends to come and stay with me . . ."

She began to cry.

"It would have been different if it had been one of the girls," suggested John—"even Mimi. . . ."

"Yes, different because you could have got off with her! I suppose that is what you mean. There's no harm in Jeff. He is not a teetotaller, I know, but there's no harm in him. You'll accuse me next of being in love with him."

"Oh God, no!" gasped John. The idea was fantastic.

"Then what do you mean by wanting to get rid of him?"

"The man is a leech."

"A what?" Suddenly she threw up her hands and flung her head on the pillow. She began to cry, in the way in which he had come to believe that only Belle could cry. The heavy sobs shook the room. She wept noisily; she wept with the intention that people should hear and pity her; she did not care to what depths of horror she dragged John.

He knelt beside the bed. Every detail of the room seemed to be impressed upon him, written into him, stamped in flame. The bed with its crenellated posts, with its vine leaves and flutings, with its trails and tendrils; the cretonne curtains flapping in the wind and undisturbed by the heaving figure on the bed and the wailing and hiccoughs that savaged the room.

"Don't, Belle," he besought, "don't take on like this. He shall stay. Of course I don't mind . . . Belle . . . !"

Chapter Three

> I cannot sink
> So far—so far down, but I shall know
> Thy voice, and answer from below.
>
> TENNYSON, *Eleanore*

I

THE rehearsals proceeded. Les Jefferson began to pull things into shape. From the snatches of conversation which John heard at different times there seemed to be some small resentment caused by Les Jefferson's interference. The company were not pleased with him. John heard of it through Roy, who alternated between being "fed-up" with the whole proceedings and delighted with himself as Whittles. He had long ago decided that without him the show would fall flat.

"But of course Jeff is a pest," he confided in John one day; "and between ourselves I am rather sorry that Belle ever got into it. They are running the show. It will be the last time either of them is asked to act, I can promise you."

But John said nothing. He had given up defending Belle, because time had taught him that there was no defence of her attitude towards life.

He wanted to think. These days his life was not his own; his home wasn't his own; he had no time to himself whatsoever. And he knew that now he must decide upon a course of action. The pack mule was conscious of the reins chafing, of the whip being applied, and knew that it was a case of now or never. He could feel himself growing pulpy under Belle's heel, and was ashamed of the white-livered fear in him which acknowledged her as master. He must think. Not here in this bewildering, perplexing city, with the drone of the trams and the North Hill for ever flowing past the house, with the people pressing to and fro. Not in the house, which was full of the hostility of Belle and the ridiculous chatter of Mrs. Barnes, for ever full of her own doings. He must be alone.

That was why he went to Craye that bright morning in late October, when the world was a riot of gold and russet loveliness. He told Belle that he was attending a sale, which might make him late—but there was no sale. He descended from the important little train chuffing and jerking at the wayside station stuck on a hillside sedgy with grasses, stretching down in a long even shoulder towards the sea. The station had been built a good half-mile from the village, which was small and compact, and in which he had no interest.

The day was hot with the mellow, lazy heat of autumn. He turned out of the station yard and crossed the lane thick in white dust, and began climbing the hill. Once before he had been here, and he had niched it then as a wonderfully lonely spot for self-communion. From the hill-top, where the red brambles trailed and a single yellow-leafed larch blew its amber finery against a hyacinth sky, he could see the silvery stretch of water which was sea.

It was one of those flashing days that are the last brilliant flags of a departed summer, waved in triumph to the dulling autumn. The road was lost in a tide of gold leaves as it led down to the village. Even the station, with its chains of trucks noisily looped together, its red brick buildings, and its drab slate roof, took on kinder tones. There was a glowing claret about the bricks which stained them the colour of crushed mulberries, and the slates glazed kindly by the ardent sun took on blue shadows. John left the road and climbed up the hill with its short, thick grass protruding from the sandy earth. He came to the thicker undergrowth, the brambles glowing ebon with fruit, lustrous like beady eyes peeping up at him, red where the sun had not yet speared through the thick shelter of leaves to colour the berries to ripeness.

He sat down, for the day was hot, rising out of the mist above the marshy bulrush beds which lay in the dip between him and the sea. He sat there staring down at the hill and thought of it as being like life, dusty, heavy-going, unaccountable. He saw the little world which lay beneath the hill, lying like a tranquil pool and stretching far. Villages that were discernible in the dispersing mists; little square church towers, tall, prim spires; the sea flinging a pearly arm about the islands dotted here and there, dark smudges like giant thumbprints on the sheen of the silver sheet of water. He glimpsed the gleam of wet, gold sands, soft and pale in the light, reminding him of moist flesh. Here a man might think.

His thoughts composed themselves to climb the tower of Babel which was his mind, confused, perplexed; a hundred emotions seemed to have been tossed together and to have built up that titanic tower, whose slippery walls afforded his equanimity no foothold. He did not know which to dissect first—the error of marriage, or the attitude which he should adopt now. He could not run away, for after all, he owed Belle something, and it was as bad for her as it was for him. He had disappointed her. He had been at a loss to understand her more passionate moments, and amazed by her sensuous demands.

He owed her something. But he owed himself something too, something more than this misery which convention insisted should last a lifetime, this ceaseless grinding against his better emotions. He was naked to Belle's taunts, to the resentment of those sullen eyes.

And now, as an added difficulty, there was Jeff. He was unbearable, utterly beastly. Somehow John recalled how once before in his life he had packed his bag, and had scuttled like an affrighted rabbit out into the world from the derelict prison house that had called itself home. He had found himself in Holland, standing on the edge of a great adventure. What would happen if he scuttled now? Was the adventure offering itself again?

But then he had had no ties. His urge for respectability had been propitiated. He was not a shirker, and did not wish to shift those responsibilities which marriage had brought him. All the same, the harness was pressing close against him; it had rubbed a sore on his swollen neck, and on his back.

He thought desperately, here on the pinnacle of this pleasant hill, looking down on the world now spattered about in haze, and the sea, and the islands below. If only he could stay here! But he could not. Time is for ever pressing onwards. We cannot stay it for one hour; we have got to go on, spun round with its rotating circles.

He heard a child's voice ringing sweet through the air. Someone was coming. He wiped his face with his handkerchief, rubbing away the sweating agony that had painted it. A small girl of some nine years, carrying a little basket in which she had put a few blackberries, ran chattering out from among the amber bushes on to the grass. She was calling excitedly to someone else, and, seeing him, paused, confused and surprised.

"Oh," she said, and blushed; then she went on more soberly, as though ashamed that she had chattered so loudly. He thought, "Would a child make a difference to my life? Would it make my marriage happier?" and he knew that it would not help in the least.

He watched her turn and run down the hill. He heard sedater footsteps coming out of the undergrowth. A second shadow flickered across him and died away again as an older girl passed. The girl was walking on the grass. Her light grey frock blew about her airily; her hair, soft and yellow, was like the river irises in the spring sunlight; her face was a cameo.

It was Maddalan.

II

They recognized each other instantly. He could not have stayed the little choky cry that he gave, her name rising to his lips. And he had thought that she had become mere statue in the niche of his heart, white virgin carved in stone. Fool! Fool!

She called the child back with amazing composure, for women are more composed than men in such emergencies. She sat down beside him, Maddalan, more beautiful than he had remembered her. He drank in the sweetness of her in long draughts as men drink wine. Yet she did not bemuse him; she quickened his pulses, sharpened his senses, set him delirious and thrilled.

"Oh, my dear," he said.

He held her hands in his, with the frail shadows of bones lying like brittle stalks under the soft white flesh. Glowing beneath the pellucid whiteness of her face he saw the faint warmth of emotion. Just at first she seemed to be as a miracle of carved ivory, but now she lived. It was not a dream. It was as Hermione coming to life for Leontes . . . she lived again for him.

"I have wanted you so much," she said, and her voice was broken, for through it there ran glad rivers of joyful tears.

"You did not answer my letters."

"How could I since I never received them?"

"Never had them?"

"The *Mevrouw* . . ."

"Ah yes"—he nodded contemplatively—"the *Mevrouw*," and the lime tree lifting its brave arms sunwards, clothed amber and glorious in leaves, sent a rain of fluttering gold down upon them. It is not well to be too trusting in life. He had forgotten the *Mevrouw*.

"Tell me," he whispered, ravenous for all her secrets—"tell me everything."

She sat there limply, her hands lying in his; he could sense the delicate presence of her—it fused his senses. "Last spring the *Mevrouw* died. It was the heart, the apothecary said. I had always wanted to come here to England and to find you. Just at first, after that last time, I hated you. They tell me women are like that. I was afraid, you see."

"Afraid?"

"Minna had a child. Her lover at Edam, the cheesemaker, he gave it to her. He did not marry her, and she left us in disgrace. It was terrible. The *Mevrouw* preached a lesson, and for a while I was insanely afraid, and it was dreadful because I could not escape it. I was afraid that I might have a child too."

"Oh, my sweet, my sweet!" He could understand the horror that she must have endured, and he put her little hands to his mouth, kissing them where the blue veins lay in twining patterns in their marble. Life is cruel organizing that woman should suffer so. Poor women, bearing all the brunt of procreation, of parturition, all the responsibilities of birth! It is unfair. Around them the day swept; the heat haze lifted, the sea, crystal and cobalt, flashed around the green islands and became fringed whitely against the peninsulars of cliff.

"Then I did not care if you wrote or not, because I was concerned only with myself. I thought you a coward to have been so thoughtless for me, and the *Mevrouw* enlarged on it. She was able, and she knew how to play on the feelings. Then I grew wiser; I understood more. I found that I wanted you badly. There were other men. One was a student from Amsterdam whom the *Mevrouw* encouraged, and the *Mijnheer* liked him too. He was a cousin of the family, a nice enough young man, going to be a banker, but he was not what I wanted. All the time I remembered you. You, John, who were so sensitive, more tender than most men. I could not believe hard things of you for long."

Her hands stroked his softly, like the gentle wings of some tired bird who has flown too far.

"John, do you remember the Franz Hals, and the Buitenhof, and the Haarlemmer Hout like a great cathedral?"

He said rather bitterly, for the memory hurt, "I have never forgotten them, Maddalan."

"I went on; I tried to find out things about you, but it was difficult. I tried to trace you. But you cannot trace people from across the seas. I wrote to the cousins in Tooting, and then when the *Mevrouw* was dying she told me that you were near here. She would not tell me where, but she said near here. I suppose she was sorry. She opened her eyes. She could not see properly, for she said that it was dark, and it was not dark—we had the lights on. She said, 'That man, the one who loved music and pictures, he wrote. He is in a city, near Harwich. . . .' She tried to tell me the name of the city, but she had left it too late. A whole lifetime, but she had left that too late." She clasped her hands together in a little desperate gesture, and then went on again. "The *Mijnheer* went to his brother. I wrote to the cousins in Tooting and came to them. Tooting is not much of a place. They got me the appointment here as governess. The little girl—her name is Carol, and her mother is Dutch. She wants her child to speak Dutch, and she had some difficulty in getting a governess for her. I was the only one who applied, and I came here because I knew that it was near you."

He caught her slender waist between his two hands,

and said rapturously, "There is some power that shapes our ends . . . there must be. This is not coincidence, it is fate. Oh, Maddalan!"

He kissed her then, with the glittering hyacinth of the sea beneath them, and the leaves burning the colour of dim tapers. The kiss was consummation. It was the healing of a breach, the beginning of a fresh adventure. Lip to lip, breast to breast, they swayed, with the exquisite crimson and gold of the day sweeping about them. Then she released him, her face pale with tears retreated a little from his, her hands slender and blossomy laid upon his arms.

"Now," she said, "tell me about yourself."

III

He drew her down to him again and sat there hushing her against himself like a child. So they sat, tensely still.

"The last thing that I remembered," he said, "was seeing your face in the darkness of that room, with the dawn coming in cold white, and the *Mevrouw* looking exactly like an indigant haystack."

"Oh, my dear," and she laughed.

"Well, but didn't she? She stood there overpowering, and I felt myself growing smaller and smaller. When you asked me to go . . . I can see your face again as you said it. For a time I was always seeing your face, then it became unreal. Now it has become real again. It is here, here with me."

They kissed again. The unsheathed wind sang about them, tossing aside the bramble leaves, darkly red like long-spilt blood.

"I went, but I meant to come back. Then when I got away everything conspired against me. There is so much of that in life, the fatal element of chance. I did not know what to do. I wanted to claim you for my own, but there was the *Mevrouw*. I wrote to you, and you did not reply. It was all frightening, rather engulfing, like the first wave when you are bathing. I wrote and you did not answer. I wrote again and again, and you did not answer. Then I got piqued. Oh, my dear, aren't we rotten? *Aren't* we fools? So easily swerved from our goal, so doubting."

"You suffered," she said—"so did I."

"Of course I suffered. Mr. Oglivy had arranged things for me and I had to come here and start work. I got the loveliest old house in Condering. It was just the sort of house and shop that I had dreamt about, not too definitely shoppy, you know. I started life and wrote to you again. You did not answer."

"I never got the letter."

"Then I don't know what happened." He came to a halt, seeing all the circumstances sweeping along in their flood tide, carrying him over far.

"But, darling, it is all over now," she whispered confidently, "all over now. We have each other at last."

Despair trailed like a weed through his brain; a weed in water, muddy, brackish, thick. "That isn't all," he said wretchedly.

"Tell me? There is nothing that we cannot fight together."

He thought desperately to himself, "Everything except this," and then he began: "I suppose I am weak, but it became lonely living like that. You had become a carving, a figure in marble gleaming out of the darkness of some niche in my mind, no more. You weren't real any longer. And I needed reality. I wanted it desperately, and that was when I met . . . I met someone else. . . ."

The wind had hushed itself. There was a stillness about the hillside, and the leaves, and the warm, crumbling soil—a stillness of expectancy. No bee flittered by them, no bird-wing brushed the bronzing foliage. Half-way down the hill, the child was poring over her basket of blackberries. He was conscious of it all being cut into her mind, as lead letters are incised into stone.

"It wasn't love," he said at last; "she knew that. She was a good deal older than I was, and not attractive. It was just that we understood each other, or perhaps we thought we did. She was an actress, terribly afraid of age, and she was getting on. Youth had passed her by and had not given her much fun. Life was passing her by. We had things in common." Then, in a very low voice, "I married her."

Still Maddalan sat there, and her resolute eyes were looking without vision into the distance.

"You mustn't think that it was because I had forgotten you. I had not. I thought that you had forgotten me. We were married last spring."

At last she said in a low, throaty voice, "You are happy?"

He wanted to lie, but the lie stuck fast within him. He felt the loyalty fighting the truth, hand in hand, striking blindly. Now he knew everything, all his future depended on the success of this battle. Should he pretend? He ought to pretend for Belle's sake, but the truth in him was fighting grimly. The words came finally: "I am miserable!" and, shamed, he turned from her. He hid his face close to the earth, among the short, pricking grasses, with the smell of clay and orchids and dead leaves all at once in his nostrils. Life and death blent together in dust! He felt the agony of defeat within his soul, and yet the fierce tumult of an acknowledged and victorious truth. At last her voice, littlish, maternal, the voice of a Madonna, and her lips very softly upon his neck, tenderly kissing the thin hairs:

"Tell me, John, tell me everything."

IV

He told her then, brokenly. He told her of the suffering, the absorbing passion of Belle, and her resentment. Of Les Jefferson, of Belle's attitude to Mrs. Darsy, the dragging down of his soul into the quagmire of her vulgarity. His desperate search for a way out and finding none. He knew that if he were true to himself in this, he could not also be true to Belle. His whole future depended on the truth now. He had to tell her the facts. Long after his voice had died down they sat there in silence. They sat there seeing the world glittering about them burnished with autumn, yet choked in the ashes of their frustrated love. Then she spoke.

"We ought never to see each other again."

"I can't do that, Maddalan. I can't do that. That is the very last thing."

"I don't want to do it either."

"Don't you see that to have found you again is to have found life? I simply can't cut my own throat. There is no going back now."

"It is now or never," she said calmly; "and if we go on, it may lead to anything."

"Not to that again. You can trust me. It wouldn't lead to that again. I promise you faithfully, Maddalan."

"There are other things in the world beside that. Other people beside ourselves."

"I know."

"We ought to think of your wife a little. Would she understand?"

He said, "No," and repeated it, because Belle would be burnt up with hot flames of jealousy—she would never understand.

"We have got to make up our minds. We must say good-bye now, or . . . or go on. . . ."

He took her hands, pressing them flatly against his ribs, holding them there as if to stay his heart-beats. His eyes stared down into hers. "We are going on," he said.

They kissed coldly, as two plaster saints who, standing in a church, desolate images of what once was, turn their faces each to the other. They had arrived at a momentous decision.

"We are going on," she said.

She turned then to the child. "John, I must take you into the village. You must come and be introduced to Carol's people. Her father is the clergyman here. We have all got to know each other. You must do this for my sake."

He agreed that there must be nothing underhand about it. They got up, sweeping the small, broken pieces of grass from their clothes. They went down the hill slowly, because the dry surface was slippery. The child chattered. She was not shy, and held out her basket of blackberries to John invitingly.

"I've got a lot," she said. "See! Maddalan won't let me eat them raw, but I like them, don't you?"

"I love them," he said gravely.

Would a child have helped? Maddalan's child, yes. But never Belle's child.

"Perhaps she will let you eat them," suggested Carol, and held up a fat berry between small, firm fingers stained darkly at the tips, purple with juice.

"That wouldn't be fair," said John, and laughed. He felt to be gaily young at the moment, just as though life had changed. The grim, stern tide of the river had turned him into some pleasant backwater, glittering with sunshine; that was life at the moment.

They talked as they went, the child running in front of them, delighted with every phase of life. They turned in at the Rectory gates, a wide low entrance across an ill-weeded drive. Laurels flanked it, cut back among the blue yews, and beyond stood one of the biggest holly trees that John had ever seen. The holly tree marked the beginning of the lawn, where the Rector, a young man in shirt sleeves, was walking to and fro, pipe in mouth, and pushing a lawn-mower. He stopped abruptly, was in the act of lifting the hood with its burden of short clipped grass, and, seeing them, halted.

"Hello," he said, and then, "what's this?" and advanced towards them. Carol skipped ahead to meet him. He was a pleasant type of man, whom one naturally associated with sport and amusement rather than with the Church. Maddalan led John forward.

"I knew John when I was in Haarlem," she said, "and imagine it, he lives in Condering! We met to-day on the hill. Such a surprise!"

They shook hands across the lawn-mower smelling of green new-cut grass and paint. "Any friend of Maddalan's is welcome here," said Mr. Hunter; "and you must most certainly stay to lunch. Heaven knows what there is to eat. It is always a case of pot luck with us. I hope you won't mind."

"I shan't mind at all."

"You've caught me in a bad moment. I can't afford a gardner, and this grass grows so quickly. I spend a third of my life walking up and down trundling that bally mower. I was trying to count up, and I find that if I stay here until I am seventy I shall have walked some twenty thousand miles. How many years shall I have wasted cutting this perishing lawn? It is a vile thought."

He went on merrily. Life amused him. The day, now mounted high in the sky, was almost overpowering. It beat down on them with much of the fierceness of June, allied with a September maturity. John saw the ray standing out in his life, something predominating, shining as a cameo against the dark background of everyday dullness: young Mr. Hunter troubling over his garden; Mrs. Hunter, large, placid, amiable: Carol. . . .

The Rectory was one of those houses in which you become automatically at home. Wide hall, stone-flagged, a little untidy perhaps, with the friendly untidiness of home. The dining-room on the left with a big open hearth to which comfortable chairs were drawn, dented and impressed by the bodies which sat in them. The drawing-room the other side was more reserved and little used. It boasted lace curtains, furniture that did not match, obvious wedding presents. It was a helter-skelter jumble of a room with no definite plan of decoration about it.

"We don't use him much," said Mrs. Hunter; "we are not the drawing-room sort."

All the while there was Maddalan floating in the background, ever present. When he had awoken this morning in the room above the shop, where Belle slept so heavily and late, he had forgotten Maddalan. Think of it! No, not forgotten her, but she had isolated herself, stepped aside into her niche, and now she was back again living in his life. It had been as a century of emotional nights and days lived since the morning. A century dividing his life. What did he do next? He knew that he must not think. Not now. Later perhaps, when he could whip up his resources, galvanize his efforts, but not now. Nothing should spoil the beauty of this hour.

He sat under the trees with Maddalan and Carol. Cedars, resinously scented, blue-green trees, pines and firs. Mr. Hunter moved up and down the lawn, laughing to them. Mrs. Hunter brought out cake and lemonade and bottled ale, setting the tray on the grass bank, and herself beside it. She was young, but growing a little fatter, threatening *Mevrouw* proportions. Blonde, with Botticelli colouring, and a light voice which John found attractive. She was intrigued with his knowledge of Holland. She had come from Leyden. The three of them sat on the close soft grass, drinking beer and eating homemade cakes, and talking of Leyden. Each saw it through different eyes. Mrs. Hunter saw it as home: the low house with the bright windows, the old Rhine flowing by it, the Hooglandsche Kerk, where Sunday after Sunday she had sat in her pitifully suppressed youth listening to tedious services, and counting the stout Cupids who blew china trumpets about the roof.

To John and Maddalan it was love. It was that day when they had wandered there to see Rembrandt's hill. Day of loveliness, with the old mill as shrine. A day just like this, at the same time of the year. There had been sails, wind-driven at moments, at others bravely four-pointed to the sky. It had been glorious, and, looking back upon it, it had seemed that they had been too young, so young that they had not known how to deal with the immense problem of their love. Now they were older, and, of course, far wiser. Something would have to shape itself, something, but what? For the moment a halt, a truce, an armistice with themselves. For the moment a hostage.

It was so pleasant to sit here on this bank, the three of them, with now and then the leaves blown down like golden curls across the grass, and the faint creaking of pine masts against the sky, as though the trees dreamt of ships. Perhaps, thought John, grown thoughtful in his sentimentality, this was a ship, a ship speeding him out of his destiny. A love ship. . . .

Mr. Hunter pushed the mower disgustedly into a corner and came across to them. "I think it is my turn for a bite and a sup," he said. "It's hot work tootling about with that mower. I shall have to do it all again before the end of the week too." He helped himself generously to cake. "My wife makes good cake. When you marry, you take care to choose a good cook. It goes a dickens of a way."

Something choked within John. Ought he to tell

them now that he was married? He felt the first faint pricking of conscience within him, moistened his lips to speak, and waited too long. The opportunity swam past him on the wings of the moment into the abyss of things lost.

"But then all the Dutch girls are good at housework," said Mr. Hunter joyously; "they do know a thing or two about dusters and frying-pans." His eyes wandered adoringly from his wife's face and across approvingly at Maddalan. "So when you're marrying," he added with a youthful cheeriness, "you'll know where to go. . . ."

Again the moment sped past him. A sick moment, when he felt himself quaking with indecision. Now he knew what Hunter and his wife thought. They believed that he was in love with Maddalan, and they were right! Of course they were right. He could not deny that, and he had no wish to deny it; but would they understand about Belle? Could anybody ever understand? Looking back through his life, he doubted whether he himself understood all the networks of circumstances which had brought this moment about.

Mrs. Hunter gathered up the tray with the cut cake, and the beer bottles like so many ninepins. "Now I'll go and see about lunch," she said.

"Shall I come?" asked Maddalan.

"No. You take your friend round the garden; there is lots for him to see." Mrs. Hunter got up and lifted the tray in her hands, calling Carol. They went towards the house together.

V

It was a walled-in kitchen garden. You entered it by a red wooden gate, and shut it after you with a clang.

Sometimes the latch stuck, making the hearty rasp of iron against brick. Then it shut. They were alone in here, screened by the high wall that surrounded it. They were standing and staring dully at each other in the little avenue of plum trees, gold tendrils adorning their shapely rounded heads. Ahead lay long green rows of potatoes, neat earthed beds, kale growing scraggy on sere and moulting stalks. In one corner the hens paraded glumly the soured, stamped-down earth of their pen. A simple cucumber frame made believe that it was crystal glistening in the sun. It was a little world shut in, away from the others, a little queer world of vegetables and straight paths, smelling acridly of mint growing in profusion beneath the long jade ribbons of horseradish leaves.

"Maddalan, this thing has got to be fought out."

"I know."

"They think I am unmarried. It isn't fair to them, it isn't fair to me, and most of all it isn't fair to you."

She stood before him, her hands on the lapels of his coat. "Don't you see, John, when I came to them I told them that I was looking for someone. I told Mrs. Hunter one day when I was homesick and a little lonely—you know how one gets. They believe we have found each other."

"We have found each other," he said tensely, "only how——"

"Things are difficult, my precious, but they will right themselves. I can trust you," she whispered.

Maddalan, with her little face against his coat; Maddalan, with her soft gold and white loveliness, with her brave eyes.

"I know you trust me," he said, "but I feel that they ought to know. They ought to know that I am married."

"They wouldn't understand."

He said suddenly, poignantly, "Would anybody understand?" The thing was too difficult for that.

"If you tell them they will forbid you the house. It would be the right thing for them to do. They would not countenance an intrigue with a man who was married, and that is what it would seem."

"That is what it may be," he commenced bitterly.

"John, there is some way out of this."

"Yes, but what?"

Supposing he asked Belle to divorce him? Supposing he went to her and told her the truth, what would happen? He had not money enough to induce her to grant him that divorce. She was better off as she was now, and as she was she would choose to remain. He had not been married so long without knowing Belle's true self.

"There must be some way," he said after a while. "Supposing we ran away?"

Her voice was insistent. "No, I could not do that. That would be horrible. I—I feel terribly guilty about that other time. There must be no more mistakes."

They could not think then. Not that day, the first day of reunion after such a long, long separation. Their joy was too keen. They wandered round the orderly kitchen garden; they traced exquisite moats in the pools which lay between the celery trenches; they imagined delightful forests out of the potatoes in their dull rows, the greens in their upstanding starkness. The whole world was lit with the bright candle-flame of their vivid imagination. It was joy, Eden, love!

"Just you and I. No one else matters, at least for to-day," said John.

"An armistice with life," whispered Maddalan, and kissed him under the plum tree preening its golden leaves.

They had lunch in the warm, friendly dining-room, scattered with magazines, the rector's socks rolled up and lying in an open-work basket, with the gleam of natural wool suggesting more intimate underwear. Lunch, which was homely. There was the gay chatter of pleasant conversation. Mr. Hunter presided over the cold beef and laughed at the roast potatoes. Mrs. Hunter superintended the "spotted dog" pudding. Beer was brought up cold from the cellar by a maid. Red Edam cheese cluttered up a too small dish, flanked by biscuits and wide pats of butter. It was all friendly and jolly with a very pleasant intimacy. They were five children playing with life, five carefree, happy children, and Carol was the only sedate one of the party. Aphrodisiac, ambrosia, never common-or-garden beer and cold beef and "spotted dog".

"You must come again," said Mr. Hunter, when the afternoon slipping into dusk suddenly quivered under the bitter tang of frost sweeping through the air. "You must come often. Any friend of Maddalan's is welcome, any friend, and more especially *the* friend," he laughed gaily.

Across the flagged hall, just when John was striving desperately for words with which to explain, came Mrs. Hunter's voice:

"Charles, the man from the village. . . ."

Her face swam out of a dark background of hall. "That baby has arrived. It isn't strong. They want you to go down and christen it."

"Oh Lord!" Mr. Hunter grabbed for a hat out of the hat-rack. "Then you'll have gone before I come back. Babies do this on me quite often. It is a way they have—so trying of them. You'll have gone, but come back again, any time, any day you like. We are informal people, if you don't mind and can take us as you find us. . . ." He went off gaily, quite unaware of the true facts of the case.

"Maddalan walks to the station with you," said Mrs. Hunter, in her pretty imperfect English. "It is the time that I give Carol her music lesson. I teach the music, you know. She hate it. So did I when little. We go so far as *The Joyful Peasant,* and we find him not much joyful."

Maddalan came to him, with her hat secured over her hair; she slipped her hand in his arm.

"Well, good-bye"—from Mrs. Hunter in the doorway; "come back soon. I'm much glad that we met," and then impulsively she crossed the wide step, with the two Georgian pillars holding up the stucco porch. She came gladly, caught Maddalan's face between her hands and kissed her. Turning to John, it seemed that her kind eyes had tears in them. "I'm so glad," she added, and then as hurriedly left them. The door shut.

VI

They walked to the station. The day had grown cold again. There was a chill in the air, *soupçon* of frost. The mist was wrapping the trees once more in shrouds, so that they stood as ghosts along the road. There was the promise of a hot day to-morrow, another sweet day, but never so sweet as this one.

They had not much to say. They were both conscious of a few hours of serene happiness before slipping into the abyss of tide and time. They were both conscious that now they were nearing the precipice of a grave decision. The fading light had sobered the first rush of their emotional enthusiasm.

"I cannot believe that to-day has ever happened," said Maddalan as they approached the sombre station fitted into the dip of the hill. "It has been like that afternoon in the Haarlemmer Hout, something apart, something that never really was."

"It has happened," said John, and then sickly: "oh, Maddalan, it will go on happening. We've got to take tight hold of ourselves or something terrible will happen. I'm afraid."

He stopped, shuddering. She put her arms about

him, solicitous for him. She drew his head down to her own slight shoulder. "You mustn't feel like that. Nothing can happen save of ourselves, and we are strong."

"You don't know Belle."

"I am thinking of Belle. Whatever happens we have got to remain loyal to her. We have got to be wise, John. This thing will take some thinking out."

He felt the innate strength of her in the firm grip of her hand. It was amazing, the life force which throbbed in so fragile a body. For one tense moment they clung together, and he felt the strongly clear flame of her burning and firing his own inner being with strength. Then they heard the shriek of the approaching train bearing down on them out of the darkness. They broke apart and began a little stumbling run towards the station. They had hardly any time. He climbed into a carriage and, leaning over the window, stared down into her upturned face, suddenly conscious of the woman weakness behind her strength. It was the pitifully helpless weakness of all women, the dark background to the flame of their strength.

"You'll come again?" she asked, and her hands reached up to his.

"Of course, quite soon."

Her eyes spoke the words that her lips refused to frame. Behind her was the sordid little station with its one loutish ticket-puncher lolling against the door, picking his teeth with a used ticket, cap set back, staring out unblinking upon their love. There was the ugly, jaundiced glare of a stable lamp, wind-blown against the tender dusk. A limping porter raucously calling to the guard, and out of all this ordinariness Maddalan's face swam out to him, a white and lovely star in a dark hemisphere. Maddalan, her eyes large with fear, her small crushable mouth protesting.

He had time to say, "I love you," which conveyed but one quarter of his meaning, of the surging of his passion, of the terrific sea of emotion pounding against his heartsick soul in giant waves. Useless little words! Little words that did not convey any depth, any profundity. But there were no words left with which to express his feelings, no words, only looks, and actions, drawings down, comminglings, possession. . . .

Her face receding—a star fading before the dawn. The scream of a whistle bringing him back to realities, and the station slipping away. Yellow, guttering light, wind-swayed; loutish ticket-collector still picking his blackened teeth; doors labelled blatantly in blue and white lettering announcing the waiting-rooms of the divided sexes; and against it all her face . . . her darling, white face. . . .

Chapter Four

Let me not know, since happy some have died
Quickly in youth, or quietly in age,
How faint, how loud the bravest hearts have cried. . . .
JAMES ELROY FLECKER

I

HE reasoned with himself as men must reason out such things, and there seemed to be no solution. He wanted to play the straight game, to be honest about this, but he could see no means by which he could be fair to both Belle and Maddalan.

"There's something on your nerves, old chap," said Roy a few days later.

"No, nothing!"

"Oh yes, there is." Roy was joking, jaunty about it, and the thing was desperately urgent. "Did you take my advice and find a 'popsy', or what's the trouble?"

They were facing each other in a corner of the Corn Exchange, where rehearsal was in progress. John had called in to see how the play was going. It was going badly.

"But it is no use talking to you, you aren't listening," said Roy. "I am sure if I had known this blinking play was going to be such a hotbed of chaos I'd never have joined up. The thing is a volcano. It has a crater a mile wide, and it keeps on throwing up all sorts of muck. Everybody is at everybody else's throats."

"Why can't you be reasonable about it?" asked John. "Why can't you all get on together?"

"Get on together, with your wife kicking up such a fuss? I like that!" Roy turned from him contemptuously. "Just you watch, that's all."

John was piloted behind a huddle of wicker baskets and broken kitchen chairs. He sat himself down on a dusty piece of scenery of the woodland variety. On the empty stage, looking peculiarly tawdry and dusty, Belle was rehearsing the last act of the play. The vicar leant against a pile of properties and was surveying the scene in much the same manner as that in which Napoleon is reported to have surveyed the field of Waterloo. Belle, flushed and hostile, was arguing with everybody. She held the centre of the stage in a way which horrified John, and her full attack was being directed on Bert Hickman, who had woefully bungled Sir Brian's part.

"Well, I ought to know," said Belle. "I've been in this business years; know it inside out. Jeff knows it too. If you won't do what we say, you'll regret it. I'll chuck in my hand. The play's mouldy. It wants some pep put into it. It isn't alive; it can't be alive with you all looking like a party of undertakers about to screw down a coffin. This thing is supposed to be a comedy, a farce, not a tragedy."

In a corner Les Jefferson tittered, like some insistent, meaningless bell that has someone leaning inadvertently against its button. Then he made an effort, pulled himself together with that absurd dignity of his, and paraded forward.

"That last scene once more," he said. "Yes, I think we shall have to do it once more from the Lady Rowena's entrance. Now then, Lady Rowena, are you ready? The dean? Ah, not ready?"

The vicar pulled himself together and advanced. Something about his attitude made John feel sorry for him. The whole play was slipping into hopeless jumble. "I think I'd better get out," he said to Roy.

"Now you've seen what it's like. Why don't you take a stick to that wife of yours, John? That's what she wants. Gee, I'd enjoy it."

"I daresay," agreed John, and then with bitterness: "only this thing has got beyond me."

He stumbled out into the street.

II

He never knew why he confided in Mrs. Darsy. Perhaps in some hearts, more particularly those with a feminine complexity, the love of the confessional absorbs and guides their actions. In John's nature there was a strong streak of feminism, and the feminine must ever tell.

He had always felt that something had stood in need of clearing up since he had asked Mrs. Darsy to call on Belle, and Belle had received her so volcanically. He had longed to broach the subject, and yet had been unable to do so, for a certain loyalty had held him back. After all, if a man cannot be loyal to his wife, to whom can he cleave? His wife is part of himself, but he knew now with a cruel certainty that Belle was no part of himself. Looking into his life, he saw it now staring up at him. Belle, who was demanding in passion, and contemptuously hostile in their life together. It was against his wishes that Les Jefferson was here, and that had been a pill that he had not yet swallowed. Jefferson was here, and intended to stay here. He was inescapable.

Now he knew that he had married Belle in an excess of pity, in the madness of one irrevocable moment. Love flowed through his veins again, firing him with desire. There was the ache to love and to be loved. But

Belle was not part of him; it was Maddalan who had always been his true partner. What should he do next?

He found himself telling all this to Mrs. Darsy in her little room tucked away in a corner of the Chantry. He had come in to see her about some furniture that she wanted, and had stayed to tell her this. He had not premeditated the confessional; it had just happened. Perhaps it had been the pleasant intimacy born of the room which had caused him to start—the warm home atmosphere. The fire leapt invitingly in the burnished grate. He saw it across the grey sea of comfortable fur mat. There was a sofa on which he could sit, and opposite to him Mrs. Darsy, understanding, wise with that wisdom of years that have bought and paid for their experience in the hard cash of adventure.

She went on with her knitting. He was glad of that. Somehow it was easier to tell the story to a woman who sat and knitted. At last his voice stopped.

"I—I don't know why I am telling you all this," he ended lamely.

"It is because you trust me. You feel that I can help you, and I'm proud. I want to help you, you know."

"I can't see what comes next in life," he said wearily. "I cannot see what I ought to do."

"I think you ought to leave your wife."

"Leave Belle?" he echoed, amazed.

"Yes, I do. The marriage was a mistake. It ought not to abide. You have never been happy with her, and you never will be. The whole of your story is one of frustration, and the fact predominates that you must abandon your marriage."

"But——"

"No 'buts'. You ought to have married this other girl then; you ought to marry her now, the moment that you are free to do so."

John felt his mouth parch. He stretched an acrid tongue round it. "But how can I get free?"

"That is the point. Belle is one of those women who

would probably refuse you a divorce. On the other hand, it might be tolerably easy to divorce her."

"Oh, I don't think so," said John feebly. "I don't know much about these things, but surely not?"

The world swam round him, a world that came and went in waves. He was a little afraid of it. He was floating into the wide river of his life, and the tide was too strong for him; it was terrifying. He was undergoing all the emotions that he imagined men in peril of their lives must undergo. The horrible consciousness that soon something must snap within him, a dynamo of self that was revolving under titanic pressure but that could not go on like it for long. There would be some weak link, and that would snap; he had no conception where the actual weakness lay, nor what could happen. He was almost sorry that he had met Maddalan again, sorry that she had come back into his life. Perhaps it would have been better if she had remained as a statue in the cool niche of memory, not eventuating into flesh and blood. Flesh and blood! Suddenly he realized how devastating they were.

Opposite to him Mrs. Darsy knitted. She went on, her eyes bent on her silk, and beside her a calendar enumerated the days to be in hard, crude letters. He found himself wondering mechanically if, by the end of the year, the termination of that piece of cardboard, he would be free.

"You can't do anything in a hurry," said Mrs. Darsy; "you must remember that. You have got to think. But I am sure that the right course is for you to leave your wife now."

"I believe you are right," he said humbly, "but I can't do it. I'm horribly weak. There is something that falters within me. I carry a burden well; it is when it comes to putting it down that I make such a hash of things."

She put out her hand, fragile, with a papery skin under which ran the dark tree-like lines of veins; it was the grave hand of experience. "It is your humility that is so charming," she said, "the fact that you cannot help yourself that makes me want to help you. Do let me help you, John."

"You shall," he promised huskily.

III

About every tenth day he made some excuse and slipped to Craye to see Maddalan. Those were exquisite days, those glad, radiant mornings of autumn. It seemed to him that there was something magical about Craye too. Afterwards those days blurred together in his memory; like pages turned too quickly and ill-blotted, they became mottled with confusion. Temporarily he and Maddalan had called a hostage with time. They had as yet no definite plan of campaign, but did that matter? For a while they were content to drift.

These were glad days of amber and claret-coloured leaves, romping in the garden with Carol, or maturely quiet days talking in the meadows wet with the heavy tears of autumn mornings. Always together! Colder days when they knew that the year was riding to the chill, when the first sharp arms of frost clasped the world closer. Then days when there was a glimmer of crystal on the road puddles, when the spiders' webs hung dewy, turned from grey nothingness into a lovely iridescence. They were all changes such as had gladdened the heart of Gerda as she rode ever north on her reindeer. They were riding towards the origin of things, towards crisis, apex. . . . Life spangled and mature was a lovesome thing.

"A halt," he told her—"and after this what will happen?"

"Nothing dreadful can happen as long as we are together," she replied. "Now, looking back, I see the long years between as gap, hiatus, not mattering. . . ."

"Grey years," he agreed, "nothing in them. Meaningless days merging into unimportant nights." Then his arms would creep round her and draw her to him. "There must be something of importance again."

"Yes, like that one exquisite, immortal hour in the dark room. Do you remember?" she asked.

Her fingers, unaware of their actions, were playing in his hair. Stroking down the back of his neck to the nape where the full tide of hair was cut short and only just a few stiff hairs remained. She fingered them caressingly. "Do you remember, John?"

"Remember?" he whispered chokily, and then, "I am afraid to remember. I am afraid to remember how lovely you were, or how wonderful that night was." He felt a pulse throbbing tenderly in his throat, so that he could hardly articulate. "I am afraid of it happening again, Maddalan—so afraid."

"It can't happen again," she promised him, and suddenly her slender, childlike hands became supremely strong. They gripped his arms so that he could feel the support trickling out of her taut fingers, propping him.

"Life is so difficult," he whispered huskily. "It is so easy to be strong when there is no temptation. With us there is temptation. There must always be temptation for people who love."

"I know, and because we know it is easier."

"Oh, Maddalan, it is never easier."

They clung together, these two, with the road winding before them pooled white with ice. At the roadside there was bracken, pale bronze, silvered by frost. The world was old in its year, old as in time the two of them would become. Time has a silvering frost to set upon a man's head, upon his skin, upon his hands. It has a chill cold to clamp down upon his heart, to numb his passions and to choke his instincts. Youth is too swift, maturity speeds by; it is age, stagnant, dissatisfied age, with only the remembrance of what has been, which dallies.

"I want life now, while I'm young," he whispered, recalling this; "I want all the beauty spilled about the world."

"You shall have it," she promised. Maddalan! His love! His Maddalan, ice maiden, with the blown red leaves behind her. He felt the wave of his strength receding a little. A breaker that had swept demandingly over him and left him the cooler for her brave perception.

"That's better," she said.

"You are so strong, my dear, so strong, so precious. How did we ever manage to live apart?"

"We didn't live," she explained; "we existed. The two things are not the same, John, not at all the same. Half the world exists, few really live."

"We cannot go on like this, drifting. . . ."

"Something will shape the course," she told him.

After seeing her he would always return determined to face Belle with the truth, but the truth refused to embody itself in expressions. Belle was preoccupied with Les and the theatricals. The vicar had retired with dignity, and refused to be associated with the affair any longer. He complained that rehearsal was degenerating into a brawl. John tried to reason with Belle, he tried to persuade Jefferson to reason with her, but they ignored him. Life was a triangle—whichever way you turned it round, whichever way you looked, there was still one of them at each corner.

"Oh, Belle," he implored her, "do try and let the play go on without any further fuss."

"Fuss?" she retorted. "Who do you think wants a fuss? I'm sure I don't, but I'm not going to be put upon by a lot of potty people who think they know what's what when they don't. Somebody has got to stand up to them, and the somebody's Jeff and me. We're doing the standing up all right."

Across the table where they were supping, Jeff nodded. "Belle is a wonder," he said; "don't know where we should be without her. Isn't she the only piece of pep in the piece? Of course she is."

"Don't you see," John asked, "you are losing my friends for me? You may not bother about friendships, because that only hurts me, but if you offend all my customers you will hurt yourself, and that will matter."

Belle sneered a little. "A damned lot of customers they are," she said. "The only thing old Atkins ever bought here was that coffin stool, and then he brought it back and said he had paid too much for it. Pleasant sort of customer to have, I must say."

"Well, it matters to me," said John, and he drew the cheese-dish closer, trying to assume an attitude of indifference.

"You are a darned sight too mealy-mouthed," said Belle; "so smug and respectable. I can't stick it."

Jeff shot out a shaky hand and gripped the decanter by its neck. There was something about the sight of the crystal tube in Jeff's clawlike grasp which irritated John.

"I put up with your friends," he said darkly, "I don't see why you shouldn't put up with mine."

Belle dropped her knife with a clatter. She pushed her chair back raspingly from the table. "Oh!" she said, and then again, "Oh! Hear that, Jeff? Hear that? That was meant for you. I suppose," she challenged John, "you want Jeff to leave?"

It was a difficult moment with Les Jefferson leering at him across the table, his hand still on the throat of the decanter. "I don't want him to stay here indefinitely," John admitted.

He felt himself to be cold with sweat. He could not stand scenes; they scraped him all raw, and made him want to shrink away. Before a third person too! He felt himself shudder.

"Well, I tell you this, right here, now," said Belle,

"Jeff is staying as long as I choose. He's my friend, and I've got few enough friends, heaven knows, in this stuffy, one-eyed town. Now you know."

Jefferson drew the decanter towards him, rattled the stopper free, and poured out a generous helping.

"Then," said John, though still showing fight, "it isn't my house any longer. You're running it."

She settled herself heavily into the chair again. "I am doing what I think is right and proper. I don't see why I shouldn't. We are married, aren't we? What's yours is mine. Jeff's staying."

John felt rising within him an impotent desire to strike her. A longing to set his hand at her throat, feel the flesh growing bruised to pulpiness beneath his fingers. He felt the desire, acute, insane, surging within him, and was appalled at its keenness.

The clock ticked away the moment of opportunity. From under his lids he saw the joss smiling imperturbably from the opposite shelf. "Poor fool," the slotted eyes seemed to say in pity; "weak fool. . . ."

IV

More days with Maddalan, happy days at Craye. The weather was too cold to be out of doors much, for the frosts had come early, so that they were in the house, in the comfortable, friendly house, with the well-used, intimate furniture, and the general air of homeliness everywhere. Mr. and Mrs. Hunter found all manner of excuses for leaving the two of them together. Carol was whisked out of the way. These two were accepted as lovers, they met as lovers. For a time love had called a truce with life. It might be a dream while it lasted, but for the moment each was glad to bask in the beauty of it.

"Maddalan is getting the bottom drawer ready," Mrs. Hunter purred over the tea table: "It is the time, too."

"I don't believe in long engagements," announced Mr. Hunter; "we married in penury and didn't care two hoots. Carol came along in the first year, and we were just gloriously happy. Nothing seemed to matter, though heaven only knew how I should get a pair of new boots."

"We have not the regret," explained his wife.

"Of course we haven't. A little effort doesn't hurt a couple. We knew our own minds. John and Maddalan know their own minds."

Across the table John's eyes met Maddalan's miserably. He knew that he ought to tell the truth. The Hunters were kindly, trusting people, who had accepted him in good faith, and whose very credence he was betraying. He ought to shatter their illusions, and he had not the heart. Just a little longer, he told himself, just a little longer; after that destiny will shape the course. Everything will be easier to-morrow; do not hinder the happiness of to-day, he warned himself.

A week later Destiny stepped into the breach.

Maddalan came down to the station to see him off. They were early for the train, and walked slowly, arms intertwined. It was a crisp bright night, luminous with star eyes peering incuriously down upon them; a lovely night when later, in the small hours, a shattering frost would spangle the world with cruelly brilliant scintillations. They talked of that other night, until they were no longer walking together down this simple English road but were back in the dark-panelled room, with the music of the *gracht* in arpeggios of sound without.

A car coming from behind them picked them up in its lights, and, expecting them to move, approached nearer. They were so occupied with each other and the ineffable sweetness of those memories that they did not hear it until, when close to them, a hooter warned them. They sprang apart and turned, facing the car. There was the jangled grinding of brakes, and it jerked to a standstill.

"Now what's up!" thought John. It was Roy who leant out towards him.

"Upon my soul!" said Roy, and his face was crinkled with suppressed laughter. "If this isn't a go! I thought it was some village lover and his lass. You. . . ."

Maddalan came round to John's side. She stared into Roy's face; John saw him look back at her. Somehow he sensed the loveliness of Maddalan soaking in upon Roy's rather usual intelligence. Roy, who had expected some painted harlot, suddenly brought face to face with Maddalan. He gave a gasp, drew back his head and, pressing on the accelerator, the car leapt forward again.

"Who was he?" she asked.

"His name is Roy. He is a friend of mine."

"Will he tell?"

"No. To-morrow I'll warn him. Of course he won't tell. He is sporting enough for that."

She came closer, laying her hand on either side his rough overcoat, staring up at him with mildly protesting eyes. "John, I'm frightened, frightened. Something is going to happen to us. These days have been too sweet to last. Something awful is going to happen."

"Nothing can hurt us, my dear," he whispered, "save our own selves. Nothing can come between us. Nothing."

He could feel her quivering, and drew her lips up to his, to find her chilly. As he kissed her he heard the distant thunder of the approaching train. The noise of it was sharpened into pistol-shots by the frosty air.

"I'll have to go," he said.

V

Two miles out of Condering Roy encountered Belle and Mr. Jefferson. They had been out to tea at a well-known local hotel, which gave an affair described as a "tea dance" twice weekly. They had left it a little late, and, having missed their train, were walking home. Roy, seeing them, slowed the car down. His sole companion was Bert Hickman, whom he was finding dull enough, but since the theatricals he and Bert had been thrown together a good deal. Bert Hickman was the only son of wealthy parents, who had spoilt him sadly in his extreme youth. Roy had taken him out on occasions when he could not possibly avoid the obligation, but he always did so protestingly. This time Mr. Hickman had urged it. Mr. Hickman was an amiable old josser, in Roy's terms, and he had the finest cellar of brandy in the city. Roy had no wish to fall foul of Mr. Hickman and thereby to jeopardize his chance of further sippings of the very excellent brandy. He had taken Bert, but he was bored with him, bored stiff with him. Lout of a fellow, thought Roy, cad of a fellow! Great oaf!

He slowed the car down. "Hullo, you two," he called. "Want a lift? It's a pretty nippy night."

Belle climbed into the back with Bert. "And serve him right. Just what he has deserved all along," thought Roy, until he realized that Les Jefferson would have to sit down beside himself. The car purred forward.

Bert felt himself under the painful necessity of making conversation with Belle. He delved into the poor resources of his small brain for a thread of an idea, found the only available one, and fished it up into the light.

"You're the second member of your family we've seen to-night," he said graciously.

"John?" enquired Belle. She was amiable and condescending, because she had been glad of the lift. The tea dance had proved itself to be a fiasco, and her feet hurt. She had not relished the idea of walking home with Jeff. "John went this morning to Salingwood. There was a big auction there."

"Ah!" said Bert, and he wagged a finger at her. "Ah, that's what you think! We saw John at Craye, and he was not alone."

If he could have seen Belle's face he would have become aware of a leaden hue that spread itself over her features, like an ugly pall.

"What fun!" she said, with a painful suggestion of mirth. It was the only way to draw Bert, and she was clever enough to know it. Belle understood human nature. Her life had been one long and dreadful experience of human nature, of gauging the susceptibilities of managers, of understanding the pretences of landladies, delving into petty meannesses, seeing through the cheap veneer of humanity. She was impregnated with suspicions, eternally conscious of the hand of fate against her. Now suddenly, starkly, she was conscious of it fighting against her again. She would find out! Oh yes, she would find out!

Bert was too feeble-brained to realize the volcanic nature of the land on which he was treading. He swallowed Belle's assurance that if he would tell her everything they could play some enormously amusing practical joke on the luckless John. The idea intrigued him. Gladly he confided the truth in Belle.

"Frightfully funny! We saw two people standing in the middle of the road, arms about each other, kissing, you know. . . ."

"I know," said Belle grimly.

"They never heard us until we got close, and then they fairly leapt apart. Roy stopped the car because he recognized him. I didn't. Lord, it was funny!"

"But the girl," said Belle impatiently—"who was the girl?"

"Never set eyes on her before. A very pretty girl; looked foreign. Poor old John," and he tittered, "he didn't know what to make of it."

Belle pulled herself together with an effort. "Ah yes," she said, and she forced a laugh, "poor old John—very funny that! Poor old John."

From the wheel Roy called over his shoulder. "All right you two at the back?"

"Rather!" from Bert.

"Right as John was when you met him just now," remarked Belle loudly, and laughed in a forced fashion at the joke.

The car skidded violently. Roy slowed down, tried to regain his hold, and went on solemnly. He felt suspicion pricking him to action. "What's that about John?" he demanded over his shoulder.

"Oh, I know all about it," chuckled Belle. "Very funny! I know all about it. Bert told me. You met him."

"We did *not* meet him." Roy brought the car to a standstill, suddenly aware of what had occurred. "What the dickens has Bert been burbling about? The man we met was an entire stranger. He asked me to tell him the way. You know he asked me the way, Bert."

"Ye-es," commented Bert.

Roy wheeled round sharply. "You see, Belle, he's been pulling your leg."

The stream of traffic sped past; ribbons of gold from the headlights lit the road ahead. The first lamps of the city were behind Roy, and Belle could not see his face.

"I don't believe you," she said.

"Well, it's true."

"What's all this?" asked Jeff. "Time we were getting

home. Quite time. I'm chilled to the bone. Could do with a glass of something warm, could I not? Of course I could."

"Don't you believe a word Bert tells you," Roy warned Belle, and slowly they mounted the North Hill and stopped at the door.

"Well?" said Belle from the pavement.

He thought that she looked queerly old, pinched, as though the hand of senility were already laid arrestingly on her heavy shoulders. She did not ask him in. She did not even thank him for the lift.

"We . . . we must be getting along," said Roy, and he eyed her furtively. She came closer, lurching a little, and the yellow headlights showed that her eyes were hard.

"About John?"

"It was a leg-haul."

He hoped desperately that she believed him; he had been dismally conscious of the effort at truth strained in his voice. She turned contemptuously.

"You're a damned dirty little liar," she sneered.

VI

They heard the door clang on her and Jeff.

"Now," said Roy grimly, "we must go straight to the station and catch John and warn him. You see what you've done, you blasted young fool."

"But it *was* John," quavered Bert from the back.

"Was John? Of course if was John—poor devil. If you were married to that infernal woman, you'd do the same thing. What did you want to tell her for, you filthy little cad?"

The car jarred sharply down the hill as he set his foot on the clutch; his shaky hands turned the wheel abruptly to the right. They took the corner far too abruptly, for the frost-bound road was treacherous. The car skidded out of his control, swerved violently and came into clattering contact with a milk-cart which had been standing beside the pavement. There was the sudden screeching of brakes allied to the kettle-drum clank of milk-cans, a sound like a death rattle as the car shuddered itself to a full stop.

"Oh hell!" said Roy.

He sprang out; Bert lumbered after him. People appeared from nowhere, urged from all quarters in that strangely stream-like manner in which people swarm to the scene of any accident. The horse was hurt. A policeman came and took laborious notes. Hostile faces glared at Roy, idiotic questions were catapulted at him. In vain did he murmur about catching a train; the police constable was determined that no train should be caught. Roy knew the law too well to risk impatience or flippancy; he knew that neither would help him. Finally, when able, he climbed back into the car only to find that something had gone wrong with it and it refused to start.

"The garage, sir?" suggested the policeman.

It took further time getting to the garage and leaving the car with the mechanics there. Finally, when he and Bert rushed into the station yard it was only to find that the train had come and gone again.

"Now what do we do?" demanded Roy, and he was getting furious with himself and life in general, and more particularly furious with Bert. "If we follow him home, we shall burst in upon a family row. It is too late to warn him."

"Telephone," suggested Bert.

It was the first bright idea that he had put forward. Roy blundered into the station telephone box, ill lit, and suffocating with unhealthy air. His hands were numb with cold and he could not find the necessary knobs. "Hell!" said Roy. "This all comes of bringing that damned fool out with me," as he fumbled about and tried to attract the attention of the exchange. "Oh hell. . . ."

"Number, please?" enquired a cold voice from the other end. He gave the number. He inserted the pennies and listened to the sound of their fall like pistol-shots close to his ear.

"Hullo!" he said.

A woman's voice. Belle. 'Blast!' he thought to himself. "Who are you wanting?" she enquired.

"Mr. Carrick, please."

"He's not in. Who is it?"

"Thanks."

He crashed the receiver down. John wasn't back yet. Hope rose once more in his breast. He dashed out and seized Bert by the arm. "He's not home yet. Let's sprint up the hill and perhaps we'll overtake him. We've got to do something to put this thing right."

They went up the hill. They could see dim lights reflected in the garden of the house, but nothing more. Perhaps he was coming by a later train. They waited two solid hours, with the cold numbing their hands and feet and gnawing at their hearts. They waited until a suspiciously-minded policeman seemed to be taking an unwelcome interest in them.

Finally they gave it up. John had apparently not come home at all.

VII

But John had caught the train, and had jogged peacefully onwards in his sublime innocence towards Condering. He had got out at the big station echoing with the sharp chatter of people's feet, and had walked quickly homewards. The night was far too cold to brook delay. His latch-key rattled into his lock. In the back room Belle was sitting, her chair drawn up to the fire, reading the evening paper and eating chocolates out of an imposing-looking box. He hung up his coat and hat, and drew close to the fire, slapping his hands stiffly together to promote circulation. Then, as he drew nearer, he saw that Belle was not reading at all—she was watching him from under her heavy-lidded eyes. When he first realized what was happening, a vague uneasiness assailed him. He said:

"It's a bit sharp to-night," and stood against the fireplace, putting out his feet one by one to warm.

"Yes." She seemed lethargic. Unusual for Belle. "Where have you been?" she asked.

"I went to that sale. Poor sort of affair. I bought nothing."

"You came home through Craye?"

His eyes turned; stared at her; his mouth opened to deny it, and then closed again. Why throw a few more useless lies on to the smouldering pyre of his own burning? He had no use for falsehoods at the best of times. Did she know? He could not be certain.

"You came back through Craye, didn't you?" she demanded a little more loudly.

"Yes."

"With that girl?"

He used the old foolish evasion that all men use, realizing in his utter helplessness that it was hoary with age and dotage. "With what girl?"

Belle flung down the paper. She tipped forward on her chair, setting clenched fists on either knee. "You think I don't know? You think I'm a poor fool to be tormented and teased and bamboozled? Well, you are wrong. You're a damned liar, and I know it. I know all about you."

"There isn't anything to know."

"Nothing to know!" She turned from him contemptuously, and then back again. "Nothing to know! Oh, my God! Going off when my back is turned, and canoodling in back lanes with some fancy woman. Isn't that something to know?"

"Belle, you've got it all wrong. Somebody has been telling you things."

"Yes, somebody *has* been telling me things. Poor fool, he didn't mean it. It just slipped out, and he was such an ass he couldn't hold it back. I've been suspecting it for some time, and now I've found out."

She glared at him, nodding in ugly triumph. He was horrified that he could not feel ashamed, because in a sense he was glad that this had happened. The drifting has been delicious, a wild delirium of emotion, but underlying it all had been the knowledge that sooner or later discovery was inevitable. Some crisis must shape their course. They could not have gone on lying and scheming; truth had to assert itself. He was glad that Belle knew. "I want to talk this thing out," he said.

"I want to talk it out too"—her tone was grim. She realized with an innate craftiness that if she could restrain the desire to let fly the full fusillade of her attack she might find out more. She wanted to find out more. At present she did not know the girl's name, and she must know that. "Supposing you tell me from the beginning?" she suggested cunningly.

He had not supposed that she would be so easy about it. Only too gladly he began at the beginning, eager to make a clean breast of it. "I met her in Holland that time. Stayed in the same house. We fell in love at first sight. She had a mother who hated the idea of her marrying, and finally one night she came upon us, and . . . and she turned me out."

"What were you doing?" asked Belle coldly.

He shot her a frantic glance. He wanted the truth. He wanted the truth badly, because he believed it to be the only masthead to which he could satisfactorily nail his flag. "We were in love," he said simply. Boggling at truth, evading it. He hated himself, but he could not tell her the fact. She would not understand.

Belle choked a little. "Once," she said, and her face was mottled, "you told me that there had never been any other woman in your life, yet you solemnly stand there and tell me that the mother turned you out for sleeping with her daughter. You——"

"It wasn't that . . . not that," he besought, and his tongue clove sickly to the roof of his mouth. It was that. Of course it was that really, only it hadn't seemed the same to him then. Now he visualized Belle churning up mud with her large and capable hands and flinging it at Maddalan's virgin whiteness. The difficulties of it all beset him. It was horrible.

They stopped to stare into each other's eyes. Into the silence jarred the telephone. Instantly she went to it, took it down and set her lips to the mouthpiece.

"Who are you wanting? He's not in. Who is it?" No reply, and she hung the receiver on its hook.

"Was that call for me?" he asked.

"Yes, and what of it?"

"I have come in. Somebody may want me."

"Well, they'll damned well have to go on wanting, that's all. Tell me more. Your story interests me." She sat down on the chair again, pulpy, blowzy, her resentful eyes staring purposefully at him.

"Belle, I ought to have married her then, but I didn't. I was a fool. The *Mevrouw* kept the letters back. We were lost to each other."

"She was too much of a fool to file her affiliation order, I suppose."

He threw up his hands, clutching rather wildly at his hair. He felt as drowning people feel when they reach up for a hold on something, weed, tree, rushes, trembling bough—anything to constitute a hold on life to them. "Don't, Belle, don't throw mud at her. It wasn't like that. I tell you it wasn't like that at all."

"Wasn't it?" She spewed sneering contempt on him.

"Wasn't it? I know what it was like. I've done it myself long before you knew me. I know what it was like. Only you wish to make mine seem sordid and your own beautiful. I suppose she was a little short of cash and you were a rich man, eh?"

"Don't!" The word clipped out sharply. Across the room he saw the joss grinning. Sardonic thing. A melodramatic desire rushed through him, setting his cold blood racing. It was the desire to fling the joss at her, hit her, maim her, but to silence her—anything, even death to command her silence. "It was the only beautiful thing in my life, and you shan't sully it. I thought she had forgotten me, and I came here. I married you. We never pretended that it was love, Belle, at least we were brave enough and truthful enough for that. It hasn't been very successful, and you've felt that too. The other day I met her again. She did not know that I was married. She is governess to a family at Craye, and I have been seeing her, trying to think out some plan."

"They know that you are married?"

"No, they don't know anything about that. There hasn't seemed to be a plan possible, nothing at all. Only this one, Belle: you will have to divorce me."

She stared at him sullenly, silent for a long while. When she spoke it was in the tone of someone still weighing the pros and cons. "If I divorce you I shall be entitled to a third of your income."

"Anything you wish."

"I am better off as I am. Besides, I don't want to lose my husband. I don't see why I should hand him over to the first little harlot who takes a fancy to him."

"She wasn't that," he flashed, and he felt the itching, consuming fire within him.

"She was a pretty good imitation." She rose slowly, as an old bitch-wolf draws herself up on stiff haunches. Her face was sharp, treacherous, bitch-wolf too! It seemed to him that she would never have done drawing her stiff body out of the chair. The pulpy flesh. Belle, with the seal of age on her, loose mouthed, sensuous, hard eyes. "You've left me to commit adultery with this woman. . . ."

"I haven't; there has been nothing like that between us."

"There was once."

"I wasn't married then," he protested.

"As if that made any difference! As if that ever changed any fellow! You can't kid me. I knew it, you poor fool. You think I am going to set you free, let you go unscathed. Well, I'm not. The sooner you know it the better. I'm not going to help you. I'm going to have the last farthing out of you, and even then I'll keep you tied to me. But I'll make it hot for her—dirty little cat! I'll wring her filthy neck, you'll see."

He heard her breath coming in pants. Then there sounded his voice, far off, jerky. "If you do anything to Maddalan, I'll kill you, Belle. You mayn't believe me, but don't try me too far."

"Fool!" she shrieked. "How dare you threaten me? Fool!"

"Be quiet," he said, and his tone might be smooth, yet it was as sharp as a razor-edge; it cut. His eyes slotted. Something in him rose. He could feel the titanic force of that something welling up within his being, grown bigger than he was. "By Jove, I shall kill her in a moment," he thought to himself; "there's a brute in me which won't stand much more. . . ."

"Be damned to you," she said, and struck him with her flat hand full across the face. He felt the sharp sting of it, swift hand on flesh. It struck down into his heart, curled there like a whip lash, and for a moment he saw a hundred confused red devils dancing in a dark pain before him. When he recovered she had flung herself from the room.

END OF PART THREE

PART FOUR
Pack Mule

Chapter One

That still, despite the distance and the dark,
What was, again will be.

ROBERT BROWNING

I

EVENTS, quick relentless whirl of events, spinning round and round in the diabolical circles which formed the tide that was his life. Bewildering, remorseless, inescapable events. . . .

He slept that night on the sofa in the sitting-room. He remembered it but dimly afterwards, and in that sleep he was tormented by the pattering feet of a toiling mule, struggling up and down a hilly road, burdened by its load. He was tormented by the woman who had struck him. In and out of the haunting, mocking nightmare there darted a brute who had lived all along in his mulish heart and demanded expression. What would the brute do if he allowed it out? He did not know. He did not care much, not now. But he must protect Maddalan. The only thing that mattered in life was Maddalan.

Morning crept greyly through the window, with all its disillusion, all its discernment, all its terrible preaching of caution. The caution of the morning is responsible for more woe than the illusion of the night. At night he could be brave, he could do things, but morning was chilly. He epitomized his life as a triangle, and at each of its corners stood one of them: he, Belle and Maddalan.

Mrs. Barnes came early. He heard her key shuffled into the lock, the clatter of kettles, the plop of gas, and the general stampede in the small kitchen. When she came in and saw him lying on the sofa before a dead fire, she expressed surprise.

"Well now, if this doesn't beat the band!" she declared, and added to herself, "my word, you've had a fine old shineup, ho yes!"

John went to the Chantry for breakfast. When he returned to the shop, Jeff was eating an enormous meal in the back room, entirely alone. He informed John that Belle had gone out. Jeff was unshaven. He was in possession of John's morning paper, clawing out with emaciated hands to help himself plentifully to toast and marmalade. Jeff feigning a Sherlock Holmes cult, in a cheap dressing-gown of art silk grown thready with use. His hollow eyes glittered like hazy lamps in the sunken caverns of sockets. "The oily beast knows a thing or two," John thought, "and the sly devil won't tell."

"Where's she gone?" he asked.

"Gone? How should I know? Of course I should not know. Mysterious are thy ways, oh Charmer!"

"What did she say?"

"She said nothing at all. Do see if Mrs. Barnes has another egg. I could fancy one lightly boiled, just two and a half minutes, not a full three. My digestion is not what it once was. Alas, none of us grow younger."

John did not move. "I shall ask Mrs. Barnes nothing of the kind, and you will do without the egg. There's your breakfast. If it isn't good enough go elsewhere. Go to hell for all I care."

Les Jefferson made a little gesture of indifference. It seemed to be a matter of unconcern to him whether he went to hell or not. "My dear sir," he explained amiably, "you are not quite yourself this morning. Not quite yourself. The best thing is to say no more."

"I am entirely myself. Where did Belle go?"

"That I do *not* know." With amazing innocence Jeff looked up from liberally buttering his toast. "Why should I know? Am I thy wife's keeper?"

John blundered out of the room. He felt that incidents and speeches were swimming about him, driftwood on the tempestuous sea in which his better self was drowning. He was busy with customers most of the morning; business was brighter and it kept him from thinking. Mr. Atkins came in about a William and Mary table.

"My dear wife has a William and Mary complex," he explained, "and I thought I'd give her a little birthday present. Now that is charming, most charming . . . the price?"

"Twelve guineas," said John.

"Ah!" The vicar ran a meditative finger along the gleaming surface of a rounded edge. He viewed it thoughtfully. "I had thought about eight," he murmured apologetically.

"That is exactly what I paid for it at a sale," said John, "when it was in vile condition. It had to be done up, and that cost a great deal. The workshops are expensive, you know. Then there is my profit."

"Oh, but come, four pounds is a large profit," beamed the vicar remonstratively, "isn't it?"

"The workshops cost over two. There was a lot to be done. They don't give their services." He felt that in a moment he would snap. He did not want to be rude, but he was not at his best, and the haggling irritated him.

"No, no, certainly not, of course not." Again the fat meditative finger thoughtfully ran along the rounded edge. John was thinking, "Where can Belle have gone? What the devil is she doing?" They stood there sheepishly. "Well, supposing I offer you ten?" said Mr. Atkins at last with the air of someone conferring a gracious favour. "That is two pounds more than I meant to pay."

"And two pounds less than I mean to take."

"Ah!" the vicar drew down the corners of his mouth. "Very unfortunate, and such a charming little table. Still, one must not be extravagant." He buttoned his worn coat closer. "Ah well, I suppose I shall have to wait until I'm a dean."

"I hope that won't be long," commented John with the politeness expected of him. He was saying to himself, "Damn him, I hope he'll never be a dean. What the devil is Belle up to?"

But Mr. Atkins, busily drawing on his neat woollen gloves, was not prepared to let it go so easily. "If you should change your mind . . ."

"I can't, I'm afraid. It isn't that I want to rob you; the table is a good piece and well worth the money. Honestly, it is not a fancy price for it. It cost me over ten."

"Yes, yes, of course. But if you *do* change your mind . . . " He moved towards the door, the thin sunshine lighting up the grease-spots on his frayed old coat. "Thank God he's going, and why the devil doesn't he buy himself a bib?" thought John. But on the step Mr. Atkins turned round benignly.

"I am keeping your pew warm for you, you know," he explained. "Quite a brief service, nothing dull or boring. Bright singing, and all that sort of thing . . . a welcome for everyone. . . ."

"One of these days," promised John vaguely.

"There is no time like the present," said Mr. Atkins, tapping him with a suggestion of familiarity on the chest. "No time like the present. I shall be looking for you next Sunday. Now don't forget it, mark it down. Next Sunday! A red-letter day in both our lives."

It was doubtful if even then he would have gone save that an extremely fat lady, a stranger to Condering, was trying to edge her way in. He had to stand aside for her. The fat lady was interested in a tallboy. She wore an expensive coat and she seemed to have a mania for French polish. She did not impress John. When she had gone a boy came about some china that John had bought the week before, and which had been improperly packed. He had little time to think clearly until lunch time, when Mrs. Barnes called him in, and he found Jeff still alone in the sitting-room. Then the gusts of thought which had blown through his mind at intervals all the morning became steady hurricane. Panic gripped him.

He thought of suicide as affording the explanation. Most people think of suicide, though it is habitually the wrong solution. John banished it at once, knowing that Belle was too fond of life. He thought that she might have gone to Mr. Atkins, but again banished it as a stupid idea, seeing that she hated Mr. Atkins, and that the vicar himself had been in the shop that morning urbanely drivelling, with no hint of any message from Belle.

John thought bewilderedly, and whilst he was turning it over in his mind over the cold beef and pickles, with Jeff watching him like one of the birds of prey, a gaunt vulture with beady eyes set too closely against his hooked nose, Roy burst in. Roy came in upon the two of them without any warning. He was obviously disturbed.

"Well," he said, "you have got back then? I rang you up last night, tried to get to the station to meet you, waited outside the house for two damned long hours, with that fool Bert. . . ."

"Oh."

"Where's Belle?"

"God knows. I don't."

Roy came round the table to him, stood beside him making queer little indented patterns on the white tablecloth with his thumb-nail. "John, I must speak to you alone."

"Come into the shop."

They went across the room with the humpy floor side by side. They saw Les Jefferson staring after them with that evil, birdlike smile of his. John thought bitterly, "He's the sort of beastly thing you'd see flying over a desert, emaciated, cadaverous, smelling death out a mile off. Hovering above it, then swooping down to peck out a dead man's eyes! Ugh!" Inside the shop he turned to Roy. "A —— mess you've landed me in for."

"I know. That blasted fool Bert did it. I could have killed him. I tried to get to the station to stop you, and ran into a milk-cart. By the bye, I'm up before the Bench on Wednesday, for the horse has died. When I rang up, Belle said you hadn't come home. I made Bert take up his stand with me outside the house for two solid hours. Two solid hours, I tell you, in last night's frost! Our feet stuck to the pavement. I hope his are frostbitten and that they drop off."

"I was in here all the time."

"I know. That wife of yours had me. Now where is she?"

"I can't think."

"Then she's up to no good. There is no such luck as her running away from you. She's up to mischief. I suppose you didn't tell her the girl's name?"

"I'm not the fool I look." They stood there in the dark shop, lit only by filaments of thin sunshine. Then suddenly it dawned on John what might have happened. Belle knew that Maddalan was at Craye, that she was Dutch, and a governess. Craye was a small village, twelve labourers' cottages, a couple of farms, a school, a church, a rectory. He became rigid. "Lord, she might be there!" he said.

"There? Of course she's there. Belle mustn't get at the girl whatever happens. We must get over there as fast as possible, and that confounded car of mine is out of action."

"We'll hire."

"I know: I'll get the garage to loan me a car and drive you over."

"Yes, of course."

They went out of the shop together into the street beyond.

II

They sped along the road to Craye. Progress was difficult, for the surface was not to be treated with contempt. They skidded here and there down narrow lanes. They hardly spoke to each other. Finally the car drew up with a slither outside the Rectory gate.

"I expect she's here," said John bitterly.

"I expect she's gone. She'll have done the damage by this time. I know her kind." Roy wrapped a rug closer about himself. "I'll wait for you, old chap."

"You're a sport."

As he got out, Roy leant across the wheel to him. "I'm damned sorry about this. It is, in a sense, my fault. I ought not to have trusted Bert. You know I'll do anything I can to help."

"I know."

Handclasp of a friend in the dark and gloomy night. He felt it set his pulses quivering; something stung his eyelids, as in his infancy he had felt the smart of tears. The moment passed.

He went inside the Rectory gate. The garden seemed to be tensely still. The holly tree stood a dark hulk against the dull sky. The day had clouded over, and a rime or rain was coming up. You could not tell which. John stood on the mat and rang the bell. The echo of it came out to him, with the same metallic, joyless tinkle that the echo gives in a dead house. He thought to himself "Something dreadful has happened here, and I don't know what it is."

Presently the maid came, smiled at him in pleasant recognition, and ushered him into the drawing-room. He would have rather that it had been the dining-room, for that was more intimate, more kindly. This room was not lived in. It had not shaped its atmosphere to the conditions and kindlinesses of the people who dwelt in the house. Their personalities had not flowed about it. It was a prim room, furnished by jangling furniture of odd and unfriendly periods. In the corner stood a broken wireless cabinet, alongside the piano on which Carol played *The Joyful Peasant* with such joyless care. He sat down on the sofa with its starched muslin cushions laid out like gospel cushions on either side a velvet-hung altar. He felt now that he was standing on the edge of a volcano, peering down into the crater; at any moment it might erupt. The crisis was hemming him in, and in a sense he was glad that it had come about. He was glad that this was the moment of action after weeks of indecision. His pulse pricked hard in him.

The door opened and Mr. Hunter came in. As he entered John knew that he was no longer the merry fellow whom John had known before. He was a new man, grave, uncomfortable. His atmosphere was almost formidable.

"You wanted to speak to me?" he said.

Gone was the *bonne camaraderie*, the "hail-fellow-well-met". John felt something crumple within him. He experienced all the whimpering wretchedness of a child who desires to be pardoned. He wanted to stretch out his hands and to say, "Whatever I've done, don't be like this to me. I haven't been so bad really." Instead, he said, "How's Maddalan?"

"She's packing her things."

Then it had happened! The volcano had shot up. The boomerang had left his hand in youth, whirled the full circle, and returned straight to his own heart to kill! He gulped wretchedly, "Belle's been here?"

"Yes, Mrs. Carrick has been here."

Mr. Hunter staring at him, calmly listening to him, his misunderstanding eyes quite cold. Assessing him, piling up his sins high against him. Mr. Hunter thinking of John as being debauched, filthy, soiled. And, worse still, thinking of Maddalan in the same way.

"I want to tell you everything," said John, and his voice had become tinny with despair. He told. He told the man in that alien room, with its too clean cushions still reminding him of some strange altar decked out for Eucharist, but with no true Eucharist to offer. He told him of his love for Maddalan in Holland, of his return and his mistaken marriage to Belle. Of the subsequent meeting with Maddalan at Craye. All the while he realized by Mr. Hunter's face that Belle had made good her story first. That she had been here and laid her subtle poisons against him, and that her poisons had been absorbed. He ended his story brokenly. It was sincere with truth, it echoed of human nature, but like all truth it sounded artificial on poisoned ears. There was silence. At last Mr. Hunter spoke.

"I'm sorry for you," he said. "I don't suppose you will believe it, but I am extremely sorry for both of you. The fact that I am sorry, though, does not justify me in keeping her here. You deliberately deceived me. You know I should never have sanctioned your meeting as you did, had I known that you were married."

"I knew. I meant to tell you."

"But you didn't tell me. Why didn't you tell me? Because you knew that I should put my foot down. It was immoral, it was extremely wrong of you."

"There was nothing immoral in it," John declared, and he knew that his eyes were growing hard—"nothing at all."

"It was grossly unfair to your wife. She came here today, and she was most upset. Poor thing! I could not help but be intensely sorry for her."

John was silent; he knew the sort of scene that Belle had staged. He remembered now before he had proposed to her, her ability for posing as a martyr. Belle wretched about her, age, Belle evoking streams of sympathy, attracting them to herself with a magnetic force.

"She is a good deal older than you are," went on Mr. Hunter severely, "and therefore it makes it all the harder for her. If you had not intended to remain faithful to her, you should not have married her. You were not a child; you knew what you were doing."

Age. Belle's trump card. How she used it, twisted it with the cunning cleverness of her tricky brain, and produced it inevitably as her ace of trumps. John stared at Mr. Hunter dumbly. If that was the man's attitude, then there seemed little to be left worth saying. Wretchedly he began again. "What is going to be done now? Have you arrived at any decision?"

"We cannot keep Maddalan here. I am sorry, because we liked her, and naturally we never thought such a circumstance could arise. It is incredible. She is going back to her cousins in Tooting. I sent them a telegram this morning."

"I see."

John felt as though some force had driven right within himself, had pierced through his body and down into his soul. An icy force or blazing hot, he could not tell which. A huge nail spiking him to the grim cross of consequences. Something from which he could not possible escape. He wanted to know the worst. He said humbly, "Do you think I might see her?"

Mr. Hunter was doubtful. He was fingering his watchchain, his brows knit together in perplexity. He was obviously ill at ease, and he turned. "Carrick, this is difficult. I have no wish to be hard on anybody, or to condemn anybody, but can't you see what a dickens of a mess it is? I do think that you might have trusted me with the truth."

"If I had done, you would have forbidden me the house."

"I don't know. Perhaps I might have understood. Lots of us make mistakes in life, and especially over marriage. I know the difficulty, but now that it has happened like this there is only one course open to me, and I hate taking it. It is so doubly difficult because I am a parson. You see that, don't you?"

"I do," said John, "and I am sorry to have been the cause of so much worry. I am ashamed, too, but, looking back on it, I don't see what else I could have done."

Mrs. Hunter, tapping at the door, asked if she might speak to her husband for a moment. John did not see her. He stood there staring into the desultory fire, seeing among its few grey ashes the greyer ashes of his own life ground together in a fine powder of hard mistakes. He must do the right thing now; only by truth and honesty and steadfastness of purpose could he hope to put matters straight.

When Mr. Hunter came back again he was holding a telegram in his hand, and looking more worried than ever. "Maddalan's cousins can't have her," he said; "they have a case of fever in the house. We are in a nice fix."

A thin wisp of paper decided their fates. John saw it as a flag of truce to their hostilities. "I think," he said, "that after all this is my affair. I could arrange for Maddalan in Condering."

"But I could hardly consent to her going off under your protection, could I?"

"I think you could if I gave you my word that she would be safe."

"It is a difficult situation."

"I have a friend who runs the Chantry hotel. I am sure she would put Maddalan up, anyway for the time being. She knows about the whole affair, and she is a most understanding woman."

"Mrs. Darsy?"

"You know her, then?"

Mr. Hunter nodded. "Yes, I know her. The point is that I feel, rather than her coming with you, Maddalan ought to stay here."

"Perhaps she ought to decide for herself," suggested John. "We are discussing her as though she were a parcel, to be handed about from person to person. It is Maddalan's life; isn't she going to have any say in it at all?"

"You're right."

They talked it out, threshing it this way and that. Now John was eager and thrust his point home. Finally Mr. Hunter consented and went to call Maddalan. Alone in the room John waited for her with a thrill. This unfriendly, unlovely room that now had become the shrine of something rather exquisite within him. He felt the whole of his body growing still, the whole of his life concentrated on this particular moment. It was like an unwinding spool that, nearing its end, flies wildly round and round and then as suddenly slows down. . . .

III

She came in seeming frailler than usual, her face whitely ethereal, no longer a live personality but like a ghost. She had her hat on, and beneath its grey brim her eyes were haunting.

"Well?" she said, and then happily, like a tired bird returning to its nest, "John!"

"Has he explained to you?"

"Yes."

"My dear, what are we going to do about this?"

She drew in a little sharp breath, raised her head, and said with the deliberation of one who has considered, "I am coming with you."

They clasped their hands on a pact, a solemn pact, and she lifted her eyes to his face. "Only don't let me see Belle again. She was dreadful. It was all so horrible, John. I can't speak of it. So soiling, so sordid. What an awful day. Thank heaven it is nearly over."

"Thank heaven to-morrow will be new."

"Yes."

They went into the hall together; crossed it, their feet clipping on the flags, muffled on the multi-coloured mat. The wide door swung to on them, and they passed down the gravel drive, frozen fast, past the holly tree cloaked whitely in rime, to the waiting car. "This," thought John, "is either the beginning of everything, or the end. I don't know which."

The unwinding spool was starting to revolve rapidly again. . . .

IV

They drove along in silence, through the world grown bluey with twilight. Roy had asked no questions; he had understood what had happened, and had maintained a wise silence as they climbed into the back of the car. Maddalan nestled close to John, and he found that almost at once she had fallen into an exhausted sleep. He sat there counting the telegraph poles as they flashed by. It was an absurd rotation of his brain, and although it frenzied him, he could not stop himself. Tall poles like gallows, long taut wires, another pole! Avenues of them! Black flag masts from which the flags had been hauled down. Rather death-like, that. It made him feel uneasy. As she slept in an exhausted coma he wrapped the rugs closer round her. She had suffered, poor child, and for him. He knew that he had no other course open to him than to take her with him. They could not continue in their old aimless rut.

The car drew up alongside the Chantry, and still Maddalan slept.

"I'll leave her here with you," said John to Roy, "and go in and see Mrs. Darsy first. That will be the best plan."

His feet were numb with cold, and his shivering fingers faltered at the door-latch. Inside there was warmth. It assailed his face as he crossed the hall and into Mrs. Darsy's sitting-room, where she was eating buttered toast and drinking tea before a roaring fire.

"Oh, hello!" she called to him gladly. "You are just in time for a cup." Then she saw by his face that something had happened, and her tone changed. "John, something is wrong?" she said.

"Maddalan is here."

"Here?"

"Yes. I have taken a risk. Belle found out from that fool Bert Hickman last night. She went over to Craye this morning and kicked up a frightful fuss. They turned Maddalan out."

"Good heavens!"

"No, perhaps I oughtn't to put it like that, for Hunter was very nice about it. It was one of those things that could not happen under a parson's roof, and he realized it. He wired to her cousins in Tooting, but they could not take her in. I have brought her here. She is in a bad state, exhausted, bewildered, all that. Will you put her up for a night or two, until something is settled?"

"Of course I'll take her in. Where is she?"

He felt relaxation, blood streaming down his thighs, hammering down his arms. "Thank God," he said, and in spite of the cold his brow had become pearly with sweat. "What a dear thing you are."

"Am I, John? Yet this is what the world knows as encouraging vice."

"There isn't any vice in it," he protested, "truly there isn't. There shan't be either."

"I know that, John, else I should not be guilty of encouraging it," and she smiled bravely at him.

He went out to the car, and together he and Roy brought Maddalan in. She seemed dazed as she crossed the entrance to the Chantry, clinging to John's arm. She came into the warm comfort of the sitting-room, stared at it as though it were totally unexpected. She drank in its comfort from the great chair by the fire.

"You'll have some tea?" asked Mrs. Darsy kindly.

Maddalan did not answer. The bewildered look in her eyes hurt John as nothing else had hurt him. He had experienced sabre wounds of thoughts and actions, the sharp knife-thrusts of cruel words, but never this dulled, deep, mortal pain of her reproachless eyes. He felt that he should go on seeing the pain in them, the bewilderment at life, the hunger. . . .

"Tea will make you better," said Mrs. Darsy, and she set the cup by the girl's side, gently smoothing the fair, soft hair.

Maddalan looked up. She looked full into Mrs. Darsy's face as if for the first time recognizing the friendship, the connection with herself. As if she had come back and found all this was part of her own life, and not a flickering cinema on some strange screen, viewed but for the passing moment. She stared up at the face, and into her eyes there swam the first moisture, the first indication of collapse. Then it was that Mrs. Darsy, with an exclamation of pity, took her into her arms.

"Leave us," she nodded to John and Roy, across Maddalan's bowed head. "I'll take care of her. It will be better like that."

V

"That blasted little swine Belle," said Roy, "Lord, I'd wring her neck! Going over there as the injured wife and kicking up hell's own fuss!"

"Belle believes that she is the injured wife," said John. "There are two sides to every question, and the worst of all this is that I am so confoundedly conscious of having behaved badly to Belle."

They were in the corner of the bar, at this time of day deserted, and they had drawn close over a small table.

"Behaving badly to Belle? God, as if anybody could! She is up to any double-crossing there is going. I bet you she is living with Jeff; I don't mind staking my all on that, only you will never catch them."

"You've got to admit that she has a side to this argument," said John, and he thought wretchedly, "Lord, if only I didn't see her side, see her cause for complaint and realize that it is a just one! If only . . . !"

"You're too damned honest," snorted Roy. "When I saw that poor little kid . . ."

John took down a gulp of whisky and set the glass chinking against a stone ashtray advertising Apollinaris. "Don't you go falling in love with Maddalan," he instructed Roy. "That would settle it."

"Me? Good Lord, no! It's just the rottenness of the thing. Old Belle leading you such a life and then going over there and blubbing. I bet she blubbed hard on them, and did the pure lily. I can imagine Belle glorying in the pure lily."

"Don't let's talk about her. The thing is what next? There must be some definite course to pursue, something that we can hold on to?"

They sat there staring stupefied at each other. Roy drummed the table with his fingers. "I suppose she won't divorce you?"

"No, she won't."

"Nothing will make her change her mind? I mean an extra drop of boodle?"

"I haven't the boodle," said John, and then he burst out frantically: "You see, my money is nearly all of it locked up in the shop. I could not realize much even if I tried. And anyway she is in possession there too. Much as she hates the house and the place, she'd stay. I know Belle."

He left Maddalan with Mrs. Darsy. She had explained that the girl could stay there some time; perhaps, she suggested, Maddalan could get a job in Condering, something that would enable her to pay for her room, instead of John being under the obligation. When he passed out of the hotel into the street, treacherous with rime, he had arranged for Maddalan for the time being. But the difficulty was appalling. It had its financial side. Finance is too often the limit that hedges round our loves. At the moment, John was living expensively, for Belle had no ideas as to economy. She never attempted to draw a rein on Mrs. Barnes' extravagant methods of housekeeping. If it were suggested to her—and John had suggested it quite often—she would declare passionately that she hated meanness in any shape or form. Belle believed that she had married well, and she intended to get the last farthing out of John. He had invested all that he could spare in his shop, and, although it was paying, most of the money was locked up. He could not realize too quickly. It was going to be difficult running his own home and paying for Maddalan at the hotel too, and misleading to the world, who would undoubtedly put the worst construction on the facts.

He hated the whirling boomerang of circumstances. He hated the network which hemmed him in, the intrigue, the accusations, the hundred difficulties. He thought, as he plodded down the North Hill through the sharp air, "This is love. Love which is the most exquisite beauty in the world, but which brings you to this. Jan was right: love is the most exquisite beauty but the most agonizing pain; death is sweet to it." Morbid thoughts! Hateful fancy! He set his key into the latch and the door opened.

Belle and Jeff were sitting on either side of the fire. It struck John that Jeff was a little drunk, and that Belle was afraid. Perhaps she had gone too far and was wondering what the consequences might be. Anyway, it was certain that she had lost some of her brazen assurance by the sudden way in which she looked up. He hung his hat in a corner, and came forward rubbing his hands together.

"A cold night," he volunteered.

Jeff eyed him cunningly. Jeff, more vulture-like than ever. His yellowed skin glazed on his high cheekbones, two pits on either side his sensual mouth. Jeff, a Lazarus of a man, too long dead.

"Where have you been?" asked Belle abruptly.

"I've been out."

"You've been to Craye?" she challenged. "I've been there too. I've been there . . ." She was getting excited; her eyes, beady bright, stared up at him.

He said passively, "I don't think we need discuss this before a third person, do you?"

"Not if you're ashamed," she retorted. "Jeff doesn't matter; he doesn't count. He's one of us."

A hoarse chuckle came from the man on the other side of the hearth. The chuckle was a croak, the hideous, raucous croak of a raven who has found food.

"Well, I refuse to discuss it," said John.

She cast him an evil glance, but he had parried her. He did not care. They ate a melancholy supper together, made all the more melancholy by the fact that in the middle of it the electric light failed and the place was plunged in darkness. Mrs. Barnes came to their rescue by carrying in two candles. She reminded John of a white-clad nun, carrying candles to place at a bier-head. His bier, perhaps.

"I don't know whether it's all the street," she said, "or something just wrong with our swish-board." She turned to Jeff. "Do you know anything about swish-boards?" she demanded. "I don't understand the things."

It appeared that Jeff knew nothing of "swish-boards".

In the unaccustomed darkness lit by the two dismal candles Jeff drained the decanter. Afterwards he floundered up to bed, leaving Belle and John alone on either side of the fire. He hoped that she would restrain her curiosity until Mrs. Barnes had gone, but she did nothing of the kind. Belle could not play a waiting game, she was avid for news.

"Well," she demanded, "and now what's happened?"

Pasty, pouched face of Belle staring at him out of the grotesque twilight. He said, "I have been to Craye. I have interviewed Hunter and have found out all that you said."

"Oh."

"I was amazed that you had the face to do it."

"I wasn't going to have that girl here at my very doorstep. I determined I'd get her sent back to Holland. I meant to do it. She had no business there in a respectable house, the common little tart."

He ignored her tempestuous indignation and went on slowly. "I brought Maddalan back here. She is here now."

"Here? In this house?"

"No. She is in the town." His desperate attempt to cleave the tumultuous difficulties with the axe of truth sent him forward. "She is here; and I ask you for the last time, will you divorce me?"

"Certainly not," said Belle. "Why should I? We are

married, and I—I am fond of you." She broke off into a laugh. He thought the laugh was ghastly. Hyænas in the desert, wolves barking across the prairies, the desperate screech of wild birds hastening to the kill. This was Belle. Belle hastening to the kill of Maddalan—because that was what she intended: the plucking of Maddalan's cool, delicious flesh from her stark bones. Death, that was Belle's desire.

The laughter broke into screams, short, sharp screams that pierced through the night stillness. Belle was in the throes of hysteria. Belle shrieking, jerking, twitching to and fro with lolling head. He had an instinctive idea that she did this sort of thing to shame him to the neighbours, for when she behaved like this he could feel the loathly desperation of acute shame bearing down upon him and pulverizing him beneath its heel into its slough of despond.

He would not bandy words with her. He called Mrs. Barnes, and passed out into the street.

Chapter Two

> Happiness is the only sanction of life; where happiness fails, existence remains a mad and lamentable experiment.
>
> SANTAYANA

I

THERE ensued days, long days, in which he felt himself being gyrated in the inescapable whirlpool. Three of them spinning round, caught in the tricky current of life, and with little chance or hope. He would have run away with Maddalan had he not held the predominant determination to do nothing of which he would be ashamed, to take no false step. He wanted to make no more mistakes. It was difficult.

He believed that he had taken the advice of others for too long, and that now the only satisfactory method was to follow his own star.

Maddalan procured employment at a house in Leyton, the better-class suburb of Condering. She visited daily to attend on three little girls, superintend their lessons and take them for walks. The three little girls quickly learnt to love Maddalan, and Maddalan loved them. Their mother was a Society woman seldom at home, and of small, rather petty, intelligence; she did not mind so long as she was not bothered by her children. She had, however, a flighty husband.

The salary was excellent, and Maddalan believed that she was established, when through the first winter days she took her charges out and about and lived in the warm, snug schoolroom tucked away under the eaves of Morlingott House. In the evening she returned to Mrs. Darsy's roof, slept in the small attic, and busied herself mending the linen as some small return for the kindness and sympathy she had received.

Then one day the master of the house saw Maddalan on the stairs. He approved her slender ankles and long line of body, and her white, blossomy face. He saw in her that foreignly attractive air which spelt for him—connoisseur in women—enchantment. He made the most of the opportunity, and developed after that a stupendous and hitherto neglected interest in his paternity. His three small daughters had not interested him. Each should have been a son, and most especially of all the last. When the youngest was coming, his wife had said firmly and distinctly that it was definitely to be the last. Son or no son, she was having no more, and she had abided by that statement. Her disappointed husband had sulked. But suddenly he found great attraction in the schoolroom; he poked his head in for lessons, and trespassed on their tea. He took a delight in tweaking small flaxen pigtails and making remarks that could be applied either to pupils or governess.

His wife discovered that he had some affection which detained him from her side, but she did not interest herself too keenly, for he had long ago ceased to charm her in any way. That was about the time that Belle discovered where Maddalan worked, and immediately put on her best hat and marched up to the front door and sought admittance.

In the futurist drawing-room, where the lady of the house languished on sea-green cushions against cold tubular steel furniture, Belle wept the tears of a stricken and deserted wife. She confided all her woes with more than a little emotion, and stressed the point that nobody's husband was safe with such a sly little vixen.

Whilst this pathetic scene was being enacted in the drawing-room, Maddalan in the schoolroom was wondering how she could avoid the master of the house without giving offence. She had never encouraged him by a single word, but that alone had been sufficient to attract him all the more. He was not used to retiring women, and he rather thought that he liked them.

The wife did not want her husband for herself in the very least, but she assumed the attitude that if she couldn't have him nobody else should. The moment Belle had left, she sent for Maddalan. In cold, cutting terms, as though they were sliced out of her glacial interior by an ice axe, she informed the girl that she had had enough of her intrigue, and that she would leave with no recommendation.

Maddalan left, bemused.

She would never have known that Belle was at the bottom of it save for the fact that Belle was somewhat over-triumphant, and, having to confide in someone, told John.

Maddalan found further employment. This time it was the daughter of a grocer who wanted to learn Dutch before going to Holland to take up her residence with a Dutch family. The grocer was a highly respectable person who lived at the St. Barnabas end of the town, and therefore knew little of what was going on on North Hill.

Belle, enquiring about, discovered Maddalan's new employment. She felt it to be her duty to march down to St. Barnabas and face the grocer across his counter. An ardent supporter of Zion's chapel, he was amazed, dumb-founded. He did not like Belle's attitude, and he would have taken a wider outlook on the situation but that his respectability was shocked. As an ardent Zionist, he could do nothing but dismiss Maddalan at once.

In Mrs. Darsy's small sitting-room John and Maddalan tried to face the thing out. They were pursued by the hounds of petty prejudice. They had done nothing wrong; their only fault was that they loved each other, and from this besieging love of theirs they could not escape.

It was Mrs. Darsy who offered Maddalan employment in the hotel. She suggested that perhaps she could make herself useful enough to justify her free board and lodging, and under those conditions Maddalan remained. Mrs. Darsy well knew that anything the girl attempted outside would meet the same fate. Provincial towns are narrow. Little scandals flit from street to street, gathering impetus as they go. You cannot escape them.

Meanwhile in his home John fought a fierce fight, perhaps the fiercest of his life.

Although "When Knights were Bold" had been acted, it had not meant the end of Jefferson's visit. He still stayed on, and although John had tried by every conceivable means in his power to remove him, nothing happened. In vain did he hint, in vain did he protest. Belle was entirely adamant. John felt that in some way Jeff was supporting her.

You could never tackle Jeff. He had ingenious methods of trapping you when you ill-advisedly supposed that you had trapped him into some admission. He was habitually semi-intoxicated, but never hopelessly so. His conversations tripped easily from sense into nonsense, and were always very lightly interspersed with exaggerated truth. You could never hold him to any of his statements, because the moment you did so he would plead that at the time he had not been entirely sober. John cornered him alone and asked him point-blank when he intended to leave. Jeff had no idea. He stood there swaying in his long, slender-fitting black coat. He waved a thin spike of a finger at John. He was, he stated, going to obtain a most important rôle. He was in treaty with Drury Lane. They were staging a new play and they wanted him for lead. At the moment it was merely a question of salary. He did not intend to act for them for nothing—why should he? He was well known; he was streets ahead of anyone else in the profession, and he had no intention of cheapening his art. They had offered him twenty-five guineas a week—his fee was thirty-five. He talked about guineas in the airy manner of a pauper who has not seen half a crown of his own for weeks. Undoubtedly they would come up to his price, for the simple reason that they had no one else to act the rôle. Svengali. Ah, but what a Svengali! John knew that Jeff was entirely fitted for Svengali, and through the mere mention of the name permitted dust to be thrown in his eyes. He waited.

Needless to say, the Drury Lane contract did not materialize. Not that it was of the slightest importance, explained Jeff airily, because he was in treaty with the Lyric. A far better part. More in keeping with himself. He hated the rôle of a Jew. And during all this delay there was Belle watching them, her face grown larger, fatter; it struck him as being swollen, bulging a little, with cheeks that hung pendulously. She had lost any pretensions that she ever might have had to a rather brazen type of good looks. Belle was now obviously growing rapidly older. Marriage had not treated her well.

At one period she had raved and stormed about Maddalan, but now she wrapped herself in an even more dreadful silence. They had split by common consent, John taking the small bedroom at the end of the passage, and leaving her in possession of the big bedroom with the exquisite bed in it.

Sometimes when he went up at night he heard her crying. The sound smote horror to his heart. He was ashamed that he had behaved badly; the error had been in not discovering about Maddalan before. He should have gone back to the Renaissance house on the *gracht;* he should never have left part of his love behind him, but should have been sure before he had allowed Belle to enter into his life. In this way he was sorry for her; it might be weakness, but he had to admit that he was ashamed of himself.

"I've behaved badly to you, Belle," he told her one afternoon just before Christmas, when he came in to find her alone looking through catalogues of presents. There were traces of tears in silver rivers down her cheeks, though the eyes she turned on him were hard.

"It's no use saying that."

"We've drifted apart. I think you ought to divorce me. Like this we can't be happy. You aren't happy, neither am I; neither is she, for the matter of that."

"You only think of her," retorted Belle.

"I think of you too. If I were not thinking of you I should have run off with her ages ago."

"You needn't imagine that I think it is your virtue that keeps you straight," she flashed. "It is all only too easy with her just round the corner, isn't it?"

"Belle, that is unfair."

"Well, why did you get her here? And that horrid Darsy woman protecting her, too! Vile, I call it. Vice, the most filthy backing up of vice."

He turned away. He might have known you could never meet Belle half way. She refused to meet you. His heart sank within him. One of these days he would elope with Maddalan, slip back to Haarlem. The shadow of a giant barge fell across his thoughts.

II

At this time he was losing his friends. The younger generation clung to him, Roy, Bert, and that type of person, but gradually the older generation, shocked and surprised, was slipping from him. Mr. Atkins when he saw him in the street no longer hailed him with a would-be-boyish friendliness. He did not negotiate for furniture. He seemed anxious to rush through any meetings, to pass before John had time to stop him. He was typical of many people, all of that same generation.

Once, desperate and unable to see the way before him, John deliberately stopped Mr. Atkins. He went across to him on top of the North Hill, with a cold stinging wind blowing straight from the sea.

"I want a word with you," he said, and he laid a hand on Mr. Atkins' bicycle, looking straight into his eyes. "I want to know what I've done that you should be like this with me."

The vicar turned pink. He always had a baby face, and he turned rosy with the wind or the heat of the moment or with sheer embarrassment, you could not tell which. "It—it isn't anything," he said lightly.

"Pardon me, it *is* something." John still kept his retaining hand on the bicycle. He stared Mr. Atkins full in the eyes. "I want to know the truth, please."

"Well, well, this is hardly the time or place to discuss it," said the vicar uncomfortably, and tried to move the bicycle forward, but John had anticipated the movement and held it close.

"I want to know—*now,*" he said grimly.

"Well, perhaps evil tongues have been wagging," said the vicar. "I daresay it is only a little foolishness, but we all feel sorry for your wife. She has had a hard time. She has told people about it, and I hardly feel that your example is all that it should be . . . not all that it should be . . . " he trailed off miserably.

This from Atkins! Atkins who had been so indignant with Belle over the theatricals, who had glared at her, yet who now apparently took her part! John had no doubt that she had made her story very good. Trust Belle for that! John began gently. "There are two sides to the question, you know."

"There can be no two sides to the question of morality," said the vicar sententiously.

"No, but you have got me wrong in this. There is no suggestion of immorality. I have asked my wife to divorce me."

The vicar turned disturbed blue eyes in John's direction. "One cannot obtain a divorce without grounds," he stated emphatically. John had not thought of that.

"Something could be arranged," he suggested miserably.

There was a silence, an awkward, harassing silence. The stream of traffic swerved past them and down the North Hill, the heavy drays lumbering along, wheels rolling like drums; there was the lighter sound of small cars, the heavy regurgitating movement of the trams. John felt despairingly, "This is life flowing past me, and it is leaving me stranded high and dry. Just the vicar and I. Absurd, ridiculous. . . ." And then he saw the bland baby face of Mr. Atkins embarrassed to a degree, and the foolish fluttering hands encased in their black woollen gloves fumbling with the glittering bicycle bell.

"Well, I am afraid I have a day's work before me," said the vicar benignly. "Must set about it. No good delaying, is it?"

"No good at all."

"Good morning." Mr. Atkins raised his small saucer hat thankfully. He was so grateful to get away that he became quite jocose again. "And don't forget when you think about it there's always room for you in the church. Plenty of seating accommodation, lots of seats and nice bright singing. . . ." He rode off quite pleased with himself over what he imagined to be a skilful turn to the conversation.

The high tide had washed Mr. Atkins along with it. Now John was standing, it seemed to be entirely alone—standing there on the pavement with the flotsam and jetsam of life riding by, and from the distance senility bearing down upon him. Every day a little older. Every day a little nearer the end, and nothing garnered out of the bright harvest of life. Armfuls of tares, golden glitter lying shorn to the ground, and no grain in his barn. He felt the sudden urgent need striking up within him, the hungry need for something to happen. Youth tires of eventless nothingness, of days each like their sisters, of nights pitifully sterile. He wanted something more. He could not let the tide flow for ever past his door without stepping out into its frothy blueness. He would run away. He made the momentous decision quite calmly, and felt the spool stay its unwinding within him. He was conscious of silence—ominous silence.

Crossing the road, he went into the Chantry.

III

They were talking together, he and Maddalan. They had come upstairs into the hotel drawing-room to talk, because it was deserted; they had forgotten that it was also fireless. The stinging cold wind had driven in at the small diamond-paned windows. It was an eerie room, without beauty, old with a crumbling age that was dotage. The beams that propped its time-greyed ceiling were gnarled. Its humpy floor was hidden here and there with mats, dull pools of faded colours blent together. Its fireless ingle was not inviting. They sat down on the wide leather sofa side by side. The cheerlessness seemed to penetrate into their very souls and freeze them. What can be worse than an unused hotel drawing-room on a bitter winter's day, impersonal, impartial, austere?

"Something has got to happen," John was saying, and he was numb not only with the chill of the biting atmosphere; his eyes were hard and glazed like a dead man's. He felt that he was dead. He felt that he had died a long time ago and that afterwards life had gone on, but that now he was viewing it from the other side. Another side dissociated from the grave and the hump of grass and the marble headstone, but more as if he looked through a half-transparent curtain. Life was a play, and he the solitary tired audience. Its jokes were stale, its music jarred. "Something has got to happen," and his voice was not his own. It had grown hoarse and it rasped. "We can't go on like this. We must run away."

He felt her hands lying in his, cold and soft as vine leaves. She was shivering a little, and her lips trembled. "John, we mustn't make a mistake. Don't give Belle a chance to say things. There is no truth in what she accuses us of. Don't let us give her an ugly truth to distort."

"You don't seem to see. This can't go on. It can't, Maddalan; it has gone on too long. We should be better if we ran away and started again somewhere else."

"It would mean desertion," she said slowly, and then she shook her head. "I cannot believe that if we go on like this something will not come to relieve us. Life does not run along in monotonies; it changes its course if you give it time."

"Yes, if only we might take the initiative and change it," he suggested whitely. "Maddalan, I feel such a poor-spirited, comfortless wretch, but I have the feeling that if this goes on something awful will happen. Belle has everything in her favour, and we are shunted and treated contemptibly; if it goes on, I shall do something desperate. Maddalan, I have come to you to save me from myself."

He was conscious that it was melodrama, and that it sounded cheap and fantastic, but for all that he could not withhold the words. He knew the spool within him was unwinding rapidly again, flinging itself round and round. He wanted to save himself from the something, the elusive, furtive something, which menaced him.

"Don't you see, my dear," she whispered, "that by refusing to come away with you, that is exactly what I am doing? I *am* saving you from yourself. That is what you are afraid of. That would be the mistake. Whilst you stay here you are safe, quite safe."

"I'm not," he said, and groaned.

"It is only that you think you are not. Belle will change her mind. She will help you and free you. I feel that will happen if only we are patient. We must wait."

He thought of her again as the white saint in the shrine. She was remote from him. She did not suffer the same tempestuous emotions; she did not have to combat the same difficulties, nor probe the same sobbing depths. "You don't know what it is like," he said. "If you did you would sympathize."

"I do sympathize, John; you know that I sympathize. I want to help, but what can I do?"

"I suppose there is nothing to be done," he told her. Still the tide of people was rushing down the North Hill, flotsam and jetsam of life, and he was left by that tide. "It is something that I have missed," he exclaimed suddenly, "something that I shall never find now. Freda . . . you . . . Belle. . . . Nights and days totting up against me, and no memories!"

She drew him down with cool, kind arms. "Hush, you shall not say so. The Haarlemmer Hout, Rembrandt's mill; that day we met again on the hill by the station, with the red brambles on it. There are always lovely memories in life, and their loveliness is so exquisite that it blots out the dark pain. There are lovelier memories still unborn."

He turned and kissed the arms that held him with that brave Madonna clasp. There might be lovelier memories ahead, but surely none more beautiful than this moment in her embrace. He was conscious of his panic steadying. "I feel so dreadful having brought you to this," he said reluctantly at last.

"There is no need to feel dreadful."

They kissed again. Her lips were like marble. It was like kissing a stone effigy on some prone tomb. Once he had done it as a boy, overcome with an impulsive pity for the poor crusader who lay there, with nobody to "tuck him up"! The kiss had been so cold to his hot childish lips that he had shrieked with the fright of it. Maddalan's lips were like that. They had the ice of the *jung frau* on them. He thought with a morbid yearning how wonderful it would be to escape now, to carry her far away to the cold North, and live at peace beyond habitation, unpursued by the darts of malicious tongues. Then he realized that his ideas were becoming distorted, as a man's ideas when he climbs very high or travels to the extreme North or South, losing his sense of perspective. He pulled himself up short.

"Now come down and have some coffee," she suggested. "I will make it for you. Mrs. Darsy says that she likes my coffee. Come down and try it."

They left the austere drawing-room with its shadows slipping into senility. They went down the sloping stairs together.

They had gained no further ground. As he groped for the banister he wondered if she understood how he was suffering. . . . It hurt . . . it hurt tragically.

IV

Chance opened the door at last. Maddalan was right. Things could not run along in the dead rut of monotony too long. There was a way; there was always a way out if you waited for it.

It was Belle who gave him the opportunity.

It happened early in the new year. During this time he was at home as little as possible. Firstly, because he objected strongly to the presence of Jeff, whose jobs never materialized and who seemed to have taken up his permanent abode with them. Also Belle was detestable. He was sorry for her because it seemed that there had flowed back into her all the old bitter resentment against life. It permeated her being nowadays. Belle had seen her hopes of cleaving to youth falling away. She knew now that she was old; she was so old that her husband no longer cared for her and another woman had taken her place. It was impossible for John to blind himself to all that Belle must be thinking and suffering. In his own deep abyss of pain he felt a certain sympathy for her anguish.

One night he came home late. The house was locked, and they had gone to bed. He moved noiselessly across the unlit sitting-room, afraid lest he should wake her, and he took off his shoes, to steal with caution up the stairs. As he did so he heard voices. If they were in bed they should be asleep. Jeff, probably in a drunken stupor, in the spare room; Belle in the room that once John had furnished as a setting for Maddalan. But he was convinced that he had heard voices. A husky laugh disturbed the silence, played with it; whispering purred softly like the sound of up-flung spray. Under Belle's door there was a long yellow pencil of light. She was obviously awake, but then she slept badly, and at any rate he had only supposed that she would be dozing. He climbed a step or two higher, listened again, conscious that the atmosphere was pregnant with presences. He was certain that there was someone in Belle's room.

He wondered if Mrs. Barnes had been persuaded to stay the night. This had happened once and once only. Instantly he dismissed the idea. Suddenly a sharp barb of suspicion darted through him. Supposing that Belle were ill? Supposing that something serious were amiss?

The idea sent him panicking. He did not want anything to happen to Belle, because she still struck him as being a pitiful object; in a way she was appealing. He strode across the landing and set his hand on the latch of her door. It did not yield, and he knew that it was locked on the inside.

There came the sound of scuffling; then Belle's voice, sharply defiant. "Who's there?"

John challenged, "There is somebody in your room," because now doubt was squirming in his heart as a snake writhes in thick grass. He struck the door with the fist of a strong man, of a man who suddenly sees his future shape its course, and a way out offering its promise to him.

"Don't be a fool! There is no one in here!"—angrily from Belle.

"Then open the door."

"I shan't do anything so silly. Go to bed and sleep it off." Then the husky laughter, as though she had said something clever.

He paused a moment, cold sweat dribbling on his forehead. He went across to the spare room, opening the door cautiously. As he had thought! The bed was empty. Jeff's untidy clothes were sprawling about here and there. His pyjamas and thready dressing-grown, relic of past grandeur, were missing. John nodded in approval to himself. So this had been going on all the time, under his very nose! He had been a fool; he had been an utter fool not to have suspected her. He went back to the door of the room that he had prepared for Maddalan.

"It's no use," he announced, and there was victory in his voice; "the game's up. I know that Jeff is in there. Do you want me to telephone for the police?"

Silence! A sharp silence confused by the suggestion of awkward sounds. He could imagine Belle's panic, Jeff, half drunk, protesting feebly, probably smothered in a clothes cupboard. Then, unexpectedly, the door opened; it opened slowly, as doors open on dramatic entries in plays, and framed in its square oak frame stood Jeff looking grotesquely tall and angular in his ridiculous dressing-grown.

"Well?" he challenged.

A Lazarus of a man! And, beyond, a vision of a bawdy woman, bitch-wolf, half naked, peering over rumpled bed-clothes.

"You get to hell out of this." John's voice sharp as a pistol-shot, rapping through the silence.

"You over-estimate the position," said Jeff fawningly; "you think that we are in love. Absurd, my dear sir! Belle has a bad cold coming on. I took her some throat lozenges. We began to talk. . . ."

John drew his watch out of his pocket. He tapped the dial significantly. "I give you exactly ten minutes to be out of this house," he said.

Power! Triumph! The spool stilling its unwinding within him. He felt the certain savage victory of it stinging his throat, flying to his head like wine, fusing his senses.

Jeff shrugged gaunt shoulders. "At this hour of the night? But, my dear sir, where could I go?"

"Where you've been before, I don't doubt—the gutter."

"Dear sir, I am a man of peace! I do not take exception to your allusions, but I am a little surprised. I do protest."

It was then that John kicked him. He had been aching to do it for months. He kicked him heartily, almost expecting to hear his meagre bones rattling together from the impact. "Ten minutes," he warned him, "and not a second more. What you haven't got together you damned well leave behind you. . . ."

Victory flowed through him! After all, things were turning out rightly. He turned once and, looking back, saw through the half-open door Belle, a huddle of flesh in the great bed, with one of her suggestive nightdresses slipping from her nude breasts. She reminded him in some eerie and disconnected manner of the joss. Flesh, mountains of it, leering face . . . sex. . . .

Ten minutes later Les Jefferson left.

Chapter Three

Every worm beneath the moon
Draws different threads, and late and soon
Spins, toiling out his own cocoon.
TENNYSON, *The Two Voices*

I

THE situation wanted thinking out. This was no time for some breathless conclusion, nor for hurried action. John left his house ten minutes after Les Jefferson had gone, and he spent the night at the Fountain. Early in the morning he presented himself at the Chantry. Although the Fountain had given him a good bed, he had not slept at all. How could a man sleep under such conditions? He was gaunt and haggard, yet in his eyes there burnt the glad satisfaction of the man who has at last glimpsed the first faint light of the silver lamps in the distant shrine of his seeking.

Mrs. Darsy was having her breakfast. Maddalan was not yet down. "Good heavens! You look like death!" she exclaimed. "What is the matter?"

"I am going up to London." He took the proffered cup of coffee and began to gulp it down. "Last night I found out things. Belle and Jefferson! I am going up to see Mr. Oglivy straight away. It is, I think, the only thing for me to do. I don't want to take any false steps, whatever happens. This means that, after all, I can divorce Belle."

"Oh, John, I *knew* something would happen."

"Yes, something, anything. The uncertainty has been awful. Until now I never knew a man could suffer so much. If it had gone on longer, I should have gone mad or killed someone. It had got to end."

She was eating toast in a totally abstracted manner. "Perhaps," she said, "it would be as well for you not to see Maddalan? I believe the laws are fairly rigid, and one cannot be too careful. What do you think?"

"I think you are probably right." The coffee was steadying him. He felt a new man again.

He scrambled down a hasty breakfast and hurried to the station to catch an early train. He was grateful for the sharp January air that bit. He could feel it stinging his nose and throat as he went. It shook off the hunger of his intense fatigue, set his blood flowing, eased the strain. The station was full of City men, who went up and down, and who disliked the chilliness of bleak mornings for the journey. The train came in; he thought once more of the steel python writhing its way along the shining rails, silver with the shine of an earlier trail. He had become part of that python on his wedding journey.

It was a fetid train, and he was uncomfortable. The heating apparatus, fully on, was so hot that it set him dozing. The carriage was full of foul pipes and strong cigarette-smoke, and men who talked mechanically and laughed too loudly.

When John eventually arrived at the London terminus he went into an hotel for coffee before continuing. He realized now that his long night hours had jaded him, and that he was feeling the full effect of wakefulness. He was tense; cold and quivering at moments, keyed up to a pitch which he found difficult to control at others. The cup chattered against his teeth in the long hotel lounge, with its cane tables and chairs, and its red-coated porters. Opposite to him he stared at the enquiry office where impersonal women moved busily with letters and papers. All a cinema . . . a revolving screen . . . no rest.

It was no use, he must get on. Something urged him forward. He rode along dull streets in a full omnibus, through a city wreathed in fog and smoke. They turned round the corner to the Mansion House, which loomed out of the fog, grotesque giant of a house in the strange lights. They lumbered up Cheapside, with yellow street lamps swung overhead and jaundicing the blue mist. He arrived safely at Gray's Inn.

He passed into the maze of little orderly squares picked out by the tall leafless trees, with straight houses rising in long rows around the green lawns; sedate houses; houses that had made history. He passed into one, climbed two flights of stairs, and knocked at a dingy door on which was written in white painted copper-plate, 'Messrs Oglivy and Barton'. He had never heard of Barton. He presumed that Barton must be dead, or existed only in Mr. Oglivy's imagination. Just as, when he was a boy, he had invented people who had participated in his life.

There was a clever brother of his by the name of Clem. Mr. Barton must be a sort of Clem to Mr. Oglivy. Clem had won cups at the school sports and had shown promise. Clem had done all manner of things in all manner of ways which made you intensely proud of him. A fine fellow, Clem! Yet the world had never met him. He had lived only in that greater world of imagination. John had a queerish fancy that he would like to bring Clem back into his world again and let him live on the North Hill with him. Clem would be amused over Mrs. Barnes; yes, he must think about Clem.

He rapped again.

The door swung open and a small pimply clerk enquired indifferently as to what John wanted. Inside was a bare office, with a passage from it leading to other offices. In the far corner a girl was perched on too high a stool, and typing on a large and old-fashioned machine. There were papers strewn about the room, musty-looking papers, yellow and sere, yet each, John supposed, bearing somebody's tragic life-story, some fevered battle that an individual had fought within himself. Funny that the raging, passionate tragedy should be so tremendously live when it was you, and so tremendously dead when it was scrawled monotonously in chronicle on deed and parchment! A gas fire plopped badly on the hearth, and before it was a small grubby office boy, doing something that entailed the use of a saucepan of boiling milk, two cups on a tin tray, and a long taper with which he was trying to relight the gas-ring.

"I want to see Mr. Oglivy," said John.

The pimply clerk, who was fair-haired, and who wore a suit that had obviously been handed down by a brother of a different stature from himself, and sharply, "I don't know where he is. He mayn't be coming up to-day."

John stood there undecided. This he had not anticipated. "But I must see him," he explained; "it is extremely urgent. Please telephone to his home."

The pimply clerk looked as if he would much rather do nothing of the sort. He stared at John for a moment, as if doubtful whether to kick him downstairs or not, and then he said with an ill grace, "Oh, very well then, come on inside," and motioned him to a comfortless chair with a jerk of his head.

The girl left off typing, and the office boy drew his small frame erect to watch John as he went to the chair. He was conscious that they were interested in him, that he looked queer, and that they probably thought that he was mad. Oh, well, let them, anyway! The clerk, in no hurry whatever, went to the telephone and, leaning indolently across a small table, enquired languidly for a number. It seemed, however, that when he eventually did get through to Mr. Oglivy's house he became more attentive. He gave John's name, and said that it was urgent, and then replied to a long conversation, the gist of which seemed to remain entirely at the other end of the line, "Oh."

"He's on his way here now, started half an hour ago. I suppose the fog's held him up," he announced, and after that left John severely alone.

It seemed that both the clerk and the typist were interested in the hot milk. At this hour of the morning they drank it. Most of their conversation was in tittering whispers, and John had not the heart to try to catch the few phrases that were uttered aloud. He was furious with the office boy, who, having finished cooking the milk, had settled himself down to suck his teeth in between intervals of entirely tuneless whistling. For the next hour John sat on, and it seemed to him that a whole third of his life had been spent there. During the time three people came to the door. The milkman called for the milk-bottle, and with him the typist and the clerk were jocular. Their humour was ghastly.

"Not so much water with it to-morrow, Jock. Why, it almost froze."

"There is a seventh commandment"—from the pimply clerk.

"Oh, I say now"—with giggles from the typist. "Isn't he a one? Oh, I say, I should never have thought of that. Hark at him."

The next caller was a gentleman who travelled in a particular brand of legal paper. The pimply clerk was extremely offensive to him. You would have supposed that he was the head of the concern, and that with him lay all matters of decision. He dismissed the commercial traveller with a wave of his hand. He really could not be troubled with that sort of unimportance; call again another time. He shut the door on the poor little man with scorn.

"That's the way to treat 'em," he nodded, winking to the typist—"next time you're passing, pass."

She was immediately convulsed with her ridiculous titters into a small cheaply-scented handkerchief.

The last caller was a client. He said he would also wait. He was large and burly, and he had a short, sharp way with the clerk that was impressive. He sat down beside John on a small kitchen chair. John felt that now they ought to have labels, Exhibit One, and Exhibit Two, so as to make it easier for the office boy, who was steadily staring. Last of all Mr. Oglivy appeared.

The impression of Mr. Oglivy in his inner holy of holies was not vivid. A small room, smelling of mustiness and fog and leaking gas-stove all in one. A small room lined with books and black-japanned deed-boxes. A table strewn untidily with papers, and tin fasteners, and green tapes in odd lengths. Before this table, which was to John in grim likeness to the confessional, he told the truth. He asked for help. The point was that from this moment he and Belle could not be under the same roof. Any reconciliation would be fatal to John's cause; Mr. Oglivy was most emphatic on that point. But John's roof was his business. Belle must go. But where?

"Leave it to me," instructed Mr. Oglivy. "Give me three days. I will go down and see her. She shall come here, somewhere in London; that will be the wisest thing. It may be a little costly, but to gain your ends this must be arranged."

"You're very good," said John helplessly. He had had time to get over the excitement in the exhaustion. Time to see it all with the supreme caution of the morning, and the office of Mr. Oglivy sickened him. It was ugly and sinister, this breaking of marriage. It might give him Maddalan in the end, but at the moment he was only seeing the sordid side—the dreary office, the mustiness of decay, the smell of boiling milk in a rancid saucepan, beautiless whistling, the pimply clerk. . . . All repulsive to him, vile. . . .

"And now," said Mr. Oglivy, "whatever happens, whilst proceedings are pending you must not see Miss Maddalan. On no account must you meet Miss Maddalan."

"No," John promised. Just as Mrs. Darsy had said.

"For three days you remain here," said Mr. Oglivy, "while I settle things. Then it will be advisable for you to get back to work, and to lead a simple life, and be careful that your behaviour is beyond suspicion. Ah—um—yes—beyond suspicion."

John did not like the emphasis that Mr. Oglivy put on the words; it savoured of the suggestion that he did not believe John always to behave beyond suspicion. The suggestion might be veiled.

"I shall lead my normal life," said John firmly. Mr. Oglivy could put that in his pipe and smoke it!

John saw a sharp look cross his face; he was quite sure that Mr. Oglivy would much rather that he did not lead his normal life, but John wasn't going to bother about his feelings. That was if lawyers had feelings. Perhaps they hadn't! They could not have many to allow their clients to be sat on cheaply uncomfortable chairs and to be stared at by pimply clerks and vulgar office-boys. "Your ordinary life with certain reservations," suggested Mr. Oglivy from across the paper-littered table. So he hadn't put it in his pipe! He had distinctly scored over John.

"Do you suggest that I racket about with women?" asked John, feeling the rising tide of impatience within him. "I can assure you that I lead the simplest life. There is no need for me to change so much as a thought of it."

"Quite," agreed Mr. Oglivy, in just the tone of voice that showed that he had all along nursed grave suspicions, and now was quite convinced of the truth of them—"quite. One can never be too careful. There is a personage called the King's Proctor, whose business is

. . . ah . . . entirely other people's business. One cannot guard too closely against his interference."

"By doing nothing suspicious one can," said John, again warring with Mr. Oglivy's insinuations.

"Ah! That's the point. By doing nothing suspicious."

John gave it up. It seemed that you could never suppress the foul doubts which grew like fertile weeds in the soil of the legal mind. He gave a grunting assent, gathered up his hat and gloves and umbrella, and went towards the door.

In the outer office the boy was collecting the hot milk cups to wash. He was whistling as before. He stopped both the washing and the whistling to have another earnest stare as John went by. John passed through the dingy door, into the dingier landing of bleak stairways, and as he did so he heard the boy say to everyone in general:

"Bet 'e's in some sort of a mess, not 'arf. All holler eyed, and dazed like. I bet yer a million pounds that 'e's . . ."

II

Belle had gone.

John was blessedly, unbelievably alone. In his own mind he thought of himself as a marathon runner, with his ebbing strength galvanized for the last lap; for this was the last lap. You could afford to take no risks with such a proceeding. He had written and explained to Maddalan, and she had replied agreeing with all that he had said. For the time being the Chantry was barred to him.

He had ferreted out of the kitchen a cheap grocer's calendar which had been brought with the Christmas order. It had a picture of a sailor swinging a bald-pated baby above his head in an extremely dangerous manner while his wife looked on in stupid approval. A usual picture with a nice suggestion of geraniums on a window-shelf, spotless pots and pans, brand new linoleum and table-cloth. But what had intrigued John was the fact that underneath this picture there was a calendar of ample proportions, with the numbers written in bold white figures easily discernible. Far ahead, at a probable date fixed by Mr. Oglivy, right into the autumn, John had marked a day in scarlet ink; that would be the first possible moment when his marriage to Maddalan could take place. He carried the calendar up to his room and set it beside his bed, and every night he marked off the white figure of the day in rich black ink. There was a lot of satisfaction about the black splotches that crawled across the sheet like so many round, shining beetles. They hid the glaring numbers underneath their blue-black bodies.

He had not the strength to look ahead and perceive how many days there yet were before the one marked in a halo of pleasant scarlet ink. There was the case to come before the courts first. Mr. Oglivy had been quick about it, and he had it all properly arranged, docketed and ticketed. Carrick versus Carrick, citing Jefferson. John understood that Belle was putting up no defence.

That was unlike Belle. He had not supposed that she would let him go without a murmur. In her own way he believed that she had been fond of him, and queerly enough in his own way he had been fond of her. He presumed that she was not living in Hoxton with Jeff. He could not imagine where else she would be, and he knew that the letters containing certain remittances from Mr. Oglivy were addressed to her there.

But John had some idea of the miseries of Jeff's domestic arrangements, for at times Belle had treated him to graphic descriptions. The cheap lodging-houses with the frowst of cooking, and of unwashed human bodies, and ill-ventilated rooms all blended together in one fetid stench. The food, sometimes scarce and always coarse. In such rooms they lived from hand to mouth, putting on decent clothes only when undertaking one of those dire pilgrimages to agents' offices in search of employment. The eternal hope of a "shop" flamed dismally within their hearts, and with it the dull despair of failure to obtain that "shop".

That wasn't Belle's idea of bliss. It did not coincide with her ideas of living, and as against her life in Condering it would show up badly. Yet apparently she had given John up without a protest. She had made no demur about leaving the house, Mr. Oglivy explained, but had gone without a word.

"And you've something to be thankful for in that," said Roy. Nowadays John need no longer keep up his pretended loyalty to Belle. Roy could say what he would. "You got rid of her easily, so easily that I half believe there is a catch in it."

"Oglivy says that there can't be."

"He's too respectable to suspect the sort of catch."

"Anyway," said John, "I'm taking no risks. This is too great an undertaking to risk chances. I'm being careful."

"You'll have to be if you want to outwit her," agreed Roy.

John engrossed himself in business.

After all, in business you could always forget. It was essential to their future peace of mind that the business should be properly established, and run comfortably. Maddalan was interested in it. She understood art, and would be both a help and an encouragement to him. Belle's attitude towards life had undermined the artistic cult far more than John chose to admit. The public opinion of Condering was against him, and had been growing steadily stronger against him since Maddalan had appeared at the Chantry. Belle had seen to that. He could imagine Belle going about with her eyes swollen by jealous weeping, holding herself in so that the biting words she would have usually expressed took on a more tragic tone.

She would say that she was a deserted wife, and so soon too; what could she do? She had used her age again as her glorious trump card. Belle and age! Belle, pitifully afraid for her departing youth. Perhaps that dread of the toll of the years was her greatest help. It had brought John to her feet; it had been waved as a pitiful emblem to Condering, and Condering, its emotions disgracefully played upon, had responded bravely enough. Poor old thing! It was a shame, they said. If John had married her, he might at least have remained faithful to her. After all, argued the world, it was not fair. He had known that she was old when they married and he had deliberately made a fool of her.

Now the news of the divorce proceedings being started against Belle divided the town into two distinct armies of prejudice. One backed John up, and believed it to be a good thing; the other thought that he was behaving badly, and that he was doing this to cover his own transgressions. Mr. Atkins remained firmly seated on the hedge of public opinion. He had the usual clergymanic genius for remaining neutral. He did not believe in divorce. He did not take sides. It was all a great pity. Ah yes, a great pity. So very sad! And this attitude he maintained throughout.

John believed that, given time and circumstances in his favour, the divorce could be lived down. The fatal marriage to Belle would be forgotten. These things are nine days' wonders; they set a small town re-echoing, but the moment that another storm occurs in their teacups off they go chattering about that. They are never long faithful to one adventure. John was too ordinary a person, and too respectable, to give sufficient cause for their tongues to wag long. The whole affair would end with his marriage to Maddalan; the long even years ahead would provoke little comment.

Looking at it reasonably, John thought that when he could arrive at those smoothly serene years nothing else would matter at all. Ahead lay calm pastures, unruffled by the breath of suspicion. Once reached, all would be well. But would he ever reach them? At times he had a hopeless feeling born of acute depression. He could not see Maddalan. If only he could have spoken to her sometimes, just sometimes. From her he would have been able to draw sufficient strength to go forward. He could not look back to her for strength, because of late their meetings had been so fraught with pain and the agony of Belle. And the former meetings seemed to have been tricked away; either there was something wrong with his memory, or they were hidden in a mountain of mist and anguish.

He must look far, far ahead. He visualized Maddalan shining as the dim tapers of some far distant altar, seen up the long round alleyway of a nave. A terribly long nave, longer than St. Albans Abbey, bluish, dim, difficult to pierce. If only she were not so far away, so difficult of access—with all the long nave in between!

No, he must busy himself in business. He must remain indifferent to the difficulties. He must fight the torments of his heart, and not be swayed, like a reed bending in the stiff tide of a flooded stream.

He tried desperately hard.

III

It was Roy who suggested the gramophone.

"You need cheering up," said he. "You'll grow positively mouldy living alone. A good gramophone is what you need."

Mrs. Barnes approved. It seemed that she and her

husband had a particularly good one which they had purchased on the hire deposit system. With the improvidence of that class they had afforded the best, though they had difficulty in keeping up the instalments.

Mrs. Barnes beamed on the cabinet gramophone which Roy ordered at John's expense. Roy chose half a dozen records.

"Nothing dull," said Roy brightly; "something to cheer you up."

For one dreadful evening the gramophone churned out its torturing medley of jazz. At the end of the evening Roy, well pleased with his efforts to bring old John out of himself, returned home. The next morning John gave the half-dozen records to Mrs. Barnes. She firmly believed that he had gone mad, but approved of the generosity of such madness.

Left to himself, John bought new records. The delicious music of Stravinsky, Koff's unforgettable *Midnight Sun*, Paderewski's *Minuet and Trio*, the Chopin Nocturnes. He chose Beethoven, grand, passionate, tremendous. Liszt, flaunting, extravagant, swelling chords which spoke of dissatisfaction, wild abandoned dancing of tune. Liszt, who flings himself from rapture to abandon, jangling, shrieking, defiant Liszt. He bought violin records too, delighting in the querulous demands of the thin plucked strings.

"Of course," said Mrs. Barnes to her husband, "he's balmy! No one who wasn't cracked would chuck away all those beautiful records for the miserable, mouldy ones he's been and gone and bought. There's no tune in them!"

Tune! Tune! What was tune? A pattern of sound in space: Perhaps. Something strident, something usual, something orthodox. But now he was himself an instrument in a minor key. He was the minor key of water, tinkling into the space of the wind-blown sky, the tranquil space of air. He thought of himself as music, and it helped. It soothed those untranquil depths within him, silenced those disturbances, so that the spool which insisted on unwinding at such titanic speed slowed up. Music salved him in some undreamt manner.

And he needed it! Heaven, how he needed it!

As he sat evening after evening listening to the gramophone he realized melody as the keynote of life. Everything has a melody of its own, and he dreamt of it. Large *piano* melody of cornfields; tender, suppressed melody of fields upturned by the plough. Crescendo of a wing brushing the pizzicato water of a ford. Rallentando of cows chewing in their stall, with rough chords, in triplets, for the grating of their chains against the wooden posts that kept them there. Arpeggios of hoofs stirring among the stones. Each to his own harmony. Impossible to make an impression on the world, impossible to move save that you stir some answering chord. Each in his turn. It is the unfinished sonata of life. Each man to his own overture, his own rondo, his own tremendous adagio. That was where he stood now—adagio of the soul!

Adagio!

But it would change. There inevitably follows the allegretto. A pause—he thought—a hesitant moment as the last notes of the adagio die away. The conductor looks round apprehensively. The violins wait with their bows far across the strings, the fingers of the players grouped about the bridge, all ready to start again. The gay grace of the allegretto! The new morning—facing Maddalan in the registry office, new vows . . . such tender little chords. Then the melody, lilting, with the basses soft, urging harmonies of sound, the 'cello with no sadness on its strings, but a new enquiring tenor. The wind instruments chirping in, mellow as bird voices in spring-blown boughs. The allegretto. Maddalan's footfalls across the humpy floor of the room . . . pert triplets. Maddalan's voice as she called to him from the doorway . . . soft chords. Maddalan reaching down her cool hands, so soundlessly that all the instruments faded into nothingness, drawing him to her, holding him to her; his at last! No sound, it seemed, at all, only the long sucking kiss, only the trembling of his fingers on her hair, only the faint distant Chopinesque melody.

Allegretto.

As he listened tears came into his eyes, and trickled coldly through his fingers. He heard them gushing, sound of tears, the minor echo of the tremendously sad adagio.

The adagio of a soul in travail, he told himself, as he wept. But soon . . . soon. . . .

IV

Were they years or only weeks? Perhaps only days. All alone, the drear monotony of rotating morning, noon and night, and again starting unwilling morning again. Dreadful monotony, dreadful unwinding spool of self, and life churning its routine into him. His being was the red soil that the plough cuts ruthlessly upwards. He was sun-soaked earth, which if you cut deeply enough is wet with the water of a million tears. This life had cut deeply enough. He could not think any more. Self-pity had bemused him.

He saw Mrs. Barnes; he saw Roy. People pottered in and out of his shop, and none of them were people who mattered. These passed in and out of his life as thread in and out of a loom. Just customers, no more. To none of them was he of any importance, to none of them did he signify anything at all. Just a common little salesman, whose heart they did not pause to consider. They came, they stopped to talk awhile, then they went off again.

They chatted of the unimportances of life. And all the while as he discussed his prices, the weather and the markets and all the matterless lumber of living, his heart was screaming, "I'm bleeding, I'm tortured, I am being cut into a hundred pieces by my own grim loneliness. Help me. . . . For pity's sake, can't any of you *see?"*

But none of them could see.

Roy came in and out. Roy, it seemed, was too bright, too gay. Now, when John was racked with such pain, Roy's brightness jarred. He did not dare to go and see Mrs. Darsy, in case the temptation should prove too much for him and he would see Maddalan. For it was urgent that he must take no risks. He kept on impressing that on himself. He must take no risks at all.

Queerly enough, through all this time of trial, of waiting, of grim and grinding monotony and adagio, he thought of Belle. What was she doing? What was happening to her? Funny that he should think of her when she had not cared for him really. But he had cared. The strange thing was that one part of him went on caring, he supposed just because she had stood for a definite chord in his life. He did not want her to suffer. Memory went back, and recalled the pleasanter moments. Memory is fickle. It cheats. It glosses over pain, and exaggerates joy. He realized that it was cheating him, but he could not remain deaf to it.

The sounds in the eerie house at night worried him. Roy suggested that he should do something about the rats—for rats assuredly they were. John went round to the chemist at the corner, and enquired for poison timidly enough. The chemist, a little bald-pated man, with owlish eyes peering through magnifying glasses, looked at him accusingly from between enormous bottles.

"You'll have to sign the poison book, you know."

"It's for rats."

"I daresay. But you'll have to sign the poison book. You might do away with yourself or something."

So they thought that of him! Stupid little man peering from his niche behind the bottles and jars. A little man much like some caged animal pattering to and fro in the limited area behind his counter. Treading out his youth there, his middle age, now his bald, peering senility. A silly little man!

"Of course I'll sign the poison book," said John, and he signed with a flourish. Because it was for rats. If he made away with himself he would not be fool enough to take strychnine. Why should he make away with himself any old way? Soon everything would be all right. It was only a case of hanging on steadfastly, of holding hard and everything coming right in the end.

Mr. Oglivy sent word that the petition had been filed. John had little idea what that might mean, and Mr. Oglivy's letter was extremely involved with technical phrases. He did not intend to enlighten John as to its real meaning. Mr. Oglivy could be very sententious, and this letter was a triumph of his sententiousness. John could imagine it as being typed by the tittering girl, while the office boy boiled the milk and the pimply clerk uttered commonplaces. What an office! What a mortuary chapel for dead loves! Pitiable! Rather ghastly. People bringing out their dying romances and laying them out like corpses on biers. The girl typing out labels, and docketing the corpses. They were ugly in their deaths, these dead romances. Once they had been exquisite, joyous, ripe with full and fragrant beauty, yet in their death they were unlovely, as are all bodies. They were rotten, putrid, greened and slimed.

John wrote an answer to Mr. Oglivy and posted it. In it he asked a few questions, but apparently Mr. Oglivy thought these to be unworthy of a reply, for he made no answer. There was John waiting for something to happen. Waiting for something. He did not know what.

Perhaps the postman would bring the answer to the something which perked its head within his very soul and asked for a response. Every time that he heard the rat-tat in the street John felt himself dithering. "Nerves getting rotten," he told himself, "nerves getting bad. I must take a tonic." Perhaps it would be a telegram? He would eat his meals staring solemnly in front of him, trying to imagine Clem with him. Seeing only the joss with his supercilious grin. Gargoyle of a joss. Perhaps he would bring about the crisis?

Perhaps. . . .

It happened at night. A wild March night, with the wind tearing the trees thickening with buds. A wind that rollicked up the North Hill, and screamed gustily as it turned the corner, pulling with titanic force at the eaves of the houses, and sending slates and loose tiles scattering crashingly to the street below. A night that was riddled with rain. Thick strings of it, scuffling against the walls in a pelting fury. Looking out of the window when the dusk swept up ominous and contemptuous, John was reminded of when he had looked out of the port-hole and had seen the black water of a harbour through its wide, round eye. Harwich, with the yellow eyes of Parkeston quay evenly spaced along its thin outstretched arm. Up rode the night, a fiercely staggering, intoxicating night.

He put on the gramophone, some of the lovely music of Solveig, but even under its spell he could not forget the outside conditions. For they refused to be forgotten. They surged, boomed, and slid like the tempestuous waves of a giant ocean. It seemed that the wind laughed. By ten o'clock he felt a certain awesome fear encompass him, just as though he were not alone in the room. A premonition of presences. Uncanny. Nerves, he told himself; he really must get that tonic.

At eleven, just as he was going up to bed, he heard a knock at the outside door. Was it storm or fact? He did not know. He listened, and somehow his heart beat so loudly that it deceived him. He was afraid; the throb of blood ran faster; he experienced the prickings of small hairs along his spine, and the drying of his throat.

Across the room the joss smiled imperturbably.

He listened, and the knocking came again. He had been at the foot of the stairs, but now he hurried across to the door in answer. "Some poor soul half drowned out there," he thought compassionately.

He unlocked the door raspingly, opened it wide. There came the scream of wind, and the scud of rain, jangling, shrieking, defiant, like Liszt.

A figure hurried in and staggered exhausted against the wall. He shut out the night, ramming the door to, and shooting the bolt, with the hair blown across his eyes and his face wet with rain. He pushed the damp hair back, faced the figure, and then recognition flowed through him.

It was Belle.

V

"You?" he said at last when he could speak. She looked ghastly, soaked through. From her clinging red frock there ran small rivers of rainwater, and they oozed into little pools on the floor at her feet. Her hair was plastered and shining on either side of her face; she was thinner. Her eyes seemed to have receded into her head as though they lingered in deep hollows, like the eyeless sockets of a skeleton. She coughed too. She leant against the wall convulsed in the paroxysm of coughing, too exhausted to speak. The sight of her filled him through with pity.

"Come," he said kindly, "you had better come across to the fire. You have no business to be out on such a night. Why, you are soaked through. What are you doing?"

She tried to answer, but could not, for the cough racked her again. He sat her down in the big chair and drew off her shoes. They were pathetically cheap shoes, with some flashy attempt at smartness, now merely poor imitations. He held them in his hands, soaking, shapeless pads of brown paper, with trodden heels. The artificial silk stockings were soaked too.

"Where are you staying?" he asked. "Why have you come here?"

After a moment she began to speak in a voice that was husky and strained. "I haven't anywhere to go, I haven't any money. I came here because I could think of nowhere else. Perhaps I've done wrong."

"But Jeff . . ."

"I left him. He was a beast. I always knew that he was a beast." She hid her wretched face in her hands. As she did so, a thin rivulet ran down from her hair, trickling through her fingers till it fell to the floor. John was appalled to see her in such a state.

"You'll die of cold," he said desperately. "What can we do? You must take your things off, and I have nothing here that I can possibly lend you."

"A blanket?" suggested Belle.

"Yes, but where can you go?"

"I . . ." She began to cough again. The coughing was terrible. When it had finished she lolled back against the chair, utterly tired out. He took her hand in his. He thought desperately. He thought without being conscious of actual thinking. His brain spun round giddily. There was a strong growing pity welling up in him. The pity suffusing his being made him for the moment incapable of action. It was obvious to him that he could not turn her out into the night again. Common charity would not allow him to turn her from him.

"Look here," he said at last, "go up into the bathroom and get a hot bath; you're frozen stiff. Get some blankets off the spare room bed and put your wet things outside the door, I'll bring them down here and dry them."

"You're good," she gasped.

"You seem so rottenly ill. How did you get like this? I can't understand it."

"It's a long story . . ." Then she coughed again, rackingly, distressingly. He could not bear to hear it, and he held up a warning finger.

"After your bath," he suggested. "You must get out of those wet things. I'll make some hot coffee while you are up there. Belle, please. . . ."

She went away. There was a trail of trickling silver where she had walked, and outside the pirate wind blew bombastically against the corner of the house. Blustering, malignant wind, a barbarian who did not care who suffered. John heard Belle coughing; the sound was mingled with the splashing of the bath water. He went upstairs, collecting the dripping garments from the mat. He brought them down, spreading them before the fire to dry. The shoes were papery; their condition distressed him more than all the other things; it seemed as though they would never be dry and shapely again. He filled them with wads of newspaper as his mother had once taught him, and set them a little aloof from the direct heat. Out of the red-coloured frock water dripped, and it was stained like blood.

The underclothes were shoddy, the cheap stockings in holes. He spread them out as best he could. In the tiny kitchen he had lit the gas-stove, putting a kettle on to boil. Queerly enough he was enjoying this. At last the monotony was relieved and he was doing something for someone; he was glad to do it. The coffee heated, smelling fragrantly as it cooked. He arranged a tray, taking care to make it bright and dainty. He made a bungling attempt to cut some sandwiches, believing her to be very hungry, and he brought the meal in triumph into the sitting-room.

Belle had come down again wrapped in blankets. The bath had washed every vestige of make-up from her face, and she sat there, an old, heavily-built woman, with drooping pouches under her tired eyes, and wrinkles like lace at their corners. Her age now stood out and impressed itself upon him forcefully. She drank the coffee, and ate the sandwiches hungrily. For a little time she made no attempt to talk, but ate greedily, and was intermittently convulsed by the coughing. All the while the joss smirked at them from his place on the side; a gargoyle, urbane above his replusive nudity. John was remembering Belle as she had been before, taunting, tyrannical, driving. "You'd like to brain me with that joss," she had sneered.

At last, when she had finished the impromptu meal, she sat back in her chair appreciating the comfort. She talked. "You're good to me, John. I thought perhaps you'd turn me away. I had nowhere else to go."

"How did you come to be this way?"

"Tramping," she said. "Sleeping where I could. I have been trying to get a job, and I wanted to join a repertory company at Manningtree. I couldn't afford the train fare. Had to walk it."

"But, Belle, surely you have some money?"

"Nothing but a pound or so. I daren't spend that."

"But Mr. Oglivy sent you a cheque only a week ago?"

She shook her head. "I never got it."

"But you ought to have got it."

"I didn't."

"That must have been Jeff."

She nodded as though it did not interest her. "I suppose so. He was a cad. You don't know what he has done to me."

"I don't want to know," John interposed.

From outside there came the swinging sound of the rain against the roof, and the boisterous screaming of the wind as it flung itself gustily round the street corner. Rain swinging like scythes in grass, wind screaming like wolves on the trail. And in a sudden panic he thought of himself as the grass, as his own the trail.

"I suppose," she said awkwardly, "I'll have to dress again and go out and try to find shelter."

"You can't." He glanced at the clothes steaming in their little heaps, the papery shoes, the two dark pools that were stockings. "You'll have to stay here all night."

She began to speak, but broke into a fit of coughing. She did not seem able or well enough to agree or disagree.

"You must have my bed. I don't think the spare room one is aired, and that would be dangerous with you in this state. I can make up a shake-down here on the sofa. I'll be all right."

"You're so good," she said, and there was something pathetic about her realization of his virtue.

"The sooner you are in bed the better," he urged.

She rose, dragging the blankets with her, and she moved towards the stairs. "Good night," she said, and then in a low voice, "God bless you." He watched her as she went slowly and ponderously out of sight, grim ghost of the love that once had been. There was something almost ludicrous about her, with those ample proportions, trailing with a pile of blankets upstairs, ludicrous and yet so tragic that it brought a lump to his throat.

He went back to the fire, stoked it up, and drew the sofa round so that it stood alongside. He would sleep here. He might have done the wrong thing according to law and all the rest of it, but according to kindness of heart he had done the right thing. Absolutely the right thing. He felt the spool steadying. It no longer flew round with him; nerves and pulse quietened.

He fell asleep contentedly.

Chapter Four

Our life is but a pilgrimage of blasts,
And every blast brings forth a fear;
And every fear, a death.

QUARLES
Hieroglyph III, 4

I

JOHN awoke before the light had penetrated through the uneven chinks of the curtains. He remembered that Mrs. Barnes had not been coming until late that morning, and he had intended to get his own breakfast. He got up, stiff from the unaccustomed position, and busied himself in rekindling a fire in the grey ashes, sweeping and dusting the room, and laying the breakfast. Belle's things were dry now, all except the shoes. He doubted if they would ever recover. They were soaked through, and had swollen out of all semblance to their origin. Grotesque, bulging. . . .

He took the clothes up to Belle, and laid them outside the door with a can of hot water. She was awake. She called to him and said that she would be down soon.

Later, when he had the eggs boiling and the toast browning pleasantly, and the room was sweet with the smell of hot coffee and burnt bread and frying bacon, she came down. She did not look so pitiful by morning light. She had powdered her face and rouged her cheeks; this had brought back to her much of her old swaggering insolence. Her hair was drawn closely and pinned in a hyper-young manner at the side. Two auburn curls—red these days with the mahogany of wrongly applied henna—lay on her brow. The red dress had suffered severely from the wetting that it had received. It had shrunk, and it clung unkindly to her person, revealing too much of her masterful legs in their shoddy stockings, and the feet disported in their absurdly misshapen shoes.

"Belle, I'll have to get you some more shoes," he said; "you can't walk in those."

"I suppose I can't," she admitted. "Shall I ring up the shoe shop? They'd send me some pairs round at once."

"They aren't open yet."

"No, but the people live there. I'll ring up." She seemed set upon it, and took down the receiver. She entered into what seemed to John to be an unnecessary conversation with the shoe shop. She told them that she had come home last night soaked through in all the rain, and that her shoes were completely ruined. She laughed jarringly, and all the while John bit his lip and stood by unable to stay her. As she clamped the receiver back to its hook, he said severely:

"Was all that necessary? Now it will be all over the town. They know this divorce is afoot, and they will open their eyes. I think you might have had the decency to hold your tongue for my sake."

She came back to the table straightening her hair with her hand, a little remembered gesture of hers. "It is because of that," she said, "just because of that, that I did it. I wanted them to know that I was here, and that I had been here all night."

"But, Belle, can't you see how difficult it makes my position?"

"It makes it impossible," she announced, and she attacked the egg that he had prepared for her. In a sudden frenzy he noticed for the first time that she had not coughed this morning. That distressing, nerve-racking cough which had shattered his scruples the night before had been miraculously cured. "You see," she went on, "I wasn't going to give you up without an effort to the first tart who came along, I can promise you. I think now you will have difficulty in proving your divorce, seeing that you have condoned my infidelity."

"I *condoned . . . ?*" . .

He felt his ears stinging, his throat smarting. The spool started unwinding again, flinging itself round and round, so that it became colourless and shapeless, a mere blur within him. It seemed as though he were suddenly seeing the world formed differently, altered, a new world, of very definite colours in grotesque relief.

"Yes, condoned." He hated the indifferent way in which she sat there pulling his life to pieces, knocking his dream castles into nothingness, and all the while vigorously eating the egg that he had cooked for her, and buttering her toast. "Who but a fool will believe you? It is too simple. I came here off the train last night. I travelled down with one of the Maxton girls, and told her I was coming to you for a flying visit. I took care that the policeman on point duty saw me come in. There was no mistake about it, because I damn well couldn't afford a mistake. The weather was kind to me, and it was easy enough to get soaked. My God, how cold I was!"

"You mean you were acting?" It was not his own voice any longer, but something hard and metallic within him. It was rather a frightening voice, clipping as the spool clipped round on its hub. It snapped, this new hard voice of his—pistol-shots snapping out of the avenging night. Firewood kindling sharply on a fire new lit. A great fire this. Through his head there flowed a quotation long forgotten, but now suddenly shuttlecocked through his mind.

A little fire is quickly trodden out
Which, being suffered, rivers cannot quench.

"If you put it like that, yes. I stayed here for the night. Early this morning I rang up the shoe shop, as they will prove. I shall tell the court that we were together; you will say that we were not. I wonder which of us will be believed?"

He felt the blood going from his head, the dreadful feeling as though he were falling from some dizzy height. Waiting for the force of impact. The spool spun into the space that has no time, no pattern. It shot round and round until it no longer stayed within him but had drawn everything into its circle. It was himself. He spoke jerkily, yet curiously master of himself.

"You did this on purpose?" he asked.

"Yes, you poor fool." She looked up and laughed at him.

He felt his hands groping blindly for aid, closing over something cold and bronze and hard. It was the joss. He crashed it into her face. He held it in the palm of his hand and hit with the maniacal strength of a man who has suddenly realized the futility of life, that all has slipped through his fingers. One minute, two minutes. He did not know how many. He did not know what he did. Love—rapture—life—it all lay in ruins. Then the spool came to a standstill, spent. It was dreadfully still within him. A little, little thing, lying cocoon-wise in his heart. Then he saw that Belle had toppled from her chair and lay in a limp huddle at his feet.

II

He felt her carefully with quaking fingers. He brought water, bathing her brow, and tried to wipe away the bruise on her temple. He tried to moisten her blue lips with brandy. He spoke to her, tenderly, in a funny, frightened little whisper.

Finally he realized that she was quite dead.

In the first panic he found that he was rushing round and round the room, which seemed on the instant to have become a prison from which there could be no exit, save that direst one of all. Then caution and the sense of self-preservation gradually overcame his fear. He had killed her. Although it had been without actual intention, he had murdered his wife, and for that murder he would hang. The law cannot take such circumstances into account, and all these circumstances could be argued away. He could do no more for Belle. He pulled himself together. His one idea now was to hide her. He tried to lift her, and found that to be impossible, for he had no idea that she was so heavy. He determined to get her upstairs and to conceal her for the time being. With a super-human effort he dragged her to the foot of the stairs, and gradually jerked her up them. In doing this he was nauseated by the way in which her head nodded and fell forward on her full, high breast. She was so utterly plastic in his grasp. She was unwieldy, even more unlovely than in life; her mouth bulged open in a hideous gape, like a fish which he had caught. Her eyes were shut, one of them almost hidden by the huge swelling bruise.

He dragged her along to the spare room, though why the spare room he did not know, save that he could not bear the thought of her lying thus in the room that he had once prepared for Maddalan. He hoisted her on to the bed there. Again he did not know why, save that in some morbid fashion he hoped to make it easier for her.

He could not hope to hide her for anything more than a few hours. He had no intention of attempting to escape the guilt or to get away, but at the moment he realized that he must have time to think. He was confused. Thought was now a clashing discord within him. It jumped and jerked, it evaded his attempts to order and control it. He laid her there, trying to arrange her with some semblance of decency, smoothing down her common clothes, placing her hands beside her. He even attempted to shut the mouth. A dreadful mouth. Once he had kissed it adoringly. Oh, horrible! He went out and leant against the banister, retching.

He locked the door. A Bluebeard's room. A chamber of the Borgias. And he a murderer.

He found that he was inclined to weep now, and all the while he knew that weeping could not help him. Action was what was required. There was Maddalan to be thought of. The moments when he could help Maddalan were limited. He must get his thoughts into order, link them consecutively, and think properly. He decided that he would get Roy to help him. He rang him up. Roy would come at once.

"Urgent," John emphasized. "Now don't be silly and delay; come at once, old chap—bring the car. You've got to help me."

And then the receiver clicked back again and the ghost silence lay on the house like an atmosphere that you could cut. And the dead thing lying there upstairs. He told himself that he must not think. If only you could switch thought off like the wireless, like a telephone! But you couldn't. As he stood there uncertain, a shadow passed the window on the way to the back door. Queer shadow! A man with his head cupped in a helmet. "Oh, God, they've got me already," he whimpered to himself, and he felt his body become sweaty at the thought. He went to the back door. Mrs. Barnes' husband stood there.

"It's me wife ain't too well this morning," he said, "and she wondered if you could leave the work till the afternoon?"

"Rather!" said John. That would be all to the good. By the afternoon—no, he wouldn't think of it.

"You don't look none too fit yourself, sir."

"Toothache," lied John—"all night long."

"Ah!" said the policeman, and he went away again in those grimly silent boots of his that should have clattered across the crazy paving.

But he would return. Of course he would return. He would come just as silently, but not so politely. To him it would be merely a case, a common and ugly murder with no qualifying conditions.

John waited for Roy with a dry taste in his mouth. The pack mule when it kicks over the traces is shot. You cannot let the dangerous pack mule live. What it has once done, it will do again. He wished he had not thought of that. Shooting, they said, was a quick death, hanging was instantaneous, yet he thought at the same time that both seemed beastly. It was so additionally beastly knowing that it was going to happen, even though you deserved it of course. He deserved it as much as anybody else, he told himself.

Roy at last. Roy, boisterous, very hale and hearty and pleased with life, poking a wry face round the door. "Well, this is a God-forsaken hour to rout a chap out. What the hell have you been up to?"

"Sit down," said John, and he pointed a shaking finger to the fireside chair. He had not realized before that he was shaking so much.

"What's the trouble?"

"You've got to help me."

"Of course."

"Swear?"

"Rather; whatever it is you've done."

"I can rely on you, Roy?"

"Absolutely."

He began haltingly. "Last night Belle came back. She was soaked, in rotten clothes, and she had a cough. My God, what a cough it was! I couldn't turn her out; it was past eleven when she got here, and she had nowhere to go."

"You never took her in, John? What a damned fool you are!"

"I tell you she was ill, she was cold. I had to take her in. How could I turn her away?"

"Is she here now?"

John laughed. The laugh was hard and frosty, and faintly within him the spool started again—very slowly. "I don't know. Some of her is. God knows where she is. She slept here anyway, and came down early and rang up for some new shoes. People knew she was here, and when she had done all that she turned on me and told me that I had condoned her infidelity and that it was the end. I'd got to stop proceedings, because she would swear I'd condoned it."

"God! What did you do?"

"I killed her."

"You *what?*" Roy stared at him owlishly; his under lip fell forward, a sudden shelf in the ordinary lines of his face.

"I killed her. I took up that little Buddha, I don't think I even knew I'd got it, and I brained her. Afterwards, when I came to, she was lying on the floor dead."

Apprehensively Roy glanced down into the fireplace and saw on the hearth some of the dye from the red frock that had not yet been mopped up. "Blood!" he whispered.

"No. That was dye from her frock. There isn't any mess, so you needn't worry."

"Where is she?"

In upon this astonishing conversation came the merry, ordinary sound of the milkman clattering up the alleyway, whistling as he came. "Half a moment," said John, and went to the back door. The strange part was that now the ordinary things seemed to be peculiar. The ordering of half a pint, and the exchange of urbane remarks as to the weather. All wrong, queerish!

The milkman had gone again; John came back to the sitting-room hearth. "I dragged her upstairs; she is in the spare room. The thing is, Roy, that I shall have to give myself up, and before I do so Maddalan must be got out of it. That is where I am looking to you."

"But can't I help you personally?"

"No one can help me." Tears whimpered to the back of his throat. He must not think of himself or he would break down altogether. "They are bound to get me, you see, and if you try to help you will only get involved in it too. But you can help Maddalan. She must be got out of the country, slipped back to Haarlem before she knows what has happened. I want you to take every penny there is in the house and see to it for me."

"You mean run her along to Parkeston this morning?"

"Exactly."

"I'll bring her here first?"

"That's what I want you to do. I will talk her into going, otherwise she may think it is funny. Then you take her with you. . . ." His voice broke again, rasped rawly, died away. "It is rather awful making all these arrangements," he whispered whitely.

"You're marvellous. Of course you'll be acquitted." Roy put out a hand and laid it steadily on his shoulder. Good to feel that. Handclasp of a friend, strengthening.

"I can't be. I did it."

"And I don't wonder."

"Yes, but a man may not kill. I did not mean to kill her, but then all murderers say that. The thing is what is decent to do now? Go and fetch Maddalan?"

"Of course."

The door closed, and there ensued the eternity of time when Roy was away. Eternity . . . yawning stretch of it. . . . How it hurt. . . .

III

He could hardly believe it when he heard her step. They seemed to have been so long, so much too long. In that time he had lived through the past and the future, and a hundred such futures, and the hurt was a burning, blistering scar. He could not go through with it. How was it that he had been so brave? How? You could not tell. He was terrified that now, when he needed it most, his courage was ebbing. Already he was beginning to imagine sounds from the spare room, horrible furtive sounds, pluckings, pullings, tearings. Once he had wondered if Belle were not really dead after all, and had contemplated the possibility of her having fainted. Perhaps he had imagined all this. He had crept upstairs, choking back his nausea, and had lingered outside the door. The silence was a knife-thrust. Grim silence, inexorable silence. and through it a rope, swinging solemnly this way and that!

It was the silence that had been Belle.

What an end! And yesterday he had been unsuspecting of it. He had gone on living his simple little life and believing it to be absorbing. He had been content with his music, and his antiques, and his daily routine. What would he not give now to have that routine back again? Everything that he had.

He jerked himself back to realities.

He was hot at times, burned by a ghastly fever. Cold again, consumed by the ice of apprehension. This way and that he turned for relief, and found nothing. He knew that he could not hope to find anything. Then he heard the sound of her voice. Her voice in a short-lived allegretto.

She came into the room with Roy, rather white, behind her. Maddalan! She seemed to him more lovely than he had pictured her in all his lonely pain. Older perhaps with trouble, a little less aloofly virginal than she had been in the Haarlemmer Hout, a little more Madonna. She came to him, put her arms about his neck and lifted her cold blossom of a face to his.

"John, something has happened? What is it? Roy won't tell me."

"Nothing has happened, my sweet," and he prayed hard for strength to control the rising weakness in him.

"But it must have done, it must have done, else why have I had to pack my things? Roy says that we are going to Haarlem again. Think of it, John. It is our dream come true."

"Yes," he repeated dully, "our dream come true."

She turned to Roy; she was suffused with joy, so that she did not sense the tragedy. "You know, I had almost thought that it was something dreadful by the way you looked. So odd. Now I know it isn't anything dreadful. How could it be like that when it concerns our love?" She looked again at them both and laughed. "It couldn't be, of course."

Roy murmured something about the car and went back through the shop. They heard the door swing to on him. They were alone. John sat down in the big chair, and Maddalan dropped to his feet, kneeling there between his wide open knees, her arms lying along his thighs.

"Everybody is being most mysterious," she said. "Why is it?"

"I don't think we mean it." He smoothed her hair, and remembered how often it had reminded him of feathers in its softness. "Fate has taken a hand in this grim game, my sweet. It has shaped the course."

"Is the divorce through?"

"No. There are reasons why I want you to go home. You have got to wait for me."

"But how shall I know that you will come?" she asked, with a woman's quickness of intuition.

"You will not know." Somehow he could not deceive her. He did not attempt it. "Things have not panned out as we expected, Maddalan, and there is a hitch. But it will not be for long. I promise you that we are doing the wisest thing in sending you away."

"You are getting rid of me?"

"Not as you suppose."

She hesitated. "Is there danger?" she asked, and before he could stop himself he had nodded assent. "Then I will stay with you. Nothing shall make me desert you. Nothing at all."

He told her, "Your love for me and the knowledge that you would hurt me terribly by staying will make you go. I ask you quite solemnly for my sake to go away, my dear. There is a reason for all this, and it is as much for my sake as for yours that I ask it. I do beg of you, Maddalan, not to refuse me."

"You know," she said brokenly, "that I can refuse you nothing. But this is terribly hard."

"It would be far harder for me if you stayed," he told her.

"There is some trouble? It is something to do with Belle?"

"Yes, but not as you think."

She sat there undecidedly, trying to fathom the meaning of the words. At last she said in a very low voice, "Supposing you never came to me?"

"Only one thing could stop my coming, and that would be my death."

"Belle?"

"No, she could not stop it."

"You promise you will come whatever happens?"

"Unless I die."

She wrung his hands, clutched at them, clasped them in her own, and laid them over her heart. He could feel the pulse under the small round breast which fitted into his hand. "You must not die," she pleaded.

Quite truthfully he answered, "I do not want to die."

They kissed then. His lips were cold as Belle's upstairs in the spare room; Maddalan's were hot with their bright, strong love. It seemed to him that the life of his being floated from between his lips into her body. No more was needed.

"Supposing," he began, and he knew that it was only the piteous pretence of a man striving to gain a few more moments of life, "that the world tells you hard things about me, what will you believe?"

"Nothing but what is good and beautiful," she answered.

He had a sudden ghastly, rather paralysing picture of Belle as he had dragged her up the stairs, hideously limp, sagging, inert. The sickness assailed him again. He realized that he could not control himself much longer. The spool was going on spinning again, and soon it would be too much for him. He must hurry his adieux. "I think Roy is waiting. He has all the arrangements in hand," and he knew when he said it that it was farewell to life.

"John, cannot you come too?"

He thought of flight, guilty flight. Of Holland and lying there in hiding. There would ensue a merciless extradition. Worse than all that, there would be the publicity for Maddalan. She would be a titbit for gloating newspaper reporters and callous constables, who would allude to her as an accessory. No, that could not be. If his escape entailed any danger for her, then he could not avail himself of that escape.

"Not this time, dearest," he said lightly.

She got up, drawing the light woollen cloak about her. She tied its strings, folded the wrap over. She stood there ready. "I hate leaving you, John. I feel a cat's-paw."

He wanted to scream, "Stay! stay! I want you more

than I have ever wanted you before! I must have you! I must!" but with a supreme effort he silenced himself. He said, "It is the only course of action to pursue."

"I still think that you need me."

For her own sake, her own very urgent sake, he insisted. "You must go."

They kissed again, but the kiss was like the pale sunlight that precedes the winter. It has no true gold in it; it lights only on the first hard crystal of hoar frost. It is bright, but harbours no real joy. What was it Jan had said? "Love is the greatest beauty, but the most exquisite pain. Death is sweetness to it." This was love combined with death.

John watched Maddalan go across the shop to the door. He felt as though he himself had become elephantinely clumsy because he could not move with her. Just a flutter and her shadow on walnut and mahogany. One fleeting impression of her face, white with its scarlet mouth; her eyes, iris . . . no more. . . .

IV

He went indoors again.

And now he and the thing were alone. The dreadful, ominous thing that had to be faced. The crisis was approaching. He must allow Maddalan time to get away, and after that, come what would, nothing could save him. He did not know that he wanted to be saved.

The lonely, silent house became mysterious with strange disturbances. He thought that eyes watched him, fingers plucked at him, curious little faces perked out of corners enquiringly to him. He realized that all this was his imagination, but he could not stay it. He could not walk about because of the echo that his footsteps awakened. It frightened him. It reminded him of drumming, the tom-toms beaten with ominous thunder by natives, and the drumming was of death. He was linking things like that in his brain. Everything pointed to the same morbid conclusion. He could not sit still because he was starkly terrified of that silence. He set the gramophone going, the exquisite music of Solveig, his swan song. But the spool unwinding noisily within him would not let him listen. He had to stop the record and was alone with the naked silence again. Oh, horrible!

Upstairs was the thing, and along with it lay the fatal fascination, grim partner in a gruesome crime. He had not meant to kill her, but who would believe that now? No one at all. An unwanted wife put out of the way when she came back to plead with him to stay the divorce. He knew just what the prosecuting counsel would say, and it would resound with truth. It would be fired with sympathy for the deceased. Bewigged and black-gowned gentlemen would argue about it with impartiality. To them he would not be a human being but just a fat fee. They wouldn't understand; nobody would understand. He wept in acute self-pity again.

He wanted to stay down here by the fire, even though it had been in this very room that the end had happened. This room with the joss smiling queerly, flung into a corner, his sensuous face smeared in blood. Only he couldn't stay in this room. Not here; anywhere but here. And he certainly could not go into the spare room. Why, the thing might be changed by now, stiffened.

Yet for all this he found himself drawing his body furtively upstairs, creeping up as though hating to be heard. He found himself in his own bedroom, with no set reason, only conscious of the tremendous physical disturbance within himself. He was making little pretences of life: washing his hands apparently as usual in a bowl of water; drying them on a towel. Standing there he fingered the soap, and the tooth-paste tube, and put them into their places, one by one. A gargle bottle lay askew. He opened the medicine cupboard above and put it back. Everything tidy, shapely, just as he liked it best, as though nothing had happened.

In the medicine cupboard, close to the little door that he had swung open, lay a small parcel which had never been opened. It was the strychnine that he had bought from the chemist.

His heart suddenly ceased its machine-like hammering, steadied itself, normalized, and the silence came again. He knew now that all the disturbances, all the noises and the eyes that had looked at him, had been part of himself. Part of himself accusing the other part. His ego stopped dead. It stood before him in definite shape, staring at him with round solemn eyes, urging him on.

He heard a step on the courtyard below, and, glancing down through the window alongside, he saw shadows on the cobbles, painted definitely by the bright morning sunshine. Oh, wickedly gay sunshine! Two helmeted men. He heard their sharply imperative rap on the door, the rap which took no denial.

He paused to think, blinking a little, uncertain. . . .

John took down the packet of strychnine, his mouth curving into a wise and thoughtful smile. . . .

THE END